Desperation!

Clyde Bowers rose and walked over to Gideon and glared viciously down at his captive. Grinning, Clyde reared his leg back, swinging a kick. Despite the ropes, Gideon managed to jerk sideways, causing Clyde to stumble. One of the men laughed. Clyde spun with amazing speed and glared at the man, who cowered and looked sheepish.

"What you laughin' at, Hooch?"

Hooch paled. "Nothin,' Boss."

"You laugh again at me and it'll be the last thing you do! Do you understand?"

"Yes, Boss."

Clyde Bowers turned back and suddenly went wild, cuffing Gideon repeatedly, sending shooting pains through his head. Bowers kicked him in the ribs, and then kicked him again. It was as if the pent up anger of the man broke loose as he kicked and slapped Gideon for several minutes. Unable to protect himself, Gideon tried to squirm as much as he could to lessen the blows, but enough connected to cause him to scream in pain. Clyde suddenly stopped his attack, walked back to the fire, reached for his cup and took a sip of coffee.

"How's it feel, Gideon?" He put his cup down and walked over and began to strike and kick Gideon several more times.

"Doggone, Clyde," one of the men spoke, "You gonna torture him?"

GIDEON'S
REDEMPTION

Mark Herbkersman

Collect all volumes of *The Henry Family Chronicles*:
Book 1: Prodigal's Blood
Book 2: Revenge on the Mountain
Book 3: The Branding of Otis Henry
Book 4: Gideon's Redemption

ISBN: **1543117201**
ISBN 13: **9781543117202**

In loving memory
of my father,
Robert Arthur Herbkersman
April 13, 1931 - March 6, 2017

He was proud of my books and it meant a lot to me.

ACKNOWLEDGMENTS

How can thanks be given to all those who make a book possible? In the process of specifically naming people there is the danger of leaving out someone who has played a role over the almost 13 months of writing. And yet, there is the need to single some out.

Joni and Kay: What would I do without you? Your love of this project was priceless. Faithful to a fault, you have read and re-read, corrected, suggested, cheered me on, slowed me down at crucial moments and even kicked me in the backside a couple times! Your gift to me is beyond both value and measure.

Jeffrey S. Dowers: You have been the key person in my book covers. From the start we chose simple and consistent. You are a blessing.

To all those who keep telling me you are waiting for the next book: Here it is! It wouldn't be happening without you telling me you love my books and prodding me to get on with it!

To my family: you put up with so many post-it notes and slips of paper lying around with ideas. You tolerate – barely – my stacks and piles and general disorganization around "my" chair. Thanks for your support!

Marilyn: It's been 28 years now as husband and wife. We have weathered storms and blessings together. Thank you for all the Wednesdays that you go to work while I run off to drink coffee and write. I love you.

Above all, thanks to God for the blessing of this fourth book, the gifts He's given me and for the special gift of His Son.

1

CRASWELL, COLORADO

Frantic lungs sucked air hungrily like a drowning dog. Chest heaving, he lay beyond desperation and past weariness, only sheer will commanding his body to continue. It seemed he might be found by the labored rasping, for to his own ears it seemed like a beacon unmistakable to those seeking his blood. He was as a wild animal, cornered and pushing to survive, clawing through the rocks above the gorge, seeking a hole, anyplace to hide.

There was none to be found.

Blood smeared his face and arms, oozed from the cuts and tears in his body, sapping his strength with every lost drop. Eyes wide, he looked pleadingly for hope in the terrain. His ears grasped for sounds of pursuit – and there were many.

In all directions were the metallic sounds of horseshoes striking stone and the calls of riders to each other as they sought their common prey. There was cockiness in the voices, anticipating a sure kill.

"He can't get away now! There's no way across that gorge! Tighten the circle! A hundred dollars gold to the man who puts a bullet in him first!"

Exultant voices were dangerously close and the sky began to glow with a deadly dawn. The night darkness had been his friend, if such could be had in these circumstances; less a friend and more like a distant cousin. Now the morning sun was clawing it's way over the mountains like the Grim Reaper leering over the side of a coffin.

Trying to keep low, he pulled himself along while his muscles screamed to be allowed to die. He slid like a limp rag over the top of a jagged stone, cutting himself viciously because he had no energy to hold himself away. Nor did he want to raise his body any higher than necessary and risk being seen.

It was too late. As the first dreaded rays of dawn burst upon the rocks, a rider looked the right way at the right time and saw the man-animal illuminated as he pushed over the rock. The victim lay with his face drawn, staring at death yet determined from deep inside to live.

"There he is!" A bullet threw piercing shards of stone in his face. Desperate hands clawed the rocks from his panicked eyes as he looked around.

There was nowhere to go! To his front was the gorge his pursuers mentioned, and they were right.

Peering over the edge, he despaired at a hundred foot sheer drop to a raging torrent. Wiping blood from his eyes, his heart cried out for help from anywhere, seen or unseen. He was finished! Something inside dearly wanted to lay still, die and have peace and rest. Yet, from an even deeper reservoir came a yearning for life – and revenge.

Anger built within him when realization came that to die meant these men would win. And he had never liked to lose. Yet he had no options. Unless...

He looked over the edge of the rock, startled as another bullet blasted the dirt by his side. The fast-moving river coursing far below looked like certain death. And yet...perhaps less certain than where he lay.

"I got him! That hunnert in gold is mine!"

"You didn't hit him, Tabor! But I will!" He heard a horse swiftly approaching through the rocks.

Drawing from the remaining vestiges of desperation, the prey rose to see a half dozen approaching horses. He half stumbled, half leaped from the cliff as bullets laced the air, grasping and pinching at his tattered remnants of clothes. A ripping pain tore through his side as all went dark, his limp body plummeting downward.

2

ST. LOUIS

Two months earlier, on the outskirts of St. Louis, he was comfortably seated at his usual table in the usual café eating his usual fare when not on the trail – eggs and side meat and a slice of bread to sop the yolks. He dabbed his mouth with his napkin and raised the coffee mug to his lips.

Seeming to be completely at ease, his awareness was nevertheless complete. His eyes had already noted the man on the street, seeing the furtiveness as the man pretended to be looking around in general, yet actually seeking. Bystanders would have no clue what the man was seeking.

But Gideon Henry knew.

Without actually looking directly at the man, Gideon sensed the situation when the man's eyes, gazing through the window, rested on him for a flickering moment. He had been sought in such a way too many times. The average diner would notice nothing, but in those few moments Gideon perceived much.

Survival had honed his perceptions to a fine edge. Much could be gleaned from the man's eyes and his clothing.

Visual evidence and the knowledge of man in general revealed not a man of strength, but a mere hired dog. Small of stature with sunken cheeks and beady eyes, the man – if such he could be called, for the word seemed too generous – was obviously weak, prone to do the business of another for a pittance. The odds were that this creature was merely a middleman, scouting the lay of the land or bringing a message, but Gideon had survived this long in his business by never playing close odds. It was always best to play the odds in one's own favor.

Somebody was seeking Gideon Henry.

What remained to be seen was the reason. Was his gun being sought for hire, or was he the target? Both were his lot over the past few years.

A careful man, Gideon had few patterns. One was his table here. It was chosen for its view of the street and dining room, and for its proximity to the back hallway with three doors to choose for a quick exit, either to upstairs, the alley or another store-room. All the exits had secondary exits, for he was a careful man.

Awareness of the seeker brought neither sigh nor panic. A man of confidence and physically stronger than other men, Gideon was dressed in a nice suit common to those living in a town. He was not ostentatious, deploring attention as dangerous. Average in height, his dark hair was neatly kept yet curled over his collar and framed a face that attracted women, yet was capable of sapping the confidence of many seemingly strong men. A man of many experiences, he was not easily intimidated. Piercing and intelligent eyes took in his surroundings in an instant, noting tables, chairs and who was sitting where. Though having already noted these things as he ate, he noted again for any signs of change. He was a man of acute awareness. Moving smoothly and with cat-like surety, he set the cup gently down and stepped nimbly backwards into the hallway behind. A hard yet strangely kind man, respected yet mysterious, Gideon gently placed a gold piece on the table as he moved away. The young waitress, whom he knew as barely getting by and raising her siblings, would be grateful of the windfall.

Moving like a wraith into a corner of the hallway just out of the dining room, Gideon palmed his gun and awaited the inevitable.

Senses fully alert, he stood unmoving in the shadows. Early experience taught him how movement attracted eyes. Often the first man to move was the one who was planted six feet under.

Hearing clumsy footsteps, he readied himself and at the subtle sound of rustling cloth, reached out his strong hand and jerked the hired dog roughly into the hallway. Staring wide-eyed at the gun barrel between his eyes, the man went limp as a rag doll.

"Speak." Gideon hissed at the man. It was a tension between worlds inside Gideon Henry, that he could charm with a voice of honey yet turn almost instantly to vicious brutality when needed. The men who sought his services rarely did so themselves. Rather, they sent cowering minions as messengers. More than one had tried in their clumsy ways to do him in themselves for what was in his pocket. Not knowing the mission of the man before him, Gideon assumed the worst. There was another door to the alley nearby where the man could be left if necessary.

With eyes as big as saucers, the man stared and shook with fear.

"Please, mister! I'se just passin' a message!"

"Then pass the message and I'll decide what to do next."

A grimy hand held out a dirty and crumpled piece of paper. Keeping the gun to the man's head, Gideon unfolded the paper against his coat front and glanced down. It was blank except for the letterhead: Hankel and Hankel, Attorneys.

It had often been so. A mere piece of paper with a name, a location, sometimes a time. It was the way of his life.

3

Moving quickly along the boardwalk, Gideon noted the messenger rounding a corner in the distance. Probably returning to complete another errand for a pittance, he thought.

There were too many such men in the world. They were men who somehow cowered to the world during their early life, by example or by necessity. Many became defeated before they even began to live. Perhaps beaten, perhaps threatened, perhaps just weak inside, they went through life with no happiness other than basic animal happiness usually of the temporal and carnal type, living for the sickly women of the dirtiest cribs on the back streets. Throw in a bottle of cheap and often deadly home mixed liquor and such people were content as they could be. Through the years he had pondered this and had surmised that a good many children seen on the streets of St. Louis were what people referred to as urchins. It wasn't so much the name as the tone in which it was said. Many used the same inflection and look as when speaking of rubbish. More than a few of these children would go through life as this hired dog with the letterhead. For most, the future meant to die some day without notice, just another pauper's grave with no stone over a nameless heap of hastily thrown dirt. There would be one smile at their death - that of the undertaker who took the pauper's fee from the town council and dropped the body into a shallow grave. Recently, what began to disturb him was how many of these street urchins realized what was ahead, yet could find no hope or any alternative.

Pausing to casually glance back, Gideon looked at the surroundings, noting changes as he walked down the street. Within a matter of blocks cleanliness and style gave way to a more ramshackle look. Whereas in his part of town there was a man paid to pick up trash and sweep the boardwalks, here trash remained where it fell unless there were coins to be gained by its collection. It would be hard to find a discarded bottle, for the local makers of the homemade poison they called whiskey had a standing order for containers. Blowing them off and maybe giving a rinse with already overused water, the funnel would be placed and the bottle refilled. Those buying such liquid on the back street had no care if there were stray particles in what they drank.

About to move on, a movement caught his eye and he looked to an alley across the dusty road. Garbage was piled at the edges of the narrow alley and as he watched, one heap moved again as a rat scampered out and into the shadows.

It brought back memories of two years ago when, walking by an alley at night, Gideon heard a groan. It sounded like the groan of a child. Only a child could touch his heart in such a way to cause him to check it out.

Wary of trickery, for so many lost not just their pokes and purses but also their lives to such tactics, Gideon pulled his gun and stepped into the alley. Hearing the groan again, his eyes sought the deeper shadows and found a girl, rumpled and wasted, lying in a trash heap. Still wary and looking in all directions, he noted no nearby doorways or hiding places. Kneeling by her side, the girl lay staring blankly upward, seeing but without vision. Picking her up, he realized she was mere skin and bones. She seemed no older than five, yet malnutrition and the resulting small stature of many such children may have clouded reality.

A hesitant doctor looked the girl over only after Gideon Henry placed coins upon the desk. It was a brief examination, but as thorough as necessary.

Turning to Gideon, he spoke with the callousness of one accustomed to such things.

"Probably eight or nine, though her size would make you think five. Malnourished, obviously living in the streets with all that that means. So many of these urchins are old before they even have a chance to grow up."

Gideon noted a brief look of compassion flicker over the man's eyes as he looked once again at the tired and emaciated girl.

"Will she live, Doc?"

"No. Even now she is on the precipice of death. Her body's worn out. God only knows what she's lived through. But worse than that, she's dying from lack of hope. My guess is she won't live the night."

Gideon Henry sat by the bedside that night, wiping the poor girl's brow as life faded, talking softly to comfort her. There was a woman cleaning the Doc's office who pitched in to help as the night struggled against the faint glow of the lamp. Somewhere in the pre dawn the girl died.

Paying for her to have a decent burial, Gideon persuaded a preacher to say a few words for this unknown child.

It was a moment of change. A crack appeared in the hardness of his life as he stood watch over the too-soon ebbing of a life – a life that held no hope from the beginning. Gideon quietly funded the start up of a home for homeless children outside of town at an abandoned farmstead. Though often dropping out of sight for weeks at a time, he made sure sufficient funds were given to the matronly Mrs. McClinder, the woman who had been cleaning the Doc's office that night, who took on the role of mother to at first a handful then quickly a dozen needy street children. The number waxed and waned. When he returned from being away, Gideon could be glimpsed on horseback approaching the home with children running to meet him. Known as Mr. Henry, he would spend some time with the children crawling over him and playing as a father with his children.

Yet always there remained a hard wall in his emotions, a detachment of sorts, protecting him.

4

Eyes roving left and right, he walked the several blocks to the law office of Hankel and Hankel. While many men would mount a horse for such an errand, Gideon relished the chance to stretch his legs.

It was definitely a seedier part of town. Then again, such lawyers as Hankel did not belong in the best part of town. Experience long since taught that lawyers tended to gravitate to where their morals fit most clearly. It seemed to him it would always be that way.

As he neared, he noted furtive eyes watching from a nearby doorway. Where there was a hat brim and an eye peering around a corner, there just as quickly was nothing. Gideon's style of clothing, along with his being alone, identified him as a target in this part of town. Pretending to adjust his coat allowed him to loosen his gun. How many times had he been though this?

Reaching the doorway, his hand flashed downward. The club wielding man faced Gideon's gun and froze in mid motion, standing in amazement as Gideon never lost a step, but continued on, lowering his gun when past the doorway. Yet the message had been sent and the man quietly slipped away.

Facing Gideon was a nondescript office. Stepping inside, a bell over the door jingled his arrival. A voice in the inner office spoke, not fully masking the cocking of a pistol.

"Who is it?"

"Henry."

Papers rustled suddenly.

"Come in, Mr. Henry."

It was the standard office for a lawyer in this part of town. Dirty, smelling of cigar and pipe smoke, the room mirrored the character of its occupant, sitting in a greasy chair, wearing a suit with greasy lapels with scuffed shoes resting on greasy papers on the chipped corner of the cluttered desk. Making no effort to get up, Hankel remained leaning back in his chair with one hand resting on his ample belly, the other just out of sight under the desk. Bloodshot eyes held a look of guarded wariness. On his chin were the greasy remains of his lunch, crumbs decorating his bulging shirtfront, buttons strained to their limits such that hairy tufts in the gaps sprouted like weeds in a fencerow. A greasy handkerchief holding the remains of a chicken lay on the cluttered desk. Two flies flew circles over the pile of bones and shreds, finally landing to enjoy the plenty.

"Gideon Henry?"

"Yes, and I'd appreciate it if you placed your gun on the desk. I'd feel more welcome if I could see both hands."

Hankel slowly brought his hand out, holding the cocked weapon. Under Gideon's sharp eyes he placed the weapon on the desk. It was not missed by his visitor that the gun remained within easy grasp. Disturbed, the flies made a circle of the room and returned to the mess.

"A man cannot be too careful, Mr. Henry." It was a chuckle with fake aloofness.

"Are you Hankel?"

"I am he."

"State your business."

Again the chuckle.

"My, you are direct."

"Yes. No need for small talk."

"Your reputation precedes you, Mr. Henry."

"Yes. What do you want?"

A slight pause as Hankel looked at him, obviously getting the measure of the man standing before him. Accustomed to being respected – or at least feared – in this section of town, Hankel was uncomfortable with Gideon's surety. Dropping his feet to the floor with a thud, he sat upright and placed elbows on the desk. Hankel's eyes widened as Gideon Henry flashed his gun when the greasy hand brushed the gun on the desk. Fast draw, he noted. Hankel's eyes were large, but he recovered quickly, swishing away flies which rose startled from their bounty. Annoyed, Hankel briefly tracked one and slapped it to the desk. A look of triumph flickered briefly as he wiped the hand across his shirt, leaving a fly wing dangling off a button.

"I...er...have been contacted by a client out West who desires your special services. It seems there is an aggressive rancher encroaching on his personal land and he wants the man...er...removed."

"He knows my terms?"

"Yes, though he considers it excessive."

Gideon stared Hankel in the eyes until the man looked down, breaking the contact and placing Henry fully in charge. His silence caused Hankel to shift in his seat. Impatient with needless quibbling, Gideon turned to leave. He used these ruses many a time, watching seemingly tough men quaver. It happened now.

"Mr. Henry. I said he considered it excessive. I did not say he would not pay. My client is prepared to meet your terms."

"Ten thousand, in advance."

"Understood. You work on trust, Mr. Henry." Still the man sought to get an upper hand.

Deigning to respond to the seemingly snide comment, Henry asked a question.

"Where?"

"Outside Craswell, Colorado"

"A Thousand extra."

Hankel's jaw dropped. His client had allowed a couple thousand dollars more, but he intended to pocket it himself. Now this Gideon wanted part of it.

"A thousand extra! What the…."

"Long ways. Travel expenses." Gideon knew the ways of such transactions and, though not knowing the amount, knew Hankel would pad his own pockets.

"That's a lot of travel expenses."

"I travel nicely."

Hankel rubbed the stubble on his chin with a greasy hand. Henry smiled inside at the renewed attempt of the plump lawyer to place himself in charge.

"I don't know."

"Good day, Mr. Hankel." Turning to leave, he heard the chair creak as Hankel arose. Gideon Henry spun and the disheveled lawyer stopped, hands raised as crumbs fell from his shirtfront to the floor. Once again he faced a gun barrel and stood wide-eyed, realizing how fast and dangerous this man was.

"Don't try me, Hankel," he spoke firmly as Hankel stepped back, alarm bells going off in his eyes.

"No harm meant, Mr. Henry." Hankel wanted this business over. It was obvious on his face.

"Deal or not, Hankel?"

"Deal." Holding one greasy hand up as he reached to his desk drawer, Hankel moved slowly, took out a poke and counted the money swiftly on the only clean corner of the desk. Along with gold was a small sheet of paper.

Taking another way back to his room, Gideon watched carefully, knowing that such people as Hankel might likely put someone on his tail, or else someone watching Hankel's office might assume anyone leaving would have extra gold jangling in their pockets. Taking a side street, Gideon finally entered a small shop, emerging very few minutes later.

Later that night Gideon Henry planned his trip. Extra money was arranged for Mrs. McClinder to care for the children. She was one of the few trusted persons in his life, though she knew nothing about his profession and, if she suspected, said nothing. Now, laying back on his bed, hands intertwined behind his head, he relaxed. In his mind was the name of the rancher and the town. A match had burned the original slip of paper into traceless ash. The name of his employer moved across his mind as he slipped off to sleep.

Dan Bowers, Craswell, Colorado.

5

CRASWELL

Dan Bowers liked being in charge. At an early age he began preferring to give orders rather than receive them. For many years his orders were reasonable and without enmity. He himself was subject to orders from his wife, who helped carve the ranch out of the wilderness. There was a clear delineation of duties – she in charge of the house and he of everything else.

Five years ago his wife died during the long and agonizing birth of a late child. Grief-ridden already, Dan watched as the baby – a girl – soon followed into the shadows of death. Something inside Dan Bowers also died that day, and he focused his life upon his ranch and his only child, Clyde. Yet, in his grief something else entered the picture – the bottle. Drinking became frequent. Old hands noted calculation and concern for others giving way to a sickening sense of ego and privilege. Obsessed with his land, Dan Bowers viciously protected it from encroachment. How it first happened no one knew, but one day a squatter on a mountain spring in the boundaries of the Rocking-B was found dead with a bullet through the heart. No one ventured an accusation, but it was noted that Dan Bowers was in the Gold Horse Saloon early that day and was sullen.

An unnaturally strong man to begin with, Bowers began visibly to thicken as he rode less and ordered others around. Much time was spent brooding in the confines of his home - with a bit too much help from the bottle. Now he was a heavy man, with much of his weight forming a mass of pillow-like fat around his neck, looking like as a chipmunk with its pouches stuffed. It was odd-looking, but none dared do more than cast a furtive glance at the strangeness of it, deigning to keep their own thoughts to themselves. It was the better part of wisdom to do so.

Dan Bowers became something evil; it was something lying dormant in earlier years. Some say it was the loss of his beloved that opened the deep well of instability. Others claimed to have seen signs of an inordinate desire to lord it over others all through the years. Comments or speculations were made only between dearly trusted friends and only in the kitchen with windows shut and curtains drawn. Thoughts caused even stalwart men to look furtively around for a Bowers man lounging for no reason nearby. Not a few experienced merciless beatings for mere comments.

A different type of hand began to ride for the Rocking-B. Working hands gave way to men with no intent to do physical labor but rather rode with a hand always near a gun.

Several times newcomers settled on his land. They received a warning – or so it was told – and then were seen no more. In one case it was known that a woman also disappeared. It afterward was recollected that a traveling cowhand stopped to whet his whistle at the Gold Horse and was heard to say he spent the previous night in the barn of the newcomer's family. He made mention of a young child. It seemed odd to townsfolk that a family would supposedly quit the country yet leave everything behind.

In the past several years, Bowers showed increasing obsession with his holdings. With plans to increase his herd and a drive to become well-known and important, Bowers set his sights on the ranches surrounding his own. One of those was the ranch of Vern Schmidt. Vern's grandparents emigrated from the old country, but Vern himself spoke with no accent, having been raised in America. His wife, Ruth, was from a family who sent many men to fight with General Washington. Her brother had fought with Sherman at Atlanta.

Something in Dan Bower's mind succumbed to degradation and he began to publicly question Vern's integrity. Vern, hard-working and not unexposed to prejudice, shook his head in wonder. Though never overly friendly, both he and Bowers were at least cordial before the relationship became tenuous. Ruth Schmidt had even helped nurse Elizabeth Bowers on that fateful night. Perhaps it harkened back to that, but Vern would do nothing but shake his head and hope for the best. He did not want to start a war and figured cooler heads would prevail. Yet, Bowers allowed no other heads to prevail.

No one dared say a thing, as Dan Bowers was by then of erratic temper, likely to act harshly and quickly if someone challenged his authority. There was a time a year ago when a traveling cowhand questioned the disappearance of a friend and did not take the hints to let the matter drop. Dan Bowers evaded the man's questions with a calm that should have been a warning. Early the next morning the cowhand's horse was in the stable but the man was seen no more. Men glanced around knowingly, yet nothing was said.

Capable of long periods of seeming rationality, Bowers was astute at business. There was awareness that others feared both him and the men on his payroll. When he spoke, others listened. None challenged him. Yet, there was also a charm that at times rose to captivate others, drawing listeners to honestly shake their heads in agreement. At other times, there was merely quiet agreement as others granted subservience to their fears. If Bowers declared he wouldn't do business with a particular merchant, the implication was clear that he expected others to follow suit or be subjected to the same ban. Other merchants could either toe the line or be quickly driven from business. Over just a very few years he had become a power in the area, and others deferred to him.

Tonight he stood in the Gold Horse Saloon facing the evening crowds. He bought drinks for all, but it was more than drinks he bought in the process. Men have always supported those giving greater gifts.

"I tell you, folks, I just don't trust those foreigners. They just ain't the same as us Americans."

A man who worked at the livery spoke without calculation.

"Bowers, Schmidt has been here a long time and ain't done nothin' to make me wonder."

Bowers glared at the man until the man dropped his eyes. Glancing at the minion next to him, Bowers went on as two of his men made themselves obvious near the man who dared to speak.

"They have different ways, different thoughts. And he's got them no-account Mexicans working. All his self-respecting cowhands has moved on. I tell you, Schmidt is no respecter of our ways." He enunciated the word "our" as his hand swept the room. At a nod from him, one of his men spoke.

"I done seen some stock of ours gathered on Schmidt's land, in a hollow. Looked to me they was there a'purpose. Seen some tracks circling them." He glared knowingly around the room.

Bowers shook his head, giving pause to some as they curiously watched his neck, the pillow remaining in one spot while his head turned.

"Folks, that's rustling." He paused, letting his eyes rove the room as his words sunk in. "We can't have this! I think we've got to make sure Schmidt knows he's unwelcome. I don't want things to get violent. Those days are behind us. I'd say you all need to watch your stock. Ain't no telling where the man will strike next." Pausing, he raised a finger and looked around. "I also would consider it unkind if'n the storekeepers show undue friendship."

He said nothing about his wire to his lawyer, Hankel. There was nothing to stop him from getting rid of this German and taking his land. It would nearly double the size of his holdings and create a fine kingdom over which to finish his days and pass on to Clyde. Hankel sent a wire assuring contact had been made.

"Another round of drinks on me! Bartender, put it on my bill." Bowers raised his glass, emptied it and turned to the bar, where the bald-headed bartender hurried along, slopping whiskey into proffered glasses. He was frustrated, as the whiskey was a big outlay and Bowers always showingly demanded it be put on his bill. The problem was he never moved too quickly to pay his bill and the owner of the saloon, Mansfield, instructed Bowers was not to receive credit. Yet, what was he to do? Questioning Bower's honor would not end well, so he shrugged, filled the drinks and figured that detail was up to Mansfield. After all, he himself was just the bartender. Bowers stood and surveyed who reached for free drinks and thereby sealed their loyalty.

Those friendly to Schmidt lowered their eyes and felt the pressure. If they showed friendship to the German and his family, or even the Mexican hands, they risked the ire of Dan Bowers. It was unknown what Bowers would do, but there was a guarantee it would not be good. So, one after another, these also reached their glasses over the bar.

There was one man present who spent considerable time thinking of Mary Schmidt, Vern's daughter. He could not get her out of his mind and hoped to ride with her soon. A shaking hand brought the glass to his lips and he gulped his drink dejectedly, for his heart was weak and knew he would not defy Bowers.

Late that night Bowers rode quietly amidst his men back to the ranch. One man, looking over to his boss in the bright moonlight, saw a smirk on the old man's face.

As Bowers strutted out of the Gold Horse Saloon that night, he passed a man who could have been a statue for lack of movement. Ol' Ridley was at his usual spot at the rough-hewn bench just beyond the swing of the batwings. One end and an armrest were worn smooth where Ol' Ridley sat day after day, year after year. The story was told that Ol' Ridley was blinded in both eyes by a single arrow in some unremembered Indian ambush in an unremembered year. His face was divided top from bottom at the eyes by a nasty scar where the arrow gouged more deeply across the cheekbones and as it sliced across his eyes. Sitting in a rotation of seats around town, Ridley walked with an old knobby Cedar branch held to the ground before him. Some said he knew the town so well he really didn't need the branch, as now and then there would be a report of him walking alone by the stables and other areas with the branch held to his side. Like a fixture, he brought no more notice than a table or chair. His presence was so expected it was unexpected, so common it was ignored.

For some reason, which made him smirk inside, people thought that a blind man was also deaf and talked loudly to him. In actuality, his hearing was keen. Certain sounds came easily to his ear, such as the rattling of the dinner dishes around town. It seemed people took care of him, a plate rattling on the bench beside him with a mumbled, "Here ya go, old man," or, "the missus sent this over," or some other such statement. Ridley never missed a meal and, if timed right, he could slip one plate out of sight until some other tender soul brought him a morsel also. An unnatural bulge above his belt testified that starvation was not his lot.

It was not unknown for rambunctious children to come running by and, seemingly seeing him for the first time, skid to a halt and stare, wondering if this apparition was real or a wooden figure clothed in cast offs. He could almost hear their minds going and took pleasure in sensing the tension and even the way children would lean close to examine him or to stare at the scar and at the eye sockets holding mostly opaque eyes that sometimes quivered involuntarily. As boys stared at him, Ol' Ridley would suddenly clear his throat loudly, hearing the unfortunate child jump and sometimes fall off the boardwalk. Spitting to the ground, he would chuckle to himself and sit quietly, ears tuned to the goings-on of the town.

Tonight Ridley listened to Bowers' ranting with disgust. Why anyone fell for Bowers' lies and half-crazy statements he would never understand. Confronted with the man's instability, many showed themselves cowards with hardly the backbone of an earthworm.

Schmidt was a good man, kind to all, ready to drop everything to help another. He recalled a couple years ago sitting by the general store and hearing

Schmidt come to town. Schmidt spoke kindly to him as always and started into the store. Ol' Ridley's keen ears listened vaguely to voices inside the store, hearing Mary say, "That would be nice, Pa." Next thing he knew Schmidt and his daughter placed a new flannel shirt on his lap.

Ol' Ridley knew Schmidt treated his Mexican hands no different than any others. They were good hands, and the Garcia's had toiled by his side for years. Schmidt also had other goings-on that nobody knew about, but Ridley knew. It was amazing what a set of ears could find out if a man just set quietly and let nobody take notice.

Bowers himself never put a hand to helping anybody any more unless it somehow benefitted him.

6

ST. LOUIS

Wang Chu looked over his glasses towards the shop door and wondered when Gideon would next appear. Gideon Henry had been patronizing Wang's laundry for years because he said nobody could clean his clothes as well. Wang suspected it was more because his shop was on a back street. Over time they got to know each other in a limited and careful way. Both had their own reasons to be discreet. Wang held strong hunches as to Henry's long absences, but made a point of keeping his thoughts to himself.

On his own part, Wang did not leave his shop often, except at night, preferring to work quietly. Yet, his fingers were far-reaching and he knew key people not only on his own street, but also on the streets of those who looked upon his people with suspicion.

Wang spoke excellent English and did a lucrative business with the whites and others who deemed it necessary to farm out their laundry. It amazed him that even some not-so-wealthy women now looked upon washing as somehow beneath them. Even some of the freed slaves farmed their wash to him, though few could really afford it. It was as if, being slaves for so long, this one act made them feel they'd moved up in the world. Sometimes he pondered this, but then always smiled when the money was in his hands. Several different sources of income kept him busy, yet it was the simple task of doing laundry that maintained his reputation and brought in a constant trickle of coins. It all added up. Of course, he no longer did the actual scrubbing of the clothes. His daughters took care of that under his watchful eyes, after the death of his wife. Many of his clientele came regularly because of the extra care and he purposefully kept the quality high. Perhaps a bit of extra for Gideon Henry, but then again a favor given may be returned later. Over time he found himself with a growing respect for the quiet man who showed discretion and wisdom not often common in a man not long out of his youth. While others in this bustling town treated Chinese with derision, commenting about their short stature as well as their color, Gideon never treated Wang as anything but a man, and an equal.

Shaking his head, Wang leaned on the counter and glanced along the street. Sometimes ladies would send for him to pick up their bundles of laundry and, if he did not have a boy to fetch, he would go himself. Ladies would act like they were doing him a special favor by "allowing" him to do their clothes! Humbly bowing and thanking them, Wang played the ritual game and later smiled at the clink of coins in his pocket. Every now and then there was some overly pompous matron or maid making unkind comments about his "kind" and asserting extra demands. Smiling, he recalled one such case when a woman persisted in insulting him and making demands. Bowing his head and acting the part of the beaten laundryman, he later carefully cut certain threads on garments so as to begin unraveling. Wang again collected coins later when receiving the same garments for repair. There was a certain amount of guilt, and it never happened again, but still there was a smile of satisfaction.

One day Gideon came to the shop to pick up his weekly laundry. Pausing to note no others in the shop, he approached Wang and inquired as to a gunsmith who was both close-lipped and competent to make some modifications. Wang quietly asked what type of modifications and Gideon placed a well oiled and immaculately cared-for Colt on the counter and explained what he wanted. Wang found the man for the job – another Chinese who was astute in the ways of gunsmithing.

Over time there developed a mutual trust and respect uncommon between both races at the time. Gideon Henry was a man of contrasts, Wang mused. Though hard and aloof at times, he also observed Henry intervene when two abusive and cocky white men accosted one of the Chinese youths Wang sent to collect laundry. When Gideon Henry stopped the men they turned on him but when the dust settled – and it settled quickly – the two men lay in the dirt and the grateful Chinese youth would not forget. Neither would Wang forget. Word spread among his people of the deed of the man many had seen but whom only Wang knew beyond the surface.

Mutual respect grew into a friendship of sorts. Many white men of the day not only looked down upon his people, but also turned their eyes and minds from the thriving economy under their very noses. Gideon Henry knew that several of the Chinese, though unknown to the whites, were wealthy beyond that of the cocky white men who looked down their noses at the industrious subculture. He also knew that though Wang was not yet wealthy, he was astute and slowly building. Wang well remembered the day Henry approached him with a business proposition.

It had been a fairly average day. Wang was brooding and frustrated. A white man – a prominent town businessman not hurting for funds – refused to pay the laundry delivery boy to the tune of several dollars. Such not-uncommon situations usually were accompanied by trumped up accusations regarding the laundry. As he shook his head he heard the clink of the bell on the door and looked up to see Gideon Henry. He smiled genuinely at his customer and friend.

"Good morning, Gideon!"

"Good morning, Wang."

Gideon surveyed the shop in a casual manner. Wang knew this for what it was – a precaution to see if they were alone.

"I do not believe I have any laundry for you, so I surmise you are here for a different reason?"

Gideon smiled. "You surmise correctly. Are we alone?" He nodded towards the back of the shop, separated by a bright curtain from where they stood.

Wang turned from the counter and looked behind the curtains to the back of his shop.

"We are alone."

"I heard you say that you plan to grow your business?"

"Yes."

"Would you be interested in taking on a silent partner? My involvement and investment would be between you and I."

Wang trusted his instincts and long since deemed Gideon to be trustworthy.

"I had not thought of such things, Gideon, but yet I have several ideas and opportunities for which I do not have resources. What might you be thinking of as far as return?"

"I am not looking to get rich quick, Wang. I would seek only twenty-percent of the profit while you keep eighty-percent."

Wang's eyes betrayed surprise, as these were unusually generous terms. Gideon noted the look and knew Wang was pleased.

"Those are generous terms. How much are you thinking of investing, my friend?"

Gideon Henry once more looked around for prying eyes, then pulled a thick envelope from his pocket and handed it to Wang, who opened it to peer inside. Wang ran his thumb over the bills and could not help expressing surprise at holding over ten thousand dollars. He kept his voice low.

"Gideon, this is an exceedingly large sum. I will be honest with you that I cannot guarantee all success. But I would be very careful."

"I know there are no guarantees, Wang, but I trust you. Also, I would ask if there might be a bank, or its equivalent among your people, where you can arrange to make deposits and where I might withdraw?"

"Such things can be arranged."

Gideon started to turn away and paused, turning back again.

"Wang, should something happen to me or you do not see me for a while, could you make sure sufficient funds go to Mrs. McClinder at the home for children outside of town?"

"I will do so."

As Gideon left the shop to the clinking of the bell, Wang shook his head. Gideon definitely was a man of contrasts. Feeling the thickness of the envelope inside his tunic, Wang smiled and ducked behind the curtain.

Since that day, Wang carefully watched over the children's home. During Gideon's absences there was money delivered to Mrs. McClinder regularly. And still the money entrusted by Gideon grew in Wang's trustworthy hands.

7

CRASWELL

Vern sat his horse atop a small ridge, looking out over a valley a few miles from the ranch house. Elbows on the pommel, he found himself caught in the beauty before him. Wildflowers dotted the landscape, giving accents to the green. More rain this spring meant more green and the beauty was refreshing after a couple of relatively dry years. Now and then Vern liked to sit and store up thoughts in his mind. Sometimes he sat for an hour, drinking it in like a parched man at a mountain spring.

Today his mind was troubled.

Years ago he and Ruth came to this land with all they owned in the back of a Conestoga wagon that rattled on its last legs. They joked for days that they would stop when the wagon finally gave up the ghost and broke down for good. Despite his worry-furrowed brow, Vern chuckled in recalling how they stopped the wagon in almost this exact spot and got down to stand together. Something in them said this was home. Slipping his arm around Ruth, a silent union in their hearts, he snuggled her to his side. Ruth's arms encircled him tightly.

Seconds later, they both jumped at the crash, turning to see one of the wheels crack and a spoke jut out sideways. Turning to look at each other in wonder, they grinned and laughter filled the air. Not just a chuckle but a deep belly laugh finally ending with them laying in the grass grasping their sides. Indeed, the wagon was the confirmation of what they already knew. They were home. Vern remembered the look in Ruth's eyes, a look of peace and happiness. And he remembered pulling her close...

Rough years passed. There were fights with marauding Indians, then with rustlers and others who sought not to build but to take what others already prepared. There were ancient bullet scars on the ranch house that he often paused to touch with his fingers and remember what it took to make this land into what it was now.

Riding far and wide, Vern bought cattle to start the herd. Many were bought on credit, sold with a handshake and a drink. Proving up on those handshakes was not always easy, but he never missed a payment. Those early years of gathering and growing paid off with the hundreds of cattle roaming his land.

Vern frowned.

Cattle numbers were now decreasing in this valley and in the distant fingers of his ranch. At first he figured they merely migrated, but a sweep found nothing but cold ashes and a trail. It was a trail towards the Rocking-B.

Vern remembered how Dan Bowers arrived shortly after he and Ruth. At first they even fought together, as neither had but one cowhand to share the labors. Both of their wives were excellent shots, and six rifles made a difference. A friendship of sorts had grown. Then a few years back Dan's wife died and everything changed. Suddenly Dan was land hungry, irritable and likely at any time to pull a bottle from his pocket or saddlebag and take a swig. Growing fat, others made sly fun – at first – of the way he carried the roll around his neck. The man's irritability and way of flying off the handle at the slightest comment soon had even old friends seeking the other side of the street.

Vern tried to talk to Dan, but the man was changed. Hunger for power gave rise in Bowers to a sense of self-importance and privilege. Avoidance by others gave way to fear and that fear seemed somehow to feed the man's mind. Dan's focus became rooted in a grab for land. Scarier was his push to hold his own land. Nesters were troublesome to all ranchers, but somehow nesters on the Rocking-B either disappeared or left the area looking like the persuasion had been harsh. There were rumors of even a woman and child disappearing, though Bowers claimed they moved on. No one dared push it further.

Dan's focus became making a kingdom for his son, Clyde. Clyde himself was self-absorbed, often strutting like his father. Vern pondered that Clyde seemed to give sway to his father, but noted Clyde began to look disdainfully upon his father. The obvious deference of others fed both Dan and Clyde's minds with falsehood as to their importance. Clyde also displayed a penchant for the ladies of the cribs in town, and rumor said he was brutal to any woman unfortunate enough to be encircled by his arms.

Clyde made a point of showing interest in Mary Schmidt. Yet the looks he gave her in town were nothing short of lust. Moreover, the looks were not confined to Mary, for he cast more than one lingering look upon Ruth. Vern knew Mary was strong willed and knew how to shoot and ride with the best of the men, yet even she would be unable to handle Clyde Bowers. Mary knew his concern and sought to reassure him, but his fatherly instincts could not rest.

Approaching Dan one day about missing cattle, Bowers reached to his pocket for a bottle and, swigging generously, wiped his mouth with a stained sleeve. Leaning on the pommel and looking at Vern with a look of superiority mixed with barely veiled anger, he glared at Vern for a few moments before speaking.

"Schmidt, are you accusing me of rustling?"

Vern was shocked at the danger he felt from the man.

"Dan, we fought battles together and I've been your friend for years."

"Well, I don't take lightly to being accused. As far as I'm concerned you ain't welcome on my land. Fact is, if you can't keep your stock corralled you may as well just pack up and leave!" Dan reached for his gun, resting his palm on the handle.

"In fact, Schmidt, if you accuse me again I will take it personal. I will also take it personal if I find anybody riding on my land." Turning, Bowers glared once back at Vern and rode off. Since then, Vern heard occasional comments accusing the Lazy-S of rustling cows. In actuality, it appeared Bowers' men were bleeding the Lazy-S and others dry. Dan Bowers' seeking of more land – of a kingdom – became common knowledge.

Ruth and he sat on the porch in the evening, listening to the birds and other sounds of the night. Their talk ranged from holding on in the hope something would miraculously change, to waging a new war. Neither had stomach for a fight with the Rocking-B. This was a foe they neither anticipated nor sought. What finally resulted was a plan to hold tight for a while to see how it all played out.

Some of the hands left, making the odds even worse. Jose and Manuel had been with him for many years. Paulo came later, and then Conner. Others in the area initially frowned upon the Mexican hands, but they slowly were accepted and local merchants found their wages just as collectible as white wages.

Could he hire gunhands, as Bowers clearly was doing? His heart would not bear the thought.

8

KANSAS CITY

"This is real nice, Otis. I'd just about forgotten what it was like to be waited on at the table." She winked at her husband.

Otis Henry winked back at his wife. "I'd forgotten what a good cup of coffee tasted like."

"Otis, now you behave!"

They both laughed! Otis looked at Ella. "I just wish they knew how to make coffee like you do, Ella. It's like they poured it half-done. Can't hardly taste the beans!"

"I've had a lot of experience, Otis. I think people nowadays – maybe just back here in civilization – don't understand that a good cup of coffee should float a horseshoe."

Laughing again, they watched as the waiter came to their table and once more filled their cups. Dressed in white with a bow tie, he seemed a bit sullen, though effective in his job. Remaining quiet for a few minutes, they looked the room over. It was early morning and the crowds were slim, but the bustle of Kansas City was beginning. There were wagons already traversing the streets and the rays of the sun found their way through random openings to touch the street in front of the hotel.

For several years now, Otis and Ella came to Kansas City for a month. They started after an embattled time when a scoundrel from back east, named Boss Carter, tried to kill them and take the ranch. Their prodigal son, Bill, returned and it had been a very difficult time. Otis' old army outfit had gathered and put the fear of God in the enemy and destroyed their plans. After it was all over, Bill noted how worn his parents looked, and suggested they go east for a bit while the ranch was cleaned up from the battle. They reluctantly agreed but found great relaxation in the trip. This was now their fifth trip in as many years.

Ella Henry saw her husband's thoughts were far away. She looked at the man whose life was entwined with hers for so many years. His once deep brown hair grew mostly silver now. His shoulders were not as muscular and wide as in younger years. Yet he still walked with vigor and was strong in mind – especially attitude – and not a man with whom to trifle. Always prepared, he continued to carry a gun even in Kansas City. It was a smaller caliber Colt in his waistband.

His gun belt was back in the room with his .44's. She smiled, thinking of the derringer she had in her bag. They both had survived by being prepared and old habits were not to be left aside as they saw the changes around them.

"Otis, where are you? Otis?"

He startled.

"Huh?"

"You're a thousand miles away, Otis."

Meeting her glance, he smiled wryly.

"I was just looking back, Ella. All we've done, all that's happened. Then that trouble we had and how it was so rough. But I sort of felt more alive then. There's something I miss about when it was rough, when we had to be sharper and we were building. I guess in ways I'm glad it's gotten beyond that, but I miss it, too."

She grinned and nodded.

"I know what you mean, Otis. We built well and we raised strong boys – now men. And here we are, sitting in luxury while they muck the stalls!"

Both of them laughed.

"Been a while since I even had to do that, Ella," shaking his head at the thought. It was, indeed, many years since he mucked a stall! He wondered if he was getting soft.

Taking a sip of coffee, Ella dabbed her mouth with the linen napkin and reached her hand across the corner of the tablecloth. Placing her hand over that of her husband, she felt his fingers curl over hers. It was a protective feel giving much comfort over the years.

Both looked up as the front door opened. It was a man barely into adulthood. Walking with a slight stoop, he glanced around the dining room, and approached their table. Both Ella and Otis instinctively felt for their weapons, though something in the visage of this young man told them there was nothing to worry about.

Drawing near, he removed his hat, revealing hair parted in the middle and slicked down. Though the style of the day, both Henry's found it a bit odd. His clothing, though not of a destitute faction of society, did not seem to be far above it, either.

Cheeks drawn and sallow, he appeared sickly; yet a firm gaze came from eyes that were strong, yet tense. Accustomed to judging men quickly, Otis and Ella saw this young man was on a mission of some sort. He appeared weak but held an inner strength.

Nodding to Ella, the young man spoke with a voice that seemed feeble. He would be hard pressed to yell and sound any different.

"Mr. and Mrs. Henry?"

Otis Henry rose to his feet. "Yes, young man. Can I help you?"

"My name is Nate Baker – at least now." He smiled. "I'm sorry to be so bold, but may I speak with you a few moments?"

"Certainly." Otis waved him to a seat and looked up to make eye contact with the waiter. "Coffee, Mr. Baker?"

"Yes, please, Mr. Henry. I will pay."

"Absolutely not. You are a guest at our table."

Bringing a fresh cup, the waiter warmed theirs also. Both Ella and Otis looked at the young man, waiting for him to speak.

"That's good coffee."

Ella glanced at Otis, to find him flashing a sparkling glance her way. Placing his cup on the table and sitting stiff and awkward, the young man spoke.

"Well, I realize this is nothing you expected. I heard last year that there was a couple with the name of Henry here from out Colorado way. I tried to get a chance to meet you but you had already left for home. So this year I kept checking so I might speak with you. You see, I think we might be related."

Otis Henry jutted his lower lip as he responded. Was this man seeking something untoward, or was he genuine? Ella found herself looking at his face, seeking any sign of familiarity with her relatives. She found none.

"Young man, you catch us off-guard."

"I realize that, ma'am. I'm sorry, and perhaps I need to tell you that, despite my appearance, I am not seeking anything from you. Except maybe information."

"Well, Nate. Now that you've startled us a mite, why don't you fill in the gaps?" Otis never was one to dilly-dally when piecing a puzzle.

"I was born Nathan Henry. When my father, Artemis, was killed in a robbery, I was thirteen years old. Mother never recovered from the grief and died. My younger sister and myself were farmed out to others. A family named Baker took me in and over the years found it easier to just call me by their surname to avoid having to explain all the time. I just – became - Nate Baker. My older brother turned a different corner and lived in the streets. His name is Gideon Henry."

At the mention of the name, Otis and Ella raised their brows.

"Thank you, since your response tells me you know of my brother."

"We've heard of him." In reality, they met Gideon Henry three years back when he passed thru on his way to a job. Having some acquaintance with Lem Teague, a gunman known as "Preacher," both men stopped by the ranch one evening and headed separate ways in the morning. Lem left troubled; Gideon left determined. They were two men, related but with different motivations.

9

ST. LOUIS

Matronly and beginning to show gray wisps in her hair, Margie McClinder wiped flour from her hands and tucked a stray lock back into a tightly wrapped bun at the nape of her neck. Children playing in the yard caught her attention and she stood, lost in a few moments of thought as she looked out the window. Just that morning she went to town for supplies and, as usual, had plenty of money to buy what she needed.

A smile crossed her face as she noted children running through the yard. Most of them had been living in such a way that meals were sporadic and mostly insufficient. Several were little more than skin and bones when brought to her door. Spotting Jimmy running after another boy, laughing uproariously, she tilted her head in wonder as she recalled how he was brought by the sheriff after being caught stealing an apple. Jimmy was a mere wisp of a boy with a look of desperation mixed with fear and anger. Knowingly, her first interaction was to slap the perpetual flour from her hands, forming a sort of cloud in the air as she led Jimmy to the kitchen of the big house and sat him down with a gesture and a glance towards a chair at the worn table. Without a word she placed before him not one, but two, cookies, and poured a large glass of milk. Jimmy's eyes bulged with wonder and her heart melted as it had with the others.

That day was a turn around for Jimmy. His small frame soon filled, ribs disappearing as plentiful food changed both body and attitude. Well she recalled the day a peal of laughter erupted from this once scared boy.

An early widow, Margie spent the past few years struggling with various jobs in order to bring food to her table and existence was not exactly something to look forward to. Yet she never was a quitter and put one foot in front of the other. Always attentive to others, Margie spent much of her hard-earned money "feeding strays" as she called it – the children that wandered the streets.

Her new life started that night at Doctor Baker's office as she was cleaning floors. A strange man came in carrying a fragile and barely alive young girl. Doctor Baker examined the poor thing and Margie heard the hopeless diagnosis. She stayed late that night after cleaning and kept to the background as the stranger held solemn vigil by the bedside as the young girl eased into eternity. Unasked, Margie brought a glass of water to the man and rested her hand upon the girl's brow a few times, brushing matted hair from her face and at one point taking a few seconds to straighten the filthy dress. Once she met the eyes of the stranger. Looking sorrowfully upon the dying girl, Margie perceived many of the same things she saw regularly in the wandering street waifs seeking food. There was hardness, yet also loneliness, hurt, deep anger and a host of other things she could not fully define. Margie alone heard the subtle, isolated sob escaping the man as the girl took her last breath. A moment later he brushed an eye with a finger and continued to look at the girl's face as he spoke, one hand on her hair.

"Will you see to her? I will pay everything."

"I will, and gladly. It is little enough that she had in life." Tears already dripped to her apron as she grieved the girl. "How might I get hold of you, sir?"

"No need. I will get hold of you." Then he walked out.

Funeral expenses were paid and, a few weeks later, the man suddenly appeared at her door. Identifying himself as Mr. Henry, he outlined for her his thoughts on a home for wayward and street children and explained he already held title to a large two-story home outside town with many acres surrounding to allow for children to play. He offered her a steady job and generous wages. Over coffee that day, arrangements were made and Margie found herself in charge and walking with a spring in her step and a joy in her heart. Word spread and a few children were brought, but others just wandered in from who-knows-where until there were a dozen sitting at her table at mealtimes. She never tired of the wide-eyed looks on newcomer's faces as they surveyed the heaps and bowls of food before them. Of course, they quickly were taught to wait till she was seated and thanks given with bowed heads before they ate.

Very soon she enlisted the help of Hessie, who grew up as a slave in the Deep South. After the war her family talked of heading west. Her husband soon died and there was nothing causing her to stay. They were barely past St. Louis when her parents died from smallpox. Hessie began life anew, taking odd jobs to support herself through the years. The two met when Margie, who saw Hessie cleaning at a restaurant, suddenly noticed she was no longer working. Inquiring, she was told Hessie was very sick. Margie found Hessie in a run-down shack appearing more rat hole than home. Nursing Hessie back to health built a deep friendship. After Mr. Henry gave his approval, Hessie moved in and began helping with the children. The sadness and desperation of her life disappeared and a smile became common to her face and her laughter – which was loud and shook her entire body – became a mainstay of life and worked medicine upon the sadness of many children. Very soon her lap was popular. Her skin color made no difference, just as the color of the children mattered not.

Each day Margie saw hearts changed with love and many of the children were as her own, not a few coming to her for hugs and even crawling onto her lap as she knitted and sewed, snuggling their heads under her chin. Jimmy had not hugged her yet, but did his best to sit next to her, glancing sideways at her as he did so. She knew he would find her lap soon!

Startled from her reverie by a knock at the front door, Margie straightened her hair once again and walked the hallway to the large front door, where she found a young man extending a thick envelope to her. It was always the same young Chinese man. Though she tried, the young man would never reveal his name. Out of her nurturing, she began to call him "Happy" for he always brought happiness.

"I bring this to you."

"Thank you, Happy. And my thanks to our friend."

With a nod Happy was gone. This was the way from the beginning. Always the envelopes came, always regular, always generous and always extra when there was a special need. It was as if someone knew when she needed more. One day Happy also delivered a carefully written note stating money was being deposited in the bank in her and Hessie's names, in addition to wages.

Never questioning the money, she knew that somehow Mr. Henry provided. When Mr. Henry came calling, he never broke the formality of addressing her as Mrs. McClinder.

Margie shook her head in wonder, tucking the envelope into her apron and turning back to the kitchen to get bread from the oven. Hessie, who was at the mercantile fetching a few things, would be thrilled when Margie told her of their latest gift.

10

KANSAS CITY

Nathan leveled his eyes on Otis and Ella Henry and spoke in serious tones.

"I don't want to keep you, so here is why I approach you: I spent several years trying to locate my sister. The family that took her in moved west. I finally received word of her through a friend who went west but returned. Said he couldn't handle all the wide open space after living so long in the city." He smiled, looking out the windows. "Imagine that! What I wouldn't give to escape this constricting life. I've been stocking shelves for years for my – father. His focus is on business, but he really sort of assumes I am there to do his bidding with no question of the future. He's probably seething right now, wondering where I am. And yet, look what living like this has done to me." Both his listeners noted a frustration in the young man's voice as he gestured to his physical body. He raised his hand.

"I apologize…back to my story. My sister and I have exchanged a couple letters. I am seeking my brother to try and bring some sort of unity back to our family. I need to find Gideon."

"What are you asking of us?"

"I thought you might be able to help me locate him."

Otis Henry looked into Nate's eyes. Having already noted his appearance, he now looked to the young man's soul, admiring how Nate Baker did not waver from eye contact. There was something within, waiting to be awakened. There was truth in the young man. Glancing sideways at his wife, who seemed to know his thoughts – sometimes before him – he saw her nod assent. She knew what he was going to do.

"Are you married, Nate?"

"No, sir. Just me."

"We are leaving in three days to head back to Colorado. In the meantime, I will send a few wires to see if I can find any indications of Gideon. I can't make any promises."

"Thank you, sir. And ma'am." He nodded to both and started to rise.

"What do you see as your future here, Nate?"

Nate settled back to his seat and looked pained. Looking to Otis, his eyes seemed to bore into the distance.

"That remains yet to be seen."

"We leave in three days. We'll take the train as far as Boulder and ride from there. Got horses waiting and going to seed." Seeing Nate still did not understand, he smiled at Ella. She spoke.

"What Otis is saying Nate, is we'd love to have you join us. Get out of this place and start a new life. We're needful of help on the ranch."

Startled, Nate's eyes were as big as dinner plates. He stammered. "Why...well...doggone!"

"Just say yes, Nate." Ella smiled.

"Yes!"

11

Trains were familiar means of travel for Gideon. Riding in a private sleeping car when possible for the beginning of a journey, his pattern was to switch to coach at the end so as not to draw attention. The final ride to a destination would be horseback.

Traveling light, the main tools of his trade were strapped to his hips. A carpetbag contained a couple changes of clothes with an extra pistol tucked between. A derringer was tucked in his vest pocket. As always, he carried a folding knife clipped behind his belt. Winchesters were available in most towns and he would pick one up after buying a horse.

Boarding the train and entering his tiny sleeping room, Gideon locked the door, lay back and soon was asleep.

A week and a half later he rode into the small town of Craswell, Colorado on a sure-footed sorrel in the heat of an early afternoon. Experience taught him over the years how to pick a horse for his business. It needed to be well muscled, with a look in its eye saying it was tamed but not broken. He wanted spirit, for spirit could keep a horse running long after muscles faltered. Those extra miles could make a difference between life and death.

Trips in the past created connections, and this horse came from a man he met before who kept a few horses tucked away out of sight for those who were willing – or needing – a fast horse. The deal was swift, as Gideon Henry knew the value of horseflesh and did not haggle over price. The sorrel was bursting with energy, responding willingly to his new master's slightest pressure on the reins.

Craswell. Not intended to become a town originally, it was a piece of ground like all others until circumstances conspired and a town was born. It just so happened few of the locals really knew the unique story behind the name. Around 1840, a group of early settlers paused for a night, cooked their meals, let the children play, set a guard and bedded down. Early the next morning there was arguing between some wanting to stop the endless journey and settle versus those planning to move on. Any loss of numbers also meant loss of weapons against Indians, causing the argument to get quite heated. Sudden wailing near the tail of the wagon train arrested all talk as curious eyes turned to see Elizabeth Craswell kneeling by her motionless eight-year-old, Dorthea. Elizabeth's wailing grew and others rushing in saw her daughter lying as dead upon the grass. Seth Jackson, with the most experience of them all, knelt and put his ear to her chest. Raising slowly and shaking his head, he stood and placed his hand on the shoulder of Dorthea's father, Micah, in the time-accepted sign of male support. It was assumed Dorthea succumbed to heart weakness, as no marks were found upon her body.

With the sun warming the air and the need to move on, Joseph Tanner and Levi Cooper grabbed shovels and, walking to a nearby knoll, dug a hole then waited while Dorthea was wrapped in a blanket and slowly brought up. Micah cradled his daughter's head, his eyes almost blinded with tears. Overcome with grief, Elizabeth Craswell rushed to her daughter's head and, in the ensuing disruption, caused Micah to lose his grip. Dorthea tumbled and slammed to the ground. Everybody gasped - including Dorthea! It was never understood what happened, whether she ate Monkshood or was spider bit. All they knew was Dorthea was suddenly back to normal. Some just plain saw it as a miracle. Micah and Elizabeth Craswell saw it as a sign this was a place to give life and chose to settle on that very spot. They waved goodbye as their friends moved on, leaving both the Craswell's and the Jackson's to start a new life on that sacred ground they now called Craswell, feeling the name would give possible Heavenly favor to their endeavors. Perhaps four or five years later the Craswell family perished in a fire, but the name was there to stay.

After all those years, Craswell was like so many other small but growing towns in the West – a dusty main street with a few offshoots and a backstreet. Amidst the General Store and other businesses and the bank and homes of the prominent citizens was the Gold Horse Saloon. Staples of the western land-scape, saloons were clearinghouses for information. A stop at a local saloon was enough to fill one in on many local happenings – good or bad.

Gideon needed information. As he neared, he mentally placed the other buildings, such as livery stable, blacksmith and sheriff's office. He also not-ed the cribs on the outskirts. Many a man lost his stake and future in such places. A careful and self-controlled man, Gideon Henry early on decided he would not fall prey to that vice. Besides, much of the refuse of the West prowled these areas and he pre-ferred to avoid unnecessary trouble. He preferred comforts of a better part of society.

More than once Gideon found himself wonder-ing why so many towns had straight streets. There were rare exceptions, one of them being a town where he stopped a year or so back in Kansas. Gideon remembered standing on the boardwalk of a saloon. Looking both ways saw the curving streets. Inside he inquired about it and was told the original settlers chose odd lots for defensive reasons against marauding bands of various types, causing the curves. A later group of interlopers moved in from the East and tried to straighten the curves, only to be met by gun barrels and threats, resulting in the interlopers suddenly deciding curves added beauty and character.

Craswell apparently opted for straight streets. Looking around, he admired the beauty of distant foothills fading into the Continental Divide. It was a wet year so far, evidenced by lush grass covering the hillsides, with Aspen filling lower slopes with a few stray Lodgepole pines, usually reserved for the higher slopes in the distance. The town itself seemed to belong there, nestled on high ground above a river, surrounded by a few stands of River Birch and a stray Choke Cherry or three. There were many such places around the country, where a man could look out from his porch and feast on the beauty of God's creation. Coneflowers and Black-eyed Susan filled much of the lower meadowland. Gideon shook his head how anybody could deny a creator when mere observation witnessed to the variety of plants and animals and the intricate way all interacted. All were provided for from the bounty around. Even in the desert there was more life than many believed. If a careful observer took a few minutes to sit quiet and unmoving, it did not take long to note the appearance of insects, small animals and birds flitting to and fro.

It was the same in any part of the country when one was able to get away from the mass of humanity. In fact, nature was a protection of sorts, providing both building materials and warnings. A man could harvest trees to build a shelter strong enough to withstand the strongest of storms – provided he built in the right location. His mother used to read in the Bible about building a house on the rock and not on sand. That was wisdom beyond the theological meaning.

If a man watched carefully, nature itself often gave warning of danger. Signs were there when storms were about to break, through the turning of leaves, the colors of the sky, actual smells in the air and the actions of wildlife in the area. If all the animals were finding their holes, a wise rider would do the same. Many times danger could be avoided by noting the actions of birds. If a bird flew to a tree but then suddenly averted and flew away, it indicated something amiss and a wise man would sit tight and wait. Careful observation and disciplined patience revealed whether it was another animal presence or a man, hidden. Men were less patient than animals at times. Many a man lay dead across the West, their last act being ignoring the warnings of nature. Sometimes the first move was a man's last.

Danger signs showed in towns also. If there was impending conflict, scurrying bystanders and quiet streets at the wrong time of day spread the warning as quickly as a wildfire on the prairie.

Sitting his horse in front of the saloon, Gideon gazed upward at the sign. Gold Horse Saloon. As with many places in the towns of the West, the sign was more ornate than the establishment itself. Sign makers lived on the wishful thinking of their customers.

A mere few months ago, Gideon happened upon a new business owner in St. Louis involved in a conversation with a sign maker. Leaning against a post near the front door, Gideon pretended to be looking around as he observed the discussion.

"I just want it to say 'saloon.'"

"But that is so limiting. You have much potential here, but you must say more so people will come in. You need a catchy name that will draw them in."

"Like what?"

"Something like...Lady Godiva's Pleasure Palace. That'll draw everybody in just out of curiosity. Once they're in the door, they'll buy a drink."

"Yes, that's quite a name all right – it'll draw the money right out of my pocket!"

Gideon listened to the men haggling back and forth and, when the dust settled, smiled as the sign maker gained a job carving a sign saying, "Lady Godiva Saloon, Bart Smith Proprietor" – charging by the letter!

Gideon chuckled at the astute business sense of the sign maker.

Now standing in Craswell, he compared the name of the saloon to the appearance of the premises. It obviously was no golden horse. Glancing around casually, his gaze lingered for a few moments upon an old man sitting on a bench by the batwings, a livid scar across obviously unseeing eyes. Yet the man's head faced the doorway, no doubt listening. As the man's white eyes turned to him, Gideon's brow creased.

Dismounting, he carefully loosed his guns and looked at the horses, noting several Rocking-B brands. It was natural for a western man to note brands, as common as a woman would perhaps note clothing worn or the texture of dinner biscuits. This was an unusual number of horses for so early in the day and could indicate several things, not all good.

To an observing eye, Gideon would be seen adjusting his horse's bridle, but he was examining a brand on a nearby horse. Obviously now a Rocking-B, his eye told him it was once a Tumbling-8 until someone handy with cinch ring or running iron did a fair job of altering.

Grinning to himself, he thought how many such brands filled the West. A heated cinch ring held in green sticks was common when a calf was found. Some carried a running iron, a short iron rod with one end in the shape of a U. It fit handily in a saddlebag. Both methods could be used legally, allowing the creation of any desired brand, but many times the same tool was used to brand a calf over a tiny fire after a careful look around. Never mind that a calf's mother was nearby with a clear brand of the owner. Some newer outfits on the range were suffering major cattle losses from such methods, while other area ranchers found their cows seemingly birthing an unusual number of calves in any given year. In years past such activities were received with a knowing smile and many early outfits grew by such methods. If there was a question as to the ownership of a cow or calf the running iron was heated and the beast marked with the application of the adage "finders keepers." Sometimes the calf was carried across a saddle for several miles before being released amongst another group. Calves could bawl for days before settling into their new herd. Now, with the law more settled and too many cattle disappearing to faraway places where their sale brought no questions, the once-common herd-building methods were frowned upon. Being caught altering a brand without legitimate reason usually resulted in a hemp necktie in quick fashion. It was the same with horses.

Stepping toward the batwings, honed reflexes alerted Gideon and he stepped quickly aside as a man flew out of the saloon to lay crumpled and bleeding in the dirt. Horses shifted nervously as the man landed at their feet. Another man, large with the bulk of muscles and with the look of one not too long into adulthood, strutted out and stood glaring cruelly as the crumpled man struggled painfully to his elbows. Obviously beaten, the man in the street dripped blood from a cut lip, his eyes all but swollen shut. Staring at the dirt, tears mixed with blood to form dots of watery red amidst the dust beneath his face.

"I told you for the last time, Schmidt. Leave our cattle alone!" Clyde looked around, making eye contact to make sure his subtle accusation was heard. Turning back to the saloon, Clyde caught sight of Gideon and glared at him. Gideon gave no ground and stared back with eyes cold with veiled warning. The blustering young cowboy wrinkled his brow in question, looking long at Gideon before turning and strutting back into the saloon. The batwings squeaked behind him.

Waiting and listening a moment, Gideon heard an exclamation from across the street and a woman yelled.

"Vern!" The woman ran to the man in the street and knelt beside him. She helped him up, gasping when she saw his face in the full sun. Glancing towards the saloon with a mixture of hate and fear, she met Gideon's eyes and saw nothing. Heaving with determination, she lifted the beaten man from the dust with the strength of someone used to hard work.

"Why, Vern? You knew he was in there! Why?"

Vern spit blood, wiping his mouth with the back of a hand.

"I didn't expect them all to gang up on me." Putting a bloody hand to his gun, he turned back to the saloon.

"No, Vern! They'll kill you! That's exactly what they want, so they can take the land. We're going home."

Putting her arm around Vern, she slowly walked to a buckboard across the street and bodily pushed and lifted him into the back, mounted the front and slapped the reins. She glanced again at the saloon and at Gideon as the wagon moved swiftly away, stopping briefly at the mercantile where supplies were loaded and another, a younger lady, also got in after startled exclamations.

Glancing around, Gideon noted several townsfolk watching from various windows and doorways. Yet none lifted a hand to help the man.

Entering the saloon, he paused to get the lay of the land, noting doors and windows and groups of men before walking to the bar. Gideon Henry surveyed the room in the bar mirror. Cowhands sat at several tables and stood along the other end of the bar. Off to one side two men played chess, though they seemed to more stare at the board as they listened. The big man from out front glanced at him again and downed a drink. Others gathered around the man as minions with their feudal lord.

Must be the Rocking-B, he surmised. Positioned at a table central to the room, the big man sat proud.

Others in the room seemed to be keeping a distance between themselves and the group of cocky cowhands. From the numbers and the horses outside, he presumed the Rocking-B held sway here in Craswell.

Gideon watched the grown men fawning over their leader.

"You nailed him good, Clyde."

"Serves him right."

Clyde nodded and slurped another drink as he swelled his chest. Looking up, he caught Gideon Henry looking at him in the mirror.

"What'cha lookin' at, mister?" His curt words caused the other cowhands to look.

Gideon looked down at his drink and ignored the man.

"I'm talkin' to you, mister."

Gideon raised his eyes and casually looked at Clyde in the mirror, responding conversationally.

"I'm listening, though I suspect if you ever really said what was on your mind you'd be speechless."

Clyde was flustered and not at all sure if what was said was an insult or otherwise.

Anger started to well in Gideon Henry as he also realized his need to tread carefully. Anger often welled up in him when a man played the game this man – Clyde – was playing, lording it over others. Gideon despised cowering before any man. Avoiding trouble as much as possible when between jobs, there was a difference between civilization and this, the raw West. Out here, men still relied upon themselves and respect demanded it. Striking first could avert other issues. Gideon found himself changing into a seemingly more primitive creature when riding into a town in this, the newer part of the country. It took a different kind of man to survive here. When he returned to St. Louis, the change reversed.

Glancing at Clyde in the mirror, tension hung in the air like a heavy morning.

"Did you have something to say, Clyde?"

"I asked what you was lookin' at?"

"I'm really not looking at much of anything, if truth be told."

Clyde was taken aback, again unable to determine the meaning of this stranger's words.

"We don't take kindly to strangers in these parts."

"I gathered that." Gideon spoke in firm tones.

"You just remember that! You're a stranger here, and you need to find some other place to stop." Clyde looked around at his minions and nodded as they continued to fawn. Full of himself and what passed as whiskey, Clyde rose, hitched his belt and strutted up to Gideon with the bearing of one used to being treated as an important man.

"What's your business here, anyhow, mister?"

Gideon sipped, looking Clyde over more care-fully in the mirror. Probably mid twenties, Clyde was large, with chest and arms swelled by the labor of the range. A certain look in his eye testified to a man used to having things his way. Smirking at Gideon, Clyde turned to look at his grinning followers before hitching his belt again and speaking in a haughty tone.

"Mister, I'm talkin' to you."

Never able to tolerate such men, Gideon Henry felt anger well up inside him. Placing his drink care-fully down, he met Clyde's eyes in the mirror. Blustery youth gave way to caution as Clyde saw Gideon's eyes glaring like a viper. Still, he could not back down without losing face in front of his men.

Gideon realized the man's quandary and pushed hard. This type of man sickened him and he would not put up with it. Early on he learned being meek at such times did nothing but make things worse.

"Go pick on someone scrawny, Clyde." He knew Clyde was backed into a corner, but he didn't care. Muscles tensed for the obvious next step of this oft repeated dance of male confrontation.

Clyde glanced quickly and warily at his fellows, and there was a moment of silence as the gravity of the situation caused chairs to scrape. Men left the saloon or stepped aside to watch.

As Clyde turned back to speak again, Gideon spun, landing a powerful fist on the man's jaw. Clyde flew backwards, kept from falling by a couple of his fellows. Stunned, he stared for a few seconds before shaking his head and coming back with fist raised.

Easily ducking the blow, Gideon quickly stepped to the side and landed blows to the kidney and head, followed by a swift blow to Clyde's temple. Clyde dropped to his knees, stunned. Gideon's blows were practiced, learned on the streets.

"Go home, Clyde."

Clyde remained kneeling, stunned and unanswering as his men lifted him by the arms and led him to the doors. Alternately looking at Gideon and Clyde, one of the minions spoke.

"Mister, you've just crossed the Rocking-B. Your time is limited. Dan Bowers will have you hunted like a dog. I suggest you leave, though I dare say it won't do much good."

Dan Bowers! His contact! What a strange turn of events. Why was it so rare for the jobs to be simple and easy?

Returning to the bar, Gideon finished his drink while others made attempts to stare without being obvious. Turning to leave, he hesitated before the batwings. Stepping over to the men playing chess, Gideon gazed for a few moments at the table while the men fidgeted nervously. Reaching down and moving a piece upon the board, he turned and walked out.

Staring down at the board, one of the men rubbed his chin and shook his head.

"Good move!"

12

Later that afternoon Gideon entered the barbershop for a shave. Something about whiskers made him feel unclean. Though he could shave at the hotel, he enjoyed the luxury of a warm shave followed by a hot towel.

Three men halted their conversation as he entered. One, obviously the barber, arose and slapped a towel to the chair, a seemingly universal symbol that the barber was ready for his next customer. Two others were almost identical to those found in so many western towns sitting flapping their jaws in mostly idle or unproductive conversation in the middle of the afternoon. Usually they were making day wages, swamping at the saloons or hauling water and other menial tasks. Men without ambition, they spent their extra hours trying to solve the problems of a community. Yet, they also knew what was going on, by the very fact they had nothing better to do but sit and watch.

One wore stained clothes with a just-as-stained and mostly worn out hat. Obviously not here for the services of the barber, the man was disheveled and sported the wispy facial hair of someone unconcerned with appearance. It was his talk Gideon heard as he entered.

In another chair was a man wearing sleeve garters and a relatively clean shirt buttoned to where the collar would be if he chose to wear one. Likely a store clerk, Gideon mused.

"Howdy, mister." It was the man with the garters. Gideon nodded.

"Where you from?"

"Elsewhere." The man's eyes widened with surprise. But Gideon achieved his goal – the men realized he didn't want to talk. That way they would likely go back to talking amongst themselves and he could glean from the information. Pausing, he looked the room over as he hung his hat.

"Shave, please." Lowering himself into the chair, which was broken and sat too low, Gideon slipped his pistol to his stomach. Then he closed his eyes and feigned relaxing as the barber dabbed cream on his face. Eyes flitted back and forth as the conversation resumed.

"Like I said, Bowers says this here Schmidt is rustling and accusing Bowers himself of the same.

Only goes to show that you may think you know somebody but then they up and show their true selves."

"Schmidt's been around a long time. I ain't never seen him be nothin' but pleasant. Don't even have no accent. I hear tell it was his grandparents what moved to this country. That means both he and his parents are Americans."

"Bowers says they are no good and we need to understand that they are lying Germans. And they got them Mexican's working, too."

"But what about his wife? She ain't foreign. And the boy and girl? They's been some hands here-abouts been wantin' to go courtin' that Mary. And they's one of them Mex gal's will turn eyes when she gets a mite older."

"Bowers done put out the word he won't tolerate people bein' friendly with foreign trash what's rust-lin' an' lyin' about him."

"I don't know. I wonder if Bowers is telling the truth."

At the last word, Gideon felt the barber pause for just a moment.

"You just better not say that where Bowers hears or finds out. Ain't either of us gonna say nothin' but you best watch your tongue or you'll be pushin' up daisies!"

Clearing his throat, the barber was grim faced with warning.

All eyes shifted as Gideon stayed the barber's hand and spoke.

"Is Bowers lying or not?"

Eyes widened and again made a circuit of the room. None of them knew the loyalties of this newcomer, and they were talking as if he wasn't hearing. As a group they turned pale.

"I do not have any loyalties. Just an honest question." After a collective sigh of relief, the scraggly man looked to the others. With a shrug, he spoke:

"Well, mister, there's some that say Bowers will do anything to get control of the range; that he's got plans to be big in the territory."

"Why don't you ask Bowers about all of this?"

All voices paused, eyes darting back and forth. It was the barber who broke the tense silence.

"Mister, Dan Bowers has been around bout as long as Schmidt. Can't rightly recall came here first. But I can tell you this: Bowers has got some rough hands that wouldn't take lightly to questioning his honesty. He's made it clear he is not to be questioned. Been some as did who have gone missing."

One of the others raised a hand and spoke excitedly. "Ol' Ridley 'bout got the b'jeebers kicked out of him t'other day." Faces turned to him and, full of their attention, the man continued. "Bowers done made some comment about Schmidt not being of decent folk an Ol' Ridley started to laugh, then squelched it and pretended to cough. I think if Ridley didn't have them scars and such he'd had a bullet in the brisket!"

"Pity's all it is. Even Bowers ain't so low as to hurt a blind man!"

"Don't count on it."

"For an old, blind goat, Ridley sure gets away with a lot. Sometimes I think he knows more than the rest of us together. I seen him back of the stables Monday evening, staring all around like he was a'tryin' to find his way."

"Knows more than a blind man ought to know. I done set with him the other evening after I dropped off the roast my missus fixed for me to take to him. Whilst settin' I seen another plate hid behind his back! Ol' Ridley's milkin' this and getting right fat!" All the men chuckled. "But I tell you, he done give me a run down on all that's going on and I tell you that man may be blind but he ain't stupid!"

"You're right he ain't stupid. I know how it is at my house. My old lady fixes pork and I look at the platter and get my belly set on a tender morsel and next thing I know she done got it settin' on a plate to take to Ridley and I got to take from what's left! Sometimes she makes me take his afore she lets me have mine. I come back and the mashed potatoes is cold and meat's dried out. There's times I want to slap the ol' feller myself!"

"Well, your wife wears a mean set of pants!" Chuckles all around.

13

Jose shook his head. It was a long and very frustrating morning. Working for Vern Schmidt for years, he knew the range as few others, having crisscrossed the hills relentlessly, tending cattle, checking waterholes and hunting varmints. This morning they were out at first light from the line cabin, making a sweep to check on cattle. Where there should be hundreds of cattle, they found just shy of a ninety.

They all knew Bowers was seeking Vern's ranch and cattle were disappearing, but so far they had not witnessed any of the actual rustling, just the tracks of various groups being driven, usually at night, across the range. Though eager to ride Bowers' range and find any herds held in back valleys, Jose was ordered by Vern to stay off Bowers land for now. Bowers was threatening to shoot anyone found on his range, and Schmidt was not eager to give them fodder for the rumors they were already spreading about Vern and his "Mex rustlers." Most of Schmidt's hands left, usually sheepishly approaching Vern's door asking for their wages and saying vaguely it was time to move on. Jose knew they had been threatened and the fact that others were beaten gave truth to the threats. Somehow the ranch still worked with the few Mexicans who remained loyal, along with Conner.

Yet, today was a struggle. Jose knew they needed the cattle to survive. He and his family, along with other hands, called this ranch home for many years. Vern Schmidt treated them no different than his Anglo hands and, in return, received loyalty and long-term cowhands. Most had been with Schmidt for years. What would they do if Schmidt lost the range to Bowers? They would be given very short notice by Bowers to grab what they could carry and leave – if they were given any opportunity at all. Dan Bowers was unpredictable. There were strong views – unspoken in public – that he harbored no remorse about women and children disappearing. Jose and his brother, Manuel, had wives and children. The brothers stopped that very morning overlooking a valley devoid of cows where grazing beasts should be plentiful.

Jose stopped his horse and watched as Manuel trotted a half-mile to join him.

"Where are the cattle, do you think, Jose?"

"I suspect they are at the back of Bowers' ranch, along with the others. Though I suspect many are already run south through the pass and sold. The Rocking-B seems to have a lot of dinero to spend."

"I think you are right, my brother. I also think it is going to get very dangerous around here before long." Manuel paused, spitting into the dust. His wife despised this habit and he now was careful to rinse his mouth before he arrived home. It didn't fool her, but at least she would welcome him with a kiss! "Our families are not safe, Jose. There is danger to come, and I fear for them. And I do not fear lightly."

"You are right, Manuel. This is on my heart also. I wonder about moving them to someplace safe – at least until this is over. There was a time yesterday when I wondered about leaving Schmidt, but deep in my heart I cannot abandon him. He is always good to us and we are like family."

"I feel the same way. Even though I know there is a risk, I can't find it in me to leave him in this time of need. If he eventually loses the ranch, then I feel our place will be to ride with him as he leaves."

Jose nodded. "I think our families will be safe over in the mountain camp."

Manuel's eyes widened. "Ah, yes. I had not thought of that."

Since that conversation they continued to gather disappointing numbers of cattle, and few calves in their midst. He and Manuel were on the flanks as two others, Paulo and Conner, took the drag. Conner had been with Schmidt for about four years and got along well with the Mexicans. In fact, Jose suspected Manuel's teenage daughter, Alita might be one of the reasons Conner stuck around. He was a steady young man and Alita was blossoming into adulthood. Jose smiled and realized he had no idea what Conner's first name was.

The bullet holed Jose's hat and took it to the ground. Jose dove to the dirt and crawled to a boulder as, a moment later, the sound of several shots rent the air. Raising his head, there was time only for a quick glance around before another shot spat upon the rock to his front, spewing chips upwards. Jose ducked.

Manuel was down on the ground and he'd seen only Paulo on horseback, riding behind an outcropping. Crawling to the left, he peered around and saw Manuel scampering for cover, bullets kicking dust on the hillside around. Both their horses moved off, wary but not unaccustomed to gunshots. Looking to the rear he saw Conner's horse down and thrashing. Conner was lying in the grass and suddenly struggled to his feet and limped to a depression in the ground, holding his thigh. Though quite some distance away, Jose could see the man's hand covered with blood. At least he was alive. Though young, he was tough.

More shots rang out. Dust and rock shards splattered the air. Jose huddled closer to the boulder as a cow screamed in pain and surprise following a sudden volley. Peering carefully, it was clear a shot intentionally creased a cow to cause the herd to bolt. Dust and noise and gunshots filled the air as cattle ran into the distance in a full stampede. Attempting to look again, Jose jumped as a bullet cut his temple. Ducking quickly, the blood ran into his eyes and he grabbed his bandana.

Through the afternoon hours they remained pinned down, dusty and longing for the canteens on their saddles. Any attempts to move were met with a dusting of bullets. Toward evening such return volleys lessened, but still they were unable to venture out.

It was obvious those who ambushed them intended to keep them pinned down while others ran the cattle off. In such a stampede the cattle could go for many miles until only the last vestiges of exhaustion slowed them. In the meantime some of the cattle, mostly calves, would drop off along the trail.

Bowers! Schmidt could not take this loss in cattle, and now Conner down with a leg wound. Another man out!

14

ausing to pay for his shave, Gideon glanced out the window. Rarely unaware of his surroundings, his glance happened upon the window across the street and his eyes narrowed. Sun and time of day happened to cast a reflection of two men standing to the left outside the barbershop door. Moving further, he adjusted the reflection and noted a couple more idly lounging nearby. Four men. All were to the left, as that would put them to his back as he exited toward his horse. Scanning further, Gideon's eyes gave pause as he noted Ol' Ridley sitting now on a long-cut pine plank bench across from the barbershop.

"Something wrong, Mister?"

"Looks like I have somebody waiting for me." He pointed to the reflection and the barber peered out.

"Them's Bowers cowhands, though likely ain't gonna do much with cows from the looks of them." They all looked serious and nodded knowingly. "That there ruddy fella is Hansen. Hangs around Clyde. The others are newer; don't know their names. Better go out the back door."

"I guess I better just see what these fellows want." Gideon adjusted his gun belt as the three men stepped to the back of the shop. Moving around, Gideon carefully checked the reflections for more men and saw none. With a wry grin, he said: "I think that back door might be a good idea. I will ask a favor, though. Wait for a slow count of three minutes and then rattle the doorknob like I was about to leave." The barber nodded. Following the gesture of the barber, Gideon looked carefully and exited through the rear of the shop, stepping quickly to the side and working his way across the back of the next shop and up the narrow space between the two buildings. Inching slowly to the front of the store and removing his hat, he peered carefully around the corner. The men now stood off to his right and seemed to have no idea he'd left the barbershop.

One man looked to another and whispered.

"He still in there?"

"Gotta be. He can't see us, but we know he went in there."

At that moment the doorknob rattled and the men tensed and put their hands over their pistols.

Intent upon the door, none of the four sensed Gideon step up behind them. With a long back and forth sweep of his arm, Gideon knocked two of the men to the ground with his pistol barrel. The other two, hearing the sound, started to turn.

"What the..." Both men froze and faced Gideon – and his gun barrel.

"Looking for me?"

He could see both men taking stock in their own minds. They knew one of them would get hurt – likely killed – if they made any further moves. The ruddy man, sensing a lack of respect in his fellow for Gideon's gun, blurted out:

"No, Williams!"

Gideon looked to the man Williams. There was a look in the man's eyes that Gideon knew from experience. Despite the odds, the man was going to try.

"Care to try? Let me help you." Gideon slowly placed his gun into its holster. William's brows raised and a look of triumph crossed his face as his hand swept to his gun.

A single gunshot rent the air and Williams looked to see Gideon's gun facing him, a small wisp of smoke rising from the barrel. The man didn't understand for a moment until he felt a deep pain, looked down and saw blood on his hand, dripping upon his own gun – still halfway in the holster. Realization shone in his eyes an instant before he stumbled to the boardwalk, holding a shuddering hand and crying in pain. The ruddy man slowly raised his hands.

"Mister, I ain't gonna draw."

"Then I suggest no sudden moves. You boys of the Rocking-B are getting a mite irritating. And for reasons you don't even know. Now, I am going to walk down the street while you get this man to a doctor and these two sleeping beauties off the street. I will be here till tomorrow morning and would hope to not see your faces any more while I'm here. Do you understand?"

Wary, yet not defeated, the man nodded.

15

ST. LOUIS

Wang honored Gideon Henry's investment, treating the initial money and additional deposits as if his own. The investments prospered. Keeping careful accounts, Wang would occasionally show the ledger to Gideon. Though Gideon never asked to see the accounts, he never refused to see them either. Wang knew Gideon trusted him, but was also clearly keeping track. It was a good arrangement, keeping each of them on their toes.

An astute judge of men, Wang also knew that unless he kept careful watch on those with whom he invested, there would be a tendency for dishonesty. It was a lesson learned from experience.

Several had sought to cheat him, to undercut him in some way. His many fingers of business were increasingly entwined and he dealt quickly with such situations when they appeared. It didn't take much to spot those so inclined, for their lives showed the same propensity outside of business. When he found, for example, that one of his connections was ignoring a marriage contract and lying to others about his mistress, Wang first carefully observed the man, noting the truth of the matter, and immediately demanded an accounting of the business debts. He knew if this man were lying about his own wife, he surely was not trustworthy in business. By this time, and through the investment of Gideon, Wang became a man with whom to be reckoned and most men quietly settled his accounts.

Children continued to play outside the home Gideon established for the street children. Mrs. McClinder at first was taken aback when Gideon introduced her to Wang. Perhaps less so than most, still she had moments of uncertainty with the Chinese people. She learned quickly to fully trust Wang and realized there would always be funds available when needed. Gideon urged her, and she complied, in utilizing his friend's laundry services. If she had any special requests she merely need send a note with the boy delivering or picking up laundry. Any hesitancy disappeared when she delightfully noted how clean the clothes were and her own hands never scrubbed them.

Wang grew more comfortable, contributing quietly to many helpful organizations, as long as those

16

CRASWELL

Dusk settled in and shots became very intermittent. Jose finally ventured to lift his head as shadows blended with reality in the approaching darkness. When no shots resulted, he rose warily and stretched his stiffened limbs.

"Manuel! Paulo! Conner!" Manuel stood slowly, appearing as a vague shadow against the hillside. There was no sign of Paulo. Conner grunted in the distance and Jose saw him struggling.

Both he and Manuel worked their way to their horses and led them to Conner, who sat on the flank of his dead horse, drinking from his canteen.

"Boy, does that water taste good!"

"Anybody see anything of Paulo? I saw him ride to those rocks." Jose reached for his canteen and passed it to his brother. Manuel drank and passed it back. Jose took a long pull. A long afternoon of dust and sun had parched them all.

Putting down his canteen and wiping his mouth with a shirtsleeve, Conner winced as he hitched his leg around. "I saw Paulo leading his horse back around that hillside. I don't think he was hit. Likely went after the cattle."

Manuel reached down to pat the dead horse. "Sorry for your horse, Conner. How's the leg?"

"Not good. I was getting dizzy for a spell. Had a hard time getting the bleeding stopped." He looked down and felt where he had tied the bandana. "Bleeding again."

Looking at each other, Jose and Manuel knew they needed to get Conner back to the ranch and the search for the cattle had to wait. Wherever Paulo was, he was on his own.

17

Bright bands of stunning color streaked the early morning sky as Gideon left the livery stable, riding west to seek out Bower's ranch. The hostler, rubbing his eyes and hitching one overall strap over a shoulder, stumbled out yawning as Gideon rode off. Scratching his ample midsection, the man shook his head. Accustomed to interacting with various people, hostlers as a rule were fairly good judges of men. This man, he reckoned as he jutted his lower lip in thought, was a hard man on a mission. Already the happenings of yesterday were common knowledge. Little did anyone know the beating of Clyde and the gunfight on the street had already traveled fifty miles by morning, as a cowhand riding all night to see his sweetheart stopped at a remote ranch to enjoy a complimentary breakfast. From there the word spread ever further.

With awakening day at his back, Gideon rode for an hour before coming into the ranch yard of the Rocking-B. Acutely aware of eyes watching his every move, he was alert and yet not worried, with confidence in a practiced ability to handle himself. Before reaching the ranch he watched a man slip from the bunkhouse and hurry to the back of the house. Alerted to his approach, the entire ranch was waiting.

Stopping before the ranch house, the door opened and Dan Bowers stepped out, his neck thickening as he lowered his chin. Following closely behind his father, Clyde displayed bruises from the day before. As realization dawned on Clyde, barely restrained anger flashed in his eyes. Other hands filtered over and looked indignant.

"Pa, this is the man that hit me when I weren't lookin'. He shot Williams"

"That true, stranger?" This must be Dan Bowers, the man he was to see.

"Right on both counts. This idiot was looking for a fight. Williams decided to make a play with the wrong odds."

Clyde stepped forward, his pa placing an arm in front to restrain him.

"Wasn't a fair fight, mister."

Gideon bristled. Clyde cared little for Williams.

"A lot fairer than what you did to that small man you called Schmidt. You want another chance with a man who's not so small?" He emphasized the word "small."

Dan Bowers looked at his son, then back at Gideon.

"Mister, I have half a mind to have you shot right now, but my curiosity is asking me why you beat my son, shot one of my men and then come ridin' next day to my house." He leaned his girth against the porch post and crossed his arms, glaring at Gideon. At his nod several men had closed in.

"You want to sick your paid dogs on me, Bowers, go right ahead. But understand you will be the first to die." Dan Bower's shifted as he read Gideon's eyes. Standing up from the post, Bowers realized he did not want to tangle with this stranger. Already his ire was up at the man's defiance.

"Why are you here?"

"You sent for me."

"I sent for you?"

"Name is Gideon Henry. You sent word to me through Hankel."

Bowers suddenly chilled. Gideon Henry! Deadly gunman, known to be absolutely fearless!

Bowers quickly gathered himself. He was not drinking today and his rational mind told him this man before him was extremely dangerous.

"Men, you all go about your work. All's fine here."

"But, pa!" Clyde spoke and started to come forward. Bowers restrained him with the casual raising of his arm.

"Not now, Clyde!"

"I'll take care of him, pa!"

"Clyde, you ain't a match for this man."

Clyde, used to his position as the pick of the big dog's litter, visibly reddened. Reaching for his gun, he found himself staring into the barrel of Gideon's .44. Dan Bowers slapped his son's hand away from his pistol.

"Clyde! You bit off more'n you can chew here. Leave it alone." Brash youth stared first at his pa and then at Gideon Henry with open hate and challenge. It was clear that Dan Bowers had a precarious hold on his son, who was chomping at the bit to take his position as big dog.

Gideon Henry stared at Clyde Bowers with hard eyes, not believing for a minute Clyde would leave it be. No, he would have to face Clyde at some point, and one of them would die.

Inside the house, Gideon waved away the offered drink and placed himself near the door where all was visible. Clyde briskly walked past Gideon to the bottle, hitching his gun belt while glaring angrily.

Simple and spacious, the room was opulent for the day and time. While many ranchers relied upon more crude and homemade furnishings, this room sported chairs obviously shipped from the East. A large Asian style carpet covered the center of the floor. Books filled a shelf near the fireplace, which crackled with a small fire obviously meant to take the chill from the room.

"Tell me what's going on." Gideon Henry spoke sharply to Bowers, who reddened also at the commanding presence of this stranger. Accustomed to fear and at least grudging respect, he bristled inside.

Strutting across the room to lean upon the mantle with an air of superiority, Bowers sought to gain back his presence in front of this man. Speaking commandingly to Gideon as to a peon, Gideon did not take offense; he understood the man's need to keep face in front of his son.

"We've had a problem with a squatter. Name of Vern Schmidt. Many of our cattle are disappearing. He also," the man paused and coughed, "is accusing us of rustling and I will not tolerate that."

"Is it true?"

Bowers glared. No man dared talk to him in such a way. Removing his arm from the mantle, the hand tensed as it hovered over his gun.

"Use it if you want." Gideon spoke casually.

Bowers' eyes glowed with fire, then relaxed, realizing he needed this man.

"Schmidt is foreign trash. He's German. Others in the area feel the same way."

"How long has he lived in the area?"

"Nigh on to twenty years."

"And you just now decide you don't want him around? Are you just looking for an excuse?"

Bowers glared.

"I want this man, this threat, removed. That is your job. Questions are not part of your pay!"

"So why do you need me when you've got," he looked at Clyde, "your own men yearning to prove themselves. Why not take care of this yourself?"

Bowers' neck quivered with strain. Forcing his irritation back, he kept calm. In this area, he was king and not questioned. Obedience was expected. Wearing a false smile, he spoke directly.

"Gideon, you are a man of perception, so I will level with you. I plan to have a future in the governing of this area. Any misplaced accusations might be limiting. You are hired to take care of it, and then disappear. A few key rumors will be spread, I will take charge of a futile search for an unnamed killer, and then I will gain a solid hold on the territory. You have your money so it won't matter to you."

Gideon's mouth lifted at one corner and Bowers angered again.

"You are paid to eliminate Schmidt. Do so."

"Does he have a family?"

There was a slow pause and Dan Bowers glanced at his son, then turned back to Gideon.

"He has a wife, a son and daughter. We expect that they will leave once Schmidt is…eliminated."

Gideon Henry had heard the same before: the hope and assumption that a family would grudgingly but willingly depart when the man of the house was no longer in the picture. It didn't always happen that way. The West bred strong women and strong children who stood to the grindstone when the need arose. Though some tucked their tails and ran, some did not. Without knowing the Schmidt's, he could not know what the end of the story might be.

"I will not kill women and children."

"You will not be required to do so. We have other resources to take care of the urchins."

Gideon saw Clyde smirk.

"The girl's mine!" It was Clyde. His father waved him off.

"Do you understand enough, Henry?"

Gideon nodded at Bowers and turned to go. In a mere few minutes his mind had grasped more than Bowers realized. Reaching the door, he heard Clyde shout:

"If you can't do the job, I will."

"Shut up, Clyde!" Bowers spoke loudly and harshly to his son, who was unfazed and unbowed.

Gideon glared at Clyde with cold eyes.

18

Darkness on the open range was intense, unnerving to those used to the city where a lantern could be seen most any hour of the night. Thousands of sparkling stars overwhelmed some while mesmerizing others. Gideon Henry preferred to camp under the stars. It was his practice, when on a job, to stay out from underneath the roof of anyone who paid him money. Usually the man with the money preferred it that way. Best to quell any association and rumors. Further contact with Bowers would be limited - if there was any. He knew his job and merely needed to fulfill his obligation and move on quickly, back to comfort.

Pondering the events of the day, Gideon knew sooner or later he would face Clyde, unless the carelessness of the man got him killed first. Clyde was the type who rode roughshod over all, with an over inflated sense of self-importance, until he ran into someone who took the wind – or the blood – out of his sails.

Gideon had bristled when Bowers referred to Schmidt's children as "urchins." His mind drifted briefly to the home he funded just for the "urchins" of the street.

Why was he so bothered? Was he getting too involved nowadays? Shaking his head, he found himself, as he occasionally did, thinking of his own life.

His was a happy childhood, until that fateful day.

Memories came to him of his father, Artemis Henry, who had been a railroad engineer in Chicago. Gideon remembered bouncing on his father's knee, wrestling on the floor, and many times having a free ride in the engine on a short run. Early on he dreamed of being an engineer himself. He was often regaled around the table with stories, along with laughter and simple, though plentiful, food. With his younger brother, Nathan, and baby sister, Abby, he enjoyed the growing up years. Gideon was sixteen when it all came crashing down.

Father had long promised them the trip to Indianapolis and they anticipated a day and night in that growing city. Mother had packed the hamper well and he and his brother and sister were all washed and wearing their best Sunday-go-to-meeting clothes.

For once father rode in the coach with them, pointing out the sights as they left the city and headed into the farmlands to the south. Happy and expectant people filled the seats around them along with seasoned travelers who tried to nap through the noise of the rails and the passengers.

He remembered his father taking him through the other coaches to the caboose. There was a special feeling of importance in being allowed to pass from one car to another. A conductor and a brakeman who knew his father greeted them in the caboose as they played cards, with the brakeman taking occasional looks over the train from the cupola. A guard stood watch over a small gold shipment. What a special treat it was to stand on the rear platform as they neared the bridge over the Wabash. Glancing down at the water under their feet, Gideon was dizzy but his father gripped his arm securely and they both laughed as they neared the other side.

Just then they heard sharp noises and his father turned at the sound and glanced into the window.

"Robbery! Get down, Gideon!" He forced Gideon to the platform as two men burst through the door and looked surprised to see Gideon's father, who instantly jumped on the men.

One robber fell off the platform, Gideon watching in terror as the man landed on his head and his neck twisted grotesquely on the sloping bank. The other robber managed to rise up and strike Artemis Henry, knocking him to the platform, unconscious. Moving to jump off the train with the gold, the man turned and cruelly shot the helpless Artemis Henry in the heart. Pointing the gun at Gideon, the train hit a bump and the robber fell backwards off the train. Gideon stared as the wind caught the man's mask and blew it off, giving Gideon a clear view of the face.

Crying, he crawled to his father and screamed. Tears filled his eyes as he ran to the caboose for help, only to find all of the trainmen and the guard lying dead.

Later, many came to his family with condolences, but his grief was unbreakable. His mother was lost to him that day as she drowned in her own grief.

There came a day when the head of the railroad came to share his regrets. This was a big event for the locals and many surrounded the small home as the dignitary stood in the doorway. Gideon remembered the man's girth as he stood in the door blocking the sunlight, but he had eyes only for the man's security guard. It was the robber who shot his father and stole the gold!

Gideon immediately yelled out what he knew, but the robber just looked cold and dignified and moved his head side to side.

"Poor kid. Just grieving and out of his mind."

Nobody would believe Gideon.

Though he tried to explain it to his mother later, she was lost to him. Telling anybody he could find, nothing happened. The local police constable looked at him, raised his eyebrows and told him:

"Jackson's untouchable, Gideon. Just drop it."

Incensed, Gideon vowed he would get the man who took his happiness away. Filtering through crowds and seeking likely avenues, he happened upon Jackson one day leaving the station. Ducking around a corner and staying out of sight, he followed the man for several days, learning his movements, his patterns and his mannerisms. Jackson was cocky, being careless in little ways that Gideon noted in his mind. Each day he learned more. Seeming to sense something, Jackson took different routes, but still had a pattern to his variety.

One evening at dusk, the moment of revenge came. Jackson stood smoking on the bridge at the same spot as always. Secreting himself on the catwalk just below the guardrail, Gideon made his move as Jackson leaned over the rail and drew contentedly. Taking a small pistol his father had carried, Gideon rose and shot Jackson though the throat from below and threw his lifeless body into the river. Something broke within him as he watched the body sink into the murky waters.

His mother never recovered and finally died six months later. The next months passed with Gideon wandering amidst the riff-raff along the railroad and waterways. There he learned various ways of fighting along with the ways of tracking men. A quick learner, Gideon became known among those of the underworld as capable and efficient. Different families took his siblings, but he became incorrigible and fended for himself.

Sitting on a bench in the park one day, looking like any street tough, Gideon shifted warily when a man dressed in a nice but not fancy coat sat beside him. The man looked at him with knowing eyes.

"Gideon."

Gideon was startled, narrowing his eyes suspiciously at the man. Tightening the grip on the knife in his pocket, Gideon tensed.

The man smiled the false smile of someone doing business.

"Yes, I know who you are and I know what happened with your father. I also know you took care of Jackson on the bridge that night."

Gideon's eyes opened wide and he drew the knife.

"Hold, boy! I'm not here to hurt you nor am I going to explain how I know. I want to hire you. I have a job that needs to be done, a man who needs to disappear. There's five hundred dollars in it."

It had begun…

Months of working with the man, whose name he never learned, brought him increased skill and connections. Happening one day upon a man practicing

19

Into his thoughts came the realization of hooves striking stone. Easing his pistol, Gideon looked to the darkness.

"Hello the camp." It was the call of the wilderness, of the West. It was never safe to ride up to an unknown fire without making one's presence known. Men in wild country shot first and asked questions later. It was the price of survival.

"Come in slowly, but there's coffee."

Gideon heard a chuckle as hoof falls drew closer and the rider touched the firelight, showing an old man, hands resting deliberately in plain sight on the pommel.

"Light and set, stranger."

"Don't mind if I do. Coffee sure do smell home-like to a traveling man."

Easing his way out of the saddle, the man bent backwards to stretch his lower back, hands still carefully away from any weapons.

"You got a cup?"

"I do, but I gotta reach in my saddlebag to get it. Don't be to touchy with that there shootin' iron."

"If all that comes out is a cup, you got nothing to worry about."

Reaching carefully into his saddlebag, the stranger withdrew the typical fire blackened and dented tin cup that was a staple on the frontier. Made to hold the beloved coffee, it also doubled to cook if no pan was available.

Gideon Henry noted the wizened old man was careful in all his movements. Not a large man, he was lean with obvious sinewy strength. Gideon filled the dented cup to the brim, in the fire's glow noting wrinkled hands with enlarged joints of age and use, sprinkled with spots and old scars. A careful sip brought a warm smile to the creased and bewhiskered face. Though seeming old as the mountains, the man was young in the eyes. Faded clothes all but hung on a slender frame, with all the indicators of long travel and little luxury. Stiff from riding, still the man sat easily to the ground. There was one gun visible, but it was one that caught the eye. It brought a grin to the man's face to see Gideon's eyes linger on the pistol.

"I bet you ain't never seen one of these. It's a LeMat .42 revolver. Got nine shots and a middle barrel with a shotgun shell. Don't want to use that'n if you can help it. Like to blow you back off your feet. Good for fishin' though." He chuckled.

Though wary, Gideon's instincts told him this man meant no harm and was just a common drifting cowhand. Many a man had tried to charm him, but most failed. Yet there was something about this man, as if this meeting was not all chance. His mother once talked of people entertaining angels unawares. Well, this man was no angel. At least he'd never seen one wearing a gun like this. It was more designed to send a man to perdition rather than Heaven.

"Grateful for the coffee, stranger. Been a long ride today. I was about to set up camp back up the way, but seen a wisp of your smoke against the last of the sun. Thought I'd mosey over and see if I might get a free meal. I done run out of coffee two days ago." There was a jovial gleam in his eye.

Gideon chuckled. "You got a handle I can use?"

"Folks call me Skerby."

"Well, Skerby, I was just getting ready to fry a mess of bacon. You're welcome to join me. Headed somewhere in particular?"

Skerby noted that man had not offered his own name.

"Oh, I just ride hither and yon. Mostly yon. Can't seem to get used to stayin' in one place very long. Spent a lot of time wandering Colorado, Idaho Territory and such, an' places in between. This old man never was good at lettin' moss grow. I been around here a spell. Sorta like the country, so's I been ridin' hereabouts for a few weeks. Sorta wanted to watch."

"Watch what?"

"The fireworks. Fixin' to be some pretty soon, I reckon."

"Something going on?"

Skerby looked long at Gideon, then squinted his eyes.

"Just an honest question. You got me curious."

"Well, they's a bit of a dispute goin' on here. Bowers seems to think he's bull of the woods, but they's other bulls in the pasture. Bowers wants all the land and cattle hereabouts for himself and that cub of his – Clyde. But they's another fella here, a fella with a fine family. Schmidt. Right nice, I hear, with a wife and a couple children. Young son, and a daughter who's a real looker hereabouts. She's right nice – I run into her once out on the range. But Clyde done set his cap for her. Bowers wants all that Schmidt has, and Clyde wants the girl." Skerby glanced knowingly at Gideon, then spoke again while stirring the fire with a stick.

"Understand I ain't callin' anybody names. I'm just a wore out old man an' I like to sit back and enjoy a show now and then. You got a side in this?"

"Maybe." Gideon offered bacon and Skerby drained his cup, holding it out to receive the bacon.

"I sit and watch and just like to figure things out. Understand, I ain't saying nothing, just pointin' out what I see." Skerby looked carefully at Gideon. "I seen that Clyde with some of the girls back at town. Some of them is pretty rough, but even they go scurrying to hide when Clyde comes a lookin' for comfort. Most of the girls is outa circulation for a week or so after Clyde comes to their door."

"I've met him. Right unpleasant sort."

Skerby sighed and visibly relaxed at Gideon's subtle opinion. "Yep. I hate the thought of that there Mary gettin' in his clutches." Finishing the last piece of bacon from the cup, he gestured to the coffee pot and upon Gideon's nod filled it halfway again.

Gideon began to ponder the situation and the information Skerby had shared. It was not part of the job to worry about who was who or what happened in the wake of Bowers getting control. He had a job to do and skills that commanded high dollar. Yet something inside was repulsed by the thought of any girl, saloon or otherwise, being abused by Clyde.

"What's your stake in this, Skerby."

"Nothin' at all. I'll be ridin on." He paused. "Maybe, though, someone could help Mary an' her family, and keep the lid from blowin' off."

"I'm like you, Skerby. Just here for a spell, then riding on."

"I reckon. It just strikes me that everything ain't what it seems – all the way around." Skerby removed his hat, revealing the pale forehead of a cowhand. Running his hand through thinning hair, he replaced the hat and slowly rose, working the kinks out of his legs and back.

"I'm keeping my hands away from my gun, stranger, but an old man ain't so steady."

Gideon kept his hand near his gun. Dashing the last drops from his cup, Skerby stretched again. "Well, reckon I better get to riding. Want to go a few more miles tonight. No offense meant, stranger. I thank you kindly for the grub and coffee."

Gideon said nothing, preferring always to camp by himself. As Skerby mounted and turned to the west, he glanced back at Gideon.

"Yessir, things ain't always as they seem at first glance. Sometimes they's changes that need to be made. Interestin' what a fella can find out when he keeps his eyes and ears open." Looking Gideon in the eye, he nodded and slowly rode the horse into the darkness, fading from the firelight like a wraith.

Gideon waited some minutes before packing and putting out his fire. Mounting, he rode into the deep eastern darkness to find a new camp where he would have no fire. Realizing someone knew his location did not set well. It was a danger to those such as him and he would not sleep well. Best to move a mile and settle into a fireless sleep.

Late that night he lay in his blankets and his mind drifted to some of Skerby's comments.

There were times he would sit and ponder what might have been if his father had lived. He wondered what became of his brother and sister, as over the years, for various reasons, connections were lost. Nate would be a man, and Abby a young lady, perhaps married.

Within there was wistfulness...

What did Skerby mean by his conversation? The comments about Schmidt, Clyde and the ladies, things not being what they seemed, changes needing to be made?

Changes? And why did he feel the encounter with Skerby was not all by chance? It couldn't be anything else. Best just quit trying to read between the lines.

20

Vern Schmidt was a realist. It was obvious he was a target. Yet there was no getting around the fact the ranch needed to be taken care of. Bowers wanted him off, but he would not go without a fight. Besides the ranch, there was Ruth and their children, Laban and Mary, to think of - as well as the hands.

With a wince he leaned against the corral in the late morning shadow, nursing the injuries received in town. Touching a gentle finger to a swollen eye, he shook his head and remembered what happened when they rode into town.

Normally he would have one of the other hands with him, but they were all out rounding up cattle so he, Mary and Ruth had gone together. Pulling the buckboard to the mercantile, Vern dismounted and turned to help his wife down when Clyde Bowers emerged from the store and set his boots loudly on the worn boardwalk. Clyde hooked his thumbs in his belt, stood proudly in the flower of his burly manhood and looked longingly at Mary, still in the wagon. Vern saw the look under his hat brim, and it disturbed him. There was a dangerous fire in Clyde's eyes, as a bull in the pasture. It was common knowledge how the man treated the paid girls, and his heart twisted at the thought of Mary in the clutches of Clyde Bowers.

Clyde's eyes shifted to him.

"Morning, Schmidt." Raising his hat to Ruth, Vern's wife of so many years, Clyde's glance rested a little long for comfort on Ruth. It hadn't always been easy, but Ruth had always been exceptionally pretty, and despite the hardships of years building up the Lazy-S ranch, she still retained classic beauty. Vern saw Ruth's mouth tighten, as Clyde's look lingered on her then switched back to Mary.

Mary was seventeen, of prime age in the West to take a husband, but there were no serious beau's. She was not exceptional in beauty, yet far also from homely. Most viewed her as quite pleasant to look upon. Yet she was an independent girl, liking to ride the trails, comfortable being alone, and very intelligent. Whereas many men in these parts wanted a subservient wife, Mary would need more than that. She would need to be a part of her man, a part of building something together. It would take a strong man who was able to handle a strong wife. She would not be chosen, but would need to be the chooser of her man.

Clyde spoke to him that morning and stood watching as they entered the store. Vern was looking at rope, not that he needed any but wanted to stand between Clyde and the womenfolk. The brute had come close – so close it was obvious he had already been drinking despite the morning hour.

"I'd like to ask permission to ride out with your daughter." It was not a humble request, but more of a demand, an expectation. The man was too big for his own britches!

Despite the man's size, Vern was not cowed. His strength was from inside, and it was a strength that built a paying ranch. It was important he portray strength or he would attract abuse.

"Not today, Clyde. Maybe some other time." He kept looking at the coils of rope, yet could feel Clyde reddening and saw the man's hands clench. Vern tensed, waiting. Then, with tremendous effort, Clyde calmed himself. It was obvious the man wanted to push the issue, but there were several other townsfolk in the store. Bowers was a significant name in the area, but even he must pay attention to convention – at least when others were looking. Turning to the door, Clyde stalked out mad and thirsty!

It was the second time Clyde had approached him, and the brute was not to be dissuaded. Vern

Schmidt knew there would be a deciding confrontation sooner or later – likely sooner.

Rocking-B riders shadowed them as they conducted other business around town. Laban was back at the ranch. There were smirks and taunting looks, causing Ruth to urge they leave and go back to the ranch.

Something inside Vern railed at the thought of taking abuse from Clyde and his minions. The breaking point came a few minutes later.

They were walking in front of the bank when a Rocking-B rider stuck his foot out suddenly and tripped Vern. Falling to his knees, something snapped inside. Standing to find the man looking at another cowhand and laughing, Vern Schmidt grabbed his gun and slammed the man in the side of his head, knocking him senseless while his fellow cowhand looked on, wide-eyed. Vern reversed the gun and pointed it into the man's eyes. Asking the man where he could find Clyde, he was told which saloon and he stormed over, despite the protests of his wife. He had taken enough!

Pushing through the squeaky batwings, Vern noted Clyde belly to the bar, beer in hand. Clyde saw him in the mirror and turned, placing the beer on the bar.

"I'll not be insulted any longer, Clyde! Nor will I stand by and watch you glare at my womenfolk and make a mockery of me!"

"You come in here to threaten me?"

With that, Clyde stepped forward and the fight was on – if it could be called that. Vern was no match for the youth and sheer brutality of the man. Though all who watched agreed Vern Schmidt was game and got a few good licks in, he didn't stand a chance. Beaten soundly and on his hands and knees while blood dripped to the wood floor, he looked up defiantly at Clyde, who responded by accusing him of stealing cattle.

Before he knew it, the big man grabbed him by belt and collar and pitched him to the dirt outside, following and strutting.

Ruth helped him to the wagon, the tears rolling down her face saying volumes. She spent much of the evening bathing his face, alternating between tears and anger at her husband's choice to take on Clyde.

Though a man who built a tough dream, Vern was no match for these men who were determined to have his ranch. Clyde wanted even more than the ranch. Afraid for his daughter, Vern was torn inside.

Should he sell out? Bowers would not pay him what the ranch was worth, for even approaching Dan Bowers would be an admission of defeat and Bowers would mock him and offer a pittance. Vern knew Bowers commanded obedience amongst the local ranchers and townsfolk. He also knew the man was bad mouthing him as "German trash."

Why, he was as American as the next man! His grandparents had immigrated and built a new life in this beautiful land. Then his father had continued to build the mercantile back in Pennsylvania.

Vern remembered clearly that early evening he found his father standing on the front walk of the store, seemingly in a daze, eyes looking towards the sunset in the Western sky. After a few moments, Adam Schmidt appeared to wake as from a dream and sense Vern's presence. Looking to his son, then a mature thirteen, and placing his arm over his son's shoulder, he nodded towards the sunset and spoke in wishful tones.

"Vern, my boy, the future for a man is out West. Here, all I have is this minor piece of land with a store, for which I pay taxes. As my income increases, so do the taxes. It is infuriating at times that no matter how hard your mother and I work, we will never be able to put aside enough to bring comfort to our old age."

Father paused and scanned the sky as colors changed their hues, blending into a deep, almost phosphorescent orange.

"Son, I want you to go West. I want you to build a life I cannot build here. I want you to have a piece of this magnificent land. Land is there for the taking. Yes, I am not blind to the fact it will take strength to take it and hold it and to prove up on it. But you, son, have something I do not have. You see, I cannot leave.

Your mother does not have what it takes for such a dream. I will never leave your mother because of the vows I made. It is a reality of such vows that they may constrain one and free another, but my vows I will keep. Marry a strong woman, Vern. Choose well, for that one decision will mean more than you can ever imagine as the future rises before you."

So he followed his father's wish, married a strong woman, and moved west where he and Ruth built a dream together. They both stood strong, back-to-back as they faced weather and varmints of both two and four legged variety. Several years ago he received a letter informing him his father was dead and his mother had become bedridden with grief and died – two months before the letter arrived.

There was nothing back East begging his return. This western land was his home. It was within his soul now.

Something in him bristled at giving up. They spent years building a paying ranch. Now someone was skimming his herds. He had no proof that would stand a legal challenge, but he knew Bowers was responsible. Too many quiet smirks by the Rocking-B hands and rumors of Bowers making nighttime drives to far towns and selling mixed-lot cattle. Bowers now had numerous gunhands and any attempts to fight in court would likely result in more deaths.

What was he to do? His options were few.

21

CEDAR CITY, NEVADA

"Sit down, Seth Johnson!"

The boy smirked a bit to save face among the other students, then slipped into his seat.

Looking calm, Abby Henry was quite put out. Seth and a couple others were a handful today. Roundup was beginning tomorrow and they would be helping their fathers and other ranchers gather cattle to brand and tally. It was a time of excitement for the children, knowing they would miss two or three weeks of school. Even some of the girls would be gone, as some events would start at the home places and it was expected that a meal would be provided.

Glancing to the window, Abby gauged the sun. There was still an hour to go before she dismissed the children for lunch. Already Seth was poking one of the girls with his foot. Abby willed the day to move faster.

"Seth!"

Cedar City was not a bad place to live, but it sure took a wise eye to make a go of it.

Sitting in the schoolhouse watching the students practicing their letters, Abby worked hurriedly to prepare a lesson for the older children. At sixteen, she was more like a sister to some of her charges, and only through well-placed threats was she able to keep some in line. She needed the job and though she had been here but three weeks it was beginning to feel comfortable.

After her mother's death, she was separated from her brothers and farmed out, settling with the Templeton's, a distant childless aunt and uncle who owned a small dairy near Indianapolis. Though there was occasional contact with Nate until she headed west, she never saw Gideon after their mother's funeral.

Isaac Templeton did not shy from labor, yet his sense of business was non-existent and the dairy failed when the bank called in his mortgage. Always one to shrug his shoulders and go on, he quickly became enamored with the stories of free land in what was wonderingly referred to as "out West." Sometimes the term was spoken with the same quiet reverence as "Heaven," and many spent the rest of their money on a wagon and a dream. Templeton did the same, spending his stake on a wagon, a pair of oxen and taking his chance in a hope and a prayer.

Stopping in various places and finding arguments with so many others over available land and facing more than one gun barrel when he tried to put down a claim stake, he took his family on, always seeking his piece of that "out West" which seemingly lay just over the horizon. Abby learned to stand her ground among the children of the wagons as well as the town toughs who seemed to take delight in antagonizing the children of those they rudely referred to as "movers." It seemed each place they stopped she fought to establish her territory. Reading as they rode, she continued to learn, as Templeton seemed to have a corner of something deep within which recognized Abby's need for books. He traded and bartered as they went and she found herself with a variety of reading material, reading them as fast as she could so Mr. Templeton could trade again.

Abby knew Templeton was weary, but even she was blindsided when it happened.

Reaching Utah Territory, something within Isaac Templeton gave out. Some said it was his heart, but Abby knew it was the end of his dream. So many desperately sought to "find" their dream, as if it were some sort of elusive deed of ownership deliberately hidden and waiting to be found through a clever search or pure blind luck. Abby noted so many others arrived as "movers" and then took what was at hand and built something enduring. Her heart learned everyone must "build" a dream from what was placed before them. Unable to grasp this concept, Isaac faded from a bubbly happiness as they started west to a mere shell of a man upon reaching Utah Territory. Perhaps it was the inability to find a piece of "free" land fitting the picture in his mind's eye; perhaps it wasn't the land at all but the search itself keeping him going. With possibilities narrowed due to miles traveled, the need to face the truth was impossible for him. Suddenly Isaac spent hours sitting in a rocker by the wagon, staring at his back trail thinking of who knew what without any energy to do more than sweep a local saloon for a few cents a day. His wife, worn from having the same misconception as well as no dream of her own, plodded along beside her husband and came to be his mirror image. She would arise late, cook runny porridge in the morning, set the pot out and sit on the back of the wagon, staring east all day.

Abby did not know what to do until a kind sheriff, Buck Ganner, came one day and tried to talk to her aunt and uncle with the only response being a vague and empty stare. He told Abby to pack her things and Buck and Mattie Ganner took her into their home, where she became their child. No longer a "mover," she was accepted in the community and grew into young womanhood. A weed-covered double mound in the local cemetery displayed a now barely legible "Templeton" scratched upon a rough board tilted awkwardly and now barely clinging to the earth. At first, Abby went regularly to look upon the mounds, out of a sense of obligation. Visits slowly decreased until they ceased altogether. Though accustomed to the Ganner's, her mind often drifted to Nate and Gideon and all that once was. She wondered where they were. There was always a sense of aimlessness and unsettledness since her mother died and she was separated from all she knew and loved.

One day a couple years ago, Buck Ganner came home for lunch carrying a letter. It was from Nate! Through luck and a few educated leaps of faith, he stumbled upon Abby's location. She cherished the two letters she received over a period of months. Nate was living in St. Louis as a shopkeeper, but was unhappy. He had no word on Gideon.

Abby returned home recently from picking up an order at the mercantile when Mattie told her about the teaching position. Always exceptional at her lessons, Abby impressed the board of the school and was offered the position despite a complete lack of experience.

Now here she was, teaching. She wondered what her parents would think if they were alive. Still, she knew this was but a step in her dream, which was to see Nate – and Gideon – again.

22

CRASWELL

As dusk switched places with darkness, Vern Schmidt stood by the corral, eyes straining to pierce the darkness, almost willing the men to return. Jose had taken the other men still on the home place to make a sweep for cattle. Normally, they would make the gather and head them back towards the ranch, with at least one hand riding ahead to apprise Vern of the results. It was much too late and worry creased his face. Too much was happening and the risk to himself was something he accepted as necessary. However, there was great discomfort in subjecting his hired hands to danger. Reaching to his face, he felt the bruises of Clyde Bowers and imagined he must look a sight.

There was always danger on a ranch – danger of being thrown from a horse, the possibility of a stampede, the crisis of a snakebite – and such dangers and a dozen others were accepted. Yet the danger now was beyond normal.

Looking deep within, Vern still felt strength, though not near the same as when first arriving in this territory. If it were just he and the men the whole situation would be different. They could camp out and fight, with mobility as an asset. Yet, with the women and children…it was different than all those years ago. Ruth had been – and still was – strong and determined. They fought side by side and it would stay that way.

In the near distance a shaft of light appeared, with a woman silhouetted in the doorway of Jose's cabin. Vern ran his hand through his hair and frowned. Conchita must be worried sick, and he could picture her doing the same as he – straining for any sign of her overdue husband.

Vern turned again to the darkness. Taking his foot off the lower rail and beginning to turn toward his own home, a slight sound came to his ears. A horse! Looking to the Garcia cabin, he noted Conchita move into the darkness. She must have heard it, too, and hoped it was Jose.

Slowly the sound drew near and Vern loosened his pistol. Something was dragging.

A few minutes later the forms of two horses emerged from the blackness and Vern recognized the horses. Hailing them, he hurried over to find Jose's horse pulling a crude travois, on which lay

Conner. Manuel followed behind. There was no sign of Paulo.

"How bad is it?" Vern could not see in the darkness.

Jose spoke first. "Bad leg wound. We were ambushed. Pushing a bunch of cattle. They pinned us down all day and ran the cattle off. We don't know where Paulo is, but we think he went after the herd."

The men could not see Vern clearly, but they could guess the look of concern on his face. He turned to the house. "Ruth!"

Moments later the door opened and his wife stepped into the darkness. "Vern?"

"Conner's wounded! We're taking him to the bunkhouse!" Ruth disappeared and Vern knew she was collecting what they might need. She would be there in mere minutes. Conner was awake and in pain. Carrying him to the bunkhouse, a lantern was lit, showing the wound still bleeding. Conner was weak. Vern noticed for the first time Jose's bandage. Seeing Vern's look, Jose gingerly touch his temple.

"Just a scratch."

"We'll attend to it next."

"I will attend to it." It was Conchita. Maria followed close behind and reached to hold Manuel's arm.

Later, as Conner rested, Jose came to the cabin. Conchita held his arm. They sat on the porch as Jose filled Vern in on the events of the day. He was hesitant afterwards and Conchita looked downwards with a tear. Vern sensed the tension.

"There's something you're not telling me, Jose."

Jose hesitated. "Vern, Manuel and I spoke early today of our concerns for the safety of our families."

Vern's voice was strained as he replied. "I understand if you feel you need to leave. Your family comes first, Jose."

"Oh, no, that is not what I am saying! You are our family also! No, Manuel and I think, however, that we must move our families to a safer place until this is over. Conchita and Maria do not like it, but they will do this for the sake of our children and so we will not have to worry also for our families as we ride."

"Where are you thinking, Jose?"

"To the mountain camp."

Vern nodded. "I'll ride over at first light to make arrangements."

23

ST. LOUIS

Wang Chu quickly slipped to the deeper shadows as two silhouettes neared in the darkness. Hankel was bad enough, but it was the other man who widened Wang's eyes and quickened his senses. Giddy Mueller was a man he feared.

In his own part of town Wang would feel relatively safe, but he was not in his part of town. One night every week he waited till dark, changed from his Chinese garb and donned western clothes, then spent several hours slipping quietly thru the streets. It was his way of checking out the going's-on, to spy on his rivals and upon his own informants. Moving carefully and avoiding brightly lit areas, he knew various holes in which to disappear if needed. More than once he used them, but never shrank from his task, for he found the information helpful. White men, when drunk, talked a lot and, more than once, he found one of his informants' double-dealing on him.

Once he had been on legitimate business delivering laundry in the early days and was accosted by Giddy Mueller. The man abused him, kicked him and threatened to pistol-whip him. All for no reason other than he was a Chinaman. It was several days before Wang could stand again and he received no mercy from the owner of the clothing who berated him and made him do his laundry over for no charge. He would have done it anyway, but the man's rudeness only underscored the lack of equality.

Mueller saw him another day and beat him again, telling Wang he could not ever be on that street again. Others stood on the boardwalk and watched it all – but did nothing. They were afraid of Giddy Mueller.

Standing in the shadows around a corner, he pressed tight against the wall as he sensed Hankel and Mueller draw near. Just around the corner the men stopped and he heard the sound of a match and Hankel puffing. The cigar smell wafted to Wang's nose.

"You as good as they say, Mueller?"

"I ain't failed yet, Hankel."

"You ever heard of a man named Gideon?"

"The gunfighter?"

"That's the one. Can you take him?"

Wang could almost hear the man swagger as he spoke.

"I ain't seen the one I can't best, Hankel. You want this here Gideon killed?"

"Yes, and there's a thousand in it for you. Two hundred now and the rest when the job is done."

"Five hundred now."

Hankel paused and Wang could smell the increased smoke as the man puffed harder.

"Fine. Two weeks ago he headed to Craswell, Colorado. Take care of it." There was the sound of paper as Hankel counted out bills.

Wang hurried home, sweating from the close encounter with Mueller. If either Hankel or Mueller had seen him…

That night he lay awake, thinking of what he heard. His network of informants did not go far enough West to warn Gideon. Yet he did not want the man hurt. He was…well, his friend. There was the option of sending a man to warn Gideon, but there likely was only one chance at this warning and what if the man he sent failed? Men with the time to do such things were either very expensive or unreliable, and there was no way to verify if they fulfilled the task.

Dawn's early colorful fingers found Wang still wide-awake and thoughtful. Finally, resolved, he sent a runner for his trusted nephew. Full daylight found Wang carrying a carpetbag to the train station, where he secured a seat in the baggage car.

24

CRASWELL

waking in the pre-dawn, Gideon chewed a strip of jerky and set out to explore the range. Today he would begin to learn the patterns of his prey, who as yet had no idea he was hunted.

Hunting a man took special skills. The key was to learn as much of the predictability of the prey as possible, so as to be able to guess their next move with accuracy. Hunting was not just about killing the man. Any gunman could do that. Gideon Henry's special skill was in doing so without being identified by anyone as the killer. Getting back safely to St. Louis without a posse on his tail was the ultimate goal.

Fleeing before a posse was not something he ever experienced, nor did he want to start. Typical western clothing covered his frame. Whereas there were some who flaunted specially made weapons and high caliber rifles in tooled cases, Gideon had no fancy decorated weapons to make him stand out. There were those who took pleasure in being noticed, and relished people stopping and gawking at their weapons, yet Gideon preferred anonymity. His pistols were specially worked for the action he liked, but all of that was invisible to the naked eye. Most of his ability lay in a keen mind, and a methodical grasp of the science of men and their behaviors.

As he rode the range this particular morning, he worked the hillsides seeking any places a watcher could survey the countryside and stay hidden. By mid morning he was certain he was on Schmidt's land.

Gideon always felt peace in the mountains. As he rode the gentle slopes of the foothills, he looked deeper into the mountains. In the distance the peaks rose as silent sentinels keeping a watchful eye over the lowlands. In some cultures the mountains were looked upon as if they actually had life. That was not his perception, yet to ride alone under mountain peaks always gave him a sense of awe in the majesty of creation.

Noon found Gideon sitting under the lee of an outcropping affording a view for many miles. Chewing jerky and sitting for an hour gave him opportunity to see the land, to feel its pulse, to grow quiet and sense the changes. There was more to the land than many even realized and it took patience to truly feel it.

About four years ago he was on a job down New Mexico way and took a breather in the midst of the desert. While his horse stood quietly, Gideon sat under a mesquite bush unmoving except for his eyes. Though the desert appears to so many as a wasteland, devoid of life and only a harsh environment, there was so much more to it. As he sat, he heard birds begin to chirp again, followed by other sounds as his quiet presence became a part of the land. Insects, a little lizard and finally a jackrabbit came near. When he rose to leave all scampered away and the land was empty again.

It was the same as he watched the land around him now. So much difference was noticeable when observing at different times of the day, and the moving shadows now revealed dips in the land that were not visible even a few minutes before. In the same way, being still and sitting quietly, one could see the movements of man and animals and make calculations based upon such movement. For example, if a deer moved freely in one direction but suddenly veered or ran, it was indicative of danger or disturbance. A small puff of dust, the roll of a pebble, all could be sensed if the mind was allowed to relax. A keen mind could sense the difference between a pebble dislodged naturally and one nudged by a boot. Many times the first movement was sensed from the side vision. Gideon learned to let his eyes and mind work, not rushing but allowing time to become almost one with the landscape. Watching, and hearing, the land could save a man's life.

His eyes noted movement and he carefully sat motionless as a rider trotted across the valley toward the distant mountains. Reaching slowly to his side, Gideon carefully raised his telescope to his eye, shading the lens with one hand to avoid glare.

Vern Schmidt! His target! Out here alone. A good opportunity to finish the job! As Schmidt passed into a distant valley, Gideon arose, tightening the cinch and riding at a gallop towards where Vern disappeared.

A half hour later he rode towards the top of an overlooking hillside, stopping just under the crest so that he could see into the valley but not likely be seen himself. Vern still rode in the same direction, but more slowly. Gideon was much nearer. Not much further and he would be in shooting distance. He would not be rushed, but would find the right spot. If he knew where Vern was going, he might be able to set something up for his return.

Where was he going? He appeared to be going further into the hills? What was out there? Making sure to remain always out of sight, Gideon followed.

25

Paulo had mixed thoughts about leaving the others. He saw that Conner was wounded. Yet, there was the realization that Jose and Manuel were good men and could handle whatever happened there. For him to attempt to approach the hidden gunmen would require moving into the open, in which case they would either shoot him or pin him down also. As it was, whoever was responsible likely had no idea Paulo was free to move. Occasional shots seemed to hit the rocks where he was hunkered a few minutes before, indicating the hidden gunmen thought he was still pinned down. So he crept around the hillside. He would go in pursuit of the cattle. Maybe they would lead to the other hundreds of missing cattle.

Paulo became nervous after an hour of trailing the herd. It was easy to follow the tracks of the herd, but it was the other riders that kept him moving back and forth. Their number was unknown and Paulo did not want to be caught in the open. Though not shying from a fight when it was necessary, it was obvious he would be at a disadvantage out here. Several men likely would be guiding this herd, and his one pistol would not be a match, especially if the riders had Winchesters.

Why was he here, anyway? A couple times over the past months, Schmidt made it clear he would hold no man disloyal who decided this fight was not wanted and chose to move on. At first, Paulo thought of the senorita he knew a couple years ago in Taos. Was she married now? They walked many times together and even spoke of getting married, but then the pull of the trail got him and he somberly rode out one day. He never told her. She likely was not only married, but maybe even would come after him with a frying pan if he showed up! A grin crossed his face. No, returning to Taos would not be a good thing.

Patting his horse, Paulo knew he would never return to Taos. Since coming to the Schmidt ranch, something transformed within him and the pull of the trail was diminished. Many other ranches treated Mexicans with distaste and paid them less. Vern paid the same as Anglo cowhands. Ruth Schmidt was so kind, and Mary befriended him quickly. Little Laban was becoming quite a man and they often worked cattle together. Someday maybe he would have a son like Laban. Of course, there must be a woman first!

A familiar sound jolted him out of his reverie. Not far ahead was a bawling calf, no doubt left behind because it was unable to keep up. Normally, Paulo would have put the two-month old calf over his saddle and carried it to the mother. On this trip that would not do, so he looked carefully around at the landmarks, knowing the calf would not go far. He would pick it up on the return trip – if there were one. If too much time passed, the poor calf would be taken by a wolf. As much as he hated to do so, Paulo rode on and the sound of the poor calf receded in the distance.

An hour later he came to a stop, spotting a flurry of hoof prints in the grass. It was clear a group of horsemen converged here to confer before moving on. A mile further he saw a scuff in the grass and followed it to another convergence of prints. Another gathering! Only this time one man rode off in another direction. They must have suspected someone following! Hurriedly glancing to the hills, Paulo heard the shot...then all was dark.

26

J ose headed back to his cabin. After a long discussion it was determined the cattle would be
followed, but this must wait a few days until
the families could be moved. Vern would ride in the
morning to check on the mountain camp. The others would stay here to prepare and to allow wounds
to begin to heal. Conner would be going nowhere
soon.

Touching his bandage gingerly, Jose stared into
the night blackness and thought back over the meeting. Manuel was angry, wanting to go after the cattle
this very night. Vern said no.

"Manuel, you need sleep. What good will you be
with your senses dulled by weariness? In just a few
hours it will be morning anyway."

"But...what about Paulo?"

"You couldn't find him in the dark. He's probably asleep himself by the trail. I will go to the mountain camp tomorrow. You both prepare your families to leave, and spend some time with them. Children need time with their fathers. Who knows when they will see you next."

Vern quieted a moment, and the import of the words struck them. If something happened to any of them, there would be nothing but the memories for the children.

Manuel was not soothed. "Paulo may be hurt."

"Paulo is a man and will take care of himself. We all must do what must be done here."

Manuel remained sullen while they ate and discussed details, nodding when a response was needed, but still not in agreement. He and Paulo had become good friends.

After Manuel said goodnight and strode off, Vern and Jose spoke long about strategies. Vern Schmidt valued the keen and wise mind of this man and trusted his judgment. Much was discussed, even the idea of leaving and starting again somewhere else. Both agreed they must wait a while longer.

Approaching his cabin and eager for sleep, Jose veered off on an impulse and stepped to the short trail to Manuel's cabin. His brother's sullenness was bothersome and he wished to share a few more words. Approaching the cabin, he rapped his knuckles lightly on the door. The door opened and Maria stood before him. Jose noted tears in her eyes.

"I wish to speak to Manuel."

"He is not here."

"Where is he?"

"He has gone after Paulo."

"How long ago did he leave?"

"Immediately after he returned from Schmidt's. He said he must go find his friend. I packed him food and he filled his gun belt and left." Tears ran down Maria's face.

27

Gideon watched Vern head deeper into the growing foothills. What would bring a man out here? The man was taking some care to watch his back trail, but was not as watchful as if going in other directions. He rode with a purpose, as to somewhere known. This was at the opposite direction from the Bowers range. Gideon's face wrinkled as possibilities ran through his mind. Yet it was all speculation. Keeping a safe and invisible distance, he followed as Vern headed into a mountain canyon, this one sudden and surrounded by rocky outcrops.

A glare struck his eye and Gideon halted, realizing someone was on the hillside above Vern. Extending his glass, he caught movement of someone disappearing from sight and seeming to step down the hillside to where Vern would be.

Picking his way carefully, he realized whoever was on the hillside was likely talking to Vern. Gideon took the opportunity to gallop across the last valley, trusting the dust would settle or be confusing to anyone returning to the hillside. Reaching the edge of the canyon, he dismounted and looked carefully around.

Vern was there, about a quarter mile distant, talking to a child! No, wait! The child had a beard! It was not a child. It was a Chinaman! What would a Chinaman be doing out here?

As he watched, the Chinaman went behind a cabin-sized boulder and emerged astride a mule. Then both rode off together up the canyon.

Schmidt and a Chinaman? Despite the job at hand, Gideon found himself curious about this new development. Glancing to the hills around only affirmed this was the middle of nowhere. Any towns were distant and, from the looks of the trail, Craswell was not visited often, if at all.

What was he doing? He had a job to do. Here he was following his target and a Chinaman through a remote canyon when he could finish the job and be on his way home. Schmidt's body would never be found out here. Or, even if some wandering cowhand came across the scene, Gideon would have time for a clean getaway. In a week he could be back at his table, drinking coffee and sleeping in a comfortable bed! Yet here he was, following out of curiosity.

He actually found himself less intent at various times over recent months. More often than not, his thoughts strayed back to the children at the home. Gideon took off his hat and wiped his brow with a bandanna, scratching his head. Glancing to the sun, his mind strayed to the children. Jimmy had changed so much. Mrs. McClinder and Hessie were making a difference to that boy! Knowing Wang would see to the children's needs helped as Gideon left for extended periods of time, but still... he wondered if all was well. Little Susanna was sick when he left.

Replacing his hat, Gideon mounted and waited until the riders were a good distance ahead before following.

Eyes and ears open for any sound, Gideon loosened his gun and rode carefully, pausing at every turn to dismount and peer ahead.

28

Chinese village!

Gideon lay atop the bluff, looking downward to the scene below. Tents and wagons were arranged in a manner simulating streets. There was a sense of permanence. A rough glance showed near fifty Chinese – men, women and children. They mingled as they performed tasks needed for such a gathering.

Careful to keep only his forehead and eyes raised, the scene was so unexpected it brought a grin to Gideon's face. This was beyond anything he expected from following Vern Schmidt. Supplies for such a group could be freighted in, but what about water? And why gather here? Letting his eyes rove without moving his head, Gideon became increasingly wondrous as he noted further details.

To his left, at the base of a small outcropping, was a group of women. Water! They were carrying water and there was a small ditch leading to a trough. It must be a natural spring! Further on were indicators of a small garden being planted.

Still not making any sense of it, he ducked down and moved around a bend in the rock. Before he could raise his head he heard voices and lay below the top of the hill, listening. Not twenty feet away was Vern and a group of Chinese! Careful to avoid sudden moves, he strained to hear.

"...need a safe place...couple families..."

The Chinese, obviously the leaders of the group, conferred and spoke to Vern. It was hard for Gideon to pick out the words what with the distance and the broken English.

"...danger...you help...t'ank you...we help." The Chinamen were nodding, though some seemed hesitant.

You help, we help? Was this camp something of Schmidt's doing? Why was he secretly helping the Chinese? By the way of the conversation, it was obvious this was not a criminal camp or anything under compulsion. Schmidt's tone and the Chinese tone indicated friendship. There was more here than met the eye.

Creeping back, Gideon moved further along and heard other sounds. Peering carefully again, he saw Chinese men, covered in what appeared to be soot, moving wearily, wiping their brows. Following the line back he glanced at an exposed hillside where a few more men came out of a tunnel.

A mine!

Buckets of rock stood at the side of the opening. Men sat hammering at the rocks, picking bits of something out now and then and putting it into a small sack.

Gideon scanned his eyes at the surrounding hills. Basalt.

Silver! A silver mine! Yet, from the looks of the surrounding piles of waste, it had been mined years ago. Reopened?

Gideon crept back to his horse and slipped off, his mind working...his heart pondering.

If he had waited another few minutes Gideon would have noted another person he recognized. Someone was watching him, eyes wise with the passing of time and curiosity.

29

anuel found the calf in the half-light before dawn. It was clear from the size of the tracks that the rogue grizzly found the calf and the way of such encounters went to the grizzly. Pursing his lips at the sight, Manuel was focused on other sign amidst the grass.

There were the marks of Paulo's horse. So his friend had been here also, but went on. No doubt after the herd, he chose to leave the calf.

An hour later Manuel spotted blood. A story lay before him in the signs on the ground. There were the tracks of Paulo's horse and the sign of a man kneeling to look at earlier tracks. Another set of indentations of the man as he fell. Blood was on the grass. So Paulo was wounded! It had to be, as the blood was too much and appeared much in one spot.

Paulo had fallen, shot by someone hidden, but later rose again.

Glancing to the surrounding hills, Manuel pieced it all together. Paulo was following the herd and knelt to look at tracks. Someone in ambush shot at him. Paulo was wounded and fell. Looking further, he noted where Paulo struggled and mounted and moved on. So whoever shot him must have counted him as dead, moved on and Paulo, though wounded, was off again in search of the herd.

Manuel looked ahead. Paulo was not a quitter.

Moving on carefully, Manuel slowly moved ahead, balancing the need to look up and the need to follow Paulo's tracks.

He found Paulo an hour later.

30

Gideon stared into the darkness. Spending the daylight hours watching and following his back trail, he sat once again on the shelf of the hillside where he first spotted Schmidt heading to the Chinese camp. As the confusing light of dusk approached, he spotted Schmidt returning home. Sitting long on the hillside, Gideon watched the man slowly work his way across the landscape.

He remained long after dark, staring and thinking.

A mine. Vern Schmidt, a bunch of Chinamen and a mine. Schmidt had shown no superiority or control and did not appear to give any orders. It was clear he was on very friendly terms with the Chinese, and was seeking their help in some matter. Though it would be natural and easy to shoot the man upon his return, something within Gideon held him back.

What kind of a man was this Vern Schmidt?

Evidence showed him a strong man, not afraid to face danger or shy when the odds were against him. He was also a man who befriended those who had no friends; treated others as equals when others would have lorded it over them. Certainly not the attitude of a villain.

Such a difference between Bowers and Schmidt! Bowers was forceful, pushy, demanding. His men respected him out of fear. It was the same with his cub, Clyde. His hired hands were intimidated and likely followed because of a sense of self-importance through proximity to strength, however misguided. Schmidt, on the other hand, was quiet, unassuming, and gentle by nature. At the same time he held strength unseen, the ability to get up when beaten down, treating others as he would want himself treated.

Both men, so different, showed the same result. Both had thriving ranches after years of toil. After all differences, it came down to cattle, to fighting to carve a home from a wild land, to sticking through the unexpected trials of the years. Still the future was in question. It remained to be seen which style of leadership, which way would survive. To an outsider, the bet would go to Bowers, with his hard-riding, pushing manner. Those ways were necessary when the West first became settled and both men came to the territory. Schmidt must have had the same strength and nerve as Bowers in order to survive and grow. As the ways of civilization came to the once wild lands, some ways needed at the beginning became more frowned upon as a more refined society encroached. Which type of person would survive in the long run? It could go either way. Bowers might become a powerful force if he channeled his energies right. His sheer pushiness would alienate many, yet maybe not before establishing himself. Somewhere along the way Bowers would have to adapt, though. Was he capable? Schmidt, on the other hand, attracted kind thoughts. He was a man giving as much respect as he received, a man to ride the river with. Yet could he survive Bowers' push? It didn't look like it at the moment, but still...

Several years ago he was browsing in a bookshop in St. Louis. On one shelf stood a book attracting his eye by the strangeness of the title; <u>Aesop's Fables</u>. Browsing, Gideon noted a strange story about a tortoise and a hare. Taking the book to a table, he read the story and sat thinking long over the moral.

In ways, Bowers was the sure winner, the hare. To all intents and purposes, Schmidt was the tortoise and was expected to lose the race. Yet the traits making the hare a sure bet to win were the same traits causing him to lose the race. Slowly and surely the tortoise plodded along steadily toward the finish line while the hare basically lost through his own overconfidence.

Thinking long over such details, Gideon found his thoughts becoming more personal. Why did he, Gideon, not take the opportunity that had been before him? It would have been simple today to set up and wait for Schmidt, finish the job and tomorrow he could be on his return journey. It would be at least two days before the body would be found. Once reaching the train it would be a relatively comfortable journey to St. Louis and his usual table.

What stopped him?

Perhaps anger over his father's death was easing. Or was it the little girl in the alley? Something was changing within him. A noticeable lessening of his intensity was obvious even to himself, though to others the habits of his life and profession would seem unchanged.

Moving back from the hillside, Gideon sipped coffee and sat late over a low fire, thinking. It was beyond late when he heard steps and a soft call.

"I'm friendly."

Skerby!

Skerby came into the firelight as before, looking old and perhaps more tired. Gideon's pistol lay across his lap as Skerby once again dug for his dented cup.

"Bacon gone already?"

"Afraid so. You came a mite late for polite company."

"Yep, just been around, exploring the territory. Covered a good piece today. Had a nice dinner mid day today. A bit different, but tasty."

Gideon eyed him as the old man stiffly reached and filled his cup. Tasting the black liquid, Skerby made a face.

"Something wrong with the coffee, Skerby?"

"Mite strong tonight."

"Next time I'll let you make it."

"Hmph!"

Both men sat in silence for several minutes. Skerby took a last sip and reached hesitantly to the pot, glancing questioningly at Gideon, who nodded. Skerby smiled and poured another cup. Taking a sip, he stared at Gideon.

"What?"

"Rice."

Gideon furrowed his brow. "Rice?"

"If'n a fella got used to it, it might get rather good."

"What are you talking about?"

"Rice I had with them China people today. Spices kinda made me reach for the water but I can see a body getting' sort of used to it." Skerby spoke to his cup, holding it between both hands in his lap.

Gideon's eyes widened, listening as Skerby continued. It was too much for coincidence. Skerby knew he'd been to the Chinese camp!

"Right friendly bunch. What with the way they get mistreated nowadays, it's a nice thing to see them feeling safe. Not everyone would let a bunch of Chinese set up a home on his land. Though I suspect the word ain't really out much. And a silver mine. Just a small vein. It's on Schmidt's land and he let's them live there. Other men started it and he come across it after whoever it was abandoned it, thought it was played out. I guess they're finding little bits here and there. Nothing no white men want to fool around with, but they live simply and just plan to be here for a couple years before moving on. Sounds like it'll give them what they need to make it through. Probably make the difference 'tween their wee ones eating or starving. Not much coming out, for the amount of work an' all. They'll take the wagons and slip down the valleys and sell it. Or trade for what they need. Seems Schmidt don't say much about it, just sort of lets them stay there. If'n anybody knows they's there, I don't think anybody's figured about the mine."

Reading between the lines, Gideon reached over and refilled Skerby's cup again. The old man smiled as his host spoke.

"You were there."

"Yep."

"You saw me. Where were you?"

"Oh, I'm around. Just happened to look at the right spot at the right time. Schmidt come in and I was sitting across the way; looked towards him and seen your head come up. Just at the right spot. I don't think anybody else seen you."

"What was Schmidt doing?"

"What I could piece together was something about him looking for a safe place for them Mex hands of his to send their families whilst all this nastiness is going on. All-fired concerned for their safety. Kinda different attitude from others ranchers 'round here."

"You like Schmidt?"

"Just like the way he sees things. Friendly, helpful to anybody needs a hand. Ain't all-fired eager to shoot it out. Not everybody would do as he's done to help them little Chinese urchins."

Gideon stared at the man.

Later that night as he slept – fitfully – Gideon kept seeing the children he knew back east and the face of the little girl he'd watched as life ebbed away. Yet as the scenes played before his mind, little Chinese urchins began to play with the other children.

31

"I saw you coming, Manuel."

Manuel startled and grabbed at his pistol. "Don't shoot!"

Both paused as Manuel replaced his pistol.

"Paulo, my friend!" Paulo was sitting on a rock in the shade of an outcropping. Seeing the blood on the man's shirt and head, Manuel looked concerned. Paulo grinned.

"I guess you can see I had a bit of trouble. Someone tried to kill me from ambush. Bullet grazed my head and the back of my shoulder. Bloody, and put me out for a while, but I'm just missing a lot of blood."

"The herd?"

"Just as we expected. Headed to the back of Bowers' range. I tracked it further and headed back. No serious looks down their back trail after I was shot. Must have figured me dead." Pausing, Paulo looked back down Manuel's trail. "You find a calf back there?"

"Yes, but it looks like that grizzly found it before I did." Paulo nodded and asked no more.

"Your horse?"

Paulo swept his hand to the outcropping. "He's fine, just tired. There is water from a seep around the other side. Grass, too."

"Best we get riding. Vern will be worried."

32

Late on a following afternoon, Gideon rested his horse. Solitude he often disliked, for the memories that filled his mind, yet there were times when quiet allowed him to think without distraction. Despite the realization he had a job to do, his thoughts and questions led him to wander the hills for the past few days, convincing himself he was getting the lay of the land, but in reality it was time to think. His mind was racing with thoughts about his life; about Vern Schmidt; about the Chinese camp, about a lot of things.

About to mount again, Gideon stopped suddenly as he caught movement in the panorama laid out before him. There was a rider in the distance. Rather a walker. Squinting, Gideon perceived the person to be small. Unmoving, he waited another quarter hour while whomever it was drew subtly nearer in crossing the valley before him.

A young child? Looking a while longer, he saw clearly it was indeed a small boy, possibly nine or ten, leading a horse with a lame front foot. More than lame. It was hopping on three feet. Neither the boy nor the horse was going anywhere quickly.

What was he doing out here? With a horse hurt bad, the boy would be going towards safety and help. After all, a child does not lead a lame horse away from home, but rather towards loved ones. Could this be Schmidt's son?

Mounting, Gideon cantered his horse at such an angle to intercept the boy perhaps a quarter mile along his walk.

It was a matter of moments and the boy stopped. Gideon smiled despite himself, realizing the boy had spotted him. He was definitely watchful!

Nearing the two, Gideon noticed the boy move to keep the horse as a shield between them. Again he smiled inside. Gideon's smile turned to respect when a rifle barrel peeked over the saddle.

"Stop right there, mister!"

Gideon reined to a stop, facing the boy at about 20 yards.

"What is it you want, mister? You ain't from around here."

"I saw you from the hill back yonder. You've got a lame horse."

"Yep, he needs some attention. I'm heading back to the ranch." The boy squinted at Gideon, seeing the hardness in his eyes. "You ride for the Rocking-B?"

"I ride for myself. Just passing through the territory." He saw the boy look to Gideon's horse, seeing the bedroll and the sign of a man without a home. The boy was sharp! "I mean you no harm."

Squinting his eyes at Gideon for a few moments, the boy eased the hammer and stepped from behind the horse. This kid was tough. Western life had a tendency to make boys into men early.

"Sorry, mister. Been some bad doing's of late. Got a bit of a problem. They's men looking for any chance to shoot my pa."

"Mind if I take a look at your horse?" Wide-eyed, the horse was in obvious distress and agony.

"Sure, mister."

Dismounting, Gideon walked to the boy's horse and carefully stooped to look at the hoof. There was no way he was going to try and lift that foot with a horse in that much pain. And there was no need to touch it. A deep swelling in the hock, with unnatural bumps along the skin told the story. Gideon had seen it before. Broken! Whimpering, the horse stood heaving and quivering.

A tough lad, Gideon realized, but even he must realize the severity of the injury. That part of the boy was still a boy – not wanting to face the reality of the horse's condition.

"Boy, this horse has a broken leg and is in a lot of pain." He spoke with neither tenderness nor hardness but with matter-of-factness.

Eyebrows raised and deep green eyes wide, a tear coursed slowly down the boy's cheek. Unruly hair escaped from under a hat perched firmly over a slightly freckled face. About medium height, this boy was tough as nails, but still a boy.

"This is Flame. He'll be fine in a few days. Just needs rest."

"Boy..."

Shoulders suddenly shaking, the boy began to cry. Toughness was gone and what remained was a hurting child.

"Mister, he's my friend and I can't..."

"What's your name, boy?"

"Laban. Laban Schmidt."

"Laban...this horse needs to be put down. He's hurting bad and it's going to get worse. Nobody can help that leg. Look at his eyes. Not much longer and he'll go down. Only reason he's still up is he trusts you to do right."

Looking at Gideon with knowing eyes, Laban nodded. Tears streamed down his face.

"You walk on ahead a ways, and I'll take care of it." Laban cried but dutifully reached and loosened the cinch to take off the saddle. Letting it down into the grass, Laban turned and petted his horse, talking softly and with that part of him already holding the strength of the West, turned and walked on ahead with determination.

Laban's steps faltered a hundred yards later as Gideon's shot jarred the silent tension and the horse fell to the ground. Laban did not turn, but waited for Gideon to load the saddle and ride to him.

Gideon held the saddle half on his lap and swung Laban astride his bedroll behind him.

"How far to home, Laban?"

"'Bout five miles due east."

No more was said as they rode. At one point he glimpsed a fleeting reflection on the distant hillside. Telescope? Gideon furrowed his brow and tucked the information away.

Riding in silence for a time, Gideon heard subtle noises as Laban quietly grieved. It reminded him of children at the home, specifically Jimmy, when a stray came to stay and Jimmy took the lion's share of the care. One day they found the dog lying curled up as if asleep, but it was dead. Gideon came by just at that time and found the children standing round. Jimmy was trying to be strong and wept quietly.

"You say someone wants to shoot your pa?"

"Bowers wants Pa dead, so's he can take the ranch."

"Why does he want the ranch?"

Sniffles.

"I don't know. Been fine for years."

They rode silently, Gideon scanning the hillsides. Who would have been watching back there? Bowers?

"Ranch is just ahead, mister."

33

"Boss, we lost another calf last night. Found it over by that pasture nigh the north pond."

Dan Bowers rubbed his morning whiskers. Dad burn it! Why didn't he ever feel right unless he was clean-shaven? He'd shave soon. Maybe a snort or two of whiskey while he was at it. It was early, but...

"You think it was the same bear?"

"Yessir. I seen tracks and they was that same paw what was missing a couple claws. It's certainly a big one! Like to give us the willey's when we's over in them parts. Ever time we hear a noise or a snapping twig, we like to jump out'n our boots."

Bowers looked at the man. Certainly small boots to jump out of! He only kept the half-worthless man around because he was expendable should such need arise. At the same time, the man was a fair hand with the cattle. You had to tell him every little direction, but he was always ready.

"Where's Clyde?"

The man tilted his head to where Clyde strutted around the corner of the house, hitching his belt up.

"Clyde, take a group of men and clear that area where we're losing calves to that renegade bear. Haze them all back to the west. Make sure you get them a few miles away. May buy us a couple days. Make sure all of the men ride with a saddle partner, and each one needs a rifle, in case that bear shows up. Make sure you cover all them draws and such. That'll be where it's most dangerous. In a couple days we'll go on a bear hunt. By then it'll be heading toward where we moved the cattle."

"Sure, Pa."

"Clyde?"

Noting his son's eyes, Dan Bowers knew Clyde was chomping at the bit and hated taking orders. Yet the boy was not ready to be the man of the place. Nor was he, Dan Bowers, ready to relinquish control.

"Do you think you can take care of this without galavantin' off somewhere?"

Clyde Bowers' hackles went up.

"Yes, Pa." Glaring, he spoke almost defiantly. Pa had never let him forget that time he headed off to town from the branding fire and left work undone and men sitting around paid but not working. Pa just didn't understand. There was that new girl at the cribs...

34

S napped out of his musings by movement out of
the corner of his eye, Vern Schmidt squinted
and saw a horse in the distance. His brow lifted
as his long experienced eye noted the horse carrying
double.

Large horse. Small rider behind the saddle. Extra
saddle up front. A hat peeked over the rider's shoulder.

Laban!

Straightening, he moved stiffly from the fence as
the horse approached. Laban slipped to the ground
and Gideon eased the saddle to him.

"Pa!" Laban ran to his father and hugged him.
"Flame broke his leg. I didn't know what to do. This
fella showed up and helped. Pa, Flame was my favorite horse!" The boy began to cry.

"I'm sorry, son." He stooped and held his son
close.

Gideon Henry watched as Laban's father genuinely hugged him. Watching Vern, wheels in his mind began to turn. There was an obvious deep love between father and son. Not what he expected. In past times the men he was paid to remove were no accounts or bad men in their own right, often pompous and overbearing, or just plain irritants. This man was tender, a family man. A common hand turned rancher.

Vern Schmidt turned his head upward, taking his hat off to Gideon and nodding.

"Stranger, I thank you not only for stopping the suffering of my son's horse, but even more for bringing Laban home. It means a lot. My name's Schmidt – Vern Schmidt."

Gideon nodded.

"I'm called Gideon. Mind if I water my horse?"

"Not at all. Fact is, the women are 'bout to put vittles on the table. We'd be obliged if you'd set and eat with us. I can get your horse a bait of corn whilst we eat."

Pausing for only a moment, Gideon looked at Schmidt. Vern lowered a brow with something he saw in this stranger's eye. An experienced judge of men, Schmidt noted an uncommon hardness. Gideon looked very self-assured. Glancing to the guns, Vern saw they were clean and well oiled. A man accustomed to details.

Gideon dismounted and led his horse towards the barn.

"Gideon, Laban can take care of your horse. He's a good man with the stock." Gideon noted the look of pride that crossed the tear-streaked face of the young boy.

Handing over the reins, he turned and casually scanned the ranch buildings. They were well-built and designed to last. Tight seams. Care for the comfort of the family. In the distance was a wooded hillside to provide fuel and building material. A few small cabins near the woods showed tendrils of wood smoke against the blue. A bunkhouse behind the barn and a couple work sheds stood nearby, one with a stack of worn horse shoes outside. Two medium oaks stood proudly in the yard. While many settlers cut down anything that might provide cover for an attacker, here were two trees bringing beauty and shade to the yard.

"Well, built, Schmidt."

Vern smiled. "Thanks, call me Vern. I came here and decided this was where I would set my roots. Didn't want to build again later, and wanted my family to be comfortable. I intend these buildings to last at least my lifetime." Gideon Henry noted Vern's mouth lift wryly at the last word.

Hearing a door open, Gideon glanced towards the house as his hand simultaneously edged towards a gun at the sound. Vern noted the movement.

Gideon saw a very pretty young lady standing before him, noting her measuring glance even as he did the same. It was the younger lady he'd seen in town. There was strength in her hazel eyes and erect bearing. Confidence. Not haughty, but just an awareness of herself.

"Gideon, this is my daughter, Mary." He watched and noted approvingly that Gideon did not glance at her as Clyde and some other cowhands, with barely veiled lust and a lingering look up and down her frame. No, this stranger looked Mary in the eyes and gave only the briefest flicker over her body. He now felt more comfortable having the man sit to table with his family.

Gideon nodded to Mary, removing his hat.

"Ma'am."

"Mr. Gideon. Welcome to our home." She spoke with pride even as she, too, took the measure of this man.

Mary Schmidt was aware that she was far from homely, with the scarcity of women in a West filled with men making her desirable if only as an opportunity. Growing up under the harshness of the struggle to build this working ranch, she had seen and known things that built strength within her. Mary noted the eyes of the stranger and wondered where his hardness came from. Without showing it, she knew this man harbored some sort of deep story in his past. This was not unusual in men of the West, many of whom came to this part of the country to flee from something in their past. Yet something was different here.

Mary instantly felt attracted to Gideon, despite the hardness. Strength was a necessary part of life in the West. He appeared confident and strong. She felt no fear, and sensed he respected her. She gestured him to come inside.

Pounding hoof beats in the distance turned their heads. A quarter mile away and riding at a trot were seven men. Gideon's eyes narrowed as he recognized Clyde Bowers at the front. Mary Schmidt noted Gideon's hands loosening his guns. It was a movement meant not to be obvious but most casual and brief.

35

Clyde Bowers sat tall and pompous as he rode into the ranch yard with a handful of his men. Defying his father's orders by heading to town in the first place, he then rode miles out of the way to Schmidt's. Maybe he'd harass the man, threaten him good or, if opportunity arose... His mind had wandered to Mary. That was the opportunity he really wanted.

There was a time a year or so ago when a new hand questioned Clyde ignoring his father's orders. The man was taught a lesson and was barely alive when they sent him off on his horse. No, Clyde might give in to the old man to his face, but behind his back? Ha! One of these days he would be King of the land. He smiled inside at the thought. As the small but loyal cavalcade of minions rode towards Schmidt's ranch buildings, Clyde sat proudly in his saddle, devoid of any true realization that any men surrounding him would be loyal only until his money ran out.

Nearing the ranch yard, Clyde frowned as he noted Gideon standing with the Schmidt's. Reining to a stop, he looked around at his men – HIS men, for he felt money purchased ownership, in both men and women. He was accustomed to doing what he liked with either.

Gideon locked eyes with Clyde, quietly watching the man look pompous for his men. Clyde smirked and spoke:

"I didn't expect to see you here, of all places."

"A lot of things you might not expect." Gideon looked the man in the eye. Clyde Bowers knew he could not lord it over this man, despite the fact Gideon was in some ways a paid hand of the Rocking-B.

Vern and Mary both gave quick glances to Gideon, wondering what the comments had meant.

Casting a long glance at Mary that left nothing of its intent to the imagination, Clyde then glared at Vern.

"Schmidt, it's time for you to sell out." He grinned. "Them bruises could happen all over again – maybe worse."

Vern Schmidt looked firmly at the man. "Is this your father speaking, or just you?" Gideon looked at the man, knowing Schmidt had no idea of the extent to which Dan Bowers was going to get Schmidt's ranch.

Clyde Bowers turned red. "Pa's been a bit soft. Mayhap it's time for things to happen and quit waiting for pa's plan's." Mary noted the man's flickering glance at Gideon.

Mary moved closer to Gideon, who sensed her nearness but remained focused. Vern moved to the side and spoke firmly.

"Get off my ranch, Clyde. You've no right here."

"Schmidt, don't make me laugh. We already know all your men – what's left of them, are out looking for cattle – whatever you got left. Only person other than you folks is them Mex women and their urchins over yonder at the cabins. My men and me could shoot you down without breaking a sweat. But I'd rather beat you senseless. Maybe I should do it in front of your daughter." He laughed, a couple of his men also chuckling.

"Maybe it wouldn't be as easy as you think."

Clyde turned at the intrusion of Gideon Henry. His eyes narrowed.

"Well, mister whatever-your-name-is-today, you would not do well in any event. You're outnumbered." Clyde chuckled and looked at his men, who nodded and smiled in support of their lord and master. Once again Mary glanced over at Gideon.

"Whatever happens, Clyde, it's only you and me here. I'm not concerned with your men. They will fall to the side when you go down."

Clyde chuckled, but warily and not with his usual confident abandon.

"I think it would not be me who went down." Gideon knew Clyde was in a bind, having to put on airs with his men. Always quickly tiring of such men, anger welled in him even as he grinned inside. He learned many skills in his time without a home. Most were by trial and error, but he had friendships with men of many skills, some willing to impart lessons to a willing young student of the street.

"You care to get off that horse, Clyde, or are you too sore from the last beating?"

Clyde bristled, knowing he must save face with his men. And with Mary.

"You'll not have the advantage here, Gideon. No tricks. You and me. And when I'm done with you maybe I'll refresh Schmidt's bruises!" Sliding down off his horse, Clyde carefully unbuckled his guns and draped them over the saddle horn.

Gideon unbuckled his guns and glanced at Mary, holding out his gun belt. She felt the weight of the guns but did not flinch.

"This will be a pleasure!" Clyde laughed, glancing back at his men. Turning back to Gideon, he fell to the ground with a fist to the jaw that landed like a pile driver. Shaking his head, he looked from Gideon to Vern to Mary. Gideon stood, waiting.

"First rule of fighting, Clyde. Don't be stupid." Clyde's eyes widened with anger as he launched at Gideon, who faced him cold and dangerous, relishing the release.

Gideon stepped out of Clyde's punch and powerfully cuffed the man's ears. Clyde fell again. Not to be rebuffed so easily, he became enraged and grabbed at Gideon's legs, knocking him to the dirt. Gideon kicked out at Clyde's stomach as the man tried to straddle him. Grunting and falling back, Clyde rose carefully and slowly. Gideon sprang up as Clyde once again came close. Twisting away from the man's punch, Gideon clapped him on the jaw.

Wary now, Clyde came in swinging again, succeeding in connecting with a right to Gideon's jaw. Gideon stumbled, momentarily stunned. Seeing his opponent reeling, Clyde stepped in again and found himself the recipient of a flashing and brutal drive to the face. Following with several more, Gideon dropped Clyde to his knees and slapped him hard. Clyde fell to his stomach and did not get up.

Breathing hard, Gideon looked from the man on the ground to his followers. He noted their eyes on Mary and looked to see her holding one of his pistols, cocked and pointed at the group of men.

Gideon gestured to Clyde. "Get this man out of here."

Two men carefully dismounted and lifted the bloody Clyde from the dust, bodily pushing him up into his saddle. Then they glared threateningly at Gideon and rode out of the ranch yard.

Vern Schmidt stood in shock. This stranger had helped his son, then showed up in time to beat the tar out of Clyde Bowers. There was a pleasure in the way the man easily conquered Clyde, of whom so many in this area were afraid. He glanced at Mary, who was squinting in concentration at Gideon.

Without looking up, Gideon reached for his gun belt. Mary expertly lowered the hammer and slid it into its holster, then passed the belt. She looked firmly at Gideon.

"Clyde knew you. What's your connection?"

"Nothing, just had a bit of a run in the other day."

"Mister, I may look like some lame-brained girl to you, but something is out of place here. He made that comment about your name not being real. Is it real?"

Gideon was a bit disturbed inside. To his own credit he did not show it. He looked hard at Mary.

"Ma'am, I reckon there's some things you just will not know. Some things there are no right answers to. And I reckon it best that I ride out."

"I reckon not, mister." It was Vern Schmidt. "It still stands to right that you been a service to my family. We are much obliged and I'd still be pleased to have you join us for vittles."

Gideon looked at Schmidt. He realized good meals might be few and far between on this job.

Besides, he would be able to watch Schmidt and his family closely and might get some insights into the patterns of his life.

He nodded assent to Schmidt.

As they walked to the house, Mary was deep in thought.

Ruth Schmidt emerged from the house during the fight and held a Winchester. Gideon glanced from the gun to the woman. She was, indeed, still handsome for her age, but the wear of the years had taken its toll. Yet, he knew he faced a woman of deep strength. Her hands were no strangers to the Winchester.

As he came to the house, Vern introduced his wife. Gideon nodded, took off his hat and stepped aside for Mary, who glanced at him knowingly as she passed by.

36

SOMEWHERE IN COLORADO

To some he was merely a telegrapher, sitting in his office tapping the keys and watching for trains. The Dragoon Colt seemed larger than the man, yet it sat next to him each day.

It was the quiet of the job that first appealed to him. Eight years now and his pay came regular, although on the low side. Still, he ran a few cows and cut some ties for the railroad in his spare time. He and Natalie did ok.

Natalie understood the need for him to have this quiet job. The war had been rough on him and he'd seen more excitement than he ever wanted to see again.

Hefting the Dragoon, he examined it as he had a hundred times before. Originally cap and ball, he'd had it converted to cartridge. Opening the cylinder and ejecting the shells, he carefully wiped the gun down. It was a reminder of the past, as if he needed any reminders. Yet he also understood the value of the gun for today and he would not hesitate to use it if he or his family were threatened.

Satisfied, he reloaded and put the gun near to hand. Swiveling his chair and carelessly crossing his feet on the counter, he leaned back, deep in thought. What was on his mind was a wire he had received yesterday. It was from his old commander, Otis Henry. Oh, what a joy to see the name! He had proudly shown Natalie.

Major Henry – of course, he was not a major now, but always would be to him – wanted information regarding a possible newcomer to the area. Yes, he recognized the man the Major was asking about – there wasn't much he didn't know in his position. One couldn't miss the man – he fit Major Henry's description. He remembered the man getting off the train a while back and standing on the platform looking around with a knowing eye. It sort of stuck in his mind at the time that the man was on a mission.

Company rules said he couldn't use the telegraph for personal use. Ha! But this was Major Henry. Slamming his feet down, he bent to the key...

37

NEW HAVEN, COLORADO

Ella Henry looked at the young man. At the ranch no more than three weeks, already she could see a difference. Nate ate enough for two and she found herself chuckling at his eagerness to eat her food. He put on weight and, though still seemingly weak, refused to slack off on work. This did not go unnoticed by the other hands, who nodded approvingly to each other. Even Nate's back seemed to straighten, as if the curvature was more the weight of desperation than anything truly physical.

Only Matt remained in the "big house" as they called it. Buck and Chad were married and built their own cabins along the hillside. Bill lived in town, but rode out on Sundays with Becky. All commented about Nate filling out, and how he worked hard in his own way. Though nowhere near able to hold up to the pace of the ranch hands, he was gaining and didn't gripe or complain.

Nate was thankful for what happened to his life. When the Henry's made their offer he was stunned. Harsh words were exchanged with Mr. Baker, who called him many names and alluded to what would become of him if he followed this foolish fancy and how he would likely die at the hand of some renegade or get trampled by some cow and he'd be better off staying in Kansas City. Nate stood, only half hearing and hardly able to contain the excitement of escape from what he felt was a living hell existence. Baker refused to pay wages owed, but Otis and Ella took care of everything.

Riding the train had been pleasant enough, but a daylong ride by horse was another thing. Rarely having any opportunity to ride in Kansas City, after several hours he was so sore he thought he'd never survive. Both Ella and Otis repeatedly cast sidelong glances at Nate as they watched his increasing discomfort. They took a few breaks, long enough to rest the horses, but not long enough for Nate to stiffen up. Caught between his suffering and the magnificent scenery around every turn and over every hill, Nate didn't know whether to laugh or cry.

Coming to the ranch from the south, Otis explained they were bypassing New Haven and going straight to the ranch. Arriving at the bluff overlooking the ranch valley, Nate's discomfort was almost forgotten as his mouth dropped in awe of the beauty and the space.

At the ranch house, Nate slipped in slow agony from his horse and almost couldn't walk. Otis both grinned and commiserated with the lad's pain. Nate spent the rest of the day leaning on the porch rail, unwilling to sit. Sly smiles from the other hands were not lost to him, but his misery took precedence over his pride.

Within a couple weeks Nate rode all day without problem. Though still not an exceedingly experienced rider he'd proved himself a quick learner.

Sitting at the table, Ella felt proud of what they were able to do for this young man. They felt he had much to offer. Nate polished off a heaping helping of dinner, smiled and then reached for seconds.

Otis, who was in town early that morning, took a gulp of coffee and looked up.

"Nate, I have some information about your brother."

Nate looked up, eyes wide.

"It's not a lot, but there seems to be word that he was seen heading west. That's all we know so far. I've sent off some other messages to people I trust and who might have some information. May take a few days to learn more."

"Thank you, sir. Ella, this food is delicious."

38

CRASWELL

Excitement over the fight had Laban talking non-stop. Due to his age and the happenings of the day, he was hardly able to eat. At one point, Vern Schmidt found it necessary to urge the boy to be quiet enough to eat his meal. Laban plowed in, but talked while chewing until his mother admonished him about his manners. At that point upbringing took over and he straightened up.

Gideon noted furtive looks between Mary and her parents. Though enjoying the home-cooked chicken and greens, tension in the air took much of the flavor away. He wished he'd not stayed.

Looking around the room, Gideon felt a sense of wistfulness, for it reminded him of the humble house he remembered. A doily covered a small table which held a Bible and spectacle case. A clock ticked softly upon the mantle, looking down over a braided rug before the fireplace. Beside one of two matching rockers was a basket of yarn and knitting needles. It was a place built originally as a fortress in a wild land, yet the changes of the years softened not only the territory, but the Schmidt's also. This was now a home. Gideon sighed to himself.

Soon after, he rode out of the ranch yard with a brief backward glance. Mary and Vern stood under the tree watching him ride off.

Later in the afternoon, sitting in the shade of a rock outcropping, he thought back over the events of the day. A valuable store of information had been gleaned, and it troubled his heart.

Laban. He was a pleasant child, and usually children are a reflection of their upbringing. Laban was polite, respectful and helpful.

Vern. He was hardworking and sought to provide for his family. A man of strength and a builder, he built to last. Though the odds were unfavorable he would stand to protect his family and ranch. One of the problems, though, was what would happen to his family when he fell – which he would. He was a target. Not only for he, Gideon, but also for Clyde.

Gideon shifted uncomfortably.

Ruth. She was a woman to stand by her man. What they built together, they would go down defending together. She would understand her man was facing hopeless odds, but that did not matter. Ruth would stand or fall beside her man.

Mary. Strong, she also was defiant and very intelligent. She had looked deep inside him. He felt she was on the verge of understanding him and his role. She was quite attractive, not in a showplace kind of way, but something about the totality of the woman stood out. Mary had the character of a woman to stand beside a man, to ride the trails of life and have the strength to take whatever comes. Also, she would stand strong by the side of her father.

Her eyes. Her wisdom was apparent in her eyes.

Once again, he found himself questioning. Thinking over his life and decisions he had made, Gideon wondered what would have happened if he had met someone like Mary a few years ago. Would his life be different? Then again, the situations he went through did not lean themselves to meeting such people.

For some reason, he thought of his mother. What had life handed to her? It was unexpected but she did not have the strength to face it. Her eyes would not have conveyed the strength Mary's eyes held.

Gideon shook his head almost violently! What was he thinking? He'd been hired to kill Vern Schmidt and now knew more about the patterns and details of the man's life. He never before allowed his emotions and thoughts to interfere with his job. It was a vocation, one demanding a certain detachment. Indeed, his entire way of living was to remain distant, to avoid any relationships having the potential to bring about pain. Nevertheless, he noted since finding the young girl in the alley and seeing her die, and starting the home for the street children, he found himself less stern at times. It became increasingly difficult, but necessary, to compartmentalize the home from his vocation.

Was he softening? Was he losing that edge which kept him detached and single-minded and efficient?

No. That edge became visible when he faced imbeciles like Clyde Bowers. Yet there had never been a job in his past directed at someone so seemingly solid as Vern Schmidt. He was no ne're-do-well or varmint, nor an evil man. Vern was just like...well, just like his own father. A hard working man building a life and dream.

Mary. He already saw she was like no other woman he ever met.

Did he have to go through with this job? There! He'd said it! Acknowledging his second thoughts for the first time, Gideon mounted again and brooded for hours, running over events of his life and musing about the future as he rode through the afternoon and into the evening. The shadows lengthened around him.

A man usually attentive to the trail, he found himself troubled with many straying thoughts, pondering the ways of his life – until he felt the rope slip over his shoulders.

39

Mary rode out of the ranch yard in the fading light and spreading colors of early evening. Her father warned her that trouble was likely in the days ahead. At the same time, he knew Mary was single-minded and determined and would be aware of herself and her surroundings. Though she knew he was uncomfortable with her riding alone, she noted comfort in his eyes at the knowledge of the derringer in her pocket and the Dragoon Colt hanging from her pommel.

Both weapons and others were familiar to her. Early on Mary learned to shoot. Vern and Ruth taught the ways of the West as she rode with them across the land over the years. She was strong and capable. She knew her parents would one day have to relinquish her to some man, and they hoped and prayed it would be the right man. Inside she had confidence she would not fall for a no-account, sure she had the insight to see though to the real core of the man.

As Mary rode that evening, her thoughts focused at first upon objects close to her, then worked out into the distance, noting the way the evening sun settled on the distant hills and gave a sort of surreal cast to the features of the land. Her father taught her it was essential to check for changes in nearby surroundings, scanning outward to those points farthest away. She knew the logic of this; awareness that danger could lurk nearby and it was essential to avoid imminent hazards and dangers before the distance was even a factor. Her father had taught her about men killed by Indians who were literally underfoot but missed because some poor fool walked out of the house and looked immediately to the distance.

This man, Gideon, confused her. She could see deep strength inside him. He was a man both harsh and violent, a man uncowed and not easily intimidated – if ever. She had the impression Gideon had a much deeper reservoir of violence if needed, that he was merely toying with Clyde. Yet, at the same time, looking deep into the man's eyes, there was something else. Could it be a hurt, a tender spot, a vulnerability?

There was something else...the gun. Not unfamiliar with weapons, she readily noted the incredibly smooth action of Gideon's weapon. It was not the usual for a weapon of its type. When she cocked it in the ranch yard, she sensed it was modified – but for what? Only a man who used his guns for a living would take the time and money to have a gun modified.

So...what was he doing out here? She wrinkled her brow in thought and concern with the recollection that Clyde was familiar with the man. He also indicated Gideon's name might be false. Was it?

A hired gun? Hired by whom? Why was Clyde familiar with him, yet not revealing of any more information? So Gideon was familiar to Bowers. Clyde was resentful of him, resulting in the fight – if it could be called that. What Clyde said told her he and Gideon knew each other in some way. Clyde's attitude toward Gideon was the same attitude Clyde showed whenever he felt someone was more important than him. She witnessed it more than once. So, feeling Gideon was more important must have come through Dan Bowers. Why would Clyde feel that way unless Gideon was here to do a job Dan Bowers felt could not be done by Clyde? Or done better?

A hired gun...that must be it! Hired by Bowers? Who would he be after?

Daddy? But the man came to the ranch and made no attempts to harm her father. Nevertheless, it was also clear he had not planned to be at the ranch, but apparently found Laban and offered the help of any western man. He brought Laban home. Was this all mere coincidence? What was he doing on our range? Watching? Observing? Learning patterns? Then he sees Laban and uses this opportunity to walk right into the opposing camp and get the lay of the land?

As she thought more about it, the more it seemed to fit. She knew her father was a target. But why had the man not shot her father in the ranch yard? And why had he stopped Clyde?

Witnesses! That was it! These men found their prey in lonely locations, or places where witnesses could not identify, then faded into the distance and disappeared.

Gideon a killer! She didn't know for sure, but the pieces fit. Still, she remained troubled by what she saw in the man...troubled, yes, yet deeply stirred in her heart.

Looking and listening to the encroaching night, she turned south to make a sweep before returning to the ranch when she heard a distant shot in the hills to the west. Reining her horse, she listened intently. Hearing no other sounds, but wary, Mary turned her horse back to the ranch.

40

Jerked out of the saddle, Gideon landed on a sharp rock and grimaced as it punctured the skin of his back. Shrugging against the tightened rope, he groaned in pain. Then a crashing blow to his head turned all to darkness.

Clyde Bowers turned and shot Gideon's horse, dropping it. The others jumped away as the creature struggled for a few moments, lashing out as if trying to fend off the cloak of death.

"Aw, Clyde, why did you have to kill the horse?"

"Shut up! I want no sign of this man left! Tabor, you and Roscoe throw a loop on this horse. Drag him over to those rocks. Let the coyotes have a feast. Hooch and Batt! Drag Gideon over to that tree. Watch him! He's dangerous. Barth! Build a fire – we need some coffee. And grab that bottle from my saddlebags. It'll warm us against the evening chill." Smiling at no one in particular, he chuckled.

No sir, Clyde thought. Ain't no way he would let this Gideon get away with showing him up in front of his men twice and now Mary. He would make a nice slow show of Gideon. Then his men would see and know that he, Clyde Bowers, was not to be trifled with or pushed around. He straightened and threw his shoulders back, strutting to his horse.

41

Gideon Henry awoke to a staggering pain in his head. He tried to reach it but found himself pinned by rope. Remembering the musings, the lack of attending to the trail, then the rope, the pain and the sudden blackness, he cursed himself. There was wetness over his face that must be blood.

"The captive awakes to hear his sentence!"

Squinting through blood trickling to his eye, Gideon noted Clyde in the flickering firelight of the deepening night. Like a partial moon, his silhouette was illuminated on one edge, sitting by the fire, sipping coffee from a dented tin cup. Two men stood close to Gideon, one holding the end of the rope encircling him. Struggling against the rope, flashes of pain shot from his back. Recalling the pain when he hit the ground, Gideon felt wetness in his shirt that he knew must be blood. So, bleeding from his back also.

Twisting his hands around, fingers groped but found empty holsters.

"Looking for these?" Clyde twirled the cylinder of one of Gideon's pistols.

"Interesting action on these pistols. Smooth and touchy. I'll enjoy them. Tabor, how do you like that knife?"

Gideon looked to another man who sat examining the knife Gideon usually kept in his boot.

"Real nice, Clyde. Well made. Good fer skinnin' varmints." A toothless grin showed in the flames as the scruffy man chuckled and looked to the others for recognition.

"Batt, you like that derringer? You been wantin' one."

Another man smiled. "Real nice, Clyde. Thanks, stranger. You passin' by right here done saved me a trip to town. Been savin' fer one of these."

Gideon focused with one eye on the prince of the Bowers spread, struggling against the rope and the pain to wipe his other eye on a shoulder. It was only partially successful. "What's your pa going to say, Clyde?"

"He'll never know a thing, Gideon. You will just disappear – your horse already has – and then my pa will figure you ran off with the money. Of course he'll yell and carry on and then I'll take care of Schmidt and the territory will be ours. Mary will become my wife and we'll all live happily ever after." A pompous chuckle and a swagger of Clyde's shoulders conveyed a sense of triumph.

"Mary has no interest in you."

"She won't have a choice. Be a shame if something happened to her ma and kid brother."

Gideon noted the nervous chuckles of the other men. They might be rough, but there was still a code in the West. Yet, these men would do as they were told, riding on the coat tails of their lord and master.

"You think you'll get away with this?" As he spoke, Gideon slyly felt his belt for another small, folding knife kept there. He felt the clip. It was still there!

Clyde Bowers rose and walked over to Gideon and glared viciously down at his captive. Grinning, Clyde reared his leg back, swinging a kick. Despite the ropes, Gideon managed to jerk sideways, causing Clyde to stumble. One of the men laughed. Clyde spun with amazing speed and glared at the man, who cowered and looked sheepish.

"What you laughin' at, Hooch?"

Hooch paled. "Nothin,' Boss."

"You laugh again at me and it'll be the last thing you do! Do you understand?"

"Yes, Boss."

Clyde Bowers turned back and suddenly went wild, cuffing Gideon repeatedly, sending shooting pains through his head. Bowers kicked him in the ribs, and then kicked him again. It was as if the pent up anger of the man broke loose as he kicked and slapped Gideon for several minutes. Unable to protect himself, Gideon tried to squirm as much as he could to lessen the blows, but enough connected to cause him to scream in pain. Clyde suddenly stopped his attack, walked back to the fire, reached for his cup and took a sip of coffee.

"How's it feel, Gideon?" He put his cup down and walked over and began to strike and kick Gideon several more times.

"Doggone, Clyde," one of the men spoke, "You gonna torture him?"

"Shut up, or you'll be next! I'll teach any man not to make a fool of me in front of my men, and especially in front of any woman!" He kicked Gideon again with viciousness and brutality, then reached for a thick branch and began to beat his captive. Several minutes later, Clyde stood panting. Throwing the branch down, eyes glaring at Gideon with satisfaction, he drew back a boot for another kick.

"Don't cripple him, Clyde! Not unless you want to carry him elsewhere. You already done kilt his horse."

Clyde stood, panting, glaring at the man who spoke and then back to his captive.

"You all get up, we're gonna drag this man to the middle of nowhere and finish him. If'n he's lucky he'll die on the way. He'll not relish what I plan to do to him!"

Gideon writhed with pain, almost senseless from the trauma, as two men jerked him to his feet. Excruciating pain clouded his vision. Gasping and unable to stay on his feet, the two men held him up.

Clyde Bowers walked up to him and spit in his face.

"It really don't bother me one way or the other. You're gonna die. You can either walk or I'll drag you. Your choice, but there's some cactus spines might not feel too good." Clyde laughed and walked to his horse, taking a turn around the pommel with the rope that encircling Gideon's arms. The two men let go of their captive to mount their horses, leaving Gideon swaying with dizziness and agony.

Think! Gideon, from some deep well, forced a part of his mind to forget the pain, to come to reality. Everything in him screamed out. Never had he felt so much pain! Yet something inside sensed the men distracted for a brief moment as they mounted their horses. With a desperate motion, he slid his fingers into his belt and grasped the folding knife.

"Ok, tough man! You've surprised me by standing. Let's see how fast you can walk. But it really don't matter, because I will make sure your legs don't work before you die." Clyde began to walk his horse and Gideon almost fell as the rope tightened and forced him ahead. Fighting the pain, he desperately stumbled as the men moved forward.

No one rode beside him, instead riding single-file and staring ahead at the narrow trail. One or the other turned every few moments to stare at the bloody man they led to slaughter, and were amazed Gideon could even walk. Yet he himself knew his strength was almost gone and every step was a step closer to more brutality. Something had to happen soon and there was nobody to act but himself.

Wincing with every step, Gideon squinted and watched as night crept downwards. The trail became increasingly difficult to follow as it snaked between rocks and trees. The men's glances became even less as they attended to low branches. Swiftly reaching with both hands he opened the knife, keeping it hidden. There was a slow moment when Clyde passed between the rocks and Gideon slipped the knife up under the rope and made a quick slice. The knife was razor sharp, but the rope was thick. He only half feigned stumbling as Clyde looked back, grinning vilely.

Stumbling more than once and finally falling, he was dragged over some rocks before Clyde paused to grin as Gideon slowly stood. Clyde was laughing at him, the men following his lead.

Somewhere in the haze of suffering, Gideon watched for any opportunity. If he was to die he did not want it to be like this.

Passing through a small clearing in the hills, the trail soon passed between two trees. As they neared,

42

Gideon stiffly slipped into the trees to the side of the trail, a mere instant before Clyde turned. Ignoring pain, he pressed through hanging limbs, working at the rope and seeking the refuge of the deeper trees, knowing it would be a minute or two before the men quieted to listen for their fugitive. He heard Clyde's angry yell and caught the sounds of other yells and the confusion of a group of horses attempting to turn in a narrow trail in the dark of night.

It was several minutes before Clyde could quiet both men and horses for pursuit. Following relentlessly, they dogged Gideon's trail.

"Here's a broken branch! He went thisaway!"

"You men circle to the left, the rest of you follow me!"

Cursing's and yells erupted unceasingly as men pushed their horses through the trees in the dark. They seemed not to realize that leaving the horses behind would allow better movement. Men of this ilk, however, would not think of going anywhere on their feet if a horse were at all available and able. Though barely able to move through the agony, Gideon still moved more quickly through the thick stands of trees than could his pursuers.

He heard occasional grunts of horses and men as they were forced through tight gaps. Desperate for distance, he also knew his pursuers were attentive to the sounds he might make.

"I heard something over there!"

"Over where, you idiot? We can't see where you're pointing!"

"To the left!"

Thinking quickly, Gideon felt desperately along the ground and grasped a handful of rocks. Seeing the moonlight between some trees, he heaved the lot to the right, and then filtered through the trees to his left. He gasped from the effort, grasping his side.

"I heard him! He's over thisaway!"

Over the next hours he barely managed to evade his pursuers, but necessity finally forced him across a bare hummock and, just as he went over the top, he heard a yell of discovery.

"I seen him! Over here!"

Gideon kept moving, oblivious to the wracking pain. Knowing he was grievously hurt, survival itself dictated he keep moving or they would kill him on sight. Always a survivor, something within compelled his stumbling steps forward. Shutting off exhaustion's pull to lay down and die, Gideon pushed beyond the limits of the average man. He had never been average...

On through the night he moved, sometimes closer, sometimes further from pursuit, but Gideon could sense the slow closing of the circle around him. On through the night he ignored the need to fall down, knowing he would not get up. Just at dawn, it became obvious capture was near. Gideon collapsed and lay in a smattering of small boulders. Grunts of both horses and men heralded the tightening ring about him.

He could not get away! Yet deep inside a spark still burned and his jaw set.

43

Hitting the cold water below jarred Gideon awake. Seemingly underwater for minutes, instinct labored furiously as he clawed for release from the airless cocoon threatening to envelope a tenuous life in a permanent shroud of death. Disoriented and unable to shrug free of the grasping bonds of exhaustion and cold, his movement slowed and death's hungry grasp tightened. Bursting lungs began to give way as Gideon's face broke surface and starved lungs gulped deliciously at the air. Almost simultaneously he slammed violently into a moss-carpeted boulder, crying out in agony.

As the cry burst free, the torrent took hold and he plummeted once again, panicking as he gulped water, broke surface and coughed violently.

It seemed like forever that he was alternately dragged under and rolled to the surface. In actuality it was only moments before he became snagged in a nest of drift logs. Gideon lay for brief moments gasping and coughing before his mind began to pull from its fog. By this time one eye was swollen completely shut and bruises and pain almost mercifully blotted his mind from clarity. Something awakened aching and torn muscles, causing hands to reach out. A small, mostly submerged, sandbar beckoned and Gideon clawed over, dragging desperately to pull his torn body to the safety of an overhang.

It took the last strength in his being to make a final pull; with eyes rolling, compassionate darkness enfolded.

Cold once again drew Gideon's mind back to life. Chill night air brought uncontrollable shivers to his worn body. Lying immobile, his one good eye opened to face the raging torrent. Seeing an overhang above him, he lacked any strength to look around. His body shivered as never before, something within aware that his rags of tattered clothing did little to warm him. Yet it was the same cold that deadened his pain, caressed his bruised and battered body and eased him to sleep once more.

44

"I saw him, Clyde! I know it, just around that bend." The man stood on the rim of the gorge, looking downward and pointing to a bend fifty yards down the river. The rays of dawn lightened the eastern sky.

"He's dead. Gotta be. No man can take that fall in the condition he was in. I swear I seen him hit by somebody's bullet."

"Shut up, all of you!" Clyde was wide-eyed, staring downriver. "Tabor, you and Batt head fast downriver to Lander's crossing and ride thisaway. If you see any sign of his body, take note of where it stops. Go fast – now! The rest of you, fan out along the rim and watch. Gideon may have found a hole somewhere."

"Clyde, I been all over this gorge. Ain't no hidey hole nowhere."

Clyde Bowers put his gun barrel in the man's face and cocked the gun quickly. "Roscoe, you do as you're told, or do you want to go into the gorge limp and bloody?"

Eyes wide, Roscoe was immediately penitent. "Sorry, Clyde. Didn't mean to sound disrespectful. I'll do whatever you want." Removing the barrel, Clyde let the man go. He was in no mood to take any guff or defiance from his men. After all, he was the son of Dan Bowers, and he would soon be king!

Below and a few hundred yards downriver, the gravely wounded Gideon breathed sparsely. Wracked with physical pain, his mind was nowhere close to reality, having slipped to that precipice over which death was a mere half step away. There was at least a semblance of peace.

Something within registered vague sounds of yelling over the sounds of the torrent and beneath the tons of rock towering protectively over him. Gideon's hands worked spasmodically at the sand and he slept again.

"Clyde, we been searching all day. We done found nothing but his boot down by the crossing. The man's dead and gone, probably clear out of the territory by now."

"I hear tell they found a body once down by Mexico done traveled a hunnerd miles in a day. Musta been quite a site." Batt shook his head knowingly.

"That's what happened to this Gideon fella, Clyde. He done bought the farm and he ain't nothin' but fish bait now."

Usually a quiet man, Hooch spoke. "I dunno. We needs to see the body – or part of it. Just to be sure he don't pull a Lazarus on us."

Clyde looked sharply at the man.

"Who's Lazarus? Which spread he work for?" It was Tabor. Hooch rolled his eyes.

"He was that man what Jesus raised from the dead."

"Raised from the dead? How's that possible?"

"Well, Tabor, Jesus did all sorts of stuff – healings and such."

"I'll be…I had a dog once't we thought was dead. Then, of a sudden he takes this big gasp of air and jumped up and started to run in circles."

Hooch looked at Tabor.

"How long did he run in circles?"

"Just a few minutes, till we shot him."

"Why'd you shoot him?"

"'Cause he were runnin' in circles. What use is a dog what run's in circles?"

"Musta been a sight to see." Hooch shook his head.

"Shut up all of you!" Faces turned as one and sheepishly looked at Clyde.

Clyde brooded at the loss of surety of the death of Gideon. He wanted the man out of his way! Surely the damage done before the fall was enough to seal his fate. After all, the man was barely alive. At the same time, Gideon was a man of uncommon strength. The fall would have injured him and the certainty of hitting bottom or a boulder would add additional insurance he was dead. His men were exhausted, having been out for two days and a night without sleep. If they did not get rest and decent food, even their fear of him would give way. Even the callousness of Clyde's heart knew the limits of his followers. He was not exactly looking forward to facing his pa, since they were supposed to be at the other edge of the ranch, but he had little choice. Maybe pa would be drunk and sleeping and they could get away before his hangover had effect.

"Let's head back to the ranch. We'll head out again in the morning.

45

"**O**f all the stupid things to do! Clyde, you're a blooming idiot! Do you realize what you've done?"

Dan Bowers was more irate than his son had ever seen before. Red-faced, bug-eyed with anger, his hands were fisted and shook in Clyde's face. The fat roll around his neck was crimson and twitching.

Usually more nonchalant around his father, Clyde, the cub of Dan Bowers, heir apparent of the Rocking-B spread, was fearful as he had not been in many summers. Before him stood a man murderous and skirting irrationality's ragged edge. Clyde barely remembered the days before his mother died when pa was focused on building the ranch and was not so brutal. Though a head smaller than Clyde, Dan Bowers was still a powerhouse. Able to charm, able to be vicious, he built his range by fighting Indians, squatters and Mother Nature. Against all he had won. Dan Bowers followed no scruples, unless others were watching. Many an opponent was found face down or just disappeared altogether.

"You done ruined everything! Gideon was hired to make this easier for us, to keep our name out of it. You and your pig headed pride have now turned the best killer in the land against us! Now we gotta watch our backs at all times, and you most of all! He'll be after you!"

"Pa, he can't possibly be alive."

"Did you see a body?"

"No, but…"

Dan Bowers shook his fist in his son's face.

"Did the thought ever occur to you that there are a couple options when you can't find the body? Either the man is dead or the man ain't dead? Until you find a body, you can't assume the man is dead! You gotta watch your back. This man is a master of sitting back and waiting till the right moment comes along! Gideon may be wounded, and it sounds like he's gotta be in desperate shape, but he's also a man who is stronger than most, more determined than most, and will crawl off in some hole and get his strength back and then he'll be on the warpath with you and me in his sights!"

"Pa, I…"

"Shut up! Now, here's what you gotta do. Listen well, Clyde." Leaning to within an inch of his son's face, Dan Bowers breathed hoarsely, wheezing with barely restrained control. "Find him. Take the men, fan out across the country and find him. Either dead or alive. Search the river, search the banks. Look for any way he mighta climbed out of the gorge. Put a man along the river, checking it all the way down to the crossing. If you find the body, hallelujah! If you find the man, well, make sure he's dead. As long as he's alive he's a danger to us and all our plans." Looking to Gideon's gun tucked in Clyde's belt, he pointed. "Is that one of Gideon's guns?"

"Yes."

"Obviously nice weapons. Hang them in the bunkhouse. Tell the men there's a hundred dollars gold and the guns for bringing in evidence Gideon Henry is dead. Hang the gold with the guns."

"But Pa, I was hopin' to keep the guns myself."

"You got a gun. Do as I say."

Disgruntled, Clyde looked down, lips pursed in anger. Yet he held it in. "Yes, Pa."

"Keeping this spread and all the others we intend to take depends on this Gideon being dead. Do you understand that?"

"Yes, Pa."

"Now, get! I gotta think."

46

A whole day passed before the ravaged man showed sign of life again. There was slight movement of a foot, then a twitching of a leg too long in one position. Discomfort mixed with stiffness and residual pain opened the eye and the eye roved up and down and back and forth. The head twisted sideways to look upward and the swollen eye that had lain encased in cool, wet sand for so long no longer was blindly shut, and began to survey through a widened slit. Shuddering with the cold, he slowly raised his head and looked around. With vision unclear from some unknown blow in the fall, he fought to see his surroundings.

Groaning, Gideon pulled an elbow up and raised himself, bringing his other elbow up and under with excruciating pain. It took sheer will for his arm to work. A quick glance and a wince showed his right hand was sore and deeply bruised. His left was black and blue from some unknown injury. Feeling a deep pain in his side, he reached slowly downward and came near to blacking out with pain. A scream of pain wrenched from his throat as his fingers found the bullet hole. It was obviously angry and needed care.

Where he lay was a deep undercut of the gorge wall where water used to run and still might during a rainstorm upstream. Looking slowly back and forth, he saw a corner where twigs and other sticks lay jumbled from being tossed and eddied in heavy rain. About twenty feet deep, the area sloped upwards at the back. He could no more than raise his head before coming up against the ceiling. No sun reached here and cold saturated the entire shelter. Gideon realized the cold likely saved him, keeping the swelling of his body down and slowing blood loss.

Dragging himself slowly to the water, he put his face in and drank deeply. He must rest, and needed food, but the water would sustain life. Weakness indicated the loss of too much blood. Feeling his side bleeding again, Gideon reached to the moss on the rocks nearby. Scraping off a handful, he slowly reached down and gritted in pain as aching fingers packed it into the bullet hole. Crawling back to the rear where there was a bit more space, he collapsed and slept again.

47

waking later, Gideon found himself more aware. Terribly weak, something in his mind forced him to focus. Cold to the bone, he knew to lie here was to die. Any animal that lay wounded was prey to other animals and to the weather. Either could kill. Warmth and food were necessities and this shelter would be a death trap in the next heavy rain. Drawing from a deep well to find strength, Gideon crawled out from the overhang and through a side pool of the current where the warmer water gave him pause before he rested in the rocks, sleeping for a time in the sun, warmer for the first time in days. As the sun traversed a dazzling blue sky and slowly forsook the rocks where Gideon lay, he crawled back under the overhang, to the corner near the pile of sticks.

Sensing movement Gideon reached for a flat rock nearby and stared intently at the sticks. A subtle movement again and a large water moccasin slithered from behind. Coming towards Gideon, the snake coiled and struck, hitting the stone in Gideon's hand! In desperation, Gideon screamed and slammed the rock at the snake, pinning its head briefly, but long enough for a weakened hand to grasp it and slam the head upwards several times against the rock ceiling. Throwing the dead snake and panting with exertion and residual desperation, he lay face down in the sand for what seemed an eternity but was mere minutes. A deep awareness made him look over at the dead snake and, slowly inching towards it, he grasped it and dragged it to his side, half ready to feel a strike. Carefully reaching to his belt, he found the folding knife was still there!

Slowly, his hands battered and used only with difficulty, Gideon sliced the head off the snake, using the tip of the knife to flick the head further away. Most who knew of venomous snakes learned a snake head could be dangerous long after the snake itself ceases to breathe. The venom remains in the sacs and it was not unknown for a full-grown man to die of the poison after stepping on a carelessly placed snake head and being punctured by lifeless fangs.

Taking the knife, he slowly and awkwardly skinned the snake. Grimacing, he put a piece in his mouth and chewed slowly, only his quest for survival keeping him from vomiting. Eyeing the knife and the pile of twigs, Gideon began to run his hand through the rocks before him until he found a piece laced with flint, broken from the ceiling above. Inching cautiously to the pile of sticks, he drew some away and found dry bark strips. Grinding these in his hand and placing the fibers below the sticks, he reached for the flint. It took almost an hour of striking, resting and striking again until sparks smoldered in the bark. Blowing the faint glow into life, adding twigs created a small fire. Gideon coughed and his eyes ran with the smoke as it collected in the small, enclosed area. Moving aside allowed a faint breeze off the river to inch the smoke out and away, adding further life to the fire.

Hungrily forking a piece of the snake with a stick, Gideon held it over the small flames before greedily stuffing the half-warmed life-giving nourishment into his mouth. Small waves of heat warmed his stiffness. Gauging the twigs with one eye showed there was not enough to last more than a few hours.

Though only able to move slowly, he knew he must get out of the gorge. Surveying the walls before and around where he earlier lay in the sun, Gideon noted a barely perceptible path of some small animal, starting above out of sight and ending a few feet in front of him. It looked recently disturbed.

Napping once again, he awoke to barely warm ashes. Glancing upward, he began to half crawl, half climb his way up the slope. Muscles screamed in agony and barely healing cuts opened again with tearing pain making him wince. Several times he lost hold and slipped backwards to have the slide arrested by a jarring stop at some rock.

The sun shifted across the sky as he climbed. As the fleeing orb began to kiss the horizon, Gideon lifted his face and peered over the landscape beyond the gorge. Making the mistake of looking downward, dizziness hit him and only his grasp upon some ancient tree root kept him from falling again. Working slowly over the rim, gasping for breath with each exhausted move forward, weakness and the pain of his wounds wracked him. Realization of what it must be like for a pursued animal crossed his mind. Crawling into a nearby depression between rock slabs, Gideon again gave in to the sweetness of sleep.

Several hours later Gideon awoke shivering in the bitter darkness with gnawing hunger and unquenchable thirst. His situation was desperate and Gideon knew shelter and water were essential to his healing.

Glancing sideways, a large tree branch loomed over him and, grasping it painfully, he used it to slowly rise to his knees. Pushing until upright, he stood for several minutes fighting both weariness and swimming vision. There were only two choices: move forward to find shelter – or death. It would be light in a few hours. Any searchers would spot him easily in this landscape and his wounds would attract predators. He must find a place to hole up.

In the depths of his mind was awareness that any hope must come from within. Anybody out looking for him would be intent upon his death. Clyde was the type who would not give up and Gideon knew that by daylight this area might be teeming with those seeking the reward of the Bower's favor.

Stumbling awkwardly through rocky ground, Gideon Henry fought forward by sheer will. After an hour he collapsed into fitful sleep against a rock.

A vague sense awakened him. Peering from behind the rock, a quick glance showed two men riding in the distance, moving back and forth along the distant rim. Their actions indicated they were Bowers' men, looking for something. And that something was surely Gideon. Suddenly yelling, one rider pointed to the ground. He must have seen the grass pushed down at where Gideon had passed. The man looked upward to the rocks.

Inching backwards, Gideon tried to increase the distance as the men slowly came his way. Working into a deep crack of the rock, he waited, a desperate man, grasping a rock in both hands.

"You circle over yonder, Barth. I'll go along thisaway."

Gideon listened as the man drew closer. His fist tightened its hold. Desperation brought momentary strength.

48

He was just a passing cowhand.

Lazying his way across the landscape, the young man rode half dozing in the saddle when he caught the smell and scanned around, spotting the buzzards over a hummock of rock. Looking around and shucking his Winchester, he sat quietly for a spell before riding over to investigate. His mount fidgeted nervously beneath him.

Rocks surrounded a slight hollow to the west that would normally mean nothing to a passing rider unless there was a reason. Buzzards and flies piqued his curiosity. Nearing, the lone cowboy peered in.

A dead horse.

Pinch-faced, he sat and took in the signs. For some reason the horse was dragged into this hollow. There was no sign of struggle, and there was a neat hole in the horse's forehead. Carrion had torn open the poor beast and dined for several days. Ripeness filled the air with a sickly stench and the cowhand instinctively put his kerchief over his nose. It did little to kill the stink and he winced as his stomach knotted. Taking it all in, he noted the saddle with broken cinch, lying askew on the carcass and covered with dried and scattered entrails.

It was clear this horse was killed and then dragged to this hollow. It had been a fine horse. No evidence of broken limbs brought an uneasy feeling and a conclusion there was no good in this situation.

This was the way of so many stretches of the West. They were littered with marked and unmarked graves of those who came this way and were stopped short of their destination – if they even had one. So much could happen, either by gun, weather or accident. He wondered what became of the man who rode such a fine horse. Riding a slow circle around the area, he noted signs of several shod horses and, circling further, found where horses had left in a group.

Wiping sweat from his brow and looking to the sun, the rider shrugged. A man needed to rope his own broncs out here. Who knows why the horse was killed. Necessity dictated he get to Craswell tonight. Shy of provisions and needing a job, he also needed a drink to wash down trail dust.

Later that evening, gathered with friends made by the passing of a bottle, the cowhand related what had found. One man at the table leaned towards him, talking in low tones.

"Better just keep that to yourself, stranger. Less'n you want more trouble than you know."

Not too into his drink to ignore trouble, the cowhand said no more. Until he rode into Battle Wagon two days later and quietly mentioned the same thing.

Around him a few of the locals cast knowing glances, pursing their lips and looking at their hands.

49

A loud cry escaped as Gideon jerked the man down and slammed a rock to his head. Reaching up, the desperate man clasped blindly at Gideon's shirt. Gideon was too weak to fight. After another yell, an answering shout sounded in the distance.

Breaking free, Gideon stumbled back into the rocks. Though he tried to grasp the rider's gun, the thong was still fastened in the struggle and he came away empty-handed. The man himself lay wounded and made no further pursuit after clutching vainly at Gideon's ankle. The other rider was approaching.

Clawing and climbing slowly and weakly though the thick brush, Gideon changed directions several times. Knowing the man below would need attention gave little comfort, as it would only slow pursuit for a short time. Two rapid gunshots rent the air.

A signal! There must be other riders in the area. He must find another hole or get way fast.

Eyes wide, the prey dug deep within to find any residue of strength. One stumbling step after another Gideon moved onward, knowing in the back of his mind he was leaving a trail a blind man could follow. Looking upwards, it was obvious only the coming of darkness held any reprieve.

Though hearing no sounds of pursuit, it was only a matter of time. This type of men would wait for the whole pack to gather. Then there would be a slow circling until he was cornered.

Gideon stumbled and lay back against a tree, panting and gasping. A fog crept across his mind, seeping into the deep corners until the bliss of unconsciousness removed the last dregs of pain and struggle.

50

Sounds of riders became louder. More than once they came close and only their rush to look ahead missed him lying, bleeding again from both old and new wounds. Staying to the thickest trees and brush in these hills slowed pursuit, but also wore his already broken body down. As daylight wore to dusk and then to darkness, he heard the men gather and argue, far enough away he only caught snatches of the conversation.

"He's up on that hillside somewhere."

"Too dark…"

"…coffee."

They were setting up camp for the night. Unless he could get away they would be out at first light and have a solid day to search. They would find him for sure!

It was a moment of almost panic, with no answers. His mind flew briefly to all his life had become. Was it all to end like this? Looking to the sky, something within uttered a semblance of a prayer – perhaps seeking a new chance, something different. His thoughts reached upward, remembering with a brief flash his mom reading from the family Bible. Pain crossed his memory.

Exhausted beyond belief from blood loss and struggle, Gideon knew he could go no further without rest. Finding a tunnel of a small game trail in the brush before him, he crawled in, lay down and swept his hands to gather leaves and needles. Sweeping them against his chilling body, he shivered uncontrollably. Just before drifting off, there was a deep realization this might be his end. Yet he found no more strength to fight. Dozing, he had no idea how long he lay, except he knew the cold deeper than ever before.

Some sense within him registered noise, a movement in the dark not of the normal night. Sinking deeper into the leaves, he waited, drifting in and out of awareness.

There! He looked to some darker piece of the night shadows not there a few moments earlier. Another rule of seeing motion, especially in dim light, is to look not directly at an object, but just to the side of it. This Gideon did and noticed the deeper darkness shift slightly.

Hearing subtle rustling, he faded into unconsciousness.

51

Skerby heard shots in the distance. Two miles? Three? It was hard to tell sometimes. His ears said southeast, but his eyes looked south. Over the years the wise man learned to trust where his eyes landed, as something deep inside, instinctual, a sixth sense, guided him. Squinting into the distance, Skerby strained for sight and sound.

It must be some of that crowd that was roaming around. Two rapid shots were likely a signal. A signal of what? They must have found what – who – they were looking for.

Riding the other day and hearing horses approaching, he had ridden off the trail. Sitting unmoving in the trees he heard the men talking.

"...Gideon...hurt..."

So that was it! He'd headed back out to the hills and wondered what was up, but now knew it involved a pack of hounds on the hunt for a wounded Gideon Henry. Not knowing the man's name, Skerby finally put two and two together to give a handle to the man he met in the hills.

Now, hearing two shots in the distance, he sensed the hounds had their prey treed. Looking to the sky, he sighed.

Why did he always have to get involved in someone else's business? No matter where he was, he was nosey and would sit and listen to find out the news of an area, then ask innocent questions to fill in the gaps. Often a half-drunk cowhand would freely fill him in. Then, seeking entertainment, he would stick around to see how it all turned out.

To Skerby it was like reading a book, which he'd never done much of, preferring the stage and drama of the real world. In his early years he'd snagged the opportunity to see some traveling stage shows and, while fun, they were so false. Skerby developed a sense of the world itself as a stage and realized every town had a drama. Best yet, the tickets were free and no two performances were the same.

Despite preferring to sit in the audience, he occasionally found himself getting involved and acting in the drama himself. Though not the bravest soul, neither did he shy from the action. He just preferred to stay on the fringe and play a part now and then. Like that fracas down Barkersville way...

Standing slowly and stretching his back, Skerby smiled and flung the last half-inch of coffee from his cup. Pulling the pot off the coals, he doused them, then leaving bedroll and such, saddled his horse and headed on a path towards the shots.

Later that day, he sat his horse just under the crown of a hill so that only his eyes could see in the distance. Patience was the name of this game, he knew, so quietly the minutes passed as Skerby watched the panorama before him, alert for any movement.

There! Two men horseback, a mile or so away as the crow flies. It would be a mite more by horse with all the ups and downs. Looking north in the direction the men were moving, Skerby caught a glimpse of a couple more horses. Roving his eyes further ahead, he saw the deeply wooded mountainside and instinctively knew that was where Gideon would hide – if it was him being sought. After all, if he himself were trying to get away, he would head where the going was slow for the pursuers.

Likely Gideon would be afoot. Perhaps badly hurt. The hillside afforded a pause at best. Clyde Bowers would flush the prey and a wounded man would be caught before too many hours passed.

Sighing again, Skerby chose his path carefully to come at the wooded area from behind. Looking to the sky, he saw darkness creeping too slowly and almost willed Gideon to find a way out of the trap.

52

Stars speckled the sky with the intensity of a million fireflies as the mangy hound wandered lazily along the boardwalk, seeking any leftover morsels the late crowd dropped. It was a nightly pattern and the dog walked without really watching, his nose to the ground, sniffing. Maybe a bit further...

Ol' Ridley normally would be in the livery, where the hostler kept an old cot in the back with the harness. Like other aspects of Ol' Ridley's history, nobody would be able to remember when the cot was placed there, but it just was always there, a bit worse for the wear and one broken leg propped on a piece of stove wood. A colorful quilt covered him at night. He thought about that quilt as he sat on the bench and the dog innocently wandered up, expecting nobody.

Ol' Ridley belched and the dog yelped and jumped into the air, landing splay-legged, wide-eyed and hair bristled. Looking over and reaching out his hand, Ol' Ridley craned his head awkwardly into the darkness, caught between his thinking and his amusement at the dog.

Mary Schmidt had brought him the quilt. Two or three years ago he was sitting in this exact spot when Ruth and Mary came to town. Things were quieter and more peaceful – it was before this mess really took off – and Mary wandered freely around town visiting with townsfolk. Stopping before him, she stood for quite some time.

"Ridley?"

"Yes, Mary?" He recognized her voice.

"Where do you sleep at night?"

"Cot in the back of the livery, next to the harness."

"Must be cold there at times."

"Yep, them times I use my old blanket and pull an old coat atop. Snug as a bug."

After a pause, Mary excused herself. A week later he went to his cot, sat to take off his boots and was startled to be sitting on something. Standing and reaching under, he found a wonderful, fluffy quilt. It wasn't some old worn out cast-off, but a finely done quilt. Who would have left it? Then he remembered Mary and smiled, bringing the quilt to his face and feeling its softness and a subtle smell of…of what? Well, it was actually the lack of smell! No manure smell, no hay smell, no sweat. It was just, well…clean! He slept that night like a baby, wrapped up in its wonder.

A week later Mary came by his bench again.

"Morning, Ridley."

"Morning, Mary! Say, I done been sleeping better than I have in a long time. Some dear soul left a wonderful soft quilt for me. You have any idea who that might be?"

"Can't say as I do…"

"Well, it sure is right nice and makes a difference to an old man's bones."

Mary was about to respond when Ruth hailed her from across the street.

"Got to go, Ridley."

"Have a wonderful day, Mary."

"You, too and…." She grinned. "Sleep tight!"

Now there was this entire fracas going on and Mary was not around as much. He missed the visits. Every time the quilt nestled to his chin he longed for things to be the way they were before.

Sometimes he sat in one of his several spots around town, thoughts of long ago filling his mind. No matter where the memories began, they always seemed to jump to the battle. Though it was long ago, the memories always seemed new.

Ridley was one of a group of eleven men different in background, interests and ways, yet all the same in their quest for gold. They were camped near the mesa. Happening upon a spring of fresh water by chance, they decided to camp and allow their horses – and themselves – to fill up before making a big swing to the distant mountains. The heat was brutal and they became accustomed to the shimmering waves hanging on the horizon at times, distorting reality. So the chance to stop and rest was welcome and all sought a bit of shade under the scarce brush. They'd routed a couple rattlers and dispatched them and waited out the early evening before starting a fire just before dusk.

None of them were experienced with Indians. Men of the East, their experiences in battle were with gray men against blue men. They kept their eyes open day after day and saw nothing. They were just like so many seeking gold – blinded by the thought of endless wealth there for the picking in some remote valley they'd heard of. Lack of experience caused the mistakes.

First, they camped by the spring. Experienced desert travelers would have watered, then camped elsewhere, knowing all animals – and men of all types and colors – would also be seeking the spring. Second, they lit the fire. It was like a signal to others that here were men new to the mountains and not wise to the ways of the land. Third, they sat around staring at the fire and talking. This would cause blindness for valuable seconds when suddenly looking to the darkness. Experienced men sat with backs to the fire, allowing their eyes to focus on the darkness and movement perhaps highlighted by flickers of firelight. A few seconds of blindness made a difference between life and death. They found out the hard way.

Walson's grunt was not really noticed at first, until the next arrow took Keever in the hip and he hollered. Suddenly they were alert, weapons drawn and scampering for cover. There was no helping Walson and Keever at the moment. Some of them had been soldiers in the war, but this was something new, this sudden attack. Arrows flew and they huddled through the night, clinging to cover and watching, as the darkness seemed to go on forever. They seemed to hear noise in the night but saw nothing.

Dawn's first rays brought more arrows. Though inexperienced with Indians, the men were no strangers to fighting and the daylight brought renewed confidence and awakened old battle skills. Ridley well remembered one rush where the Indians leapt over the rocks at them; they anticipated this and shifted positions just before it happened. Despite wounds, they repelled the attackers.

It was amazing to him how all senses were keyed and every rock and grain of sand seemed to stand out in such situations. Everything was clear during a battle.

It happened just before the battle was over. It was crystal clear to him still today. There was silence for quite some time and he leaned out beyond his cover to peer towards some brush when he felt the searing pain and all went dark as he cried out. Drawing back, he did not lose consciousness, but lay, feeling the blood and not understanding what had happened. He groped to wipe the blood from his eyes so he could see, but it didn't work. He laid panting while the battle went on and the Indians left. As the men gathered, hard earned experience now had them post sentries as they took stock of their situation. It was Longston who first came to his aid.

"Help me wipe the blood away so I can see!"

"Sit still, Ridley. Let me get a good look at you." He felt Longston wiping, then felt the pause and heard the man curse.

"How bad is it?"

"Bad, Ridley. Arrow skimmed your face." There was a pause. "Got both your eyes."

Gold fever abandoned for the moment, the men packed and rode quickly away, wanting to elude the Indians before more came back. All day and through the night they rode, horses dragging as they finally came to some adobe buildings, where armed Mexicans came to their aid. Walson they buried at the battle site, Keever lived but they couldn't get the arrowhead out of the hip joint, and the man never walked again.

Ridley stayed with the Mexicans for quite some time, along with Keever, before they were healed enough to travel further.

After the initial concern and hopes, he accepted the reality of his blindness. He lay shuddering many nights with the memories. Slowly that faded and his world at first became very small, and knots on his head and stubbed toes became common.

Not knowing what to do and having no family back East, Ridley wandered. Some befriended him; others took advantage of him as he learned a new lesson of humanity and the ways of the human soul. Slowly he adapted and somehow wandered into Craswell with a family of settlers.

Finally, Craswell seemed like a home, as the womenfolk sent food to him and the hostler offered him a bed and life settled into a routine. At least once a day he reached his hand up and felt the scarring across his face and thought of that day in the desert when his world went dark.

How many years had he been here? An answer eluded him. All he knew was he was happy here, was well cared for and nobody bothered him. Oh, there was the occasional comment from some of Bowers' newer hands, but he knew the type and just stayed away as best he could, or just made a point of sitting motionless. Being just a part of the bench gave anonymity.

It was a couple years ago that something strange happened. One afternoon as Ridley stumbled along by the corrals, something he did every day just to move his bones, a sudden shaft of light caused him to reach his hand up before him and shut his eyes in reaction. It was a movement he had not done for many years.

Light! He had seen light. Leaning against a corral post and panting excitedly, he gingerly opened his eyes again. There it was again! A shaft of light, though narrow, was before his right eye!

Hiding his excitement, Ridley secretly enjoyed this new development. Over time the shaft of light widened and he could see just a small bit from that eye if he tilted his head just right. After a short while the widening of the vision stopped and there was no more gain. Resigning himself to this, Ridley quietly enjoyed the narrow shaft and learned to use it. Still stumbling, he would sometimes carry his stick and enjoy walking. He told no one. Life went on the same as always, except he now absorbed more of the going's on and found enjoyment. Townsfolk heard him chuckle one day and looked at each other as they wondered. Nobody knew he'd seen a cowhand stumble on the walk and was tickled by a sight not experienced for years.

One of his joys was in carefully turning his head one day as he spoke with Mary. His little window of sight showed him a beautiful young lady and he smiled in delight as she suddenly furrowed her brow and stared into his face.

53

Flickering flames of a tiny fire nestled in a small hole met Gideon's still-swollen eyes as he awoke. Fingers felt gingerly the softness of a blanket at his chin.

Across the tiny fire sat a wizened visage he had seen before. Skerby! Looking around as a breeze stirred the small fire, Skerby poked the sticks to get the fire smaller. Not wanting a fire at all, he needed the hot water. Even a small flame could be seen a long ways in the night. It was in a small hole and only rare flame rose above the edge.

"You set tight, Mr. Gideon Henry. You been hurt bad. Ain't sure how you got it so rough nor why you's still alive. I seen other men die from less'n you been through."

Gideon lay back. "How'd you know my name?" His voice was raspy, barely audible.

"Sorta guessed, young fella. I seen a group of Bower's men ridin' through, but they was intent upon watching the gorge and missed me standing in the trees right there beside them." He chuckled. "Right there in front of their faces, I was! Then they started a'talkin' about some fella they was huntin' for, name of Gideon. Said it must be something to have the tables turned on a killer. Said you was hurt. Well, I been around a piece. Heard tell of the Henry's. Some mighty tough galoots in the lot. This Gideon Henry supposed to got some cousins by the name of Teague." As he said the name he eyed Gideon.

"Preacher. Cousin to me."

"Know him. Rode a mite of a trail together. I suspect a different kind of trail than you's riding." Rising, he filled a cup of coffee and brought it and a cold biscuit to his wounded guest. Gideon took a sip, wincing with the pain of such hot drink, yet his body relished the warmth and familiarity of the taste. The biscuit was like manna to his yearning stomach.

"How'd I get here?"

"I done seen them fellers huntin' you. I circled up behind where I thought you'd be, and done found you collapsed near right in front of me. I frittered my way out and brought you here. My horse didn't appreciate it none."

"Thanks. Where are those who were after me?"

"They done argued and give up the search for the night. Just like men of that type, I heard them say they was heading to town to get a drink, said you was too wore out to get away and they'd come back tomorrow and finish you off."

Gideon looked relieved.

"I appreciate the help."

"Sounds like it's getting' a bit hot. Might be time for a man to change his trail."

"We all have our own trails to ride."

"Yep, and I've started on some trails and reached a fork and had a brand-spankin' new choice." He was looking up at the stars as he spoke.

"You're sounding like Preacher."

Skerby smiled, showing stained and age-worn teeth.

"Maybe you need some preaching. You done a good job with that moss, Gideon. Lost a lot of blood, but woulda been worse if you hadn't stopped the bleeding."

Gideon nodded and put the cup down.

"Truth be told, it was my mare Bessie over yonder what lifted her ears and I seen she was starin' at something. I took a curiosity and worked my way over. I bent over you and seen you twitch. Like to scare't me to death. You was so dirty you blended into the ground. Thought the rocks was a'risin'! Done give my heart a good thrashin'!"

"You get around."

"I do. Shared a meal t'other night with Schmidt's. Whilst we was eatin', Mary kept a'lookin' out the open door over towards the hill. It was like she was hopin' she'd see someone in particular."

Mary! Why did his heart lurch at the mention of her name? She was the daughter of the man he was hired to kill. Yet, with Clyde now being the enemy, he needed to kill him. Killing the son of the man who hired him...that was an unusual twist. How did that fit in the picture and who was the enemy now?

Something inside was forming a different picture – a picture of a new way of living. Gideon now knew what it was like to be on the other side of the bullet and what it was like to be hunted. What was it like for those other men in his past? Did they have families still mourning their deaths? Were there homeless children because of his guns? Looking deep within, he did not like what he saw...

Looking over, he noted Skerby eyeing him quizzically. It was as if the man could see within.

"Lots to think on, ain't they? Reckon you ought to get some sleep."

A twig snapped. Gideon looked to the darkness. Where Skerby sat there was nothing.

54

Mary loved to ride in the early morning hours. She never tired of watching the land come to life as the morning hours slowly dwarfed the shadows. It was a time to look over the land and a time to think quiet thoughts. Pa warned her to stay close, yet she found herself going further than he would consider safe.

She was confused. This man Gideon was a concern to her, yet she found herself strangely attracted to his mystery. There was something hard about him, yet it was also strength.

He rode away a week earlier and she had heard nothing. Perhaps he had left the area. But in her heart she felt differently.

If he was indeed a hired killer, then she should hate him. She supposed she did in a way, but yet there was something within her that wondered why a man, seemingly still in his twenties, would be such a fear? What turned him hard? And there was something about the man that reached out and held tenderness. Gideon had brought Laban home. Any truly heartless man would have seen the boy in the distance and passed by without a second thought. So there was something caring inside the man.

Riding out to the far range, Mary never harbored fear in the past. There used to be a strong code in this country protecting women from harm. Any man doing harm to a woman, no matter what type of woman, would soon find himself swinging from the lower end of a rope. She often rode far and wide. Her pa worried, she knew, but she still sought the wild openness, the lone spots in the hills. She spent long hours in the saddle. It was different now, with Bowers seeking their land and Clyde's obvious looks when she was around. She also knew of the beatings he gave the girls at the cribs. Despite the seeming common knowledge, no one dared confront him. She knew she was unsafe, yet something drove her on. Her short ride became longer. Knowing the land, her wary eye ranged ever to and fro.

Today she rode long into the afternoon, ever farther from home as she found herself glancing at the sun. She knew her parents would be looking off into the distance, shielding their eyes from the lowering sun. Maybe Pa would be riding out a ways, seeking to cut her sign, though that would be difficult given the frequent comings and goings over the past few days. Yet her pa would work it out and find her general direction, but she changed so many times over the course of the day that it would be fruitless to search, especially at night. Pa would know this before starting, but he would start anyway.

She had been forced to stay out before unexpectedly, once staying in a Rocking-B line cabin when an unexpected storm hit. She was comfortable and always armed. As always, the Dragoon Colt hung from her saddle horn. She carried a slicker behind the saddle and little bits of this and that in her saddlebags. Cold biscuits snagged from breakfast sated her hunger through the day.

Why she was staying out all day was partially a mystery even to her. Was she seeking something? Someone? Was she hoping to find someone? Gideon's face seemed to float before her through the day. Something about the man called to her, something she couldn't understand.

Dusk was deepening. Mary glanced to the sky and the shadows around, gauging there was just enough time to return to the ranch by moonlight when off in the distance she caught a flicker out of the corner of her eye. Focusing her eyes to the side of where it appeared, she moved her eyes around slowly and... there! She saw it again. It was a flame, small, showing only when the wind buffeted.

Who could it be? Must be two or three miles away. Was it Gideon? Or Bower's men? Heart quickening, Mary looked in the direction of home. After only a slight hesitation she spurred her horse to a trot over territory she knew well, headed towards the flicker.

55

Raised in the West, Mary worked her way steadily towards the distant light. Taking a look at the stars before she began gave her a solid guide as daylight's glowing orb finally faded behind dips and shadowy hills. She knew those new to large landscapes failed to fix their direction or location, and so tended to walk in large circles. Mary knew these hills like the back of her hands.

Pausing now and then, she took in her back trail to fix her return by the stars. Moving carefully through brush and rocks more by instinct of her horse than by sight, she was able to gauge when within a half-mile or so of the fire. Dismounting, she ground-tied her horse and moved forward afoot. Mary was glad Pa trained horses to be ground-tied, as she never liked the idea of a horse left tied and unable to fully defend itself. She knew her horse would be within a foot of where she left it when she returned.

To her recollection, the fire should be in the rocks to the right. It was the only formation she knew that could mostly protect firelight from being seen. Flickers of firelight were intermittent and probably only seen from her exact angle. Somebody knew what they were doing.

Approaching the rocks, she paused to let her eyes adjust to the different colors and facets of the rocks so as to know where to place her feet. A subtle crackling of a fire was just ahead. Hearing a low voice, she had just looked down when a rock rolled under her foot and caused her to step sideways to keep from falling. Coming down on a small twig, the snap was like a gunshot in the night. Instantly the voice ceased and she tensed with the realization of the mistake. She began to move backwards slowly and nearly jumped at the sound of the voice.

"Don't move. Raise your hands where I can see them in the moonlight."

She paused and raised her hands slowly.

"Move around that rock to the left and walk towards the fire. And understand I got a little itch to my trigger finger."

Slowly working her way about thirty feet through the rocks, she came to the fire and at first did not see the man in the blankets.

A man stepped around her and looked at her face. His eyes widened.

"Mary Schmidt!"

It was Skerby! The man who joined them for dinner a few days back.

"Can I put my arms down, Mr. Skerby?"

"Land sakes, Mary! I done told you my name is just Skerby! Ain't no need for no handle on the front. What in blue blazes you doing out here? It's too late for you to be out galavantin' around the country! There's them Bowers scoundrels and I hear tell of a renegade bear. You ain't safe out here!"

"I was riding earlier and I saw the fire. With all that's going on and Bowers trying to get my pa out of the way, I was just checking it out."

"Your ma and pa are likely bout half sick with worry right now! Land O'Goshen and sakes alive!" He shook his head and rubbed his chin.

"I'll go back and get my horse and head home, Skerby."

"It's awful dark and all these fellas I've seen. I can't leave right now." He glanced to the side and Mary turned to see someone in the shadows in a blanket. There was a groan. As she peered, a head turned and she saw what she thought was Gideon, but she was not sure. Walking closer, she bent down.

"Gideon?" The man was hard to recognize, with bruising and wounds and the wear and tear of his flight.

"Not much to look at," he rasped.

"Found him in the rocks a ways south of here. Like to pegged out when I got to him. Been through something mighty rough. Ain't got the full story. Been run pretty ragged and shot and looks like beat pretty bad."

Kneeling by his side, Mary eased the blanket off Gideon. Skerby had removed the shreds of his shirt so looking to the wounds was not difficult. Gideon was powerfully built, but he had been through quite the ordeal. She gently touched his side with her tender hands. Gideon winced but stared deeply into her shocked blue eyes. Looking back at him, confusion within her caused her to focus on the wounds.

"Skerby, is that coffee hot?"

"Why, yes, ma'am."

"Go get my horse. About a half-mile out." She stood and pointed to the sky. "Straight out from the tip of Ursa Minor towards that peak outlined by the moon. By a clump of brush in the middle of nothing. I'll work on these wounds."

"Mary. I done worked the wounds over pretty good."

"I'm going to clean them again."

Skerby glanced long at this confident and determined young lady, and cast his eye to Gideon. A twinkle was in his eye as he turned to fetch her horse.

"You keep close and keep the fire small, Mary. Might be they's others would like to find Gideon – an' I 'spect they ain't interested in doctorin' any wounds."

Tossing her long blonde braid over her shoulder, Mary began to take the bandages from Gideon's wounds. Bringing the coffee pot and filling a cup, she herself took a drink of the bitter campfire coffee and, grimacing from the strength of taste, tore a piece off her shirt tail. Dabbing it into the hot coffee, she bathed his wounds again as Gideon stiffened and set his jaw. Some of the wounds were starting to crust, but there was inflammation around the bullet hole in his side.

"Gideon, you got yourself in a real mess."

He barely nodded as she continued bathing the wounds with the hot coffee.

"I been doing a lot of figuring. I've decided you are not here for anything good. In fact, I'm going to ask you a blunt question for which I expect a straight answer. Are you a hired killer?" She stared intently at the wounded man before her.

Gideon was torn inside. His past few years were spent doing just that and now, in just the past few days, he found his whole idea of life challenged.

"I have been."

Mary pursed her lips and dabbed the wound with perhaps too much force, causing him to wince.

"Ok, let me ask you another question. Were you hired to kill my father?" She lifted her eyes to his face.

Gideon was unconscious!

56

"He can't ride. Least not for a couple days yet." Reaching for the coffee pot, Skerby rubbed his whiskered jaw. Using his kerchief to grasp the pot, he topped his cup.

"Pa will be worried sick about me."

"I ain't too all-fired comfortable with you riding back this late alone. Been some real scum around." He looked at Mary, seeing her lips pursed in thought.

"Ok then! Tam will take a note to Pa." Seeing the questioning on Skerby's face, she laughed. "Tam is my horse. I have a tally book in my saddlebag. If I send him off, he will head towards home. He usually gets a bait of corn at night, so he'll go even faster. I'll tie a note to the saddle, and tell Pa to bring the buckboard. We'll be home before sunrise."

"Well, I'll be et fer a tater, girl. You sure it'll work?"

"Absolutely. Gideon needs better care than we can give him out here. And from the looks of him, time makes a difference."

Skerby noted the confusion in her eyes as she focused on Gideon. He'd done a bit of thinking himself and had a hunch what Gideon's business was, but not the particulars. Sipping his coffee, he looked at Mary through the steam. She caught his glance and held it a moment before looking to her own cup.

"You taken a shining to this fella?"

Visibly fumbling for words, Mary finally looked straight at him.

"I might have, but I suspect he's up to no good. I think he's a paid killer."

Skerby met her eyes, letting her last word hang for a few moments.

"Ain't like some other fellas I had the chance to meet over the years. There's something about him. He's hard, but they's a softness inside. He's still young. Maybe someone could tap into that there soft spot. With the right training he might be a man to ride alongside on life's trails."

Was she blushing? It was hard to tell by firelight.

"I think he might be here to kill Pa."

Skerby hesitated. The same thought had occurred to him.

"Ain't done it yet. An' it seems to me he might be a bit confused about now. If'n he was hired, the only logical one to pay him would be this fella Bowers.

When Gideon was sorta out of it, he mentioned somethin' about Clyde. Now, I ain't been out here that long, but I see how things is. Dan Bowers ain't right in the head, and he's got his sights set on this whole territory. Your pa sits right in the middle of some of the best-watered land hereabouts. Bowers' boy, Clyde, is a poor excuse for a human being, done set on proving hisself. He and his men was a'runnin' around a bit afore I found Gideon. Like they was a lookin' fer something. If it was Gideon, I suspect Clyde and he got some sort of problem and Clyde and his men done this to Gideon."

Mary looked at Skerby. "So, if Clyde and his men did this, then the lines have changed and Gideon – if he's what I think – will be seeing things a bit differently."

Skerby smiled and raised his eyebrows. "Maybe... maybe not. Depends on a lot of things. Might be a good time to get Gideon on another path. Maybe he ain't all bad. Most generally, they's a reason people take a certain path. He ain't more than twenty-four, twenty-five."

"Have you heard anything about Gideon's past? You've been around."

Chuckling, Skerby squinted his left eye at Mary. "Yup, I been around a mite. Seems like I cain't do nothin' but get around. They say 'a rolling stone gathers no moss,' but sometimes I wish I had a little moss. I ain't never settled, but this ground's getting'

57

"Let him go."

Two men stepped away from the calf as it bawled and jumped up. Smoke from the singed hair of its flank tinted the air.

"Looks good, Hansen. You're a good man with a cinch ring."

"Boss, it's sure is an all-blamed pity that Schmidt's cows have had so few calves this year." There were cackles as the men joined in the humor.

"Yes, and it sure is amazing that Rocking-B cattle are so blessed fertile. Some give birth to two and three calves a year!"

Clyde laughed at his own comment and the others followed the lead. One man didn't laugh and Clyde turned on him. A newer hand, he was dark-haired and deeply tanned but somehow answered to the name "Whitey."

"What's the matter, Whitey? You got a problem with this?" Clyde glared at the man and squinted. Cowhands around moved casually away.

If Whitey had any doubts as to what they were doing, the yearning to survive held sway and he forced a grin.

"No, Boss. I just was a-thinkin' how all us hands is gonna have to work so much harder when all this range is yours."

"You better believe it." Clyde looked at the man, logging the incident in his mind. "I could sure use a beer. Let's head to town. Except you, Whitey. I ain't so sure you ride for the brand. You go make a round up to the north. Sweep any cattle you find without brands down this way. We can swing by at first light and brand them."

Whitey stared at Clyde, seeing the obvious bruises from the fight with Gideon. If anything, the fight made Clyde lord it over his men even more than before. And now this.

"I don't get to go to town?"

"No. I ain't sure about you. You got a problem with that?" His hand rested on his thigh near his gun. The air was tense.

"No, boss."

Clyde continued to look at the man, looking back as he led the others off towards the town, at least a good hour's riding away.

Whitey sat his horse and pondered this new job. Broke and hungry and riding to nowhere almost a month ago, a job at the Rocking-B was a ticket to regular meals and a roof over his head. Pretty quickly the lay of the land was clear. Don't cross the boss and keep your mouth shut. Always an honest hand, this theft rankled him. Never mind, he was going to wait till payday and move on. Just needed a grubstake. A few more days and he would have it.

Truth be told, he wanted Clyde Bowers to get what he deserved. In town the other day, he tried to visit a girl he'd seen the week before. Asking for her, the madam had told him it'd be a week or so before the girl could see him. She looked disgusted and made a comment about Clyde damaging the goods.

Whitey had already heard a few whispered rumors of Clyde beating the girls, and the thought rankled him. Clyde took pleasure in strutting and acting better than anyone else.

Sitting and pondering, he looked to the north, then to the south towards the distant cloud of dust of the men heading to town. A drink sure would taste good! Maybe he should just mosey out of this territory and this tense situation. Sure, he had no food, but he'd been hungry before.

Maybe he'd slip into town for a quick beer at that little place at the edge of town. Bowers men rarely went there. Then off he'd go. Just had to keep his

58

Old Dan Bowers emerged from the house, trousers unbuttoned as he hurried to the outhouse. Stomach pains and multiple runs out back had kept him from sleeping. Intent on his needs, he suddenly glanced up and saw the new man, Whitey, leaving the back of the bunkhouse.

What was he doing here this time of day? And why was he packing up? If he had not been headed to the outhouse he'd never have seen the man. Changing directions, his right hand released the thong from his gun as his left threw down the bottle of amber.

Whitey reached his bunk and began to get his small bit of life's accumulation together. Glancing up, his eyes landed upon Gideon's guns and the bag of gold hanging near the doorway. Didn't Bowers owe him wages? Well, he wasn't about to wait around to collect. Clyde would be incensed and Whitey knew Clyde was not in his right mind all the time. Hesitating just a few seconds, he strolled over and, taking the poke, slipped out a month's worth of wages. Beginning to cinch the poke again, he paused and weighed it in his hand. Smirking, he poured more into his hand and slipped it into his pocket.

Rolling his bedroll, Whitey threw his few possessions into his saddlebags and walked quickly back to his horse. Tying the roll to his saddle, he heard the twist of a boot sole on the dirt and stopped. A gun cocked.

"So, sneaking in the back way and loading up?" Whitey both recognized the voice of Dan Bowers and noted the slur, indicating the man had been drinking.

"Can I turn around?"

"Sure. You rode out with Clyde and the men this morning. How come you're back here and nobody else is?" As Whitey turned, he noted the man's hand near his gun.

"Clyde rode into town with the men."

"How come he didn't take you with him?"

"He...he wanted me to make a sweep to bring in cattle."

Dan Bowers had a strange look on his face.

"This ranch is a strange location to make that sweep. Ain't no cattle around the back of the bunkhouse. How come Clyde wanted you to make the sweep and not go to town?" Bowers fidgeted a mite, looking strained.

"I don't know."

Bowers' eyebrows rose. Whitey noted the man shiver and glance to the outhouse.

"I been hearing some doubts about you, Whitey. Like maybe your heart's not in this. Looks to me like you're sneakin' off. You got a problem with what we's doing?"

"No, sir."

"You get any cattle branded this morning?"

"Couple dozen calves."

Bowers nodded.

"I think you should stick around till Clyde gets back."

"Sure."

Bowers glanced again at the outhouse. Looking at Whitey, he lowered his brow.

"You wait here."

"Yessir."

Whitey watched as Dan Bowers desperately ran to the outhouse.

Glancing around, Whitey grabbed a nearby fencepost from a pile and quietly placed it against the outhouse door as he heard Dan Bowers occupied inside. Striding to his horse, he paused, glanced at the outhouse and quickly entered the bunkhouse. Reappearing moments later, he held Gideon's guns.

A few minutes later he heard curses in the distance and urged his horse to a trot.

59

Curtains blowing in the breeze were a strange sight to Gideon's weary eyes. A breeze blew them gently inward, where they riffled and settled against the window, only to riffle again with the next breeze. Glancing downward, his eyes noted the hand-sewn quilt.

Gideon looked around. Clean sheets covered him in a deep feather bed. A sampler hung upon the wall and below it laid an open Bible on a small table, along with a partial bottle of laudanum. Nearby was a rocking chair. His guns lay on the rocker. His guns! How did they get here?

Looking around again, he noted this was a home; a well cared for home and a deep sense of peace seemed to fill his soul. When had he last felt this feeling?

Reaching up, he felt of his side, noting much less pain, and clean bandages. His ribs were bound. Looking at his arm, he noted it was clean also. Someone had bathed him. Lying back again, he recalled being by the campfire with Mary and Skerby. Mary had cared for his wounds, but also asked questions. At some point he had blacked out, but something in the back of his mind vaguely recalled waking briefly to the jiggling of a wagon and the sound of soft voices. Where was he?

Gideon looked around and saw the steady influence of a woman on this room. Remembering, he realized this must be the Schmidt ranch. He had good reason to suspect that Mary knew why he was here, so why did she allow him to be brought back here?

Hearing booted steps, Gideon turned to see Vern in the doorway. Settling into the rocker, Vern smiled at Gideon.

"Good to see you awake, son. I had a fear about you. That side wound was bad infected. Mary done sat with you, dozing in this chair now and again. She wouldn't leave. She bathed that wound with liniment and herbs and finally trucked off to bed early this morning when she seen the infection was leaving. I ain't never seen her work so hard."

Gideon looked at Schmidt, seeing something in his eyes.

"Where'd my guns come from?"

"One of Bowers' hands, name of Whitey, brought them by. Said he was moving on. Asked him to lunch and he sort of glanced backwards and said he'd like to but he had some miles to cover."

Gideon nodded.

"You know, Gideon, they's many a path that leads a man through life. Sometimes we choose a path and sometimes a path chooses us. Sometimes it's both. When we came out here all them years ago, it was of necessity, an' we chose a path, but it also sorta chose us, since there were not many options. Then we picked this here valley – still the purtiest thing I've seen as far as land. Now, after all these years of building, another fork in the road comes up. Bowers is trying to take my land, and there's no way I can let it happen. I'm not sure how to stop it, but I'm on this path and it sorta has chosen me. I wondered at first if I could handle this fight, but now it's decided in me." He looked hard at Gideon. "Many a man had a path sorta choose him, but many a time they's these little game trails leading off'n the main trail. Sometimes they lead nowhere, but sometimes…" He raised an eyebrow, "they lead to some beautiful meadow or glade or…incredible valley the likes of which they never dreamed and they forget all about the path they was on before."

Getting up, Schmidt walked to the window and held the curtain aside as he looked out.

"Somebody coming?"

"I see something coming, but not today. I see changes. I see the old ways giving way to the new, but which way really wins is just not clear yet. Whichever way things go around here will choose the path this territory takes. And whichever way things go will not so much affect me as it will my son and daughter. Like any father, I want the best – happiness and prosperity – for Laban and Mary. I suspect Dan Bowers would give a lot to have me out of the way so they can just take my land. But you see, Gideon, I have something dear to fight for. No, it's not the valley, for that is just land. What I have to fight for is a wife who's done rode the river with me, and a son who loves this land as much as I do. Then there's Mary. She's a strong young lady. She loves the land, but she's not settled anymore. She's reached the point in life where she wants to forge her own way. She's seeking a path to travel. Like any father, I want it to be a safe path, though safe doesn't lead to happiness all the time. Ruth and I were not safe when we started here. Then we were safe for many years, but now…anyways, I want my Mary to find the path that is right for her. I guess what I'm also trying to say is…" He turned and looked hard at Gideon, "you also have a path to choose. I suspect the path you been on has been getting thin and it's time to explore new options. But the choice is always up to you. You are welcome here as long as need be, but it's when you

leave here that you'll have a choice to make. And…
that choice may make a difference to more than one
person."

Turning, Schmidt walked out. Watching the
man's back, Gideon found himself respecting this
man. He was a man of strength – true strength. Not
a strength based on how many gunhands he had
backing him or dependent upon money in the bank.
It was a strength based on character, determination
and the love of his family. It was the kind of character his father had before…Gideon looked back over
the events that led to his path.

Schmidt and his family loved each other deeply,
and Gideon found that bond attracted him. He himself knew it before his father was killed and his family
fell apart. Riding the trails, he sometimes wondered
what happened to his brother and sister. Did they
find the happiness that evaded him?

Well he remembered the day Nate and Abby
were collected to go live with other families. All
were given promises they would see each other
but, of course, that was just an adult way to get the
job done without fussing. Very quickly he realized
there was no intention to make sure the three of
them maintained contact. He sneaked and visited
Nate a couple times, but was unsuccessful in seeing Abby.

60

After killing the man responsible for his father's murder, Gideon Henry had slipped into a sullen state of mind. Countless hours were spent thinking of what happened and what might have been. Emotionally detached, he watched from afar as his mother fell apart, his family fractured and he went from security to living on the streets.

Something within him wanted to survive. When confronted, his deep anger and frantic quest for survival easily toppled those around him whose deepest ambition was to be king of the hill.

When approached by that first man seeking to hire him, Gideon had no idea he would start down the path traveled ever since. There were times when he had tinges of regret for those he killed, yet his targets were men of ill repute, and he rationalized that the world was better off without them. Taking the money, Gideon carefully studied his targets, becoming so adept that he commanded larger and larger sums of money. Skill also kept fingers from pointing at those who hired him, which greatly blossomed his reputation. In the process, he found his life becoming one of watchfulness and lack of true ease, knowing others would love to see him out of the way. There were attempts of some in the criminal element to gain his loyalty. They were unsuccessful – his only loyalty being to get the rest of the money after a job was done.

Only one time did a man, feeling tough and self-important, tell him he wasn't going to pay him the rest of the money owed, and the man turned haughtily away with his two bodyguards. All three were found the next day in the same alley. They were shot from the front, with evidence of having tried to draw their guns.

Ripples of that day held firm and no one failed to pay. In fact, his price went up again. Gideon now commanded sums that raised eyebrows in wonder.

He was good at his job.

He didn't care. Early on there were occasional women, but only of the type that frequented his world. One had tried to kill him...

As he gained in monies paid, Gideon ventured over to another side of the tracks and became more of a respectable gentleman. For the sake of safety he avoided most patterns. One he knowingly held was the back table at the restaurant where he could be seen for hours on end, reading and drinking coffee like a gentleman. Yet, even the role of gentleman was hesitant, for many suspected his vocation even on that side of the tracks. While others went to their jobs, he did not for days or weeks on end. Then, of a sudden, he would drop off the face of the earth for a few days or even a few weeks, returning suddenly and resuming his place at the back table.

Then came the day he found that poor young girl in the alley. Stoicism succumbed to tears that night and something changed within him. Continuing in his vocation, there was a sudden chink in his armor, a softening, and Gideon found himself working for the times with the children at the home.

What was the path he was on? As Schmidt mentioned, could he truly change his path? How much did Schmidt know? Had Mary shared her thoughts with her father? Likely.

Hearing the swish of skirts, he turned his head to see Mary walk in bearing a plate. Pulling a chair over, she sat by the bed.

"Welcome back to the real world, Gideon. Though I suspect anybody looking at you might still think you an apparition from the lower parts of the earth." She chuckled. "How are you feeling?"

"Pretty beat up. I suspect I feel like I look from the outside. Thanks for taking care of me. Your father told me."

Mary turned red. "Didn't treat you any different than I would have treated a sick calf, though I suspect I was treating a wolf." She turned from red to hard and angry. She began to spoon soup to him. Though he was capable of feeding himself, he found himself enjoying the attention. Taking couple spoonfuls quietly, he raised a hand.

"Mary…"

"Let me ask you directly, Gideon. You are fully conscious and can't evade. Were you hired to kill my pa?" She stared hard at him.

"I was hired to do a job."

Mary shook her head, then dipped the spoon again and slipped it gently into his mouth.

"You're slinking around the question like a wolf backed into a corner." She looked towards the door, then leaned forward to within inches of his face. "Is my pa your target?"

Gideon looked a few moments at this spunky young lady. Inside, his heart battled with the reality of the job, as opposed to the reality of life, of his situation, of…Mary.

Mary looked deeply in his eyes, seeing the truth and turmoil within the man. It was as if she saw the turning of a new set of gears in a machine, a shifting from one gear to another. She continued to look deeply at Gideon. Slipping another spoon in, she spoke:

"My pa and ma came into this valley to start a home. It was hard work, but they stood together and transformed the valley into more than a home. One day the Garcia's showed up in a broken down wagon with no life left in it. They stayed for supper and never left. This land became their dream also and they worked side by side with my folks. Jose and Conchita came soon and the dream became a part of them. Then Paulo and more recently, Conner. He is sweet on Alita. There is a future there – and here. My brother Ben is buried in the grove on the hill. He was thrown from a horse. It was not the first time he was thrown, but this time he landed wrong. It's his clothes you are wearing now. My parents dream has not been without deep pain. Most dreams have those moments. There's a lot of work and tears and sweat in this dream. Pa has provided for more than us – you can easily see there are other families who have a home here. It goes further than that, though. If Bowers takes this land, he will cut off the water to others and will force them out. He wants their land, too. Bowers wants the land and the power. Even Craswell, which cowers to him, will become fully his. Do you think that so many should be forced to give up their dreams, their homes – all they've worked – and sweated and shed blood for – because one man wants it all and will do anything to get it?"

Mary had continued to slip spoons into his mouth, but they had become rapid and not so gentle. Gideon's eyes remained on hers, hearing her words and her heart.

Opening his mouth to speak, Mary shoved in another spoonful and continued.

"The very people you were hired to harm have helped you. You need to make some choices. I think it goes even deeper, Gideon. You need to make some choices in your own life. I think they can be made right here in this valley."

Mary stopped, looking deep into Gideon's eyes. He looked back, lingering.

"I…will…not kill your father." He said the words hesitantly then, solidifying this change, this new determination, he said them again. "I will not kill your father."

Mary sat back, seeing the change and feeling the relief. Yet, the question remained unanswered: had her father been the target of this paid killer? Had Bowers hired Gideon to kill her father – or anyone else?

Gideon fought with his emotions. A man in his profession learned to shove his feelings inside, to bury them deeply. Mary saw the conflict in this man, saw in his eyes a torment.

"Mary…"

"Yes?" She spoke softly, yet with determination.

"There was a moment out there...I thought it was the end. A few brief thoughts crossed my mind. I was hired to kill your father. But...this is all wrong...I've been wrong."

"Thank you, Gideon." She spoke tenderly, with her heart, with tears of relief in her eyes. "I love my pa." She looked away. "He came to build a dream, a new life – for all of us. His dream has come true, and I suspect there are men like Dan Bowers who cannot share a dream, but must own it all. My pa said there is enough for all of us to raise our families and build for the future. He believes that all ranchers in the area can benefit from each other, and from mutual support. Some may have more than others- there is so much based upon weather and chance- but we can all have enough. My pa and ma have worked hard. They have built and saved and lived by a slender thread at times, all so Laban and I can have a home. That is my pa's dream, Gideon, and I love him for it."

"It is a good dream your father has, Mary. And he has the greatest blessing already – a family, love, a daughter such as you."

She looked at Gideon, seeing him differently. Then she arose and took the tray.

"You need to rest." Leaving, he admired a greater swish to her skirts.

61

A few days later Gideon heard the pounding of horse's hooves. They were of a horse pushed hard.

He was healing quickly, perhaps due to physical strength and mental determination. Yet even he recognized it was due in no small part to the food and care of the Schmidt's. Mary was self-appointed nurse and expressed pleasure with his progress. In a very short time he began to sit at the table with the family for the lunch and evening meals. Within the family he found a gentleness and friendliness not experienced since choosing his path. Usually, those who were gentle and friendly to him had something to gain from it or were already being paid for services to be rendered. Not so here.

Gideon was asking Schmidt about his cattle when they all turned and tilted their heads to the noise.

Schmidt was the first up at the sound, moving quickly to the door.

"It's Skerby."

Skerby rode quickly to the house and spoke as he quickly dismounted. Gideon winced and started to rise, his senses alert.

"Clyde and his men are heading this way! Be here in a matter of minutes! Looks to be in a determined mood. I got a hunch they's huntin' fer Gideon. Like maybe they ain't happy 'bout something." He looked at Gideon, who worked his way slowly to the door.

Gideon spoke sharply. "Where are your other cowhands?"

"They're all making a sweep of the valleys to bring in the cattle for branding. There's just the women and children up at the cabins yonder. They've been around Clyde's men before, so no doubt they are in the house watching right now."

"Get your rifle, Schmidt! Stay here at the house. Skerby! You take the barn. Mary, get my guns." She disappeared for a few moments and returned. As he looked at the belts and felt of his wound, he took a pistol in his hand and handed the belt back to Mary.

"They're after me, Schmidt. I'd rather your family not be hurt. Let me handle this." He hobbled out to the porch.

"Gideon, I don't know much about you. But I can tell you there ain't any man under my roof I won't defend. You ain't in any shape for a fight." He stepped up beside Gideon as they heard the pounding of the coming horses.

Clyde Bowers rode up like a proud rooster, looking both ways as he reined before the house. Seven men plus himself. A deep chuckle arose deep within as he spoke.

"Well, Gideon Henry. Looks like you been through the mill. No matter. Get your boots on. You're comin' with us."

"Not hardly." It was Schmidt. "This man is a guest in our home, Clyde. He is hurt and will not be leaving."

Clyde Bowers laughed.

"Two of you gonna face all my men?" He emphasized the word 'my' with exaggerated swagger to his shoulders. "We'll cut you down. Make no never mind to me." Riders began to spread apart.

Soft creaking of leather suddenly gave way to obvious cocking of a shotgun. Eyes turned to the barn, seeing the muzzle of a double barrel pointed from the window. At almost the same time, a shutter creaked slightly in the house and another double barrel pointed their way. Clyde's men looked from the barrels to Clyde. Though still more afraid of Clyde than of gunfire, the men were in no hurry to take their chances in a crossfire of shotguns. Some had seen the effects of a single shotgun blast, much less four barrels. One of the men spoke.

"Clyde, this ain't the time to argue."

"Shut up!"

"Clyde, they's always another day. Don't make no moves."

Gideon spoke weakly, but with sureness. "Listen to your men, Clyde. You touch that gun at your hip and you and a few of your men will be dead. Two double-barrels in a crossfire will make mincemeat and it'll be a toss up which grave to throw which pieces in." Gideon shifted as he leaned against the post.

Sensing reality through his initial elation, Clyde looked at both sets of barrels, at Schmidt's rifle and suddenly noted Gideon was also armed.

"Schmidt, I ain't takin' kindly to you helping this man out. It don't seem natural considering…"

Schmidt cocking his rifle, which happened to be pointed directly at Clyde, interrupted his sentence.

"Get out, Clyde, before you say something your men will regret."

Fuming, Clyde looked around. "Alright, Schmidt, we're leaving peaceably, but you ain't seen the last of us. Henry…we'll be meeting again."

Gideon Henry nodded. "That we will, Clyde. Maybe you won't have your lapdogs with you to do your dirty work."

Suddenly red-faced, Clyde barely restrained himself and turned his horse.

As the men left in a cloud of dust, Gideon turned and saw Mary holding a small pistol. He watched as she put the Patterson on a shelf by the door. She had been prepared to fight. All of this family had been prepared to fight for him!

He sagged with weariness and felt Mary's arms reach carefully to grasp his arm.

"Back to bed for you, Gideon."

62

an Bowers was incensed. Clyde glared back. "Pa! They had shotguns pointed at us. Woulda cut us to ribbons!"

"See what you started? Here I was, expectin' to sit back and let you run the place whilst I set away my years in a rockin' chair. You done upset everything with your blasted unthinking ways!"

"But…"

"Now you done shown your whole hand to the Schmidt clan. Won't be long an' it'll be all over the territory if'n we don't stop it and take care of this right now. Well, thanks to you actin' like an idiot, I done put my plans for a rocking chair away for now."

"Me and the men…"

"Shut up and let me think!" Old Dan Bowers paced the room for a few moments. Clyde shifted uncomfortably, causing his father to give him an evil stare. The older man walked to the fireplace, leaning with both hands on the mantle, staring into the remnants of the night fire and drumming his fingers with a tune known only to him. Musical fingers halted for the barest of moments. Dan Bowers stood, turning to face his son.

Clyde stood before his father, submissive in appearance, but inside seething, eager to use his own methods, to take charge. Old Dan Bowers was indeed that – old! Any love for his father ceased long ago and Dan Bowers was nothing but an obstacle. Remembering his mother reading to him from the family Bible, Clyde recalled King David wanting to build a temple, but God telling him it would be his son, Solomon, who would actually do so. He saw himself like Solomon, except he wanted his dad out of the picture so he could do what he felt needed to be done. There was a kingdom to build, with himself as the undisputed king.

So as his father looked at him, Clyde saw his father through eyes of a horse wanting to be loose while held in check by reins and a roweled bit.

"Pay attention, Clyde! Here's the plan. We gotta get Henry away from the family, so's we can kill him and claim we were ridding the territory of a killer. At the same time, we gotta get rid of Schmidt. And we gotta do it all to once. Hear me boy, and hear me good. We got one more chance to clear this up and still be able to hold our heads high. If we do it right, ain't anybody gonna argue with us about nothing. We'll be ridin' high and Schmidt's land – and a few others – will just naturally fall into our care. But you got to listen and follow what I say to the word. Understood?"

"Yes, Pa."

"I want you to put a man on that bluff a few miles west of Schmidt's place. I know that boy of his likes to ride. When we see him ridin' out from the ranch, lookin' to go galavantin' around the territory, I want you to have a couple men head him off and bring him and his horse to the high line shack. He's a sharp kid – do you think you can accomplish this relatively simple task?"

There was a tone of sarcasm in his voice not missed by Clyde, who bristled at being belittled by his father. Though wanting to lash out, he still held a healthy fear of this man who had built the ranch into a powerhouse. And yet...

"Yes, Pa."

"Good! Then we'll send an anonymous note to Schmidt for just he and Henry to come to...the crossing at the river. They'll know who it is, but nobody else will be able to pin the note to us. I'll write it so's I know it's right." He glared at his son.

"So, we trade the kid for Schmidt and Henry? What if the kid spills the beans?"

"Clyde, I don't know why you have to be so blasted dumb at times.

Clyde tensed.

Just as quickly as he'd snapped at Clyde, he switched to a smile. Clyde knew his father was riding a fine trail of sanity.

"Naturally, son, they's a lot of rough territory out there. Every once in a while somebody, even urchins, falls off a horse and they hit just right and break their neck." Old eyes looked knowingly at his son.

Clyde's eyes widened. A brutal man in a fight, he took pride in being tough and even had no fear of skirting the edges of the law. Of necessity, the occasional nester or ne'er-do-well just disappeared into the gorge. But to kill a kid? Kill Laban? Yet, it was not so much the killing as the what-if's of being caught.

It was at that moment Clyde himself smiled inside and crossed a fine line.

Dan Bowers noted the change in his son's eyes and placed his arm around Clyde's shoulders.

"Son, walk with me."

Leading Clyde to a rear window, Dan Bowers swung the shutters wide and looked out across the land, the distant cattle and the colors of the far-reaching mountains.

"It's beautiful, isn't it? Well, when I came here there were nothin' but Indians and weather that had any say over the land. Took care of the Indians and, well, the weather ain't nothin' we can ever control. We fought renegades and rustlers and then nesters got a high horse and thought they could carve a chunk out of our spread. We done took care of all of them. We've held this land with force and sometimes we just have to take desperate measures. Some of the men have been through this before. Sometimes it takes a bit of coldness to hold what one has. Sometimes I just stand and look out across the land, remembering when me an' your ma – bless her soul - had nothin' but the clothes on our backs and a couple worn out saddle nags. If'n we lose the ranch we have nothin' again and all those years will be worthless. I'm building this for you, son. You'll rule over a territory twice or three times as big as mine. And it'll be secure – if we do it right. But you gotta be a man, Clyde. And you are – it's just there's a few rough edges we gotta smooth out. Now, you just do as I say and everywhere you ride, men will doff their hats to you and move so's you get the best table. And the ladies will scramble to be seen with you."

Clyde was swayed by the persuasion of his father, but was stopped by the idea of being charged with the murder of a child. Yet, to have people respect him, give way to him - it was a thought that played with the edges of his mind. Spite for his father faded for a moment.

Dan Bowers sensed the change in his son and smiled inside.

"Just do as I say."

"Yes, pa."

63

Gideon sat on the hillside all morning, soaking in the sun and watching the activity of the ranch.

Vern Schmidt ran a good ranch. A couple times one of the hands and Vern would have a brief conversation, but then the men would go back to their jobs. Gideon knew Vern wanted to be out with his men, but was sticking close to home because of the trouble with Bowers. The beating in town and the unwelcome visitors to his ranch wore heavily on his heart. From his hillside vantage, Gideon noted how Vern stood and watched as the men faded into the folds of the hills in the distance. Yesterday he asked Vern whether he might leave some hands at the ranch for safety. Vern looked briefly at him, then into the distance.

"A ranch won't run by itself, and cattle ain't going to ride to a branding without somebody driving them. And a ranch won't make any money without cattle. No matter what happens, if I am to leave something for my family, I must keep things going. Also, we're bringing all the cattle we can closer to home for a spell. Not the best for the grass, but we've had quite a few calves suddenly disappear. Found their mother's wandering over towards Bower's place." He looked knowingly at Gideon.

"Bowers rustling cattle all around, or just yours?"

"I hear tell of others missing a few, but we've lost a significant number. I think there's a couple running irons keeping busy. My men have found the remains of small branding fires, all of them over towards Bowers' land."

Gideon glanced quietly at Vern Schmidt, pausing just a moment. Vern squinted into the distance. Gideon spoke.

"Tell me about the Chinese and the mine."

Vern glanced sharply at Gideon, the concern in his eyes mingled with a trace of anger as he spoke.

"How do you know about them?"

"I followed you there."

Vern stared at him, then pursed his lips and looked off into the distance.

"It was a strange sight one day as me and Manuel were out checking the herd. We saw dust not too afar off, over the crest of a ridge. We rode over and took a look-see. It was a wagon train. Waiting a mite, Manuel, whose eyes are better than mine, said there was something different. I couldn't see anything for the dust. Well, Manuel leaned forward a bit and said they looked like Chinese!"

"Well, they were coming closer, so we sat a while, then rode down to intersect their path, a ways away so as not to come upon them sudden. Four or five men – we thought they were boys first – rode forward to meet us. They carried rifles, but they were not very good rifles."

Gideon waited as Vern wrinkled his brow in thought.

"They were skittish. Timid, but yet with something in their eyes I had not seen before. Around here, Gideon, Chinese are seen as sort of a trash people. Good for doing chores and hard labor behind the scenes, but not taken seriously as a people. It's like they're looked upon as less than – well, less than a dog and even a shade below Mexicans. No rights, liable to get kicked if they get in the way. Not even treated fairly. Sometimes just getting enough scraps thrown at them to keep them alive. They expected more of the same with us that day. One fella, I couldn't understand his name so I called him Lee, apologized for crossing our land and said they meant no harm. Well, as he spoke I saw fear. Fear in his eyes and fear in the others."

Vern paused a moment, struggling.

"What was even worse was the fear in the eyes of the women and children. What sort of life must a woman and some little children have to show such fear? I learned a lot that day. We sat a while with them. They were heading to Oregon Territory. They said they had friends there. They didn't give many details – like I said, they had fear in their eyes. They apologized again for crossing the ranch, and said they'd pay. It didn't take much to know they didn't have much, and why would a man charge a wagon train to cross his land. Why, Gideon, all of us out here crossed someone's land to get here! Nobody ever charged me!"

Gideon nodded as Vern continued.

"This Lee fellow said they were warned about Bowers and especially Clyde and so chose to go a different way and cross our ranch. He said just a few days and they'd be across. I looked and saw the children all worn out and growing thin. No kid ought to have to face hardship like this, Gideon!"

Nodding, Gideon agreed more than Vern could realize.

"So I asked Lee if they had any food. He looked at me sort of strange and said they had enough. But I could see the hunger in the eyes of the children. Right then I made a decision. Off in the back of the ranch are the remains of an old silver mine. Not much of a mine, but it gave someone a grubstake just before we came to the territory. Just sitting there all played out, but few know there's also a natural spring there and I sometimes wondered if a little effort might turn up another vein. I told Lee that it looked like his people could use a rest. I sent Manuel with a cow and they ate well that night. Long story short, the whole kit and caboodle of them stopped there. They've found a little silver – not a lot, but enough to help them get something put away for the journey. Now, they've even got a few seeds planted and the children are filled out. They've got permission to stay as long as they need."

Gideon was curious. "Where do they go for supplies?"

"I give them a couple cows now and then."

"Hard to do with your losses to Bowers, isn't it?"

Schmidt paused again, looking thoughtful."

"In those early years here, it seemed when times got rough – and, believe me, they did – it seemed there was always someone lending a hand. I remember when Mary was born; we didn't have a milk cow. About a week or so later a wagon came through headed into the mountains to find the crossing before winter. They had three milk cows tied behind. One of them was obviously not going to go over the mountains. I traded a yearling and a week's rest in good pasture for that cow. Gave us milk for many years. My Mary and Laban never have starved. We have what we need. May not always have had ready cash, but they've had food and milk. So it doesn't matter that

64

From the hillside across from the ranch house, Gideon saw the harshness of the task ahead of Vern. The safety of his family – and the safety of the hands, weighed heavily on the man as he also balanced the needs – the necessities – of a working ranch. Bowers would like nothing better than for Vern to either just walk away or to be so constrained that the ranch died for lack of attention to the details. To top that concern, other people depended upon him. A few hundred yards away, near a cluster of trees, two of Jose's children, Isabella and Hermano, played. Gideon's mind strayed to Mrs. McClinder and the children back east. He wondered how they fared, since he was absent longer than he expected. He knew Wang would see to their needs. The last time he visited, three of the boys ran to him and there was a brief wrestling match. Smiling and lost in his thoughts, it took a moment for him to register the shutting of the door of the ranch house below. Focusing, he watched as Mary shaded her eyes and looked around. Lowering her hand, she headed towards the hillside.

Watching her walk, Gideon sensed her walk become suddenly more pronounced. For his own part, he found himself enjoying watching her approach. In his time recovering, he became used to her presence, looking forward to her changing of the dressings. Mary's hands were gentle, yet not afraid to do what was necessary. She bathed and dressed all his wounds, and made it clear to her parents that this was her task. Hesitant at first, they gave way to her determination. Gideon learned to trust her hands and the care she gave. Mary did not shrink from any task. One day in particular, as she began to change the dressing on his side, she found the bandage stuck. Leaving the room, she returned with a pan of hot water and began gently bathing the area until the bandage was freed. To distract him, she plied him with questions and mention was made of the children at the home with Mrs. McClinder.

"Gideon, you are a man of definite contrasts."

"I guess I am."

"Know what I think? Rather, do you care to hear what I think about this?"

Pausing, he realized he cared very much for what this woman thought. Awareness was in her eyes as a slight twinkle accompanied the subtle upward move of the dimple in her cheek.

"Tell me what you think."

Her reply was soft as she paused and looked him in the eyes. "I don't want to just tell you what I think, Gideon Henry. I want to know if you really care about what I think. There is a difference."

Pausing for a mere moment, he returned her gaze. "Yes, I care what you think."

Mary grinned, then puckered her brow as she bathed a difficult area. Her hands sensed his muscles tense as the wound pulled.

"I think, Gideon Henry, that you are changing. Where once there was only deep pain and vengeful anger, there is now something else. There is the need to make a difference in a caring manner." Her voice quieted. "Where there was only the taking of life, there is now the need to give life. Perhaps the children remind you, in a way, of yourself. Instead of lashing out, you now are reaching inside and changing things in a different way. There's now...room... in your heart for love." She blushed. "So the children have become important to you. You love helping them. But there's another step.

"What's that?"

"Instead of loving the chance to help the children, you need to just...love...the children themselves. It's God's opening in your life to really start to love."

Looking into her eyes, Gideon's mind worked over Mary's words, not merely hearing, but taking them to heart. After a few minutes he rolled to his side as she bathed carefully, peeling the bandage slowly.

Unable to look at her, he spoke nonetheless. "Is it time for me to 'be' in love?"

A pause. "Hush, Gideon. No…you're not ready for that." Without looking, he could sense she was blushing deeply as she spoke. Mary glanced to the doorway. "I have no doubts you know how to love in a physical way, but you don't know how to be in love. You need more time."

Pausing again, he then grinned.

"Gideon Henry, why are you smiling?"

"You don't want to know."

"You're right, I don't!" She gave a deliberate tug at an unbathed edge of the dressing, causing him to jerk.

"Ouch!"

"Hush…and behave!"

Beginning to spend periods of time together, Gideon slowly opened up about his life. Now she walked up the hill and sat by his side as he watched the ranch. Pulling a long grass stem, she peeled it and put it between her teeth. Pulling it out, she worked a moment to peel it further.

"I was thinking of you this morning, Gideon." She noted his head turning as she observed him through the corner of her eye. "I realized thus far in your life you haven't been who you are going to be."

"I'm not sure what you mean."

"All the pieces of your life are pulling at you. Some tug you hither, some tug you yonder. You have done one thing while, more than ever, another part of you tugs a different direction. I really think the best thing for you to do is let go of the way it's been and follow a tug in the new direction."

"What do you see as the new direction?"

She paused and Gideon waited as she pulled another stem and peeled, testing it for a moment before taking her hand away. Then she turned and looked him in the eye.

"I think your new path is the opposite of the old. You need to follow the path of love. You have a love for the children and you are making a difference in their life."

"The children. Is that the only direction I should focus?"

Mary blushed, but held his eyes. "Is your heart telling you something? And is it more than a casual interest? I know when I marry I'm not going to be just a woman. I will be a wife and partner."

65

Early that morning he sat at the table with Mary, Ruth and Laban. Vern was already in the barn mending harness. The work of a ranch was never done. Gideon's eyes swept the room as they ate. There was more to this home than just shelter. Ruth Schmidt's influence made it a comfortable home, from the leather upholstered chairs to the tatted doilies decorating most flat surfaces. Knick-knacks stood upon the mantle and a Bible lay prominent upon a small table next to a chair. Next to another chair he spotted a sewing basket with some current project draped atop. Over this hung an oil lamp for nighttime reading. Obviously there had been improvements over the years. Still, the placement of weapons around the room showed readiness for whatever might come.

In ways it reminded him of his home as a child. His mother kept a neat house, though an austere one out of necessity. If events had not happened the way they did, would he be sitting at the table with his mother and father and Nate and Abby? How life might be different. And yet, look at him now.

Gideon's heart pounded in his chest. He was a paid killer. Of course, he could rationalize the killings of his past were men who, for the most part, were not the cream of society and, truthfully, there were some the world was best without. Yet, with all said and done, he was 25 years old and had nothing to show for it but a list of headstones to his credit and a reputation wherein he was both feared and respected within certain circles. Of course there was also a lot of money. At the same time, he had to watch his back at all times, and could never let his guard down because of those who sought to take him down. His own headstone would boost another's reputation and there were others who sought both his reputation and his headstone.

All he had to look forward to was more of the same, until such time as he became slower or missed a detail and lay bleeding in the dust of some isolated town or mountain valley.

Would he ever have a family? The past couple years provided much time to think and such thoughts came to mind now and then. Yet it seemed he became even more silent, keeping to himself and living an existence that would cause his father to turn over in his grave.

That young girl found in the alley changed him more than he wanted to admit. When she died his hard shell cracked and he actually began to feel pain and anguish and sense it in others. Then he started the home for children. Was it to alleviate in some way the guilt of having taken lives? Was the money spent as some sort of offering to God to make up for sins he committed and continued to commit? Only he and God knew the number of lives he had taken and only God knew what the result was of those "jobs" completed. Was he just fooling himself inside to think the world was better off without those people?

There was genuine joy in his heart when he approached the children's home on those seemingly rare occasions. He felt a happiness approaching that of his own childhood. Yet at the same time there was a shadow looming over the happiness. And when opportunity arose to grow close to others he remained distant.

Something deep within yearned to be released, to break into the light of day, to be freed from the bondage of shadows in his heart.

What would his father have said to him? His father was dedicated to the railroad, a solid employee.

Every once in a while he recalled a new memory of those days gone by, and most centered on the lessons of his father. There was a day when he caught his father brooding. He saw the distant look in his eyes and stood watching and wondering. Looking up, his father caught his glance and gestured for Gideon to sit beside him.

"Son, there are many opportunities that will come your way. Always remember money is not everything. There must be purpose in a man's work, and a pride in what he builds and leaves for the next generation. All of us grow old and what we look back upon either brings a smile and thankfulness or leaves regret and guilt. One leaves a man with a spring in his step while the other weighs a man down and puts a bend in his back. I've just been offered something to put more money in my pockets, which would do a lot for our family but, at the same time, it would require me to be deceitful. Just the thought weighs me down and I can almost feel my back bending. I want my life to stand for something worthwhile, and I want my children to be able to stand tall and smile when they remember me."

66

In the kitchen one morning, Ruth paused several times, straining her ears to the conversation in the other room. All she could hear was whispering as Mary changed dressings on Gideon's wounds. Mary made it clear she would tend to his wounds. And she tended to them as often as possible.

Their daughter had shown slight interest in one or two cowhands. Many men were content to work and drift and perhaps she sensed their amorous intentions to be of the same sort. None kept her interest beyond a Sunday afternoon picnic or an evening horseback ride. In all cases, Mary returned and Ruth sensed something in her demeanor making it clear no further courtship would be forthcoming.

They raised a daughter who was sure of herself, determined and wise beyond her years. She would not settle for just some roving cowhand. She sought something more, a solid man with character and dreams. Ruth believed she sought a man building something beyond himself.

She and Vern spoke as they spent a few too brief minutes sitting on the front stoop with dusk deepening into the darkness only found in such remote places. For a brief moment the flicker of a lamp in the bunkhouse punctuated their reverie. Then it, too, disappeared Conner and Paulo sought a few hours of sleep. With the departure of the other men, the two shared the space. They would be off again in the morning for the gathering. Vern spoke as he stared into the distance.

"I think Mary's getting attached to Gideon."

"Yes, she is. Does it bother you, Vern?"

"I guess I want what's best for her. I just don't know if Gideon's the right kind of man."

"What's the right kind of man?"

Vern glanced to her in the darkness, brow wrinkled in surprise. "Well, you know, a well set-up fellow with a good family and...well, daggone it, Ruth! Do you think it's ok?"

"I remember quite a few years ago when a gangly, wet-behind-the-ears young man came calling on a young lady. He didn't have anything to his name but a dream. The girl's parents wondered and fretted, but saw determination and inner strength. And they saw the love he had for their daughter, and she for him. It was the same way they started. Perhaps the one point that gave them pause was his name… Schmidt. They couldn't even spell it!"

Vern put his arm around Ruth and chuckled. "Ah, Ruth…you're right. We started with nothing but love and look at us now." He paused and she noted the somber tone in his next words. "If this mess with Bowers doesn't get straightened out we may be back to just love again."

"Vern, I have traveled many a trail by your side. In my heart I carry both fear and trust. I see Mary and Gideon and I find a building hope. We have built something big here, and I can't help believing it will continue to live. Perhaps not in the same way it has, but it will continue. The struggles in our lives have always led to deeper wisdom and strength."

Seeing her eyes in the last flickers of dusk, Vern looked at his wife's gentle face. "You give me strength, Ruth. And though your parents wondered about the match, time has shown we have made a good team. We pull in tandem and neither one of us is afraid of the harness. It took a lot of years to build what we have, and we'll certainly not give ground easily."

67

Final preparations were underway as the Mexican families began loading the wagon to take the women and children to the relative safety of the Chinese camp. The wounded Conner would also go along, making Alita happy. While there were tears and tension as the wives grudgingly packed, it was nothing like the heat of the words between Vern and Ruth. More than once, Conchita heard bits and pieces and glanced wordlessly to Maria.

"Vern Schmidt, I will not leave!"

"Ruth, I need you to be there to care for the children. Besides, I want you safe. We have no idea what the Bowers outfit will do. Dan Bowers has gone crazy and Clyde isn't much better."

Ruth turned to her husband, dishtowel in hand, waving and gesturing like a flag in a military assault.

Her face was red and she stood firmly in front of the man with whom she'd shared the years.

"I have fought Indians; I have fought rustlers; I have fought everything we have faced standing by your side. I can shoot just as well as you – if not better!"

"But, Ruth."

"There are no buts, Vern! I will not leave this home. I will defend it and my family as long as I have breath in my body! I tell you again. I will not leave!"

Vern looked angrily at his wife, yet also with pride. She was correct – they had fought side by side for all these years and he knew of no better partner. They always guarded each other's backs and more than once survived where they felt there was little hope. They stood strongest when they were together. He rubbed his chin, realizing he forgot to shave that morning amidst the preparations and the hard silence he felt from Ruth since they arose. Now he was faced with it! Glancing out the window to gain a few moments of thought, he noted Conchita in the distance glancing towards the window. He chuckled.

"What are you laughing at, Vern?"

"Maria and the others are listening to us and looking this way."

Ruth glanced out, then gave a subtle shudder as she also chuckled. The tension was broken and they looked at each other a few moments before Vern spoke.

"Ruth, I want you by my side. But the children…"

"Vern, Maria can look after Laban and, in case you have not noticed, Mary is very much like me and she is not a little child anymore. You will not be able to get her to leave. You might as well not try."

Vern looked at her.

"What do you mean?"

Ruth smiled.

"Dear husband, while you have been working the ranch, your daughter has grown up. Mary can ride as well as anyone, herd cattle, shoot and she has a streak of stubbornness. She will not leave and you will face the fire if you try to get her to leave Gideon. It is beyond what you and I think anymore – she is a woman now. She is a strong woman. We have raised her well. It is within her to now fight to defend her home – and all that she loves."

Shortly after breakfast, Laban cast his eyes cautiously around as he rode out of the back door of the barn. Careful to keep the structure between him and the house, Laban increased the distance and finally dropped over a short ridge and was able to spend his time looking ahead.

After Clyde and his men came by the ranch, Pa told him to stay close, to not ride out as he was accustomed to doing. Now the talk of leaving confused him. He wanted to stay. Laban's mind kept going to the secret fort he was building up under the edge of a distant ridge. In an outcropping of boulders jumbled this way and that, Laban had been hauling fallen wood from increasing distances. Working for a time, he would then ride out to see how it looked from afar. Pride was strong in his heart, his young mind seeing it as a marvel of creation rather than the haphazard stacking and piling that it was.

Just some finishing touches and it would be complete. A short distance from the fort, Laban stacked some wood scavenged from a copse of trees, ready to dally a loop around and drag to the fort. It was late in the night that his father's orders to stay close gave way to youthful bravado. Hardly sleeping the rest of the night, Laban came to breakfast with barely contained excitement.

At the table that morning, Laban caught Gideon Henry looking at him as a man knowing. After the meal, Gideon seemingly sought a moment alone with him, but Laban kept one step ahead with chores. Now, with Gideon occupied, Laban decided a ride to the fort would be quick and safe. After all, it was well within the bounds of the ranch. Besides, when he returned the others would be well on the way to the Chinese camp and he would be able to stay at home. His youthful imagination and bravado obscured reality in his mind.

Fully away from the view of the ranch house, he rode freely and happily, though with an inner sense of unease knowing he was being disobedient. While oiling his saddle the afternoon before, Laban was looking down at the slickness of the pommel and missed the momentary flash from a distant ridge.

68

CEDAR CITY

A light breeze teased the students with welcome refreshment as Abby sought to keep them attentive to their lessons. It was a difficult task, given she also wished to be out of the classroom and under the trees where the shade's coolness would ease the stickiness of the summer heat.

Long blond hair lay coiled in circular braids on each side of her head. A face many viewed with a double take, Abby had grown into a beautiful young lady. Mattie and Buck made sure she dressed well and showed good manners. Like all young ladies in the west, she knew how to handle a horse. Buck taught her to shoot in a canyon outside of town. Yet, when she dressed, those abilities were missed as folks were drawn to her beauty.

Abby's abilities as a teacher greatly impressed the local board of citizens, giving her a notoriety of sorts when late afternoon gave her opportunity to stop in town. Womenfolk stopped to chat kindly, commenting on lessons learned by this or that child and would she like to come to Sunday dinner. Young men of the area seemed to come out of the woodwork and happen to be along the walk when she strolled by. Each would stand, doff their hat and greet her with hope in their eyes or a yearning to say something more significant.

Such attention by all was pleasant and the availability of suitors put her on a collision course with the traditional next step for a young lady in the territory – marriage and children. Yet there was unsettledness within her soul. More often than not, Abby lay awake at night wondering – about Nate, about Gideon, and wondering if she'd ever see them again. It had been months since she heard from Nate. Life became a pattern of teaching, strolling with young suitors and looking for something missing in her heart.

Then one day another letter arrived. Buck Ganner was an astute judge of people. Being sheriff brought awareness, and he looked at Abby knowingly as he handed her the travel-worn envelope.

Rushing to her room and laying across the bed, Abby carefully opened the envelope and looked longingly at the letter. She soaked up the words as a flower during infrequent rains. Perusing the letter, her spirit soared with Nate's news.

Nate was in Colorado with family. Though she did not recognize the names of Otis and Ella Henry, something within was elated with the mention of family.

Gideon was in Colorado, too! A place named Craswell.

Buck and Mattie Ganner sat in the kitchen, quietly holding hands. A tear coursed Mattie's cheek.

At dinner, Buck broke the silence.

"How's Nate?"

Abby looked up into the eyes of this kind man, and then shifted to Mattie, who looked down at her plate. She knew this couple cared for her as if she were their own.

"He's in Colorado. A place called New Haven."

Mattie's eyes shifted briefly to Buck's. He continued to look at Abby. After a pause, he cleared his throat and forged ahead.

"Long letter to say so little."

"Gideon's in Colorado, too. Craswell. Do you know where that is?"

"Few years back I went through a place by name of Battle Wagon. Seems like Craswell was near there."

Storing his words in her mind, Abby nodded.

69

CRASWELL

"Here comes the kid!"

Clyde Bowers rose slowly from the ashes of the fire. It had been built earlier of the driest twigs to eliminate most of the smoke. Filtering through the branches of an old pine, what smoke remained dissipated to give no indicator of their position.

"What we gonna do to the boy when we catch him, Clyde?"

"Take him to the line cabin. Gonna send a note home on his horse for Gideon and Vern to come to the line cabin."

"What then?"

"Just you never mind. I'll do the thinkin' an' you just do as I tell you. Understood?" Clyde glared menacingly at the man, who nodded and swatted a bug on his arm that wasn't really there but was effective in breaking the eye contact.

Drinking a last swig from his cup, and gagging on a mouthful of grounds, Clyde spit and sputtered.

"Doggone, Dillard, you like to gag me to death! Next time I'll make the coffee!" In actuality, he was making small talk to cover his own nervousness. His father had shown a new side, a side that included killing Laban. It shocked him at first, but through the night as he tossed and turned, Clyde began to see the need to protect and build the ranch – at all costs. Threats and danger could take various forms, and he remembered a drifting cowboy showing up at the ranch many years ago. Hunchbacked and short, the odd-looking man was stern-faced at snickering amongst the other hands. The next morning pa made a trip to the outhouse just before dawn and caught the man cutting a prized stallion out of the corral. They tied a feed sack to the man's feet to have enough weight to hang him. Yep, he thought to himself, danger comes in all sizes. Laban was small now but problems would compound later when he grew up. If it needed to be done, best do it now. In his own mind, Clyde became bolder and forced himself to walk like a man sure of himself. As he did so, he believed himself more and more.

A day earlier they chose this spot after one of his men reported seeing Schmidt's boy over in this direction several times. Sure enough, Raston pointed to a small wisp of dust in the valley below. Clyde could see it was a small rider. Laban for sure. Looking around, he gestured to the two men.

"Ok, mount up. Dillard, you sweep around the other side. Raston will go west and then we'll nab the kid at the Narrows." Clyde pointed to a distant narrowing of the ridge, where it seemed continuous, but in actuality was overlapping with a narrow gap between. "Be quiet, stay out of sight. We can't let him escape. If'n he doesn't go to the Narrows, circle behind him."

70

BATTLE WAGON

Creaking steps echoed the measured and confident steps of the dusty rider. He wore a pale duster, a bit worn, with both sweat and rain stains of a man who spends time outside in the weather. As all men of the West, he naturally noted the other horses, their quality and care, for as the horse, so must the rider be. Experienced eyes also noted there were Star-3 brands on a few. A quick glance took in the town, a town different yet so similar to the small enclaves of the West where men wearied of travel and set down roots. Pausing to slap a token amount of trail dust from his jeans and sleeves, he removed his hat for a moment, wiping the sweat off the band. Dust and sweat were part of any travel and he longed for the day he would return home. His gun was placed expertly and, out of habit of the past, he loosened it in its holster. He had not the look of a long wandering man anymore, but as one with a purpose.

Battle Wagon was refreshment at the end of a long day. The night before he stopped and shared a fire with some hands at a line cabin. Always enjoying late night conversations around a campfire, he casually mentioned heading towards Battle Wagon. An older hand pushed back the brim of his hat, spit into the fire, cocked his head and look at the traveling man.

"Interesting thing about some of these here towns out in the West. Usually the names mean somethin'. Take fer instance Battle Wagon. I hear tell it's named such because some of the early miners going through had a run in with the Indians. There weren't no buildings, just a blackened fire pit in the prairie, and those men, three of them I recall hearing, jumped up in that there wagon and stood off the Indians. When it was all said and done there were a hunnert arrows in the wagon and nigh on to half that many in the men. One died and the others come close to cashing in their chips. A teamster train come by, some stayed and some went with the rest of the teamsters. One what stayed was one of them men what fought. Sorta seemed natural to call it Battle Wagon."

As was the way of the West; names came from happenings, physical characteristics and people who figured prominently in the settlement.

Pushing through the batwings in the only saloon in Battle Wagon, the man paused as his eyes adjusted to the dim light of the setting sun in the saloon. Wanting information, he knew this would be the place. Men sat at various tables, it being past dinner hour and the saloon was gearing up for the evening. A few outlying hands would be filtering in.

Walking to the bar, he noted stray glances his way – measuring glances. He grinned inside. There was a time…

"Rye." The bartender placed the glass and poured. "Looking for a spread located near here. Dirkson of the Star-3?"

"You're close, mister. Bout thirty mile due east through the pass. Fact is there's some of that bunch over yonder."

Hearing the conversation, a dusty rider from a table nearby spoke:

"What business you have with the Star-3, mister?"

"I come to buy cattle. Also looking to hire some temporary hands to help with the drive. Got a man coming on the stage in a couple days to help."

"Well, we're headed out in a bit. You're welcome to ride to the home place with us."

The stranger nodded. "I'd welcome the company. I might get a bite to eat, if there's time."

"Plenty of time. No rush."

Downing a shot, a man at a nearby table showed signs of being a bit too far into his drink as he spoke with a slur.

"Buying cattle. I was a-wonderin' for a minute if you wasn't some gun hand. Over east of here near a place called Craswell they's fixin' to have a war. They's a lot of hired guns around. They's some fella name of Gideon. The Rocking-B done tried to kill him, but he got away. Now he's fightin' them alongside some German fella."

At the bar, the stranger stood, his drink paused on its way to his lips.

"Hey stranger, you be ridin' with us. You got a long handle?"

"Teague."

Nodding, the man went back to his drink.

"This Gideon. They say where he's from?"

"Not much known, but someone said around St. Louis."

Looking thoughtful, the stranger downed his drink and headed to the door.

"Hey, mister, where you goin'?"

The dusty rider paused and turned back to the men.

"There'll be a fella here in a couple days asking for me and for Dirkson. Lawyer-type name of Bill Henry. Tell him what you told me. Let Dirkson know I'll be back...got a side trip I got to make."

"Sure thing, mister." They all craned to see the man outlined against the last rays of sunlight streaming through the doors.

The batwings rattled as the man walked into the deepening dusk.

"Where the devil's he going?"

"I dunno, but his name sounds familiar."

71

CRASWELL

Laban looked up from his saddle and for a moment thought he saw dust on the distant ridge. Staring intently at the spot and seeing no more, he dismissed it as a play of the wind and sun. Drowsing a bit, he decided to keep himself awake by singing. A lot of real cowboys sang to the cattle to keep them calm and several hands he knew from the territory had fine singing voices.

Singing with vigor, Laban lowered his voice to sound older and imagined himself on a cattle drive riding night herd. It helped him to ignore the fact of disobeying his father. There were several miles between here and the ranch now. Looking around with unveiled concern, Laban realized he usually told someone where he was headed, just in case. This time nobody knew where he was headed – or that he was even gone.

Shrugging, he lifted his head and straightened his shoulders. Eager to be seen as a man on the ranch, he was tired of being treated like a boy. In some ways he already had responsibilities, and cherished times when sent on what were obvious grown up chores. At the same time, like any other boy his age, it felt good to be able to talk to his ma and wander freely about the ranch.

He smiled and sang even louder. Pretending to herd stray cattle along the path, Laban for a while rode waving his arms and shaking his riata at an imaginary bull that kept trying to break away from the imaginary herd before him. He wove in and out amidst the brush and his imaginary herd became quite impressive. In his mind he saw his pa smiling as he brought the cattle in. Concerns in his heart were forgotten, as he became a real cowboy, now driving a herd to market over the Chisum trail. Knowing the Narrows was coming, the path became a chute and he worked the cattle into single file.

Off in his imaginary world Laban was singing loudly and did not see the tracks in the trail. Riding around a small bend at the Narrows, the men in the trail cornered him.

Laban did not realize their intentions. Thinking it was merely a casual encounter, he tried to make small talk but one of the men grabbed his bridle and the other dragged him roughly to the ground.

"My pa is gonna be mad at you, Clyde!" Laban had yelled. The big man walked over and slapped him so hard Laban wanted to cry and, in fact, a tear coursed a dusty cheek.

72

ideon walked to the barn in mid afternoon. Gingerly forking hay to the horses and careful to avoid straining his side, he heard steps and rustling cloth and looked up to see Mary, carrying the egg basket.

"You just can't sit still, can you, Gideon?"

Gideon smiled wryly. "No, Mary, I find it quite hard to lay in a bed or sit in a chair while others are at work."

"Is your side feeling better?" She changed the subject and reached as if to touch his side, but held back.

"Thanks to your care I'm well on the road to healing. My side feels really good. I'm fit as a fiddle again."

Mary blushed, wondering why. Gideon was a killer – or had been. Why was she so drawn to him? Yet she couldn't deny it...

Gideon looked in her eyes, sensing the struggle within Mary's heart and mind. There was awareness of what that struggle encompassed. Turning to the manger, he finished forking hay.

Mary stood unmoving. Reaching over, she touched his sleeve and spoke softly.

"Gideon, tell me what it was like for you growing up."

Looking at her, there was a jumble of emotions and thoughts in his eyes. Mary saw the hesitancy.

"Never mind…if it hurts too much."

Gideon stared at her and squinted in thought. Never before had he told anyone his story. He always maintained walls. It protected him from having to face his memories. Yet, something inside him told him it was time. Leaning on the manger, his eyes looked first to Mary, then to the floor.

"It…was good…to a point…" At first, the thoughts and words were short and disjointed, then built strength as words cascaded like fresh water over a falls. Gideon found himself telling her of the wonderful times, of the joys they had as a family, the murder of his father, the death of his mother and the splitting of the children. There were times when he looked off, as if into a hazy distance.

Mary sat, attentive, wondering if this was the first time he had shared these things. She sensed it with every ounce of her being and knew that to interrupt might stop the healing flow of what needed to be said. He was sharing the deepest pain, that which was blocking a new path for his life.

With a deep sigh, Gideon's shoulders sagged and he stared off into the distance, intent upon something.

Reaching over, Mary placed her hand upon his arm. He tensed suddenly, eyes widened. Drawing back, Mary looked up at him.

"Gideon, I'm sorry…"

"Mary…?" His look was tender, but worried. He looked out the door of the barn.

"What is it?"

"Where did Laban go this morning? His horse is coming…without him!"

73

"Laban wasn't supposed to leave. Pa told him to stay close!"

"Vern!"

Vern Schmidt, knowing the tone of the call, dashed out of the house, rifle in hand. At that moment Laban's horse trotted into the yard.

Vern quickly grabbed the reins. All three saw the ragged paper tied to the horn. Gideon worked the string, took the note and read it.

"Line cabin on the ridge. Only Gideon and Vern to come. Anybody else and the boy will die. We will know ahead if you have others along."

Jose, Manuel and Paulo came running from their preparations. Vern looked around.

"They got my boy! Must be Bowers and his men."

"We've got to ride, Vern." Gideon spoke with determination.

"But Gideon, do you think you can take the ride?" Mary was fearful for her brother, but knew Gideon was not fully healed.

"I'm better than I was, Mary. Right now Laban is all that matters."

Jose stepped forward. "We will ride with you, Vern."

"No, Jose! The note specifically says Gideon and myself." Pausing, Vern looked into the distance. "Besides, it's best just the two of us go - less confusion and hesitation if shooting starts…and I suspect it will. Besides, you need to get your families to the Chinese camp."

"But what if they come while we're gone?"

Schmidt looked around, and then spoke to all three cowhands.

"My guess is they will wait to see what happens. Go, see to your families. We need them safe for what might be ahead. I think we are starting into something that will need all our attention. Go, get them settled into the camp and try to be back in a couple days.

All three looked to each other and nodded, then hurried off. Mary stepped forward.

"I'll have Ma pack something to eat."

"I'll saddle the horses, Gideon. You get your gear." Vern marched stiffly to the barn.

A short time later they mounted up as Ruth and Mary came to their sides.

"Pa, I know that cabin. That was where I took shelter the time I was caught in the storm. There's a draw comes up from the east, almost right up to the cabin. I remember because there was quite a bit of water running down and I went over and looked. Could be helpful."

"Thanks, Mary. Might be worth thinking about. You and your ma look after the place. Some rough men around these parts nowadays." Mary noted the worn yet angry visage of her father. There was something in his eyes unseen for a long while. Ruth handed Vern a small sack. The clinking of the contents revealed bullets. Ruth and Vern held eyes for a few moments. Mary saw the same intent look in her mothers' eyes. Ruth spoke sternly to Vern, gripping his hand firmly.

"Vern. I thought we might avoid a fight, but they took our son and that means war. You bring back our boy, Vern. Kind ways are no longer a choice. You do what you got to do." Ruth looked into his eyes ever more intently, pursed her lips and squeezed his hand tightly, lingering.

Nodding silently to his wife, Vern leaned down and kissed her. Straightening in the saddle, he spoke.

"Let's go."

As they rode off, Mary watched Gideon turn to look back, meeting her eyes. This was not unnoticed by her father.

74

Blindfolded, Laban was unable to see except for a small gap below his left eye, allowing glimpses of a saddle and a mite of trail. Hands tied, he lay over a horse with the pommel digging into his side and making it difficult to breathe. At least an hour went by and he focused upon getting breaths between the pressure of the pommel and the steps of the horse.

Finally they stopped and Laban was lifted roughly from the horse and carried like a feed sack. It was nearing dusk and getting cool.

"Get him inside." It was Clyde. The man scared him. Something in his eyes alarmed Laban.

Pa would be all-fired mad right about now. He had run off against Pa's orders and now couldn't get away from Clyde and his men and Pa would have to come looking.

Pausing, Gideon looked around, then spoke matter-of-factly, looking Vern in the eye.

"I have made mistakes in the past, Vern. Some I regret, others I do not. The past is now just that – the past. I now must move ahead into the future. That future begins now, with getting Laban back safely."

Vern looked at the man, seeing determination as well as sincerity, but still questioning. Gideon read this in the man's eyes.

"Someday, depending, I may tell you more."

Nodding, Vern looked into the distance. In the West, he knew, men were judged not by the past but by the present. Many men had pasts they regretted, and many had pasts from which they could not run fast enough. A man was judged by how reliable he was, how honest in any dealings, and whether he would fight when the chips were down. A man who was a coward or shirked his duties was neither respected nor wanted. Many respectable men of the West had at one time done something questionable, but later turned into respectable members of society.

Some hands he knew through the years were only a short distance in front of a posse carrying twenty feet of hemp, and they changed their lives around – and many times their names – forging a new trail in life. He himself remembered branding questionable calves and anything without a brand. It was common as the early comers sought to build their dreams. At the same time, even that had its limits.

Vern remembered he and a couple other ranchers, one of them a young Dan Bowers, sharing a drink all those years ago when the first saloon in Craswell opened on the back of a wagon. They stood, staring at the horizon, when Bowers spoke to the third man in a conversational voice with a bit of a smirk.

"Gary, I really wanta know where you get your cattle. Seems like some of your cows have three and four calves a year. Must be some sorta record."

Gary McCall smirked back. A solid man, he later became a respected part of the new community that became Craswell. A man without fear, he died several years ago when his horse fell in a stampede.

"You ought to look at your north range, Dan. Up there in the breaks of the mountains they's a lot of calves. You run a few of your cows up there, work through the edges of them sodbuster's spreads and you might find your cows suddenly real fertile, sometimes two, three calves at a time. It's like a miracle."

Looking at each other, both laughed. That was a long time ago and such practices built the ranches but were no longer necessary. Now, such behavior was viewed as rustling and dealt with firmly, usually with lead or hemp. The sodbusters became friends, though most abandoned the ground years ago after a couple very dry years.

Gideon's voice broke the silence.

"How far to the line cabin?"

"'Bout ten miles. Long ride yet. Be after dark."

"They aren't going to hurt Laban yet, Vern. I suspect their plan is for none of us to get away, but they'll wait till we're there. They won't risk having us alive to spread the word. Might be best we get there after dark, sorta scout around a bit." Pausing, Gideon scanned the country. "Somewhere they've got a man watching for us. Any idea where that might be?"

Vern looked at the ground between his knees. A strong man, he wanted to get to his son as soon as possible. Yet to approach too hastily might get them all killed.

"I reckon we might play them a mite, Gideon. When we get over that rise ahead we'll see a pointed ridge at the overlapping of two valleys. Looks over most of the approach. Likely where they'll be, as that's where the trails run."

Squinting his eyes, Gideon worked his jaw, then looked at Vern.

"Here's my idea: let's gamble on that fella on the point being in not too much of a hurry. He'll be expected to give information and he'll want it accurate. Let's split up here and mosey around the ridge ahead from both sides. He'll see one of us and wonder where the other is. Is there a way you could stay out of sight until we meet up somewhere where he can see us?"

Vern nodded. "There's an upthrust of the ridge that carries off into the valley yonder. If I stay out of sight behind it, we could meet where it folds into the flat. Might sorta surprise whoever's watching."

"Ok, So we'll play with his mind and meet up on the other side. He'll know we're supposed to come together, so he won't be sure who we are till we meet up. I'll plan on being there before you, so if you get there first, hang back till I get there. Then we'll both dismount and make a fire. Be near dusk. We'll picket the horses like we're going to stay the night. Then come dark we'll mosey off and see if we might catch them unawares."

Vern looked at the sun. "We got a bit or we'll get there too early. Best you get some sleep, Gideon. I'll wake you after a spell." Gideon nodded and willingly lay back. Though doing much better, he still tired easily.

76

Following Vern's directions, Gideon came at last through the trees and into the flats. Turning his horse towards the distant point where the rocks faded into the valley, he came into the sunlight and caught a momentary reflection off a glass on the distant hill Vern had suggested as a likely observation point. Gideon chuckled. Any watcher would be scratching his head about now, expecting two riders and wondering.

Gideon neared the point and glimpsed Vern hidden in a deep shadowed recess of rock. As Gideon neared, Vern emerged and the two men met at a copse of trees. Dismounting and gathering sticks, Gideon kindled a fire while Vern removed saddles and hobbled the horses as if for the night.

Sitting by the fire, dusk deepened to near darkness when Gideon spoke in a low voice over his coffee.

"We've got a change in plans."

Vern looked up with wrinkled brow.

"Why?"

"Cast your eyes carefully over yonder. We've got two men approaching from those hummocks in the distance. They were horseback but now they're afoot. Likely be here in about ten minutes."

Vern turned his head just enough to look into the distance without being obvious. He saw the movement.

"Any ideas?"

"Just before they get here they've got to go behind those trees on the right. Let's ease down like we're going to sleep, with only our hats visible. Then we count till we think they're behind the trees and slip off into the dark and surprise them.

In a few minutes they slipped off and waited, each on a different side of the site. Moments later they heard a subtle brush as of pants against a bush, followed by instant silence. Vern and Gideon watched as two men stepped into the vague firelight and cocked their pistols, then looked around wide-eyed when they realized the men were gone.

Gideon cocked his pistol and spoke.

"Drop the guns."

One man cocked his gun as he spun, blazing his shot into the night but missing Gideon. Gideon fired and didn't miss, cutting a furrow in the man's hand. Falling to his knees, the man reached for a second gun as Vern stepped from the bushes and knocked him cold with a gun butt.

The other man started to turn and Vern yelled.

"Drop it!"

The man dropped the gun and slowly raised his hands. His voice was strained as he spoke.

"I got another gun in my belt but I ain't gonna reach fer it!"

"Don't give us any reason to wonder. Use two fingers and drop it, too. You got two guns pointed at you."

Moving slowly and deliberately, the man carefully removed the gun and dropped it away from his body.

"Now step back. Any more of you scoundrels out there?"

"No. Just the two of us."

"Vern, put some sticks on the fire. Let's get a look at this varmint."

As the fire flared up, both looked carefully at the man. Gideon tied his hands. Vern looked the man in the face and pushed his hat back.

"You're Johnson...you work for Bowers."

"What of it?"

Gideon was momentarily shocked as Vern viciously backhanded the man, knocking his hat off and causing the man's nose to bleed. Vern was red faced as he drew closer to the man.

"You got my boy, Johnson. Gideon, you think we got any obligation to take this man to town?"

"No, it's a bit too far to burden ourselves. But we sure can't let him go free."

Stepping around quickly, Vern grabbed the man bodily and kicked him behind the knees. Johnson fell face down and Vern enfolded his collar and dragged him close to the fire until his hair crinkled and Johnson screamed, trying to rise. Pulling him back, Vern shoved him to the ground, where the man began to cry, his forehead blistered.

Gideon looked at Vern, seeing the strength of this man who had faced Indians and all manner of dangers as he built the ranch. Many years of relative peace pushed the early determination below the surface. Now someone had his son. Vern caught his eye and, gritting his teeth, grabbed the man and began to push him back over the fire.

"Where's my boy!"

"I dunno!"

Vern shoved Johnson again to the fire. Gideon nudged the sticks with a boot, raising a flame and sparks that licked the man's beard and neck. Squirming with panic, Johnson again cried out and Vern threw him to the ground.

"Mister, I really don't care if you live or die. But you will die if you don't tell me what I want to know! You need to make yourself useful to me. Where's my boy?"

Whimpering, his beard burned and neck scorched, Johnson gingerly lifted a couple fingers to his face.

"At the cabin!"

"Line cabin on the high ridge?"

Johnson nodded.

"How many men there?"

"Dunno, I weren't there." Vern grabbed the man again. "No! It's true! I really don't know!"

"How about a guess?"

"Five, six."

"Clyde there?"

"Not sure." Vern cuffed the man across his scorched jaw.

"Think harder!"

"I think he's there!" Tears ran down the man's face.

"How many of you were up on the point watching for us?"

"Just the two of us. We had orders to head to the cabin when first we seen you, but Will and I thought we'd try and capture you instead."

"Well, you thought wrong. Gideon, what do you think we should do with this varmint?"

"Hang him." Vern's eyebrows lifted. Johnson's eyes rounded and the tears gushed. Gideon went to his saddle and returned with a piece of hemp. Bending, he tied one end around Johnson's ankles and then found a nearby limb of the right size.

"Vern, lift him up and I'll tie him over the limb." Raising the man, Vern held him a few moments while Gideon tied the rope. Vern let the man go. Johnson hung just over the ground, upside down. Gideon checked the man's bonds and noted they were secure. They also tied the other man.

Johnson hollered. "Don't leave me here! I need some liniment on my face?"

Reaching to the man's neck, Gideon took Johnson's kerchief and tied it through his mouth and behind his head. Then he looked at the man lying on the ground.

"Your friend will be out for a few hours. Maybe you'll be able to convince him to cut you loose. If we see you again there will be no talk. Let's go, Vern."

77

Other men arrived at the line cabin. Laban counted six or seven. Some came inside for coffee, usually in turns. One or two looked over at Laban; others seemed to deliberately avoid looking.

These were harsh men, not typical cowhands. They were paid for their fighting skills. Though some despised the use of a child, they were paid and paid well. Riding for the brand that paid made for a lively time in town and still left plenty in the pocket. Gold coin also bought silence about exactly how things were done.

Shortly after their arrival, Clyde ordered men to take positions in the brush surrounding the cabin. Two men moved down the hillside to watch for Gideon and Schmidt.

Laban struggled against the ropes. Once he succeeded in making a break towards the door; a man grabbed him and threw him against the back wall and called Clyde. Alone, Clyde brutally backhanded Laban, flung him against the bedpost and tied him bodily.

"Try to get out of that, you little rat!"

Crying, Laban could not respond. Clyde's blow stunned him, hurting terribly. Unable to wipe his eyes, the tears flowed down both cheeks. For the first time he sensed the absolute danger of his situation. He looked at Clyde and it was as if the man knew what Laban had suddenly realized. Grinning viciously, Clyde spoke.

"That's right, you little whelp! You are finally seeing the truth here. You are the bait. Your pa and Gideon will come to find you. They have to. We'll take care of them and," He chuckled, "then we're gonna take care of you."

Laban could only stare at the man. He sniffled.

"After that, we will take over your ranch. Your ma will either cooperate and sign it over or we will take it. Your sister…well, I have other plans for her. She will be my queen."

❦

Vern and Gideon rode slowly and carefully through the trees, watchful for any other guards. They figured the two who came to their camp were the only warning system Clyde had in place. Soon, however,

Clyde would begin to wonder, if he didn't already. They best expect to find the camp ready for them. Surprise would be difficult.

Peering around a wagon-sized boulder alongside the game trail up the mountain, Vern spotted a smaller game trail curving to the right. Pausing to confer, they decided to take the less-traveled trail. Stepping forward, they heard the click of a hammer from the other side of the boulder. Pulling their weapons, they turned.

78

Laban sniffled for some time before he calmed enough to remember things his pa said. There was a time they were riding a mountain trail and his pa pointed ahead to a wind-toppled pine barring the trail about a quarter-mile in the distance.

"See, son. Many men would spend their time looking right in front of them, but most times if'n you can get wind of the problem ahead of time, there's usually something that will come to mind. For instance, now we know the main trial is blocked, and we know it before we get there, we can start scouting for various ways around. Right up by that rock yonder is a game trail, appears to angle up the hill above the tree. Other animals have gone around this obstacle. Might be a likely way. And over there on the left is another likely trail. But the one up the hill looks less troublesome. Now, if we waited till we came right up to the fallen tree, we'd maybe have to come all the way back here to go around. Time wasted. Best to spot the problems ahead of time."

Another time they were riding and his pa spoke of how many times people miss something right in front of them. He said, "Where there's a will, there's a way." Many times he told Laban to stop and ponder a problem. Usually there were different ways to solve it, and a person just had to decide which way was best.

Laban sat now looking around the cabin. Clyde was in and out but never gone for more than a few minutes. One time, Laban heard him yelling and cursing outside. Coming in, he cast a distracted glance at Laban and then sat to sullenly drinking a cup of coffee. Ten minutes later he was gone again.

Laban pulled on the ropes with all his might, but could get no slack. They were tight around his wrists to the point of hurting. He leaned back in frustration and felt the bed move. Thinking quickly because of the sound of someone coming, he lowered his head and feigned sleep while one of the men came in and filled a cup, casting a furtive look at the captive. When the man left Laban quickly pushed the bed again. It moved!

If he could get the rope and slide it down the bedpost he could get free! He scrunched as much as he could, feeling the ropes slowly work down the post. About to slide them again, the door opened and Clyde entered, glowering at him. Walking over to Laban, the big man grinned wickedly and kicked Laban viciously. Tears welled up again and he groaned with pain.

"Go ahead and cry, boy! I really don't give a rip! Two of my men are missing. Gideon and your pa may have got them, but I've got men outside and we will get both your pa and Gideon and it won't be pretty." Pretending to ready another kick, Clyde laughed and walked to the coffee pot. Laban felt tears coursing down his cheeks as he fought pain. He sensed blood under his pants where Clyde broke the skin.

Glancing quickly at Laban, Clyde strutted out the door.

❧

Many miles away, Ruth Schmidt stood a hundred yards out into the pasture beyond the barn. Staring into the darkness, her ears strained with hope, yearning to hear the men return. Not just the men, she sought to hear Laban's voice.

She and Mary busied themselves with baking and checking in on Conner through the afternoon, after the hands headed off to the mountains with their families. Manuel assured her that they would make all haste and return promptly. She sensed the men's hesitance to leave.

"Go. Take your families. We will be fine. I've fought before."

Now, standing in the darkness, Ruth began to remember the early days and an awareness reignited within her. It was an awareness of the reality of the struggles of life. Birth to death was filled with some struggle, some problem, some tragedy or fight. After several years without violence, it was upon them again. Though she did not like it, Ruth Schmidt determined she would not shy from what came.

They had taken Laban. They had taken her son. Her jaw set. Raising the Winchester at her side, she jacked a shell into the chamber.

79

"Gideon? It's Skerby. Don't shoot."

Coming around the boulder, Skerby held his hands up until he saw recognition and heard both men release their tense breath. Gideon spoke softly as the men held their heads close.

"What in blue blazes are you doing here, Skerby?"

"I were yonder in the hills and I seen men with a small boy tied over the saddle. I could tell right away it were Vern's boy. I followed. They got no idea they were followed and made no try to hide the way."

"They knew we were coming, Skerby. They want us to find them."

"Do you know how my son is, Skerby?" Vern looked at Skerby intently.

"I done crawled up near the cabin as I could get. Heard Clyde inside yelling, then heard a noise and

Laban cried out. Ain't gonna lie. I think they've hurt him."

Vern started to move, but was restrained by Gideon.

"Wait, Vern. Skerby, you have any idea where their men are?"

"Not all, but they's one up this trail a mite. I think it'd be best to take this here game trail Vern spotted. I been up this way myself."

"It'll leave the man up there behind us. That's not good."

Skerby looked at them both, then motioned them closer as he spoke.

"I said they's a man up the trail, but he won't be a bother to us. Ain't the first time a no-account made his presence known by the smell of his tobaccy smoke. It just don't blend with the smells of the woods. Tried to argue with me, he did. I sort of helped him go to sleep and hog-tied him pretty nicely. He's off in the brush a ways." He peered knowingly and both men realized what he was saying. "But someone may be coming back to relieve him soon, so's best to take t'other way. It'd be sneakier."

Skerby led them up the hillside until they found themselves looking over the line cabin in the moonlight. It lay across a brushy flat, but near to the hillside behind. The cabin appeared well built, designed to protect in snowstorms, thunderstorms and give refuge when needed in gun battles.

Laban was inside.

Gideon twisted and looked up at the full moon lighting the landscape. Sometimes beautiful and helpful, tonight it was a dangerous orb as the bright light threatened their plans and their escape.

The three men lay together looking through the tufts of mountain grass at the cabin. Skerby whispered.

"They got men scattered round. They's been one or two up on that knoll yonder, off and on. They come in fer coffee now and then."

Meanwhile, Laban knew his time was limited and sensed the need to warn Pa and Gideon they were coming to a trap. Painfully bringing his knees to his chin and folding his feet up underneath him he successfully raised himself to where he could lift upwards on the bed rail with his elbow. It hurt beyond what he could imagine. Finally, getting the corner of the bedpost an inch or so in the air, he slowly worked the rope under the leg. The bed slipped and bumped to the floor. A moment later the door was opened and a cruel-looking man stood glaring at Laban.

To all appearance nothing had happened and Laban sit just as he had, feigning sleep. Pausing briefly, the man left and shut the door. Tugging lightly, Laban knew he was free from the post, but his hands still were tied tight behind his back.

Hurriedly looking around, Laban noted a window behind him. Shuttered, there was a crosspiece holding it shut. Would the bar fall and alert those around if he tried to lift it? Was there a guard right outside the window? Whatever he did, he must take a chance and must be quick. Waiting just a moment with his ears tuned to the door, Laban stood up quickly as he could, pain coursing through his body from the earlier blows. Standing on the bottom of the bed, he used his head to push up on the cross-piece, which slipped easily out and onto the bed, making no noise. The shutter opened slightly and he nudged it further with his head until he could stick his head and shoulders out. Looking around swiftly and seeing no one, Laban squirmed out the window and dropped to the ground.

80

Gideon took in the situation and suggested they draw closer by circling through the trees, but they would have to take out guards as they went. Their options were limited and they were rising when the cabin door opened, silhouetting a form they knew as Clyde. There was a shout.

"The kid! He's escaped! Out the back window! Go!"

Gideon looked at the men and recalled the words of Mary about the draw.

"Spread out, each of us work our way around while they're distracted. Vern, you take the left; Skerby go to the right. I'll go right down the middle. Mary mentioned the draw off to the right. Head that way and we'll meet at the top. We've got to get to

Laban before they do. Get them to focus on us to give him a chance. Go!"

Landing on his shoulder on the hard-packed dirt, Laban stifled a cry and looked around. He heard the door open in the cabin and dove for the brush as Clyde yelled. Wriggling and squirming through the underbrush, he needed distance and had to avoid any open areas where the moonlight would show him clearly. There was sudden yelling as men ran around the cabin. Knowing he had mere moments before the men would have the sense to pause and listen, Laban kept moving.

Hearing the sound of men beginning to search, he paused for a breath. Spotting a game trail through some briars, Laban ignored the scratches and shimmied in to work his way along under the arches of the branches. It would deter the men for just a short time, but would not stop them.

Gunshots came from behind him.

"Idiots! Don't shoot off into the dark! Dillard's off thisaway somewhere! We want the kid alive!"

Laban did not cry anymore. Determination took over. He needed to warn his pa of the danger. Having played in the hills much of his life, he knew how to hide, knew he could evade these men, but he needed to find his pa. Careful to avoid any brush he could, Laban stumbled forward.

Hearing sounds of pursuit nearing, Laban squatted until he could grasp a rock in his tied hands and, standing, twisted and threw the rock as far as he could into the briars to the left. It didn't go far but made a loud rustling.

"Over here! Right up here! I heard him!"

Sounds of men converging gave him a moment to take some deep breaths. Shots sounded in the distance. Knowing he mustn't pause, Laban turned.

Arms wrapped around him and a hand tightly clamped over his mouth.

81

Gideon ran swiftly across the clearing as men yelled and Clyde bellowed from behind the cabin. To his right he heard a man cry out and knew that Skerby had decreased the odds against them.

Almost as suddenly a man rose in front of him and yelled.

"Hey! Stop there." He held a gun. As with many men, this tough made the mistake of thinking the man he faced would hesitate or cower.

Gideon did neither, and instead without a pause pulled his gun and fired. The man fell with a cry as Gideon moved onward. More shouting erupted from behind the cabin and shots hammered the air. Visible in the moonlight, Gideon dodged to the right towards a clump of brush. Flashes rent the night, bullets smacking into trees around him. Rolling and squirming his way into a depression in the ground, he followed it into the deeper woods. Sounds of gunfire continued. It wouldn't take long before they found where he went. The dirt was scarred by his boots and they would find his trail. Blast the moonlight!

Gideon knew they would expect him to pause or flee, so he worked his way closer to the cabin, hearing the pursuers going away behind him. They likely would not expect him to keep coming with Laban loose, but would look for him to be escaping with Laban and Vern. He would head to the cabin, then into the draw.

Laban looked into the eyes of his father and the terror faded. His father continued to hold his mouth until Laban recognized him and comprehended his signal to make no sound. Laban nodded and Vern reached for his knife, easily slicing his son's bonds. Laban hugged his father with stiff arms. Vern pushed him away, looked him in the eyes and motioned for him to follow.

Laban stayed right on his heels as they headed down the draw and skidded to a stop at the sight of a gun sparkling in the moonlight. Vern lifted his weapon.

Recognition.

Skerby!

Skerby whispered. "Seen Gideon?"

Sounds of pursuit increased. They heard Clyde yelling from not as far away as they wanted.

"Over here! Headed down the draw. You men head around over there, the rest follow me!"

Skerby and Vern headed down the draw with Laban between them. Moments later the brush parted and both men turned to face Gideon, who held up his hands until he saw their faces. He was breathing heavily. Not fully healed, they saw no quit in him.

"They're closing in. I saw more heading down below. They've about got us plugged tight." Gideon turned his head and listened to the men in the brush getting closer and drawing the noose tighter.

Vern spoke. "Getting close."

Skerby squinted at Gideon. "We need a distraction."

Gideon knew. "I'm going back up, while you both take Laban across the hillside here. Get beyond their circle; get back to the horses. I'll keep them pinned down here."

"You ain't got the strength, Gideon." Skerby looked at him, but they both knew there was no real option.

"Go, Skerby. You've got the skills to get them out. Take Schmidt and his son. Go!"

Both men looked at Gideon, knowing what he was saying. There was a good chance he would be killed. There was no time to waste, though, and they knew it. Unspoken words known only to men in such situations passed between them now. Vern quickly and silently nodded, Skerby squinted, and the two ushered Laban across the hillside.

Moving back up the hillside towards the pursuers, Gideon dodged to the right and came face to face with a startled man. Gideon hit him with his gun. The man collapsed.

Slipping off into the brush, Gideon made no attempt to be silent. Hearing men nearby, he deliberately hissed:

"Run, Laban!"

Pursuit converged quickly.

"Over here! The boy's over here!"

Darkness played its tricks as men suddenly saw what wasn't there.

"I seen them!"

"There's one right there!" Bullets flew around Gideon as he pushed through the brush and into the trees. A blow like a hammer took him in the hip. Stumbling, Gideon fell and felt the ground give way. Slipping downwards, bullets flew by the spot where Gideon stood only moments ago.

Recognition was quick upon him to realize the mud of the slope had caused him to slide and this took him out of the gunfire. Grasping the rocks beside him and slipping around a pillar of mossy rock, he grasped a tree and pulled himself up as men passed nearby. Taking hold of a stout branch at his side, and lobbing it down the slope, he heard the men shout and head towards the noise.

Listening into the night, the sounds of pursuit faded. Gideon remained immobile, knowing only a moving man or animal created a trail. From the sounds he knew the ruse had worked and felt confident that Skerby and Vern had gotten Laban safely away.

Pain shot through him and he reached to feel his hip. Blood. Catching his buckle with his hand, he drew back as he pricked his finger. His buckle! The bullet had hit his buckle and veered down to his thigh, cutting a nasty wound. It bled and hurt, but was not desperate. He sat tight, waiting.

Sometime in the night he heard hoof beats fading in the distance. Where were Vern and the others? Had they gotten away?

82

Skittering along the hillside, Vern led the way with Laban following closely, eyes wide. Skerby brought up the rear. Twice they suddenly halted, thinking they heard sounds of pursuit. Each time the sound had ceased as they stopped. Skerby peered intently into the darkness, unsettled. He stood beside Vern and whispered.

"It feels bad, Vern."

"I keep thinking I hear something, but…"

"Someone's out there."

"Our horses are not far ahead. Let's move – fast."

Moving on, they approached the copse of trees where the horses were tied.

The horses were gone!

Earlier, Clyde followed his men in the pursuit through the woods and, crouching and squinting into the darkness of the woods caught, out of the corner of his eye, movement where a shaft of bright moonlight came through the trees. Two men and...a child! One he recognized as Vern Schmidt. Try as he might, he could not place the other.

Knowing to yell for his men would alert his prey, Clyde slipped off quietly. For a large man he moved easily in the woods.

Pausing in the darkness, his mind ranged back over the hillside in the direction Laban and the two men were headed. He had been over this ground many times and ranged his thoughts ahead. The grove of trees at the edge of the lower hillside! It was a perfect place to leave horses, being right beside the trail. Looking again where he saw the movement, Clyde realized he could beat them to the spot by a few minutes if he took the direct path over the hillside.

Moving swiftly, he found the horses, untied them and led them into the darkness and up the hillside, where he paused and retied the mounts. A few minutes later there was a muffled exclamation and Clyde grinned, quickening his pace.

Skerby looked at Vern.

"Somebody done found our horses. Likely some-one of that there Bowers bunch."

Suddenly from the hillside came the sound of three quick shots.

A signal!

Vern looked at Skerby.

"They'll be here in just a few minutes. We'll move down towards the flats, staying to cover as much as we can. Down towards the bottom there's a jumble of boulders if we need."

Another shot! This time from behind and below.

"We got to go along the hillside, Vern. They've got the lower trail covered!"

"Follow me! Laban, climb aboard." Laban quickly climbed as his father squatted and Vern led the way.

Covering most of a mile, they paused briefly to listen. Sounds of horses came from above and below.

"This's got a wrong feel, Vern. They're behind us but not tryin' to get no closer. They's a'horseback and shoulda caught up with us."

Vern wrinkled his brow.

"They're herding us somewhere. Like cattle!"

"Must be some reason. You know this area, Skerby?"

"Right ahead's a box canyon. Been in there be-fore. Sheer wall, no way out."

Suddenly bullets slammed the rocks beside them.

"Box or no, we gotta get to cover." He motioned towards Laban. "We'll have to hope Gideon's out there somewhere. Let's move!"

83

Vern crouched protectively over Laban as bullets cut brush in the canyon entrance and danced around the three as they worked in to find cover. It was a small canyon, not more than a hundred yards across, but darkness would not allow them to see the full extent of their predicament.

"We've been herded here, Skerby, as sure as I herd cattle."

"They must be sure there's no way out."

Bullets panged the rocks around them as they entered the rocky enclave. Slivers of quartz flew up and around. Both men eyed each other, knowing the danger of ricocheting bullets. Looking around, Vern found a deep indentation in the wall of rock.

"Laban, crawl in here, stay low, don't sit up. In fact, dig out the bottom a mite and hunker lower."

Laban nodded and began to scrape the sand and dirt from the bottom.

"Skerby, how many shells you got left?"

"'Bout thirty. Left the rest with my horse. You?"

"No more than that myself. Have to make them count. Not sure how many are out there."

"I'd give my eyeteeth, if'n I still had 'em, to know where Gideon is about now."

As if in response, in the silence there was the sound of a shot, followed by another.

In the distance, Clyde was riding home, not sure of the news he had for his pa or how he'd react. Vern and the others were trapped in the box canyon by his men. No chance they would get away. Puffing his chest, Clyde rode tall, and knew he would be King. They had lost some men, and needed a couple more.

Creeping through the woods, Gideon paused to listen and heard multiple shots, barely audible. Turning to the sound, he set off in that direction.

It must be Skerby, Vern and Laban.

84

"You just plain can't do anything right!" Dan Bowers tossed the drink and re-filled his glass, spilling a healthy portion. Firelight played upon their faces in the main room of the ranch house. Dan Bowers had a habit of sitting in the darkness as night fell, with only the fire to see by.

"But we got them trapped, Pa."

"You shoulda had them at the cabin. Instead, you play the stupid card and lose the hand. It appears you're more stupid than the kid!"

"Pa! I just didn't think he would be able to get away."

"You're exactly right. You didn't think. See? That's your problem – you just ain't good at using the little brain you got! You not only didn't tie the kid tight enough, you left him alone with a back way out!

And why'd it take you so long to get home? I bet you stopped to see that whore at the cribs on your way!"

Clyde could do nothing but stare at his pa, fury restrained in him only out of fear of making it worse.

"You just can't do nothin' right!" Dan Bowers spat into the flames. Clyde wanted to yell back at his father, but he held it in, seething inside. His pa never was pleased with anything!

"Pa…"

"Shut up! I shoulda figured you'd mess up something simple! I can't get nothin' done right around here less'n I do it myself. I need a drink." Dan bowers turned back to the amber bottle across the room. Partway, he paused and looked back at Clyde.

"Now, here's what you need to do. Get a couple more men up there. Tell them to get those three. Kill 'em. Not you. Tell 'em where to go and then you get back here. We got another job we gotta do."

"Pa? We gotta take care of Schmidt and that son of his afore the town finds out."

His pa looked at him, a different light in his red eyes. His tone was changed. Clyde saw something in his pa's eyes. These outbursts lately made him wonder, but now the look in his pa's eyes confirmed it – it was a distant look.

"Aint nothin' gonna happen without my say-so! Now, do as I said, then get Roscoe and Tabor. We're goin' Grizzly huntin. Done lost four more calves. Can't run a ranch with Griz taking out the growth."

85

Blood trickled into Vern's eye as he tightened the bloody rag around his head. Wearily leaning back against the rock to reload, he glanced at the older man nearby. Skerby could be eighty, or could be sixty. Years of sun and wind in the West often turned men old before their times. Now he watched Skerby and the man's lithe and unwasted movements. He was a good man and one to ride the trails as a companion.

"How you doing on bullets, Skerby?"

"Ain't got but a double handful left."

"Wish we could get a good bead on them."

Sunlight beat upon the rocks as both men squinted toward the canyon mouth. Trapped through the night into the next day, Bower's men kept up a sporadic fire. Unable to move from their spot without exposing themselves, Vern and Skerby felt like cornered rats and hunkered as best they could. Looking at each other at one point, Skerby realized their best chance might be to make a run for it. Yet, looking over at Laban, he knew that option was out. So they fought on, shooting back at shifting figures in the trees and rocks beyond. Skerby counted at least six men, and an hour earlier they heard the pounding hooves of more arriving.

Skerby was grim. They were trapped and the worst thing was the reality they did not have an option. Herded like cattle, they had taken the only option available, right into the trap. Worst of all, they knew it but had no alternatives.

Vern knew his thoughts, for he had them himself. Glancing down at Laban, he knew Laban would not stand a chance if he and Skerby failed to protect him. Earlier a bullet ricocheted off the rocks and tore across Vern's scalp, not just cutting, but tearing a nasty gash across. Skerby crawled over and wrapped it, but it still oozed. It was only a matter of time before something hit Laban.

A volley spattered through the rocks, and Skerby yipped and grabbed his leg.

"Bad?"

"Just a crease across my calf, but we can't last here."

Vern looked at the man. Skerby was no local hand. Just a wandering man suddenly caught up in a mess and now likely to die here in this lonely canyon.

All three of them were likely to die. Vern grimaced with the realization that surrender would not save Laban because the men out there would kill all of them. Yes, this was a fight to the death. A fight with very little ammunition. He looked to the old man.

"Give my ranch to see Gideon show up about now."

Skerby smiled grimly back at him and nodded as another volley of shots filled the air with lead.

86

Tracking a Grizzly took time and the men were already weary from the intensity of the hunt. With a Grizzly, it took constant vigilance, and any mistake would likely be fatal. Early that morning they formed a skirmish line of sorts, riding a hundred yards or so apart to scout for sign. They rode north, alternately scanning the ground for sign and glancing ahead and around for danger.

Dan Bowers raised his hand to stop and signaled them in close. There, at the side of the creek, were the remains of a calf, with the prints of the Grizzly. All eyes quietly glanced around and knew the story. The bear had run the calf down without the slightest effort. Their horses caught the smell and shifted nervously, eyes wide.

"Calf never had a chance."

"Not much of anything stands a chance against a Grizzly. Even a man with a good rifle thinks twice 'bout tacklin' one."

"Them's awful big tracks."

"Biggest Grizz I ever did see."

"That one few years back by the north fork was a big 'un, but this'n's even bigger."

"There's four of us and only one of him." Bowers spoke firmly, but even he did not convey his usual confidence. This was a monster of a bear.

"I hear tell that story 'bout that mountain man what were mauled by a Grizzly. Hugh Glass. Lived, but ain't no woman would look at him no more he were so frightful. Men shied away. Guess there was teeth marks and tear marks ever which way."

"Shut your trap, Roscoe." Dan glared at the man.

"Said he crawled two hundred miles, with maggots eating on his wounds."

"I said shut up, Roscoe."

"Imagine crawling with them festered wounds."

"Roscoe!"

Nervous, all of them looked carefully around. Roscoe jacked a shell into his rifle. The other three looked at him and did the same. A Grizzly could cover a lot of ground in a flash.

"Where's the cow?"

"Yonder." Clyde pointed. The body of the poor beast lay not fifty yards away.

"Mama came to save her baby, but ol' Grizz cuffed and killed her and then run after the calf. Tender meat. They likes tender meat. Easier to chew."

Dan Bowers looked angrily at Roscoe. On any other day he'd send Roscoe off, but the man was good with a rifle and Dan was serious and intent upon the hunt.

"He's around somewhere. Tracks are fresh. Probably less'n a mile from here. Likely on that hillside over yonder." With his rifle he pointed to a rocky hillside in the distance.

Bowers men split into two pairs, Roscoe and Tabor swinging to the left, he and Clyde heading to the right.

"Ride quiet and ride loose. Keep your rifles free." Each man carried a Winchester and all had hunted bear before. They knew one man with a rifle could take down a bear, but it could take a lot to bring down a Grizzly this big. A wounded and angry Grizzly was a fearful thing to behold. Two men could keep a steady fire and confuse the bear from different angles, but a Grizz would run towards one of them for sure. Over a short distance a Grizz could overtake a horse. It was, indeed, a time to be alert and work as a team.

Skirting wide of any obstructions that could hide a sleeping bear, Clyde and his father rode warily towards the hill, which encompassed at least a mile of ground, some rocky and mostly tree-covered.

"Pa, when we gonna get rid of Schmidt?"

"When I say so, Clyde, and not a moment sooner. You done shown you can't do anything right. I call all the shots from now on. Understand? Now shut up."

Clyde seethed inside.

They rode on in tense silence for some time. Clyde figured the other men were around the side of the hill now, likely near two miles away. They'd heard no shots.

Rounding a rocky outcropping, Clyde began to speak. His pa stopped him with a hand. Clyde's face reddened with anger at his pa.

"Pa, you got no call to talk down to me!"

"Shut up, Clyde! I'm still the king of the ranch! You will do as you're told. And now I am telling you again – shut up!" Clyde could see a dangerous glint in his pa's eye. Still, he fumed.

A branch broke on the hillside.

Both horses shied and became wide-eyed, fighting the reins. Clyde and his father fought their horses and stared at the hillside, ears seeking any sound. They knew it was best to shoot from the ground, but the horses would not calm.

Another crack!

"Let's get out of here, Clyde!"

Turning to leave, both men were terrified as the monster Grizzly suddenly leapt off the hillside. Clyde spurred his horse and barely missed being clawed. His horse dug at the ground and ran without urging.

87

CEDAR CITY

It was a brief note; just a couple of paragraphs. Nate was headed to Craswell, Colorado. Gideon was in some sort of danger. Buck read the telegraph when it was brought to him. Sighing, he left his office to find Abby.

Buck Ganner stood quietly as Abby read the few lines. When she finished and looked into his eyes, Buck knew and quietly nodded.

Mattie Ganner's eyes were red with weeping that evening at dinner and she barely picked at her food. Buck, who never had a problem eating, was preoccupied and did not finish before pushing his plate to the side. Placing elbows upon the table and resting his chin upon clasped hands, Buck glanced first to Mattie, then to Abby. For a moment he was unable to speak. Before him was a young lady he and Mattie had taken into their home. She was a part of their lives and like a daughter to them.

Abby also picked at her food. Not wanting to make eye contact, she pushed her food around and looked everywhere but at the faces at the table. When Buck spoke, she startled.

"Abby."

She looked into his eyes. Silent words passed between them until he spoke again. His voice was softer than usual and she could feel his emotions.

"When we took you in a few years back, you became as a daughter to us. You know that and we can't deny our love for you. At the same time, we know you have another family that came before us. You've told us the story. Nate has sent letters and, to be honest, it hurt when his first letter came. We saw your thoughts become distant and you'd stare off to the horizon at times. Mattie and I both were very aware of where your thoughts were. We've known your hesitancy to be courted by the local young men. While you have been here, your heart is somewhere else. You have a need for your first family."

Abby tried to stop it, but the tear escaped anyways. She nodded and looked to Mattie, then to Buck.

"You two are very precious to me."

Buck paused again, then spoke with a slight rasp.

"We know. But we also knew when the first letter came from Nate, you would want to find your brothers."

Shifting, Buck reached for his wife's hand and continued. "When the Templeton's were buried, the town sold his outfit. They graciously gave that to us for your care and we put it away. Then, when Nate's first letter came, we started to put a mite away. Mattie put aside some of the egg money, too. All told, it's not as much as we'd like, but it's time you knew. Between the sale of Templeton's wagon and team and what we've put aside, you've got near three hundred dollars. Put that with whatever you've saved from teaching, and you have enough to get to Colorado and then some."

It was like looking through a haze as Abby sought to focus. Tears of both sadness and happiness conflicted in her eyes and her mouth quivered. Before her sat two beloved people who had made all the difference in her life. After all they did for her, it was now time to leave. They knew it and were actually going to help her go. As she wiped the tears, Abby saw Buck and Mattie doing the same.

"Thank you."

88

CRASWELL

When the bear leapt from the hillside, Dan Bowers was turning his horse and inadvertently turned right into the bear. His startled horse had no warning and caught the bear's claws across the neck, screaming in terror.

Falling from the horse, Bowers scrambled to a knoll. He had lost his rifle. With the bear distracted and busy sinking his teeth into the poor horse's neck, Bowers gaped wildly for safety and scrambled for his life over the brush.

Fresh blood running from its jaws, the Grizzly heard the sound and raised his head and looked around. Spotting Bowers, the beast rose to its full fearsome height, sniffed the air and roared a sound to shiver a man's soul. Blood and horse ran from its massive jaws.

Terrified, Dan Bowers desperately grasped for the nearest tree as the bear lunged the too-short distance and snapped his jaws. Bowers' foot was severed completely as he screamed and scrambled upward with all the strength in his arms.

In the distance, Clyde succeeded in stopping his horse. Turning, he saw his father reach the tree. Forcefully turning his reluctant horse, Clyde hurriedly rode to a small rise commanding the scene. Jumping down, he double-wrapped the reins around a tree and grabbed his rifle.

At the top he quickly checked his load and rested his rifle on the branch of a tree. Not seventy-five yards away, he could see his pa clawing up the tree. The Grizzly was incensed and fighting higher, shaking the tree. Perched precariously on a rocky hummock, the tree did not have deep roots and began to shake. The bark was wet with his pa's blood.

Squinting, Clyde could see his pa staring alternately downward and then around, looking for Clyde. His foot and boot lay thrown to the side. A cry of desperation rent the air as Bowers caught a glimpse of his son.

"Shoot him! Hurry!" Clyde heard his pa sobbing as he clawed to the highest branches that could hold his weight. Incensed by the smell of blood, the Grizzly clawed ever more furiously. A snapping root echoed like a gunshot.

Clyde Bowers set his rifle across the tree branch and took careful aim at the bear. Just behind the forelegs he zeroed his sights.

About to squeeze the trigger, he paused. Lifting his head from the stock, a glimmer shown in his eyes. Looking across the space, he locked eyes with his pa. Dan Bowers suddenly winced in lost hope as he knew...

"Clyde..." It was a sobbing whisper heard by no one.

Clyde's eyes glimmered as he whispered quietly to himself as he locked eyes with his pa's.

"What's the matter, Pa? You ain't in charge no more, huh?"

Clyde took his rifle and turned, a smirk crossing his face as he walked down the back side of the rise and untied his horse. Over the hill were the sounds of the bear tearing the tree mingled with the terror-laced sobbing of a man crying out to anybody.

Reining his horse away, Clyde heard a loud crack, a gurgled scream and then...nothing but growling as the bear tore into the lifeless body of the former king of the range.

Riding away, Clyde sat tall in the saddle, nodded his head and grinned broadly.

King of the range. He'd have his clothes moved into the big bedroom tonight.

Tomorrow…tomorrow he'd have the Schmidt ranch. And Mary. A strange light showed in Clyde's eyes.

89

Ruth and Mary stood in the brightening sunrise, hoping to see the men returning. They instead saw nothing. Twice that morning they stopped their labors to peruse the distant hills.

Nearing noon, a distant sound of horses came to their ears and, rushing out to the yard, they spotted several horses riding out of the south.

"Too many, Ma."

"The front man, see how he rides? Clyde…"

"Let's get in the house, Ma."

Ruth Schmidt set her jaw. She had no time to wonder about the fate of her husband. These approaching men could be nothing but trouble. Calmly walking to the door, she reached inside and grasped the well-used double barrel shotgun. Snapping it open, she checked the loads and reached for a

Winchester. Passing the rifle to Mary, Ruth looked her daughter squarely in the eyes.

"If trouble starts, don't hesitate – make every shot count." Ruth set the shotgun inside the door. Mary rested hers by the front window.

"Ma?"

Ruth looked at her daughter.

Mary spoke. "There will be trouble. I can see it already."

Ruth saw resolution in Mary's eyes.

Clyde led the horsemen into the yard and waved his hand. Dust billowed as men fanned out to each side. A horse blew. Mary stood in the doorway, Ruth in front and to her left. As Clyde's eyes ranged to Mary, Ruth stepped firmly in front of her daughter.

"What do you want, Clyde?"

Clyde was grinning, and looked knowingly at the men around him, several of who grinned in return.

"I come to see my future wife. And to look things over, since this will be a part of my ranch now." His eyes ran lingeringly over Ruth.

"In your dreams, Clyde. I thought Dan Bowers called the shots."

"Not any more. He got hisself kilt by a Grizz. I'm in charge now. I'm the king of this range!" His face was smug as he sat tall in the saddle.

Mary's eyes widened at the news. Ruth looked Clyde in the eye.

"Well, you are not king of this range! Vern and I have stood up to varmints for years and we're still here." Ruth was angry. "Get off our land, Clyde Bowers!"

"Well, ma'am, I hate to be the bearer of such bad news, but your husband ran into a problem in the hills and he ain't coming back."

"What happened to him?"

"Done run into some varmints." Clyde chuckled. Then he glared at Mary, looking her up and down with brutal relish. Her shocked look made him chuckle.

"Yep, little miss Mary. Looks like I done won your hand…and a mite more." Mary chilled as his eyes looked her over again.

One of the men sidled his horse toward the side of the house. Ruth Schmidt watched him carefully out of the corner of her eye.

Clyde laughed.

"Ma'am, you might as well just give up. We aim to have this place - everything." He grinned and looked Ruth up and down again.

"Leave this place, Clyde Bowers. You got no right to be here. Our hands will be returning soon."

"Not likely, ma'am. We got them all pinned down at the Forks.

Ruth spoke softly to Mary.

"Into the house." Both ladies backed quickly into the house. Mary slammed the door and dropped the bar.

Clyde waved to a bedraggled man nearby.

"Frenchy. Kick the door down."

Frenchy grinned toothlessly and swaggered to the door.

"Ma'am, I sure hate to mess up this here door. You want to open it, or do I need to kick it in?"

Inside the house, Ruth grasped the shotgun and stepped to face the door. A look of grim determination shone on her face as she eared back the hammers.

"Open the door, Mary. Stay to the side."

"But, Ma! We can't let them in!"

"Open the door, Mary. Open it wide."

Lifting the bar, Mary held it and opened the door, stepping quickly aside. Frenchy stood framed in the opening with thumbs in his belt. A grin lit his face as the door swung open.

Ruth Schmidt lowered the shotgun and fired.

Wide-eyed, Mary looked at her mother. Men outside were milling in confusion after the shock of what happened to Frenchy. Ruth calmly backed in, shutting and barring the door again.

"There's a time to talk and a time to act. That man was trying to get the jump on us. Mary, take care not to show yourself. These shutters will take most bullets, so use the ports."

"Ma! What about Pa? Clyde says he's dead."

"We've not seen a body. Until then we really don't know. Couple times in the past I thought he was gone, but he always showed up. Clyde may just be saying all this to get us to give up, but we will do no such thing!"

Outside, chaos held sway as men fought to hold their horses, some wounded by the shotgun blast. One flailed on the ground, kicking another horse and then a rider as he fell. Scrambling away, the man grasped his side in agony.

"You crazy old heifer! You done drawed the wrong card!" Clyde yelled and signaled the men to fire. Jumping from their horses, they took cover around the yard.

Bullets smacked into the house. Despite fear of Clyde, some of the men did not show a strong sense of wanting to be effective in their fire. Others, shiftless as Clyde, had no scruples about women. They rode for the paycheck. A few shots were high. Still, many shots had effect and found their way into the house. Breaking dishes hit the floor and shattered further. A lamp exploded and oil sprayed on the floor.

90

Vern and Skerby took turns crawling around, finding additional rocks to build a miniature parapet around Laban. They did so even though they knew it would be futile, that the right bullet at the right angle would tear into Laban.

Both were wounded in several places by small ricochets. Though mostly superficial, the wounds still dripped their blood into the dirt. It was the inability to attend to the wounds that made it most difficult. Skerby's calf wound continued to bleed until the constant movement clotted it with dirt.

"I got five more bullets, Skerby."

Skerby was reaching to check his own bullet loops when they heard more gunfire and instinctively ducked. No bullets came their way. Vern craned his eye around the edge of a rock, looking towards their attackers. Gunfire increased.

Soon there came the sound of running horses, fading into the distance. A few minutes later they heard the crack of a twig nearby. Both pivoted with their guns.

"Don't shoot!"

☙

Earlier that day, the stranger paused in a small shallow to rest his horse and to eat. Making a small fire out of dry wood, he knew little smoke would be seen. Placing the small pot over the flames, he sat back, dozing fitfully.

Approaching hoof beats opened his eyes fully. He stood and stepped away from the fire. Not wanting to lose the coffee, he was being protective of his investment.

Three men came at a trot around the bend. Seeing the unexpected stranger in the trail, they reined to a stop and glanced from the man to the coffee.

"Kinda startled us, Mister."

"Looks like you men are headed somewhere in particular." None of the men missed the tied-down gun and the careful way the man brushed his coat back behind.

One man, full of himself and also wearing a tied-down gun, puffed up and sneered.

"Mister. I don't know who you are, but you need to haul yourself somewhere else. You're on Bowers land and we don't need any no-accounts around here. Gonna be some doing's today and we got a man to kill."

"Must be quite a man, with three against one."

"Oh, they's more than that. Gideon will be dead by the end of the day and likely a couple more with him. Some old man what's made trouble. Ol' geezer just come out of the hills and up and butts into Bowers business. Yessir, that there Skerby will die fer shore."

"I might stick around and watch the show."

"Mister, unless you want to die right now, you got about one minute to mount up and ride due east."

Knowing the type, the stranger wryly lifted his eyebrow.

"I'll finish my coffee and be on my way."

"I think maybe we should drink the coffee. You just mount your horse and ride off." The other two men grinned and stepped their horses to each side of the spokesman. One man dug in his saddlebag and withdrew a battered tin cup. Grinning, he feigned to blow the dust out.

"I think not."

Eyebrows raised in shock, the spokesman looked down.

"Mister, you don't have a choice."

"Neither do you. You've blown your mouth, now you've got yourself and these two men into something you can't finish. You are a loud-mouthed, two-bit wanna-be and today is the end of the trail."

"What?"

"Make your play!"

Ten minutes later, the stranger rode off, content with the taste of fresh coffee. Behind him he left three men. Two were trussed tightly and the third needed no ropes.

Later, walking into the Gold Horse saloon in Craswell, he noted the sparse crowd looking casually at him. No glances lingered. It was obvious this group was used to seeing strangers. Food for thought. Along the wall near the door, two older men sat over a chess game. A couple of other small groups sat at nearby tables. Not even a dozen men.

"What'll it be, stranger?"

"Whiskey. The good bottle."

Noting the bartender's empty look made him wonder, as he had before, about these men who tended bar. Every town across the West had such a man. They heard everything, saw everything, yet never spoke. Cowboys and all who were down in their luck poured their hearts out to these men as they polished the bar with a towel, and many who connived spoke as if there was not a witness standing washing beer mugs two feet away. It was an unspoken rule that bartenders kept their mouths shut. Yet, for the right motivation they opened up – that meaning if it concerned women, children or the ringing of a coin upon the bar.

There was an extra coin now, and the bartender glanced up and saw eyes determined, calm, but... eyes that would take no nonsense.

"Looking for information about a friend."

"Who might that friend be?"

"Man name of Gideon Henry." He spoke deliberately loud enough to be overheard. Conversation paused in the room. One old man paused with a hand in the air holding a card.

"Mister, been a lot going on around here lately." The bartender scanned the room. All safe ears, but one could never know.

"He's around here?"

"Yep. Word has it he's been at the Schmidt ranch."

The man holding the queen cleared his throat.

"Mister, they's been a lot of nonsense going on around here. They done tried to kill that there Gideon, but he got away. Now they think they got him treed again in the hills, along with Vern Schmidt, one of the best men around." The other men looked wide-eyed at the speaker as he placed the queen on the board and kept talking.

"You all know what I'm talking about! Mister, I hear tell they's been shots fired at the Lazy-S. Passing cowhand heard them this morning."

"You say Schmidt is gone, up in the hills with Gideon?"

"Yep."

"Who's left at the ranch?"

"Dunno. Maybe just the womenfolk. But Ruth Schmidt ain't one to trifle with."

Throwing back his drink, the others watched as the stranger pulled his pistol, spun the cylinder, checked the loads and holstered the gun again. Turning and striding to the door, he gave pause at the chess game and nodded to the man who had spoken.

"Mister, you got a name?"

"Teague."

Eyes wide, the men sat silent and watched the batwings spring back and forth, the squeak fading with each swing.

91

BATTLE WAGON

A smothering cloud of dust rolled into Battle Wagon, rapidly overtaking the stage as it jarred to a ghostly halt in front of the saloon. Passengers coughed and squinted as the dust covered them from head to foot. Hopping down with a spring belying his advanced years, the grizzled and tobacco-stained driver opened the coach door. Two well-dressed gentlemen stepped down, followed by the worn duds of a short and rotund drummer. After reaching up for his carpetbag, the drummer threw it on the nearby steps and wobbled into the saloon to wash the dust from his throat. From his appearance, the two gentlemen figured he spent more time washing down the dust than was really necessary.

Stretching and taking the measure of the town, the more experienced man looked over the brands and, seeing a couple Star-3's, motioned to his companion.

They wandered into the bar after pausing first to re-move their hats and make a feeble attempt at slapping the dust off their clothes. They noted the drummer already slugging down shots. He had been a know-it-all and was not a pleasant traveling companion. The last thirty miles were passed in a dust-filled silence.

Walking to the bar and ordering drinks, both took savoring sips. Bill Henry looked at the bartender.

"Looking for a friend of mine, came by here a few days back likely. Name of Teague."

"He was in, spoke with those hands yonder." He nodded towards some dusty riders at a table playing a half-hearted game of poker. Turning to the men, one caught his eye. Bill nodded.

"Would you kind gentlemen have any informa-tion regarding a friend of mine, name of Teague?" Flipping a coin to the bar and tilting his head, the bartender read the age-old cue and walked a bottle to the men's table. To a one, they nodded.

A man pushed his hat back. "You Henry?"

"Bill Henry. This here's Nate."

"Teague was in here a couple days back, planning to go to the ranch with us to buy cattle. He done heard about some doings about a hunnert mile from here over to Craswell. Somethin' to do with a fella named Gideon. Changed his mind about stayin', said to let you know when you come in."

"Livery hire out horses here?"

"Yup."

Bill Henry finished his drink. "Let Dirkson know we'll be back to buy cattle. Just gotta take care of a family matter first."

A few moments later they were through the batwings.

"Don't that just beat all," the cowhand said as he rubbed his chin and ruffled the cards.

92

CRASWELL

Skerby glared at Gideon.

"Took long enough. You stop to make coffee or something while your friends were getting shot at?"

Gideon looked at the men, concerned at their wounds but relieved to see them alive. Laban crawled out of the hole and ran to embrace his pa.

"A cup of coffee'd taste good right about now. How bad's your head wound, Vern?" Gideon limped to a rock and slowly eased down, sighing deeply.

"I'll make it. You look like you're carrying more lead."

"Just a nasty flesh wound. Lost blood though." Gideon shifted his leg. "You get any of them no-accounts?"

"Couple. I need to check."

Skerby spit. "Grab some gun belts, Vern. We need bullets. I'll see if they left any horses around. They ran ours off."

Returning a few minutes later, Vern passed around a couple of gun belts and a Winchester. Gideon commented to the rocks.

"I assume those men didn't need them anymore."

"Not where they're going."

Both men held their guns ready as Skerby appeared.

"Hold your fire. I didn't find no horses, but we may find one wandering."

Vern looked at the sky and spoke.

"Long walk home. Better start. The women folk will be a mite put out. I'm ready to wrap myself around some of Ruth's biscuits."

93

Gun smoke filled the house as Mary and Ruth continued to go from window to window, making a point of not creating a pattern.

Ruth paused and looked at her daughter, smiling grimly.

"Doing well, Mary. I think you winged one pretty good. Heard him yell. I got the one by the barn, I think. Not been any firing from there since." Ruth wiped the hair from her face, Mary saw her mother's hand come away bloody.

"Ma! How bad is it?"

"Just grazed me. Take care to stay out of sight; don't linger too long with your barrel out of the port or they'll have a target." She grabbed a kitchen towel and wiped the side of her face.

Both ladies turned at the creak of a porch board. Looking to Mary, Ruth squinted and stepped back, crouching in the corner, gesturing at Mary to do the same. As Mary crouched, a shot tore through a shutter, ripping a board off and plowing into the fireplace, sending fragments through the room.

Ruth raised the shotgun and sent a blast at an angle through the shutter, creating a bigger hole, but also a cry and the sound of a heavy body hitting the floor.

Now there was a large hole for the men outside to aim for and they concentrated on it. Mary crawled to the other room and continued to fire.

94

An hour after they began walking, they spotted two horses at a small spring, reins dragging. They were saddled, with rifles and canteens. Skerby moved slowly towards them, talking softly. Skittish, the beasts balked some, but finally allowed him to gather their reins.

They rode double for a couple hours when they found Vern's horse grazing. Riding with his father, they all now made good time. Stopping to rest later at a tree-surrounded seep known to Vern, they dismounted to water the horses and see to their wounds. Suddenly the sound of approaching horses came to them and they rose quickly. There were three riders, all Bowers men.

Gideon stepped out as they approached the trees, causing the surprised men to haul their reins. As the horses stopped Gideon spoke:

"Bowers men on Schmidt range. Something must be up. Likely no good."

Vern stepped out of the other side of the brush, Winchester held in a friendly manner but so that it could be swung readily to bear on the riders. Recognizing two of the riders, he nodded, eyes resting briefly on the third man.

"Hooch, Batt. Long ways from home and you're coming from the wrong direction."

"Ain't no laws agin' crossin' land. 'Sides, this is Bowers land now."

"Just takin' land now? Even Dan Bowers knows better than that."

"Old Bowers is dead! Got hisself kilt by a Grizzly. Clyde Bowers sees things a mite different."

Vern's brow crinkled.

"There is law around here still!"

"Well, I suspect things has changed. Clyde Bowers calls the shots now."

All three Rocking-B riders laughed, but kept their hands away from their guns.

"Right now you need to drop your guns."

"Ok, Schmidt. It'll buy you a little time, but the end is the same. Time for you to load your wagon and seek the wild frontier somewhere else."

Carefully, all three riders eased their guns out and tossed them to the ground. Gideon noted the unknown rider holding his hand oddly. He cocked his rifle, a sound readily noticed by everyone.

"Mister, I don't know what your problem is, but you've got one! I want those hands in the air, and I want them up now!"

The man slowly raised his hands.

"Vern, the man has a hide-out gun behind his belt. Get it."

Vern ran his hand along the man's belt, returning with an ancient .28 Baby Patterson. He looked at Gideon, who smiled. Some said the gun was too small to harm anybody, but a hole is a hole and the right hole with a small bore is just as deadly as a .44.

"Any more weapons, stranger? Best come clean."

"Pig-sticker in my left boot. I ain't lookin' for trouble. Fact is, I been gettin' a hankerin' to see new country, maybe out Californey way."

"I'll give you that choice. I hear the weather in California is healthier than here. Stay here and face the music, or leave. But if I ever see you again, I'll draw first."

"I'm a'leavin. Can I have my gun?"

"Vern, shuck his shells and put it in his saddle-bag. Keep the Patterson."

After the man rode off, Gideon looked at the others.

"You men want to leave or stick around?"

"A few more days and this land will all be Rocking-B range. I reckon to stick around."

"Get off the horses."

Skerby tied the men securely, perhaps gaining too much pleasure in drawing the ropes tight. Both men scowled at him in turn.

Vern gathered the horses.

"Hey, you ain't taking our horses!"

Vern was grim as they mounted. Catching Vern's eye, Gideon squinted at him.

"Vern, a man ought not to be out here unarmed." He cast a quick glance at Laban and then at the Patterson. Vern understood and looked at his son.

"Laban, you been taught how to use a gun, now this one is for you. Take care with it."

Laban's eyes widened as he held the gun and, glancing back at his father, checked the loads.

"Thanks, Pa."

Gideon smiled…a rare thing in recent years.

Skerby saw the smile, squinted, spat tobacco and looked at the sky.

"Ok, y'all. Let's ride."

95

Ruth and Mary fought well in a desperate situation, taking no chances. They knew the house was a fort and the only way the men could get them out was by a stray bullet or fire. They also knew most of the bullets were not being aimed well. As vile as the men may be, there was still the chivalrous attitude toward women and the men likely would not set fire to the house – unless Clyde did so himself. With bullets they would always be able to claim it was the other who fired the shot, but all would know who set a fire. Yet there was no doubt the odds of getting hit by a bullet were high.

Their eyes stung with gun smoke. Tear lines coursed their cheeks. Ruth wanted nothing better than to open the door and windows and fan the bad air out with a towel. She squatted by the mantle and wiped the tears from her eyes. She squinted and peered through a hole. Chips flew as a bullet struck close. Wiping the splinters from her face, she stuck a shotgun through the hole and pulled both triggers, almost falling over backwards. The odds of killing a man were not good, but at least the blast would keep them hunkering behind cover and, if she did chance to hit something, it would be a warning to them all. No problem with firepower or shells in the house.

Ruth and Vern learned early they needed plenty of shells around, and though it was inconvenient at times to have a bag of shotgun shells or cartridges or even cap and ball sitting around, it was better than having to run around looking when they were needed.

Vern! Ruth fought the panic. Was he really dead? Had he found their son? He wouldn't go easily, this man of hers. She knew from experience that he would fight viciously when pushed. There was no back-up in him. She wiped a tear that had nothing to do with the acrid gunsmoke billowing throughout the room. Then a fire glinted in Ruth's eye and she set her jaw.

Breaking the gun, she withdrew the spent shells, slapped two new ones home and snapped the gun together with a purpose. Standing well back, she looked for another target. Seeing a man peering from around the barn she shoved the double barrel through and let go with both again. Hearing a scream and a curse, she smiled and broke the gun again.

Mary was firing though the shutter in her parents' bedroom. She, too, was having thoughts of her father, but the needs of the moment kept her occupied. She refused to believe her pa or Laban were dead. Brushing a wisp of hair from her eyes, Mary bent to peer from the gun port and flew back as a bullet took her through the shoulder. Falling against a dresser, she screamed.

Ruth was at her side in moments, panic in her eyes. Pulling Mary's dress from her shoulder, she peered through the murk at the wound. She felt along the back and found no exit hole. The bullet was lodged inside, probably against the bone. The blood was not surging, so Ruth jerked open the nearest dresser drawer and stuffed the corner of a shirt into the wound as Mary grimaced in agony.

Outside, Clyde heard the scream and signaled for the men to stop.

"Garvey! Go see what you can see."

A man scampered to the porch and carefully leaned to one gun port and peered in. Ducking down, he shook his head at Clyde. Clyde gestured to the next port, wider from well-placed bullets. Garvey was seen to take a deep breath. He crawled along the porch floor, rising to peer into the opening. Seeing nothing at first and raising higher, the silence was suddenly rent by the blast of the shotgun again and the man fell screaming and grasping at his head. Grazed by several shot, the man held his head and cowered against the wall. Ruth had heard the porch creak and saw the man as he dropped from the first window. She guessed correctly which window was next in line. Crawling frantically, the wounded man scampered off the porch and behind a trough.

Ruth was now a desperate and angry mother defending her child.

Clyde swallowed and gestured and a fusillade tore through the hole in the shutters.

But Ruth was seasoned and stepped back and to the side as the bullets tore into the house and plowed through her treasured kitchen cabinet. Crouching, she ran to the bedroom again and stooped. Incensed, she placed a folded blanket under Mary's head. Mary lay unconscious.

An hour later, Ruth stood firm, moving from one window to the next. She had few shotgun shells left and was carrying the Winchester. Blood smeared her face from where a shard of wood sliced her forehead.

Just like the old days, she thought wryly. Except her daughter lay wounded and needed doctoring. Needed it badly.

96

Ruth carefully sighted on a man behind the trough attempting to work closer. Peering through a small crack, she realized he was carrying a shotgun! If he got that barrel into the confines of the house it would be deadly!

She fired as the man dashed for the porch, winging him in the leg. He was out of her reach now! Ruth heard a volley pepper the front of the house as she dashed for the bedroom. They were endangering their own man! Slamming the bedroom door, she pulled Mary behind the bed.

They couldn't hold out. It was just a matter of minutes till the men would be inside. She checked the shotgun and jacked another shell into the chamber of the Winchester.

Another volley, then a yell. She waited for the expected shotgun blast, but it never came. Instead, there was a distant shot and Ruth heard someone yell. More shots rang out, but none appeared to be aimed for the house.

Someone was shooting at Clyde and the others! It sounded like a single shooter by the spacing of the shots. Peering through a shutter, Ruth saw two of the Rocking-B riders looking to a small hummock a few hundred yards distant.

Bending down to Mary, Ruth noted the bleeding had lessened. Still, she knew her daughter desperately needed attention. Careful to stay out of the line of fire as she passed shutters, Ruth filled a pitcher and went to wipe Mary's brow.

As the shots continued, Ruth once again took up the shotgun and fired from the front of the house. Suddenly there was a lull and she heard distant shots from another direction. Ruth squinted and turned her head to listen. The sound of racing horses pounded and faded. Then other horses approached.

"Ruth!"

It was Vern! She raced to the front of the house and peered through a port. Vern stood in the yard. He had Laban!

"Ruth! Open up, I'm back and Clyde's men are gone."

Slamming open the door, she ran to Vern's arms. One hand reached to Laban, who grasped her hand.

"Vern, quick! Mary's been hit."

Happening to glance at Gideon, she saw his mouth tighten. Vern ran to the house with Ruth. Gideon was about to follow when Skerby came around the corner of the barn with a man, arms in the air, dragging a leg. Blood stained his pant leg. A bandanna was tied above the knee.

"Found this scoundrel tryin' to get away. The rest of that bunch left him behind and his horse done run off."

Gideon limped to the man, grabbed him by the shirtfront and slammed his jaw with a fist. Screaming, the man fell to the ground. Reaching for him again, Skerby yelled.

"No, Gideon! We need this man!"

Gideon breathed heavily, and looked from the man to Skerby, then back to the man who cowered on the ground. The look on Gideon's face was death warmed over. He almost hissed as he spoke in a half-whisper.

"So help me, if anything happens to Mary, you will die a slow death."

Vern came out on the porch.

"Bullet's still in…gotta be taken out. We'll need the doctor. Time's important."

Skerby spoke gently. "Vern, you're right - time is important. Ain't no time to wait on the doctor. I can get the bullet out. I done it a lot in the war and in the mountains. Learned it from the army docs. I even done it to myself once." Looking to the others wounds, he pursed his lips. "You all needs to take turns tending to each other whilst we's inside."

Vern looked at Skerby and paused only a moment before nodding. Skerby looked hard at Gideon. "Tie the man up so he can't get away, but don't hit him no more!" He then hurried into the house.

A glance into the distance brought Gideon's hand to his gun.

"There's someone coming!"

A man walked slowly towards them in the distance, leading a horse. Gideon turned, gun out, to face the man, who walked casually, hands swaying easily with his walk. He was unafraid, a man aware, a man assured. Yet his right hand was swinging close to his gun. Face shadowed by his hat, the stranger drew close.

Gideon tilted his head to block the sun's glare and squinted. Recognition dawned.

Lem Teague.

97

Gideon stood on the porch as Skerby operated on Mary on the kitchen table, gently easing the bullet out with a knife Ruth boiled on the stove. Laban went to the barn, concern for his sister mingled with a sense of responsibility to do chores.

Gideon had helped open the windows, fan out the gun smoke and clear the table. Holding Mary's head as they carried her to the table, he saw her eyes flicker open briefly. She looked at Gideon and a smile turned the corner of her mouth. Touching his hand gently with hers, she winced and lapsed into unconsciousness.

Ruth looked at him, then down at her daughter.

"Gideon, it's best you leave. We got to uncover her partway and it's not fittin' for you to be here."

His heart lurched as he heard Mary cry out a few minutes later. He squeezed his hands tightly.

Standing at the corral looking into the distance, Gideon did not shift his eyes as Teague came to stand nearby.

"You're about the last person I expected to see, Lem."

Lemuel Teague nodded and smiled.

"Came out to buy cattle, then ran into some gents speaking of some trouble over to some town by the name of Craswell. Didn't think much of it till your name was mentioned. Decided the cattle weren't going anywhere and thought I'd mosey over."

"Good time to show up."

"God's timing is always good." Gideon glanced over. Lem Teague had once been a preacher.

They stood together a while, saying nothing. Though cousins by blood, there was a similarity in their lives bonding deeper than blood. Both gunmen due to tragedy, Lem Teague for years was a dreaded gunman known as "Preacher" but had settled and started a new life.

Gideon placed his heel on the lowest rail and leaned into the fence, placing his arms on the upper rail. Seeming to look intently into the distance, his eyes focused inward.

"Lem?"

"Hmm?"

"How did you know it was time to let go of your anger and get your life back again?"

Lem Teague's eyebrows rose at the question.

"It was several things, actually. I guess I realized living an angry life was getting me nowhere and it certainly wasn't going to bring back the life I wished I'd had. The path I trod was leading to more unhappiness and it was bringing unhappiness to others. Something inside told me if I continued on the same path, I would reach the end of my life without ever really having lived again. It was like God telling me He had a better plan for my life and that, like Job, He would give back to me the years the locust had eaten. But I had to stop, 'cause it seemed God was on my tail but I was running so fast He couldn't catch me. He used a situation, and a few people, to show me there is more to life than living in anger and longing for something that will never return. Of course, there was this wonderful young lady that played a part in it." He paused. "I'm a happy man again, Gideon."

Gideon squinted and nodded. Lem Teague looked to the house, then to his cousin.

"Seems to me it's thinking time, Gideon. The locusts have chewed up too many years."

Both men turned as the cabin door opened and Skerby stood stretching his back. Gideon saw the man's eyes widen and Skerby stiffly approached. Drawing close, he nodded to Lem.

"Teague. Didn't expect to see you here. Can't say as I'm any disappointed that God done sent the cavalry."

Teague smiled and retorted.

"You don't need me, Skerby. I see you've still got the LeMat. That center barrel is worth a troop of men."

"Yep, but it still ain't but worth one shot and then I got to get up off the ground. An' I can't get up near as quick as I used to. Got to turn to my knees, then look fer somethin' to hoist up on."

Teague laughed.

"Good to see you, Skerby!"

"How's Grace and Luke? Kinda miss your wife's biscuits."

"Both are doing fine. Grace is with child."

Gideon interrupted.

"How is Mary?"

Skerby shook his head.

"We got the bullet out, but she'd lost a lot of blood. Needs a long rest."

Gideon glanced at the house. After a moment he shook his head, looking from Teague to Skerby.

"You two know each other?"

"Skerby and me became acquainted back home. Had a scrap we fought in. There's not a better man to have by your side, Gideon. But he sure can eat a sight of grub – especially biscuits."

Skerby glared.

Ruth came out, looked around and called to Gideon. When he stood beside her, she placed a gentle hand upon his shoulder.

"She's a'hurtin' bad, but she's asking for you."

Walking into the room, Gideon stood a moment to let his eyes adjust to the dim light.

Mary lay on the bed, the covers over her except for her wounded shoulder. The bandages were bloody in the middle where the blood was not yet clotted as they wrapped the wound. He grimaced realizing the scar she would carry.

Ruth walked in.

"Bullet was clear against the bone. Had broken up a bit, but Skerby thinks no major damage. But she'll take some healing." Wiping Mary's brow with a wet cloth wrung in a basin, she looked at Gideon. "She's precious to me, Gideon. I want a good life for her."

He nodded.

"No running from place to place. No disappearing just to show up somewhere else."

He nodded.

"Just a regular life, a peaceful life. That's what we've worked for."

Again the nod.

"I want the same for you, Gideon."

He nodded again. Lem's words rang in his mind: "The years the locust had eaten."

Mary's head turned and she looked up at him. Weakly, she grasped his hand.

"Stay with me, Gideon."

"I'll be here, Mary." She smiled and closed her eyes.

98

Vern stood on the porch staring into the hills. Ruth came and stood beside him.

"No sign of Jose or the others. This is not good. I can tell you it must have something to do with Bowers."

"Vern! Clyde said that Dan Bowers was killed by a bear."

"Dan Bowers! He maybe was losing it, but there was still a spark of sanity there. I'm not sure if there's any left in Clyde. This is far from over, Ruth."

Ruth grabbed Vern's elbow and rested her face against his shoulder.

❦

Manuel and Paulo were in a battle for their very lives. On their way back from the Chinese camp they rounded a ridge and saw tracks of cattle and horses. A large bunch of cattle were being herded! Riding in pursuit, a barrage of gunfire took them by surprise. One horse was down and the other ran off as Paulo kicked loose of the stirrups. Manuel was hurt badly, with a bullet through the chest. Puffs of dust flew around as Paulo dragged the wounded man to a small ridge nearby affording a semblance of shelter.

Manuel groaned and looked up at Paulo, whispering.

"It is not good, Paulo. I am hit hard and I cannot be of help to you."

"Sit quietly, my friend. Jose is out here somewhere." Paulo looked to Manuel's wound and, turning him slightly, found the exit wound. He looked grim at the quantity of blood running. Pulling the bandanna from his neck, Paulo twisted a corner tightly and used it to plug the exit hole. Manuel grimaced and lost consciousness. Paulo knew his friend needed attention quickly, but there was no chance. Bullets pelted the ridge of dirt in front of him that was barely enough to shield them.

Where was Jose? He split off a mile back to follow another set of tracks. Perhaps it was best he was not with them, or they might all be pinned down. At least now there was an element of hope.

From the sounds of the guns, there were at least three to four ambushers pinning them down. Paulo dug his hands into the dirt and began to dig, to deepen their cover. Yet the dirt was hard. Rising up slightly to pull the dirt out he screamed as a bullet creased his back and plowed through his suddenly exposed calf.

Bullets pelted with determination and Paulo looked to his friend's face. Manuel remained mostly unconscious.

"Manuel, I'm not sure we're going to make it through this."

Jose rode a few miles away driving a small group of cattle. Too few cattle. There should be hundreds of cattle to be rounded up, but it was clear to him that they were being bled dry.

Stopping to give his horse a breather, Jose turned his head at the sound of distant shots.

Manuel and Paulo! The sound came from roughly where they would be. More shots. Probably three or four miles away. Spurring his horse, Jose sped off at a gallop.

99

It was obvious they were marked for death.

That they were not both killed with the first shots was a miracle of horse movements and the ground they rode on. Obviously the ambushers came close to succeeding with Manuel. From the continued firing over the past couple hours Paulo knew the intent was to keep them pinned down without access to water, letting wounds and nature take a slow course.

Paulo was weary. Each time he attempted to raise his head, a flurry of shots drove him to hug the ground more deeply. Manuel was slipping deeper into unconsciousness and his own wound desperately needed attention. The bullet entered the top of his calf and exited near the ankle. He was almost blind with the pain, but managed to fire an occasional shot to let the attackers know there was still fight in them. In reality there was little fight left. They needed help, badly!

Where was Jose? Paulo carefully wiped his brow then, fearing for his friend's life, reached a hand to Manuel's shoulder and said a quick prayer.

As if in answer, there was a sudden shot from their rear and a few answering shots that did not hit the dirt parapet Paulo had raised. Glancing to a ridge a quarter mile away, Paulo saw sunlight glimmer off a rifle barrel and heard the report. Suddenly the fusillade directed at him and Manuel was focused in the distance. Paulo heard less firing from the ambushers. Jose was an excellent rifle shot, and it must be Jose they were hearing. Paulo felt a surge of hope. He lay back, tired and worn by the sun and battle.

Shortly there was a complete stop to the shooting and, perhaps fifteen minutes later, Paulo heard approaching hoof beats and Jose singing to identify himself. As he neared, Paulo waved and Jose sprang from his horse to attend to his friends.

"Manuel is in bad shape."

Jose turned his brother and looked at the wounds

"He is barely with us. And you are not good. I will build a fire."

"The horses?"

"Manuel's is dead and yours has run off. We must attend to the wounds."

"Could you tell who the attackers were?"

"Not by sight, but as they ran off, I swear I saw a dappled mustang."

"One of Bowers' new men rides a dappled mustang."

Jose kindled a fire and heated a cup full of water and began to bathe Manuel's wounds. The man was hurt badly. Yet, Manuel had always been a fighter. He had much to fight for.

100

Gideon and Skerby used ropes to drag the bodies a good distance from the ranch yard before burying them. Neither one was in shape for extra labor, so they lay the bodies next to a brushy bank and caved the dirt over.

"Doggone, Gideon. Ever wonder how flies know when there's a dead body? They come from everywhere. I recollect the time I was down on the Mex border during the war for Texas. There were near a hundred bodies an' the flies. Land sakes, it was like one of them plagues God pulled on Pharaoh...you ain't listenin, is you?"

No response. Skerby wrinkled his brow in thought. Gideon had a distant look about him.

Later they loosed the man from the corral post and pushed him to one of the horses they caught. Lifting the man bodily to the saddle, Gideon tied the man's feet under the horse's belly and his hands to the pommel. He gave the man an unwavering glare as he finished cinching the rope.

"Now, I've got a message for you to take to Clyde. If you try and skip out before you give the message, I will hunt you down. Understand?"

"Yessir."

"Tell Clyde I am coming to town after him. Day after tomorrow, shortly before noon. Got it?"

"Yessir."

Vern slapped the horse and it cantered out of the ranch yard in the direction of town.

"You sure about this, Gideon?" Vern knew the answer.

"It's got to be cleared up, Vern. Clyde has to be stopped."

"He'll be there with an army."

"I know."

"I got to defend my family, Gideon."

"I know you have to stay here, and it's the right thing to do. If something bad happens in town, you'll need to be here. They'll be all over you."

"If you fail, I got no choice. I'll have to get out best I can. We'll have to move Mary out in a wagon."

"I have no intention of that happening, Vern."

Both men stood and stared to the sunset. The colors were grand this time of year. Neither man took notice.

🖎

The next day, Mary awakened very weak, but aware. She tried to get up but was stopped by her mother and the wrenching pain. Grimacing, she lay back gasping and fell back to fitful half-sleep, awaking again in the afternoon.

Gideon sat with Mary that afternoon, talking now and then in hushed tones in the brief moments Mary was awake. Ruth politely kept a distance, but watched knowingly. At one point, Mary's hand reached up and lightly caressed the side of Gideon's face. He did not move away.

"I am willing to move anywhere, Gideon. If it takes that to get you a new start."

"I'm not sure we'll have to do that. Not many people knew who I was. Most of those who do around here will be leaving. I just want a new beginning. I want my new life….but there's something I've got to do. As a man. I can't run. It's not in me."

"I know, Gideon. Do what you must." She then drifted to sleep.

Both he and Skerby slept in the barn that night. Without sharing thoughts, both cleaned and oiled their guns. Lem Teague faded into the hills earlier that evening, saying he was doing some scouting.

"Skerby, you don't have to be in this fight."

"It's personal now."

"Don't take chances."

"I ain't no fool, Gideon. You worry about yourself. Now, I ain't good with a gun like you is, so's I got to use my head more."

101

To any early morning eyes or those making trips to the outhouse in the confusing light between night and dawn, he would appear as a teenage child unless those same eyes managed a close-up view. Squinting, he looked for a place to hole up until he could get the lay of the land.

It had been a difficult trip. After the trip in the baggage car to Wichita, Wang had run into constant difficulties with men trying to cheat him or abuse him. In one train yard outside Wichita he was accosted by a group of ruffian youth in the early morning. Dozing by the side of the station with some time before the ticket office opened, he was suddenly kicked and fell to the ground. Looking up, he stared around at five boys with something to prove. Knowing their intent and seeing a familiar look in their eyes, Wang did not hesitate. Swinging his carpetbag, he knocked two over and took the moment of confusion to pull a derringer. Wide-eyed, the youths backed off, then turned and ran.

It would be but minutes before they would tell a story and Wang would be in jail and subject to abusive justice! Taking his leave, he dashed under the train to the far side and hurried down the line to the farthest end from the station, looking for an open freight car. Finding one near the end, he scampered inside, put his shoulder to the door and, pushing with all his might, shoved the door to almost closed when it jammed.

Outside he heard excited voices farther down. Scanning the boxcar, Wang spotted a small pile of crates at one end of the car and quickly hunkered behind the pile as voices approached and hands reached for the door. Sounds of an argument reached his ears.

"This one's jammed. He couldn't be in here!" It was a man's voice.

"I swear I seen a leg go in one of these here cars, mister."

"Boys, I got other things to do than play your games. Now git!" Running feet grew fainter and the slower steps of the man receded.

Wang sighed with relief, turning to lean against the wall as the whistle blew and the train began to inch away. As he lifted his eyes his heart sunk as he spotted another man standing at the far end of the car, disheveled and obviously not of the kind he wanted to know. As the train gained speed, the man came closer and fingered a knife, grinning toothlessly.

Getting the door unjammed and tossing the man's unconscious body out drained him. Settling behind the crates, he fell asleep.

Finding a horse took some skill and more cash than was fair. Watching his back trail was second nature, but out here he did not miss the looks of any nearby when he paid in gold for his purchases. He had to keep moving and leave the bad element guessing. His many days on the trail were focused on staying out of sight as much as possible.

It had been two weeks since he left home. Chinese were frowned upon and it took tact and skill to buy his food. Now he was in Craswell and really longed for a good meal. It seemed like forever since he'd eaten decent food.

Crawling into the woodshed behind the livery, Wang looked to make sure nobody saw him. Pulling a small blanket from his bag, he settled into a weary sleep.

102

Gideon awakened and looked around in the early half-light. Skerby was gone.

Arising stiffly, he noted the man's horse also missing. How did he sleep so hard as to miss Skerby riding off?

Sounds of dishes clinking came from the house and Laban came running to the barn.

"Morning, Gideon! Ma says for you to come eat."

"Be right there, gonna see to my horse." Laban ran back to the house. Not really hungry, Gideon would sit with the family just to be social, while in his mind and heart he prepared himself for the day. There was no way to know exactly what he would face today, or whether he would be badly wounded...or even if he would survive. In the past he faced one man, or at the most two. No telling today, except there likely would be several. For sure, Clyde would have no scruples and the unexpected should be anticipated. Clyde would no doubt bring as many men as he could.

Skerby and Teague. He knew Lem would be beside him without even posing the question. It's what family did and he and Lem had a closeness others did not understand.

Where the devil was Skerby anyhow? Somewhat of a mystery, he knew nothing of the man except he was old, had been around and popped up at odd times. Gideon knew the man could be counted on in a fight, and would stand through the gun smoke but, still, he was an old man. He feared for Skerby. Skerby really had no place in this fight, and was just a wandering man.

Sitting at the table, he sipped coffee and picked at some eggs and side meat. He knew he'd need strength, yet his appetite wouldn't come. Finally he settled for the coffee.

Conversation was minimal. Halfway through, Vern spoke.

"Confound it, Gideon! I want to be there!"

"I know, Vern. But your place is here with your family. Just in case."

"Just in case isn't helping you none."

"It'll help me most to know that you are here, protecting...your family." Neither Vern nor Ruth missed his glance toward Mary's room.

"I'll fix some fried chicken tonight, Gideon." Ruth forced a smile. Gideon looked up and locked eyes with her for a brief moment.

"I'll look forward to it. Anybody see sign of Skerby this morning?"

"Laban said he's gone. Don't suppose he's flown the coop?"

"Not that old codger. More than likely he's got something up his sleeve."

"Lem left before sun up."

"He'll be there when needed, I think."

103

Bill and Nate shared a fire the night before with a trapper on his way through to the high lonesome. Fresh-brewed coffee scented the air and they followed their noses to the campfire.

Both knew better than to ride in unannounced to a remote fire in the West. It was a good way to get a bullet through the brisket. Bill spoke softly.

"Hello, the camp!" Hearing a hammer click, they received the response.

"Come in, and welcome. Keep your hands where I can see them. I don't want to see nothin' in 'em but a coffee cup."

They helped themselves to coffee and noticed the man's saddlebags were light and the pan showed but two strips of bacon. A very small packet set to the side. Provisioned well and having stocked up at Battle Wagon, Bill reached for his pack. A pistol cocked behind him.

"Mister, you go steady with that gun. I'm not trying anything."

"Better you don't." Yet the man's eyes grew as Bill turned to the fire with a large slab of bacon. Soon several thick slices sizzled in the pan and the friendship was palpable.

"Mighty nice of you, stranger. I was a bit low on provisions. Not been a good year for cash money and figured to get up to the hills and shoot some dinner."

"Been around here a while?"

"Nope. Just planned on stayin' a few days to have a mite of town experience before heading up for a few months. Lost my wad in a poker game and headed out early. Just so happens it's cheaper to stay out here than it is to stay in town. Room is free. Board takes a bit of effort, though!" He chuckled and they joined in.

"What's the town like?"

"Not the place to be tomorrow, if you want the truth. Supposed to be some sort of fight between someone named Bowers and a stranger named Gideon something or other. Seems like this Bowers wants to control the area and Gideon done messed up his plans. Gideon fella done sent the challenge. You boys best enjoy the outside for a day before you go galavantin' into Craswell. Not telling you what to do – just a suggestion."

"Thanks." Turning to look at both Bill and Nate, the man saw their looks and grinned.

"You folks is goin' in, ain't you?"

"Yep."

Bill and Nate left before first light. The trapper listened as they loaded and then fell back to sleep. As hoof beats receded, he turned over and glanced to the fire. Beside the coffeepot rested the slab of bacon, a sack of cornmeal and a packet of coffee.

"I'll be durned."

104

Dusty from the long ride, the rider glanced up the street of the barely awakening town. Her eyes caught the parting of curtains as townsfolk wondered who might be coming into town before the breakfast dishes were put away.

What they saw was a slender young lady, thick blond hair flowing in the wind. A dusty broadcloth dress clung to her slender frame as the half-light prevented a good look from those peering with sleepy eyes. Riding astraddle the horse, her dress spent most of the fast ride bunched at her knees from the wind. Such show of flesh would have awakened even the sleepiest eyes.

Seeing a lantern moving in a mercantile down the street, the young lady cantered to the hitch rail as a still bleary-eyed shopkeeper opened the doors for the early morning crowd, or maybe just to get away from home.

Surprised to see a young lady, dusty and worn from a long ride, pull to the front, the shopkeeper rubbed his head.

"Good morning, young lady."

"Good morning, sir. I realize I surprised you, but I need to know where a young lady might find a room in town."

"Mite early, ma'am, but I might suggest you check with Mrs. Griner. They's rooms at the hotel, but you might be more comfortable staying elsewhere. Mrs. Griner has a room she lets out for ladies now and then. I think you might fit best there, miss…?"

"Abby. Abby Henry."

"Henry…hm." The man scratched his head again.

"Sir? Where might I find Mrs. Griner?"

The shopkeeper pointed up the street.

"Little yellow house on the south side of the street, just the other side of the livery."

As Abby turned her horse, the shopkeeper's eyes followed her, wondering. Finally turning to go inside, his eyes caught sight of a child between buildings across the street. Straining, he could not see clearly in the early light. His brow wrinkled as the figure turned and disappeared.

Whose child was that? Seemed to have strange clothing on.

The swamper in the Gold Horse saw the same figure earlier. Never one to sleep through an entire night, Smith preferred to get in early to clean the saloon. Sweep a couple hours, empty the spittoons, grab a couple slices of bread and take a long nap. That was his style. This morning he spotted the figure roaming behind the buildings and stared intently into the darkness, but the light played tricks with his eyes.

A child. Too early for the locals, though. Something rankled in his mind - some distant thought just out of his grasp. Standing a few moments, Smith shifted the broom and bent over when it hit him.

A Chinaman? He'd heard tell of such, but never had occasion to see one. Surely his eyes were playing tricks. Must be some town kid out sneaking around. And yet...

105

Clyde was coming off a drunk. He and the men rode hard the day before, off to the range deep on Schmidt's ranch. There for a purpose, they stared intently into the distance, holding hats to their sides so only their eyes and heads were visible over the ridgeline. One man stood further back, awaiting orders – or whatever Clyde wanted. He stood tensely, as Clyde was coiled tight lately as eagerness for conquest took its toll. When the sound of approaching horses from the rear reached their ears, they startled and hands dropped to guns.

It was his men from the ambush. Clyde's eyebrows squeezed together in thought.

Knowing one of Schmidt's men was badly wounded and the other likely the same, they rode to find Clyde.

As the riders approached, they could not miss the wild look to his eyes as he stepped back from the ridgeline, wiped his brow and replaced his hat. His eyes were shadowed, but danger lurked in their depths.

"Well?" It was not a question, but a demand from a king to a minion.

"We nailed one good, boss. We think the other is winged pretty good also. Didn't know the whereabouts of the other one, but he showed up with a rifle and was pouring lead into us, so we just took off."

Clyde, red-faced and coiled like a rattlesnake, glared at the man.

"I said I wanted them all dead. Did you not hear?"

"We got 'em good, boss. They ain't traveling soon."

"But you didn't do as I ordered." His hand moved to his gun.

One of the men looking into the distance spoke up.

"Boss, there he is again."

Glaring for a moment longer, Clyde turned to the valley.

"Where?"

"Over there by them rocks." The man pointed.

"Sure looks like one of them Chinamen, boss."

Mexicans forgotten, Clyde scratched his head.

"What would a Chinaman be doing out here?"

"Looks like a sentry. He's just settin' there with a rifle like he's guardin' something."

"We need to get some men and ride over thataway. After we clear up the issue with Schmidt tomorrow, we'll ride over and see what that there Chinaman is guardin' so intently. We'll circle in from the north. I never seen a Chinaman up close."

"They look like little children, boss. I was in San Francisco few years back and they was everywhere. Some say they's only good fer doin' laundry. I hear tell they's good at other stuff." He winked at Clyde.

Clyde grinned.

"Let's get back to the ranch. Need to get the dust washed down. Tomorrow's gonna be big. Tomorrow I take over. In a day's time I will rule it all."

"You buyin' the drinks tomorrow, boss?"

"Yep."

106

Skerby rode through the wee hours of the night, guided by the stars. Near morning he found his spot, settled behind some brush, took out his spyglass and took a look-see. A few minutes later he smiled and began to hum to himself.

By six o'clock, town folks began scurrying around, taking care of necessities while casting frequent glances toward the edge of town. Both the local grapevine and the long distance owl-hoot trail had spread the word and many slept restlessly. All knew there was to be a fight, but none wanted to chance getting hurt.

Perhaps the livestock were the only ones to be excited, as their owners fed them early. Buckets clanked and hay rustled and back doors closed again. In the rare cases where locks and bolts existed, clicks and clanks were heard as everybody sought extra security.

All over town, furtive glances could be seen as fingers edged curtains aside. By seven o'clock stores opened early, knowing some would seek to take care of business, retreat to safety and hunker down away from doors or windows. Of all the souls in town, shopkeepers were amongst the bravest as they sought any potential profit. Yet they frequently stepped to the boardwalk looking for dust on the horizon. It would take only a moment to lock the doors and rush to the back room.

It was assumed, correctly, there would be no school for the children this day. No announcement was really necessary, given the issue at hand.

Old timers, accustomed to arising early to watch the sunrise and sit on benches and talk, found other places to sit. Talk was halting and punctuated by nervous twitches at every sudden noise. Finally, all made weak excuses and wandered home.

Dogs, sensitive to change, looked around with worried eyes. Some whined and crawled beneath the boardwalk, squirming deep into the shadows and lay with heads upon paws, eyes shifting back and forth. They didn't know what was going on in a human sense, but their instincts knew and their eyes perceived the changes in town.

Old Man Ridley sat by the Gold Horse saloon, in his usual spot, eager for a front row seat. If anyone watched carefully, they might catch the special tilt of his head and the way his eyes canted towards the west. Breakfast should arrive soon, and he greeted the closing of a door in that direction with eagerness. One stray old dog, Lester, paid no attention to the trend of the other dogs and anticipating his usual half biscuit from Ridley. His approaching nails could be heard on the boardwalk.

Wang sat in his cubbyhole in the woodpile, waiting. Sneaking around town the day before he had looked and listened. Going by the side of the saloon, the voice of the swamper carried through an open window.

"So Clyde's gonna face this Gideon. That ought to be interesting to watch."

"Gideon fella needs to watch his back. That Clyde will sure as tootin' have the deck stacked in his favor."

"By the way, some strange fella been hanging out past couple days. Been to the cribs and in here, flashing a bit of cash. Cagey lookin.' Heard his name is Mueller."

Wang stood, stretched and prepared for his day.

∿

Clyde roused the men early. A hangover increased his surly mood and he kicked one man who didn't respond to his yell. About to curse, the man caught a dangerous glint in Clyde's eye and held his tongue.

With the cook more cantankerous than usual, the entire crew was sour by the time they were done picking half-heartedly at their beef and eggs. Most were nursing headaches. As was the nature of paid warriors, they argued over the jobs of feeding and watering the horses. All felt it was below them, and the three or four working hands took the brunt of the abuse, bristling inside and saying nothing for fear of the guns on the warrior's hips.

After chores they mounted and rode towards town. Besides himself fourteen men rode under his orders. Seven more he sent out to the range to check the cattle. Two of those were designated to check on the Chinaman back in the hills.

Abby washed and changed from her traveling dress. Mrs. Griner was a bit put out being disturbed so early, but readily opened her door at the thought of a few days, maybe more, of income. She talked briefly with Abby over coffee and spoke of the events of the day to come.

"You won't want to be in the streets today, Abby. They's gonna be a big to-do. It's a showdown between the Rocking-B and the Lazy-S. Really, though, it's gonna be a face off betwixt this Gideon fella and Clyde Bowers. I can double guarantee you Clyde has something up his sleeve. He intends to have Schmidt's ranch. So I suggest you sit tight till all the shootin' is over and done."

After washing, Abby glanced out the window, watching as two riders rode in. She felt the reassuring bulge of the Remington .32 rim fire in her handbag. Knowing her journey would have its moments, she went with Buck to pick out a weapon and settled for this model. Buck was a good shot and taught her well over the years. Often they spent Saturday late mornings practicing in the wash back of town.

Bill and Nate tied their horses at the livery, waking the hostler and urging the grouchy man to feed their horses. Demanding payment in advance, he received it and faded back into the tack room. The two found their way to the restaurant for breakfast. Filling their cups, the owner of the establishment frowned as tables usually full sat empty.

Wang spotted Mueller, coming out of one of the cribs on the back end of town.

Skerby headed to town, grinning from ear to ear. He didn't take the direct route, but rather swung wide.

There'd be horses coming soon and he didn't want to get in the way.

※

For an hour into the ride to town, nobody from the Rocking-B spoke. Fourteen riders followed Clyde, lost in their own thoughts, as was the usual with men headed into a gunfight and men nursing the nasty results of too much cheap liquor the night before. Several dozed in the saddle, trying to make up for lack of sack time. Rounding a bend in a trail man and beast knew by heart, one man happened to glance backwards sleepily. Sagging eyes became dinner platters as he hollered:

"Hey, Clyde!" Clyde did not look backwards. He was thinking of the little red head at the crib. She was the same one Mueller was visiting but Clyde didn't know it.

"Clyde!" Men awakened with a start. Horse's ears stood turned.

"What?" He spoke irritably.

"An awful lot of smoke back there!"

Clyde turned and stared. Lots of smoke, several miles back. Fire at the ranch! Clyde glanced to town and then back at the smoke.

"Dusty, you and four others go back and check it out. Ride hard!"

Now there were only nine Bowers riders following Clyde.

❧

Skerby heard horses coming and waited behind a stand of trees until they were past and out of sight. Then he started at a trot towards town, whistling. It didn't work too well, what with it being hard to whistle while fighting a grin.

❧

Bill and Nate finished eggs and cornbread and settled in to another cup of coffee. Nate was nervous, but had confidence in Bill's guidance.

❧

Gideon was halfway to town, grim-faced. Spending a few moments with Mary before leaving, he kissed her brow gently. It hurt to see the look of fear in her eyes and a tear slipping down her cheek. He and Lem Teague rode mostly quiet, with a few random attempts to talk.

❧

Mueller walked around town, watching Clyde's men dismount at the saloon. Being in town a couple days with nothing to do but listen, he picked up pieces of the coming gunfight. His plan was to watch how they set up and take out Gideon before the guns ever fired. If he failed? Well, he had enough of the $500 left to get to California. Hankel would never find him. Never mind the other $500. Then again, that redhead was worth staying around for a while.

⚘

Wang shadowed Mueller, always out of sight.

107

Clyde kicked open the door of the saloon. It was ten o'clock and he wanted a drink. When the barkeep told him they were not open, he strutted to the bar and grabbed a bottle. Bowers' riders poured in and one put a gun to the barkeep, who suddenly decided it was ok to serve drinks to the rest of them. Nothing was said about who was paying. Nobody worried, either - especially not the barkeep.

Throwing back a couple of whiskeys and drawing his gun, Clyde checked the cylinders and the action. Slipping it into the holster with a feeling of satisfaction, he saw the men glance his way. He stood taller and smiled confidently.

Bowers men sat in various places, most of them boisterous and loud. Most had proven their mettle, at least to themselves. They now strutted and acted tough. It was false courage, a façade men showed in an attempt to cover nervousness.

The two chess players, seeing the door opened, wandered in to play but, seeing the group inside turn their heads and reach for their guns, decided today was not a day to play chess. Never mind, they'd finish the game later today...or maybe tomorrow.

In one corner sat three of the most experienced Bowers hands. They whispered, with an occasional strained laugh. Such men as these lived realistically. Well they knew some of the men in the room would not drink another drink or see another sunrise. They watched disdainfully those who strutted and bragged, seeing false bravado for what it was.

None talked to Clyde, but quick glances fell upon him. Late last evening one of the men in the bunkhouse wondered aloud if they should ask Clyde for all money due them, just in case. The others merely stared at him in response. No, they all knew the way of such things, and that it was not a time to ask for money. It would be seen as lack of confidence and nobody wanted to face Clyde with such thoughts, especially as he grew more morose as the day came into its own.

No, if Clyde died, they would all just move on to the next job and forget missed wages. Stares lingered on the man, who lowered his eyes in discomfort. That settled, the men quietly cleaned their guns.

Nursing another whiskey, Clyde's thoughts were similar to the others, yet with a somber twist. He knew, sure as the sun rose and set, either he or Gideon would be dead today. Or both of them. At the least, there was a good chance he would take some lead. The other men knew it, too.

Still, including him, there were ten men to face Gideon. Sure as shootin' Gideon would have one or two fools to side him, probably Schmidt and that other old man. Yet no one else from the town would dare step in. He'd sent a man in last evening to spread word any involvement would result in rather unfortunate action against both the town resident and their family.

Unable to hold it, Clyde suddenly grinned from ear to ear and threw back his drink. Pounding his shot glass on the counter to signal the barkeep, he smirked as more amber filled his glass.

At the end of today he would be the absolute king of the area! He would strut and walk into the saloon and require everyone to stand! Doing what he absolutely pleased, he would have his run of the cribs... when he wasn't home with Mary. Yes, she would make a great showpiece for visitors. He wanted her, but also knew her resentment would have to be cured by showing who was boss. She would do what he wanted after a few well-placed slaps. Clyde saw her not as an object of passion, for he would take care of passion at the cribs. Mary would be an ornament for his king-dom. Still, there would be those moments...

Quick steps patted the boardwalk and the ba-twings squeaked open and eyes lifted. Earlier Clyde had stopped a lad he knew at the edge of town, tossed a gold coin into the dust and told the boy to let him know when Gideon came to town.

"Mr. Clyde, that Gideon fella is comin' onto the edge of town." At a nod from Clyde, the lad disappeared.

Throwing back the last of his drink, Clyde flung his glass violently to the floor. Shards flew and a nearby man instinctively raised a protective hand. Turning to the room, Clyde began to point and bark orders.

"You two, take the far side of the street. You...and you, circle behind the buildings and work up behind Gideon and whoever sides him. The rest of you... we'll go right down the middle."

Nobody moved until Clyde hitched his belt and walked, he thought, like a king to the batwings.

Stopping suddenly, Clyde stepped to the chess-board near the door. Glancing down, he fingered the edge of the board and scratched his chin.

"I've never understood this game."

Stepping outside, he stood in the middle of the walk as his men split around him and took positions. Crinkling his brow briefly, Clyde stretched his arm to stop the last man.

"Gabe, take that rifle from your saddle and go up that livery loft yonder. If'n you get a good shot at Gideon, there's an extra hundred in it for you."

"That's a back shot, Clyde."

"Yep." Clyde stared at the man. "You want I should give the hundred to someone else?"

Crinkling his lips, the man then smiled.

"Nope, they's a horse down the valley I want that costs just that." Going to his saddle, Gabe pulled the Winchester and headed quickly down the street. Clyde watched Gabe duck into the livery.

Ol' Ridley, the blind warrior, was unnoticed, much like a lamppost or a hitch rail. Sitting quietly outside the saloon, every one of the Bowers men passed him going both in and out, yet none took notice of him. Even Clyde was unaware of Ridley sitting right behind him.

Knowing better than to move right away, Ridley sat unmoving. These men were keyed up and ready to pull iron at the drop of a hat. Beside him was a beat up plate, wiped clean with the biscuit. Brought by the barber's wife, Ol' Ridley was partial to her gravy. Someone else had brought him a piece of chawin' tobaccy.

At the mention of the man in the livery, Ridley raised a brow. As Clyde stepped into the street, Ridley quietly and, more quickly than others would believe, stepped through the batwings. No one noticed the squeak as they swung behind him. With a hand in front and a hand to the side, he found the bar and walked quickly to the back door, stepped out slowly and carefully made his way next door. Fumbling slightly with the latch, he entered the back of the mercantile.

Another pair of eyes watched the man headed to the livery, aware of his purpose. A delicate hand gripped the pistol.

Gideon reined his horse just outside of town, watching the different activities of Craswell from a large brushy clump. A mile back, Lem headed off to come in from behind the buildings. Gideon sat with his forearms on the pommel, eyes ranging back and forth. Already the town was waiting. No children in the street. Looking to his left, he saw the school was vacant.

Unnaturally, there were many horses at the saloon. Too many for this early hour. They belonged no doubt to Bowers men, who must be inside fortifying their courage. Gideon counted ten horses? Is that all the men Clyde brought?

A glance to the south earlier showed smoke in the distance. It looked to be from the Bowers ranch, but it could be deceiving. In the back of his mind he wondered.

Accustomed to observing and finding the weakness of his targets, Gideon looked the town over, placing the stores, the horses, the occasional flash of a shopkeeper smudging the glass to see down the street. His eyes narrowed as he saw a silhouette of someone sitting outside the eatery. Another two stood in front of the livery and he watched as they moved beyond a couple storefronts and disappeared in an alley. Something about the men…there was purpose in their presence.

Hearing hoof beats in the distance, Gideon instinctively touched his gun and turned. Suddenly grinning, he moved out from the brush a few feet and waved to Skerby. The old man turned and rode his way, reining to a stop.

"Skerby, I wondered what happened to you. You've no obligation to be a part of this fight, but you disappeared without as much as a tip of your hat to the ladies."

"I know it. I got to be truthful…I give moving on a bit of thought last night – all of about ten seconds. I done traveled a lot of miles, covered a lot of trails and met a lot of folks through the years. Ain't never been able to settle down. But I guess I just figure this is as good a place to settle as anywhere. I ain't getting' any younger and I'm getting' stiffer in my bones. Yep, I think this here might be where I stay. If'n that means I settle six feet under, well, it's been a good run of years. I been around, close as I can figure, nigh on to seventy years. I guess I just sorta figure I might as well stand by you through this and see what happens. For Mary's sake." Winking at Gideon, he spat and squinted towards town. "How many you reckon?"

"I count ten Bowers horses. Less than I expected. At least three other men I'm not sure of. Lem's around somewhere." He looked quizzically at Skerby. "Where you been?"

"Well, I felt a mite inclined to even the odds a tetch." He smiled at Gideon and spat again. "Seems there was this barn over to the Rocking-B. All the animals done got out for some reason. Then the dad-blamedest thing happened! Someone dropped a match in the hay and whoosh!"

Gideon grinned. "Anybody try and stop you?"

"Just the cook. I trussed him up nicely, then sat him in a rocking chair on the front porch so's he could watch the fire and get comfort from the heat. Not another blessed person on the place. Sorta disappointin' there weren't any more fun. But ridin' back I done seen five riders ridin' to beat all back to the ranch. 'Spect they seen the smoke. Shame nobody'll be there to entertain them."

"You're a good man to ride the trails with, Skerby."

Skerby spit into the dust. "Evened it out a mite, but still not the best odds."

"Nope. Still time for you to back out."

"I reckon not. What say we head on in?"

Urging their horses on, the pair rode in slowly, eyes roving to and fro in the shade of their brims.

In the distance they noted Clyde exit the saloon, followed by his men who separated as he sent them to their places. They watched the men fan out. They also saw a man take a rifle and head out of their view. Gideon noted someone duck into the saloon.

"Well, better tie our horses here and walk on in." Both men dismounted and stood up. Gideon loosened his guns and, glancing at Skerby, began his walk. "When we get closer, angle off to the right, Skerby. Hang back a bit to stop a crossfire."

"Here they come, Clyde."

"I got eyes, Hansen! I'll take Gideon, you take the old man."

Walking in the dust, Clyde glanced back and forth and noted his men were in place. There was a light in his eyes as he hitched his belt higher. As a king before his army he walked in the strength of numbers.

"Man sitting in front of the eatery, Gideon."

"He's on our side."

"Good thing. Odd's are still not the best, but I'm feeling a mite hopeful."

Unknown to Bowers' men, the man was there for some time in the shadows, watching with careful eyes the events playing out in this once-quiet town. As Gideon and Skerby neared, the man rose and stepped into the street. It was Teague. Nodding to Gideon, he fell into step. Now three capable men walked onward. Bowers men approached from a few buildings away.

"Figured to see you, Lem."

"Scouted a mite. Couple men circling to come up behind, but I don't think we need to worry." Turning his head ever so slightly, he spoke to Skerby. "Careful with the middle barrel, Skerby."

Skerby nodded. "I hear you! I'm cuttin' over now. Luck to you."

"And you, friend."

Mueller snuck alongside the Ladies Emporium, glancing up and down the buildings to make sure he remained unseen. Gideon would pass by in a few minutes and he intended to get a perfect shot. Reaching the front corner, he hunkered in the shadows to stay out of sight. Taking off his hat, he laid the Winchester by his side and peered carefully around the corner.

There he was! Gideon. Oh, that money would be enjoyable. Might even see what else Hankel had in his office, then club him and drag his body to the alley. Probably had a couple thousand in his office. Maybe even a safe. Have to force him to open the safe before he conked him. Mueller smirked at the thought.

But first...Gideon. To be known as the man who killed Gideon Henry! Mueller's heart quickened as he slowly dropped to his knees and stretched out on the ground. Another minute and Gideon would be right in front of him and he would have about five seconds to make a good shot. He brought the rifle up and snugged his cheek against the stock.

Wang was always good at padding softly. It was something natural to him and this time it was aided by Mueller's intense focus on the street. One time Gideon shared a few words about being on the trail and how it was always important to watch your back trail. Mueller definitely did not watch his back trail.

As Mueller's barrel moved to track Gideon, there was a slight click of the cocking hammer. Taking a deep breath, Mueller let it out slowly, then held it as his finger tightened on the trigger.

Mueller body sagged as he grunted with finality. Wang wiped the blade on Mueller's shirt and slipped it out of sight. He always appreciated a sharp knife.

Gideon cast a flickering glance at the alley as he walked by. A child seemingly stood over a man who lay upon the ground, unmoving. A momentary rising of an eyebrow and his eyes once again focused on the street.

108

Since the recent death of his father, Clyde Bowers felt a sense of power, of domination of the range. In his heart and mind he was, indeed, king of the range. He now walked with the strut of a man certain of his future and certain of success. Sureness of his numerical superiority blurred the reality that being the king of the range made him a specific target.

Yet there was still a deep reserve holding a grip on reality. That reserve noted the extra men on the street not of the Rocking-B. Two men had been on the walk on the far side, but had slipped off. They were too casual to be common gunhands. No matter, they must've sensed what was up and just got out of the way.

Out of the corner of his eye he saw movement in the mercantile. A glance revealed the face of Ol'

Ridley in the front window. Clyde chuckled. That old man was like a worn-out hound dog, doing nothing but mooching food for years. Never once did Ridley treat him with any kind of respect. When this was cleared up he would make sure Ridley was sent packing. Just a matter of days!

Clyde missed the activity behind Ol' Ridley.

As men converged, none really paid attention to the weather.

A strange and sudden wind gusted in the street. Creeping clouds blurred the mountains and flickered in turn over the sun, changing the light on the scene. Swirling, the wind picked up dust and bits of this and that and flung them along the street. As the men came together and halted, dust momentarily billowed and hung nature's curtain over the act about to unfold. Cloaked in a swirling blindness, men squinted and some ducked their heads, most with an innate sense preventing sudden moves. At the same time a man on one end of Bower's army did not have the wisdom of years and reached suddenly to cover his eyes. The man next to him saw it as drawing his gun. Movement in such situations never drew thought – only instinct. Despite the dust, guns fired and dust-filled eyes wildly cast about as the street filled with gunshots and cursing and grunting and crying out and the smoke of battle and the scurry of men shifting and the cries of death scything through the street. Shots came from behind the buildings to Gideon's right. A loud blast was heard in the dust.

Just as sudden, the wind moved on, to perform its second act at the corrals down the street, where horses, already milling nervously from the sounds of battle, suddenly became engulfed in swirling dust and debris, infused with acrid smoke and the smell of gunpowder.

Just as quickly, all became silent. Even the natural sounds of town life suspended for a bit of time. All eyes – those still able to open – cast about seeking blindly for impending danger.

A subtle wisp of tail wind faintly blew and the smoke cleared quickly, showing men standing with guns forward and eyes flashing with intensity.

In the middle of the street stood Clyde Bowers, gun pointed at Gideon. In the violence of the last moments he remained somehow unscathed.

Gideon stood with his gun also pointed at Clyde.

Both men realized the doom of two men – themselves.

Gideon, experienced in the reading of men, looked into Clyde's eyes and knew the man would not draw.

Clyde heard the sounds of death and realized he was alone, miraculously alive, saved by the cloaking of the dust and the confusion of men. Sanity flowed in and the presence of death sobered him as he slowly lowered his gun and dropped it to the dust.

A quick glance revealed two Rocking-B riders lying in the eerie stillness of death upon the ground. Another writhed and clutched a leg wound while another grasped a shattered arm and cried for help.

Gideon looked around. Skerby sat on the ground, blood covering his face. Two more of Clyde's men lay on the walk groaning and crying out. Gideon rushed to Skerby's side and knelt down. Teague took only a moment longer.

"Don't move, Skerby, until the doc gets here." Gideon was concerned.

"Help me up! I ain't got but a scratch."

"Something knocked you down. Sit still."

Teague grinned. "I don't think a bullet knocked him down – at least not in the usual way." Gideon looked at Teague, questioning. Skerby broke the thought, speaking irritatedly.

"Dad blast it! Help me up! It was the middle barrel what knocked me down! Knew I needed to get them both." Skerby's LeMat revolver held a middle barrel holding a 20-guage shotgun shell.

Relieved, Gideon helped his friend to his feet and noted a furrow down Skerby's scalp - hence the blood. Looking around, Skerby saw his hat and bent to pick it up. A hole shown both fore and aft in the crown.

"Blast it! My hat!"

The two newcomers emerged from the alley to stand in the street. One was a young man with his bloody kerchief held to his arm. As Gideon scanned the street, his eyes touched upon the bloodied arm and then glanced upwards. Eyes wide, he squinted at the man with an unspoken question. Smiling, the newcomer spoke:

"Hello, brother."

"Nate? I'll be dogged!" He walked to meet Nate and grabbed his hand meaningfully, but Nate pulled him into a hug. Over Nate's shoulder Gideon recognized Bill Henry and nodded.

Gideon pulled back and looked at Nate's arm.

"How bad?"

"It hurts like heck, but I don't think it's bad."

Turning to Clyde, Gideon walked forward, Skerby at his side.

"Clyde, your reign is over."

Clyde stared, still unbelieving.

At that moment a shot ripped the air. Skerby crumpled to the ground. Gideon and the others turned to the sound. The loft over the livery pushed further open and a rifle barrel glimmered. A door opened and a rifle blasted from the mercantile. A quick answering shot from the loft brought the rifle from the mercantile to bear once again but before the man could shoot there was a muffled shot from within the loft. With an audible grunt, a man tumbled from the loft and lay motionless in the dust.

Gideon looked to the mercantile, where the shopkeeper held a rifle. Ol' Ridley stood by his side.

Yet, it had not been a .45 they'd heard. It had been smaller caliber.

Turning, Gideon ran again to Skerby. Again he knelt by his side. A bullet had taken the old man in the shoulder, the blood forming a spreading stain across his shirtfront. Skerby held a bandana to the wound, his mouth twisted in pain. Still, as the men knelt, he pointed to the street.

"Don't pay attention to me, Gideon! Clyde's gone!"

Taking advantage of the distraction, Clyde had dashed to the nearest alley.

"There he is!" Nate pointed.

Clyde was just turning behind a building, then ran through the alley and along the backs of the stores as silence held the town. A man scampered from a door as he passed and looked stunned as Clyde ran him down.

Stumbling, Clyde heard a shout from the street. Cutting sharply to the hitch post at the saloon and slipping the knot loose, he jumped to the saddle and dug his spurs viciously into his horse. Screaming, the animal lurched like never before as Clyde raked it mercilessly through another alley.

109

"I'm going after him!"

"I'll join you." It was Bill.

Gideon hitched his belt and took his Stetson off, running his fingers through his hair. As he replaced the hat, he glanced over as a beautiful young lady approached with a pistol in her hand. Eyes narrowed, he tensed.

"Hello, brother."

Suddenly both Gideon and Nate were wide-eyed. "Abby?"

Abby nodded, choked and unable to speak for a moment. Nate and Gideon approached and, with a mere moment's hesitation, embraced their long-lost sister.

As they drew apart, Gideon threw a questioning look at the pistol still in Abby's hand. His sister saw the look and glanced towards the livery stable.

"You shot the man in the loft?"

She nodded, a pained look in her face.

"He was going to shoot you."

Gideon nodded. Nate, standing next to her, put his arm over her shoulder.

Breaking the mood, Skerby brought them back to reality.

"Blast it, Clyde's getting away!"

Gideon looked to the fading dust in the distance.

"Let's go, Bill!" Looking once again to Abby and Nate, Gideon turned to his horse.

"Hold on, Gideon." It was Bill Henry, pointing.

A horse was running into town, sides heaving with effort.

It was Vern.

"Gideon!" Vern Schmidt reined his horse to a stop and the beast flung white lather to the street and blew. "We need the doctor...bad!"

"What happened?"

"Mary. I think she was coming after you. She sneaked out the back. We heard a scream and found her by the barn. She fell from the horse. Broke her wound open again. Bleeding badly. She had her rifle with her and the last thing she whispered was your name."

Nate stepped before Gideon. "We'll get the doc, Gideon. You go after Clyde!"

110

Raking his horse mercilessly, Clyde ignored the animal's screams as blood ran down its flanks and it was helpless to escape the crazed man upon its back. Its only thought was to move and avoid further raking of the spurs.

Clyde's only thought was to get away, to gain distance. Something inside him was already broken and he rode, intent upon the hills ahead and the safety therein.

Indeed, he crossed a line that day, a line where sanity held insanity at bay, and now that line lay far behind, in the dust of Craswell's street. His eyes held a different look, a vacant look, the look of a man who had lost all yet was not aware of the loss. The look of a deposed king suddenly reduced to depravity yet still certain of his right to reign. It was a land of fog, of false ideas of the loyalty of men.

Rounding a hillside several miles from town, lather flying from his laboring horse, Clyde spotted a fire and saw two Rocking-B hands holding a calf and working over the brand. As his now faltering horse bore down on them, their hands dropped to their guns. They stepped back as Clyde jerked his horse to a cruel stop. Stumbling, the horse trembled with fear and exhaustion. Both men noted blood running down its flanks and saw the wild look in the rider's eyes. Involuntarily they flinched and stepped backwards.

"I'm taking a horse!" Clyde yelled and grabbed the reins of a roan standing nearby.

"Boss, that's my horse!"

Clyde turned and shot the man in the belly and pivoted to hold the barrel on the other man. Wide-eyed, the man held his hands out.

"I ain't gonna pull no gun, boss! Don't shoot!" Seeing the fierce eyes, the man knew Clyde was no longer sane.

"I'm not the boss...I'm the King! Understand?"

Eyes wide, the cowhand nodded. Danger faced him.

"You will do as I say!"

"Yes...King."

"If a group of riders comes after me, you hold them off for an hour – understand?"

"Yes, boss," he replied.

"You ride for the brand!"

"Yes, boss."

"I'm not the boss – I'm the king! Say it!"

"Yes...er...King Clyde."

Clyde grinned wildly, jumped to the saddle and turned the horse, raking it as he had the other beast. New animal screams rent the air.

The stunned cowhand watched Clyde recede into the distance. Turning towards town he saw no sign of pursuit.

Shaking his head, he rushed to the other man. Blood covered hands grasped a devastating stomach wound as the man lay writhing and groaning. One look told the story and the lucky hand shook his head, looking downward in time to see life flee with a deep spasm. Cloudy eyes stared to the clear sky.

Squinting into the distance, he noted a dust cloud billowing as another horse crossed the mile-long valley at a run. Kicking dirt over the fire, he looked to the cinch ring just cooling from its duty. It would see no more use today. There was nothing to do but wait for the approaching rider, hands far away from his guns. As the cloud neared, he noted it was actually two riders.

Gideon reined and held his gun on the man. Bill stayed to the right. One glance took in both dead cowhand and bleeding, crazed horse.

"Clyde go by here?"

"Yessir, Mr. Gideon." Nodding in the direction Clyde had ridden, the man kept his hands motionless.

Gideon looked and glanced back at the man, then down to the dead man.

"You work for the Rocking-B?"

"Used to, but not no more. Time to move on."

"Healthy thing to do. You got other horses back at the home place?"

"Yessir."

"Good. I need your horse. Mine's losing a shoe." Grabbing his rifle, Gideon dismounted.

"Help yourself. Want I should send yours back to the Schmidt place?"

"Appreciate it."

The cowhand looked at Bill and pointed to another animal.

"I got the other pack horse. Good horse, too."

Bill nodded.

"Can I have my rifle, though? They're not cheap."

Mounting the new horse and handing the man his rifle, Gideon put his own in the boot. With a glance at Bill, Gideon looked into the distance. No dust was visible. Looking to the sun, he noted it leaning towards the west. They would be hard-pressed to catch Clyde unless fate intervened.

Spitting a dark stream, the puncher spoke.

"Mister, that Clyde just ain't right."

"What do you mean?"

"When he come by here, they was a look in his eyes I ain't never seen. Made me call him King Clyde. Reminds me of a coyote backed agin' a cliff with a pack of wolves a'facin' it. Clyde had that look. Shot Jones here fer no reason. Just shot him. He's done gone loco."

Gideon looked at the man, then nodded and rode off.

Walking to the dead man, the cowhand grabbed a leg and dragged the body to a nearby gulley. Best to knock the bank over on the body, he realized. Save some effort. Suddenly, pausing, he put the leg down, knelt beside Jones and began to go through pockets. Pulling out a small poke, he weighed it in his hand and grinned as he slipped it into his own pocket. After all, Jones wouldn't need it anymore. Drawing a watch from the vest pocket, he wiped the blood on a clean part of Jones' shirt. Standing up, he opened the watch and glanced at the time.

"Yep. Time to move on."

No more than five miles distant, Bill hailed Gideon to a halt.

"Gideon, there's no sense in going on. We're just guessing at his trail."

Gideon's felt frustrated. At the same time, the reality of the setting sun and Clyde's escape shown in the thinning of his lips and the slump of his shoulders.

"The man is going to be back, Bill. I can feel it. This business isn't done yet."

"I know. I feel it, too. But there's no sense in wandering off into the dark. Clyde could be anywhere, and I've a hunch he isn't going to stop anytime soon. He'll ride that horse into the dirt and steal another one. He's loco."

Both sat their horses and stared into the distance, almost willing their eyes to see a sign of Clyde in all the rolling hills. None appeared.

With a sigh Gideon glanced at Bill, nodded and turned his horse towards home.

And Mary.

111

Hastily throwing on a worn and stained frock coat, an older stately man with a bulging Adam's apple wobbling up and down in a neck resembling that of a turkey, hurried out and slammed the door behind him. As undertaker in Craswell, he wondered whether there would be payment for today's services or if the town leaders would expect him to provide obligatory burials. He'd been doing a few of these lately and it seemed people always wanted something for nothing. And so he went to his task wondering.

In the mercantile, Skerby lay across the counter. Teague stood by his side, looking down at Skerby as he examined the shoulder.

"Skerby, you are nothing but a mangy old coot with hardly any meat on your bones!"

Skerby grimaced and looked up.

"How is it, Teague?"

"Well, looks like the bullet went clean through and hit nothing important. Bleeding's stopped and we poured some whiskey into it to clean it. I'd say you've got a good chance of making it, but I think you'll need to rest for a few weeks."

Sighing, Skerby looked out the window. A few moments later his eyes shifted back.

"You know, Teague, I been a wandering man fer a good many years. Most all my life, in fact. But I think the time has come to settle. I ain't getting' any younger and a man reaches a point where he wants a mite of comfort. I 'spect I done reached that point."

"I'm sure there's a place for you here."

The door opened. Abby slipped in and stood by Skerby's side.

Looking upward at the young lady, Skerby could see the resemblance to Gideon. It was many a year since he'd seen such a beautiful young lady. His mouth hung open.

"Don't catch any flies, Skerby!" Teague laughed. Abby's eyes danced with playfulness.

"So, you're a dear friend of my brother?"

Skerby could only stare as Abby grasped his hand.

112

J ose and Paulo walked into the ranch yard while Schmidt headed back with the doctor. A travois followed Jose's horse, Manuel unconscious upon it. Paulo rode the other horse stiffly.

Hearing horses approaching, Ruth stepped to the doorway, shotgun in hand, placing it to the side of the door as she took in the men and the travois. Rushing out and stooping beside Manuel, she spoke the question.

"How bad, Jose?"

"It is very bad, Ruth. Bowers riders ambushed us and he was hit in the first volley. He has lost a lot of blood. I fear the worst. I regret that Maria is not here to see him."

"He's not dead yet. Get him into the house." She turned to see Paulo lowering himself to one leg. Seeing her glance, he smiled.

"It is nothing. See to Manuel."

"Sit on the porch, Paulo. I will see to you later."

Jose looked around as he untied Manuel from the travois. He noted the signs of trouble.

"Where is Vern? What's happened?"

Ruth filled him in briefly as they struggled to carry Manuel. Placing him on the table, Jose helped Ruth remove the man's shirt, exposing the wound. Both looked grim. Ruth poured water from the stove into a bowl and began to bathe the wound. Worry deepened the lines of her face.

Distant sounds of running horses once again brought weapons out until Vern was recognized, along with the doctor.

Later, after working on Manuel, then moving to Mary, the doctor straightened from his examination, shaking his head and glancing to Vern and Ruth.

"She's a strong young lady. Only a strong young lady would have been able to get out of bed and mount and straddle a horse in the first place – much less do it with a rifle in her hand!"

Ruth tilted her head. "Doctor, you haven't told us anything we didn't know. But you know the question we have in our hearts right now. Can you answer it?"

Shaking his head, the doctor lifted a corner of his mouth and raised one eyebrow. His left hand rubbed the stubble of his chin.

"Yes, Ruth, I think she'll make it – as long as she stays abed and doesn't try some other dad-blamed foolish thing and get the bleeding started a third time. She needs rest. She needs to rest for several weeks. It befuddles me why she ain't dead after that foolishness, but this girl is mighty determined. Keep her from being heroic and playing Joan of Arc and maybe she'll heal quicker!"

Turning to grip his bag on the edge of the bed, the doctor sensed a light touch of fingers brushing his arm. Looking down, he saw Mary's eyes staring at him, and he heard her whispered voice.

"Thank you, doctor. I will not be so foolish again." Her eyes closed and she appeared to fall asleep instantly.

Shaking his head, the doctor grinned.

"Don't that beat all! If that's any indicator, I think she'll be fine."

Looking to the kitchen where Manuel lay, the doctor shook his head.

"Paulo just needs time for the leg to heal. I think Mary will be ok. Manuel…it's a roll of the dice. He's a strong man, but he's torn up something fierce inside and lost a lot of blood. Ruth, you and the womenfolk have got a lot of nursing to do."

Jose stepped outside and a few minutes later a horse headed to the hills. Vern stepped to the window and looked back at Ruth. Her eyes widened in question.

113

"Clyde was running his horse hard. With day wearing on, I'm doubtful they'll catch him." Lem Teague rode beside Nate as they headed out to make a sweep before heading to Schmidt's ranch. Nate favored his wounded arm, bandana tied tightly just above the elbow.

"Looks to me like Clyde is headed to the high country."

Both men quietly looked to the distance, each pondering, until Nate spoke.

"Riders coming on the right."

Turning to their flank, a dust cloud formed between two hillsides as four horsemen emerged from the hills.

Keeping their horses between themselves and the approaching riders, Teague loosened his guns. Watching, Nate saw the purpose and did the same.

Four men against two. He would be expected to do his part. Teague spoke softly.

"Nate, I'm going to ease to the left a mite. You sidle to the right. Be ready for anything."

As they moved, the approaching riders fanned out and covered a twenty-yard front. Reigning to a stop, they looked what they were – paid gunmen. It was obvious in their clothing, from the shirts to the boots. Not fancy, but not bought with cowhand wages. They rode Rocking-B mounts.

A man with a long face and chin whiskers was the apparent leader. Riding a few paces ahead of the others, the man kept his right hand beside his hip. Sharp eyes held questions as he took in the strange brands, unknown in the area. Perhaps it was a sixth sense that hesitated for a moment on Teague. Unconsciously, he turned his horse slightly towards Lem. Teague noted the change, accepting the responsibility thrust upon him. Voice calm, he spoke first.

"Can we help you gentlemen?"

Teague recognized the danger in the man, keyed up and ready to show himself brave before the others. At the same time, it was obvious the others were only slightly less dangerous. If this lead man opened the ball, the bullets would fly and someone was going to get hurt. Nate had noted the pecking order, and focused his attention on the men behind.

"You are on Bowers range. I don't recall your faces."

"Last I heard this was Schmidt land?"

"Clyde took care of that today in town. We been on the range, gathering our new cattle. Headed to town to wash the dust away." He grinned a toothy grin showing several missing teeth, leaving gaps in the front which must have made dinnertime interesting.

"I think your celebration is a mite early."

"What makes you say that?"

"I mean Clyde Bowers lost the hand that was dealt him. He's on the run and he left dead hands behind him in Craswell this morning."

The men shifted, casting glances at each other. Their leader hesitated a moment before speaking. If Clyde was on the run, it might be their employ was no longer. Being gunmen, they rode for the brand – but only as long as the brand paid their wages. Still, these men might be bluffing. Glaring questioningly at Teague, the man pushed.

"Now, mister…whatever your name is; how do we know you ain't lying?" Lem let the question die, as any accusation of falsehood was grounds for instant gunplay.

"The name is Teague. This here is Nate Henry. We're kin to Gideon."

"Teague? You the Preacher?"

"I was called that for a spell."

At the name of Teague, gap-tooth twitched his jaw and began to sweat. Teague! Preacher Teague? A feared gunfighter, he was a legend in some parts of the West. Story was he trailed his family's killers for several years, then settled the score and made a new life. And yet, his skill was known to be deadly! The sweating gunman ran the options rapidly through his mind. Oh, to be the one to kill Preacher! A man could name his own wages. At the same time, he would become a target. Being a paid gunman held perks, but being a dead man held no perks at all. If what Teague said was true, it was apparent he and the others would receive no further wages from Clyde Bowers. Ultimately it took money to bring happiness in his world. Reputation would add nothing but trouble…or death. Also, he was a man perceptive of others and his senses clearly said Teague was telling the truth about Clyde Bowers. No sense in starting a fight if there was no money in it. None of them had anything against Teague or the others.

Lem Teague saw the change.

"Well, Teague, I think me and the men ought to ride on to greener pastures. I been told Arizona Territory is a nice place to visit."

"I hear tell the same thing. Healthier for a lot of reasons."

Nodding, the man spoke over his shoulder.

"What do you say, fellas? I'm riding on. Are you with me, or do you want to stay here – permanently?"

Indicating their agreement, the leader touched his hat to Teague and, turning his horse, led the others off.

114

Life settled into a time of healing and routine. It was a busy two months with a lot of changes. Seasons changed. Green turned to dazzling yellows and oranges only foothills and Aspens could provide, lending brightness, interspersed with evergreen and the brilliant reds of the Oaks. It was like a palette slathered across every hillside, leading up to the tree line, where dark mottled sentinels held their arms to the skies.

Skerby gimped around after two weeks of careful nursing from Abby. Watching him one day, Gideon smiled inside. It was obvious the old man enjoyed the ministrations of a young lady and worked it for all he could. Abby was aware, but also enjoyed Skerby's ways and his free spirit.

She found him staring one day – just staring – at the hillsides in the distance. His eyes held wistfulness.

Sitting down on a chair nearby, the squeak caused him to look over. Over the days he learned to trust Abby so he spoke, his words soft and interspersed with pauses of one groping for thoughts.

"I done lived a long life, Abby. I'm an old man now. Ain't healing as quick as I used to. This here's a wide and beautiful land and I done traveled a goodly chunk. Met a lot of special people. Always felt I might go back to them places and see those people again. At one time I figgered to settle down and maybe raise a kid. Even had a woman down to Abilene one time givin' me eyes and hints. But I look back and realize that were nearly thirty years ago now. Life has a way of moving on and we get stiffer of a mornin' and maybe more preferin' of some more comfort and more than a rock or a saddle for a pillow. A good horse, a clear mountain stream and an occasional visit to town are fine when you're young, but when you get...old...it seems like them things ain't as important. I been thinkin' on this a mite of time now. Seems like what I'm missing is family. Maybe what I'm doing is finding a place to settle in and pass my days, where I can have a good meal – maybe put on a few inches – and be content. I want that, and I think I can have that here. But it still don't take away the sting of realizing all those new valleys and places I wanted to see are just not going to happen."

Skerby leaned back.

"Have you spoken to Vern?"

"Not yet. I don't want to burden no one."

"Well, I already spoke to him about you."

Skerby scowled.

"Now listen here, young lady…"

"Vern said he needs good help and would be appreciative if you could stay. He said a man with your skills would be a blessing to him."

"He said that?"

"Yes."

Skerby sighed happily.

One evening shortly after returning from following Clyde, Gideon walked to the barn with Wang. The little Chinaman stood out amongst the others.

"Wang, it was quite a surprise to see you out here."

"You are my friend, Gideon. When I found Hankel sending Mueller to kill you, my heart told me there was no one I trusted to make sure this didn't happen. So I traveled myself."

"I owe you a debt of gratitude, Wang."

"You owe me nothing."

They stood in silence a few moments, staring at the magnificent colors beginning to stretch across the sky, highlighting the edges of the clouds with colors that daily brought comments of delight from Wang.

"Never before have I seen such colors. And such open space. My heart is changed with the opportunity to see for so many miles. In the past I measured the distance in city blocks. Here there is no description fitting the measure of the span between myself and the setting sun."

"There is plenty of room out here, Wang. Perhaps you might consider a change in your life."

Wang nodded and squinted. "There is merit in that thought, Gideon. Yet there must be consideration given to all aspects of this. Out here I stand out as a Chinaman. I am not sure how Chinamen are treated here. There is comfort in anonymity. Back East I disappear when I am in my own part of the city. I can fade away. I also receive a certain amount of respect among other Chinese."

"At the same time, Wang, there is the opportunity to build out here. There are other Chinese and they would be benefit with someone of your skills and abilities to change their way of life here and open the doors for them. It may take time, but somehow the changes must be pushed in order for them to happen."

"There is truth in what you say, Gideon. I will think upon our words. There would be much to do in order to make such a change. Many things need to be considered." Wang paused, but Gideon sensed there were words yet to be spoken, something the Chinaman needed to say. After a few moments, Wang continued. "There is a certain woman who has caught my eye. Yet she remains in St. Louis. She is very pleasurable to look upon. We have spoken of many things."

Gideon smiled.

Wang returned to St Louis after two weeks. It was a new experience, as he traveled in company with Teague and Bill Henry, driving cattle back to their ranches. He learned of dust and horses and long hours, yet felt invigorated. There was a comfort and a companionship unfelt on the trip out. Some of the hands were crude and not exactly friends at the start, but a few looks from Teague and Bill quieted most. One night the men were complaining about the food and Wang went later to the cook, who was a man friendly to Wang – probably because Wang never complained. Early the next morning, Wang rode out and returned with various plants and, along with things the cook carried, created a pot full of beans the next day that caused eyebrows to rise and prejudiced hearts to cool. Wang was treated differently from that day on. When they finally parted ways, all came to shake his hand.

At the train depot, Wang headed towards the luggage car, stopping as Bill Henry commented and held out two tickets.

"Who is the other ticket for, Mr. Henry?"

"Me. I figured I needed to do some business in St. Louis. And we both ride in the coach."

It was a pleasant journey, with a few rude comments and questions, but Bill Henry soothed all – some more firmly than others. No matter, the seats were pleasant.

Wang carried special letters in his pocket.

115

The sunsets were so beautiful! Mrs. McClinder began a habit of coming to the porch as colors painted the sky with a majestic brush defying imagination. Out here in the West space opened up and she could see nigh on to forever, the colors stretching from hither to yon.

Flour peppered her apron as usual as she sank into the rocker with a happy sigh. The children were in bed and she now had time to herself. Hessie rattled around in the kitchen, readying things for the morning. They took turns with breakfast, allowing the other to gain an extra hour of sleep. Though she loved the children – both old and new – she learned to relish these times of quiet, especially since the move.

It came in the usual way, with Happy delivering an envelope. Only this time the envelope contained a simple letter with an offer and Happy stood to the side of the door, waiting. Her eyes were big as saucers as she read the telegram, clutched it to her chest and turned to look to the West. Never had she dreamed of such a thing happening in her life!

Gideon was extending an offer for her and Hessie to pack up the children and come to a place called Craswell. If she was willing to accept the offer she was to send a reply and he would make arrangements.

She paused only for a few moments before wandering in to peer at the children as they slept. Most had no connection to keep them here and, she realized, neither did she. Within minutes she shared the news with Hessie – whose eyes widened at the thought - and composed a reply, which she handed to Happy, who then dashed off.

A rugged journey, she was at her wits end a few times striving to keep the children in check. Hessie, with racism still rampant, was required to ride in the rear car, so was unable to help Margie, except on the stops along the way when she helped corral the children.

None of the children ever rode a train before and scampered from window to window, climbing over laps of innocent passengers in their excitement. More than one angry look came Margie's way until the children settled over the next few days. Hampers of food were carefully packed for the journey. Mealtimes were the only time she was able to get the children together, and saying the blessing was the only silence. Stops to fill the water tanks were especially taxing as she and Hessie strove to make sure all the children were aboard again. By their arrival in Colorado Margie was tuckered out. Wagons were already arranged and they spent several nights on the trail heading to Craswell. The teamsters guiding them were both wondrous at the children and eager to get them to their destination. Many times the children walked or stood silently staring into distances never seen before, unable to fathom the ability to run in any direction. They were deliriously happy.

Refreshing to Hessie, the teamsters also were respectful to her and, aside from one man, seemed to take no notice of her skin color. Of course, her insistence upon cooking helped. She knew how to work magic with basic provisions and the men wore looks of ecstasy as food was ladled.

Now settled on the former Bowers ranch, the children were learning to do chores. Gideon made arrangements to purchase the ranch when it was found to be in arrears on a loan. Bowers apparently did not attended to his own ranch in his quest to take over, ignoring queries from the bank. The banker happily made out very favorable terms and work began immediately. New cabins were built for the boys and girls, with the scent of fresh lumber still vivid. A mere few days after their arrival she set the table for dinner and, starting to sit down, suddenly stopped half way. Something was different. Standing again, she pursed her lips and counted around the table, pointing her finger at each child as she went around. Stopping, at one point, she lowered her hand and looked at a young boy sitting with head lowered, trying not to be noticed. Her mouth lifted at one corner as she put hands to her hips.

"Young man, are you new here?"

"Yes, lady."

"You can call me Ma'am or Mrs. McClinder, but never 'lady.' Understood?"

"Yes, Ma'am."

"What's your name?"

"Carl."

"You have parents?"

A pause and the boy looked down. "No, Ma'am."

"Where have you been living?"

"Her and there, Ma'am. I was with them teamsters what come through yesterday. My ma and pa died with the fever."

Now it was her turn to pause. "Well, then, Carl, best we eat while the food's hot. Now, who would like to give thanks?"

Since that day there had been another, a young girl who wandered in one morning. One look told Margie the girl needed help. So they were now up by two children. No problem, though, as Mr. Henry had provided enough room.

In her thoughts she registered soft footfalls of approaching horses and looked up as Gideon Henry rode to the porch, another horse by his side with Abby riding beside him. Even in the dim light she could see a resemblance between the two.

"Evening, Mrs. McClinder."

"Good evening, Mr. Henry. Late for you to be riding."

She could see his smile. One of the first things she noticed when she arrived in Craswell was Mr. Henry being softened, no longer appearing angry and, somehow, much more settled. Perhaps it was the western clothes instead of the suits she was used to seeing on his frame. No, she thought, something was different. Drastically different. Later that first day she saw him walking beside Mary Schmidt and her heart knew the reason.

"Mrs. McClinder, I was wondering if there might be a need for a schoolteacher. Abby would do well, I think."

"Land sakes, Mr. Henry! I was just thinking yesterday morning about that! These children need to know their reading, writing and ciphering. You are once again an answer. Welcome, Abby. I have only one condition for you to teach."

"What's that, Mrs. McClinder?"

"When we're not with the children, you call me Margie."

Six weeks after the fight in Craswell, a wagon pulled up before the Schmidt home with supplies from town. Skerby helped Manuel slowly step down the wheel to the ground. Manuel was weary and stood hunched over. Maria was helping Ruth and hurried to her husband's side. She looked concerned.

"Manuel, was the trip too much for you?"

"It was long trip, but it felt good to be moving again. Still, I must go rest now. I fear it will be some time before I am back to the man I was before."

Skerby smiled. Both looked at him.

"You're all hunched over because you been shot. You'll straighten up eventually. Me? I'm a bit hunched and it ain't from this shoulder. Mine's from being old!"

They laughed together, Manuel holding his stomach.

Manuel and Maria had given their permission for Alita to marry Conner, who was back in the saddle again.

Skerby took to helping Schmidt with anything needing to be done. Yet, in any time off, he could be found riding to see the children...and Mrs. McClinder.

❧

Nate settled in as a common hand but after a month, his ability was clear. Gideon made him foreman of the former Bowers ranch and Nate did well, receiving some needed tutoring from a couple seasoned hands, including Paulo. Walking with a decided limp, Paulo still was one of the best hands around. He enjoyed teaching the children the ways of the ranch and could be seen grinning as children flocked around him.

Mary and Gideon took many walks together. It was a time of growing together. At first they visited much on the porch as Mary healed. She still favored the shoulder now and then. One day Gideon rounded the corner to find her softly feeling her shoulder through the material of her dress. She startled at his appearance.

"What's the matter, Mary?"

Mary paused, then reached for his hand.

"I'm afraid I have a very unsightly scar, Gideon. Someday..."

"I have some also. We've all got our scars, Mary. Some are visible, some are not."

They walked many miles and rode countless more. Gideon learned what it was to work cattle and mind the range. His peace and contentment grew. One afternoon Mary said to him:

"God can take your anger away – but you've got to be willing to let it go."

He realized he held much anger. Though much was departed, there was still a deep chasm filled with a residual burning anger. For he and Mary to have a future, he must let it go.

116

There were signs of a lone horseman beginning to appear on the range now and then.

At first, the hands reported finding evidence of small fires in secluded locations quite distant from the home place. The evidence began to draw a tighter circle.

Then came the night horses disappeared from the former Bowers place. Three were taken, with two of them being remembered as those Clyde rode.

Riders watched carefully, but no sign of the horses – or the thief – were found. The trail faded into the tracks of cattle and was lost.

A rider from Battle Wagon came to the Gold Horse in Craswell one evening. Bellying up to the bar and gesturing for a drink, he turned and spoke to the room.

"Strange man wandering the hills." They turned to the speaker. One of the men at the chessboard looked up.

"What's he look like, mister?"

"Kind of a big fella. Pinched nose, a wild look to his eyes. I'd say he ain't right. Came to my fire last night and wanted coffee. I give it to him, but I took off when he left. Left me uneasy, so I made a cold camp. Was uneasy all night."

Eyes flitted back and forth.

"Did you notice a brand?"

"Yep. Was a Rocking-B."

117

News of the rider reached Gideon and he scowled to himself.

That same morning he received a letter from Wang telling him his investments were paying off nicely and money was placed into an account from which he or Mrs. McClinder could draw. Wang also mentioned taking a bride. Gideon could not help but smile. It was the last line that gave him concern:

"Hankel will no longer be a problem to you or to anyone else. However, there was a letter on his desk. I was curious and saw it was from Clyde Bowers, seeking the return of certain monies Dan Bowers sent to hire a man skilled with a gun. The letter has now been destroyed, but I thought you might like to know Clyde is around somewhere."

Gideon was quiet that evening as he sat at dinner, Mary at his side. He'd told her about Clyde and she mentioned it to Vern and all were aware. Skerby set his mug down firmly.

"Dag nab it, Gideon! It just ain't finished yet! Let's you and me go after that varmint and take care of it once and fer all!"

Vern spoke up.

"He's right, Gideon. But I think we can take a few men out and track him down."

Looking around the table, Gideon thought of all this family had been through and hesitated to put them through any more. He looked at Mary. Looking back to his eyes, she knew.

Gideon would go alone when the time came.

It happened sooner than expected.

Arising early the next morning, Gideon went to the barn corral to rope a horse. He had grown fond of a roan mare that had a lot of leg and seemed sure-footed. Throwing the rope, he missed and coiled it again. About to toss the loop, he heard footsteps and knew it was Mary. The loop flitted perfectly over the mare's neck and Gideon brought her to the fence where his saddle rode the upper bar.

"Good morning, Mary."

"Good morning." She responded only half-heartedly. They enjoyed these moments early in the morning. Yet today she was distracted.

"I'm afraid for you, Gideon."

Gideon looked to her as he reached for the saddle blanket. Settling it on the horse's back he nodded.

"It's one of those situations, Mary. I've got it to do. I'm not thrilled to go after him, but until I do there will be no true peace around here. You've noticed how I've been preoccupied much of the time?"

"Yes, and I know it's because of Clyde. And I know you've got to take care of this. But what I don't understand is why you can't take several of the others with you."

"It's this way, Mary. It will be nip and tuck up there. Clyde and me. It's one of the realities of this life. I'm used to working alone. One of the benefits of being alone is that I know, when push comes to shove, I can pull the trigger. I don't have to worry about who else might be there. When a friend is around and the moment arrives where a trigger must be pulled, there must be no hesitation. That moment of hesitation can be the difference between life and death. I need to be able to know it is just him and me." He finished tightening the cinch.

"I understand, but it still frightens me."

"I will be back, Mary."

"You mean so much to me, Gideon."

"I feel the same way, Mary."

Gideon was leading the mare to the fence when the shot rang out. A bullet slammed into the fence just inches from Mary. She screamed and jumped. Gideon scooped her up and jumped behind the barn.

"Gideon, who is it?"

Gideon squinted into the distance.

"Could only be one person."

There was a deep anger in his eyes.

A mere few minutes later there appeared a wisp of dust on a ridge a half-mile away. By then, Vern and Jose arrived with rifles. Manuel walked up also, puffing. Skerby was at the house behind a post, LeMat drawn. Gideon turned to them.

"I am going after him."

Being men of the West, they knew and made no argument. A short time later he rode out.

Riding through the morning hours, he kept an eye on the dust in the distance. It was as if Clyde wanted him to know where he was. They wound through the foothills and deeper into the rising land. The dust cloud finally disappeared and the hunt began. Gideon paused to take care at every clearing and rode with the expectation of gunshots. He hurried when he needed to cross any rises and his senses keened with every hill and copse of trees.

Clyde could be anywhere. This time, only one of them would survive.

118

Clyde rode deeper into the hills and reason came to a shadow of its old self in his mind. Where was he going? Something in him had headed this direction. There was within him a burning urge to lead Gideon into the hills and then ambush him. He could not grasp why, but knew his kingdom must be defended. He already knew the bank had sold his kingdom. He must have revenge!

Smiling, he was proud of himself! Though he intended to hit Mary with the shot and missed, he accomplished his ultimate goal – to get Gideon away, lead him into the hills and destroy him!

Glancing back at one point, a dust cloud shown in the distance. The smile turned to anger. Jerking the reigns, the horse, wide-eyed from the abuse of many days, whimpered.

"Go, beast!" Clyde raked the horse's flanks once again. The frothing horse once again climbed a steep slope, slipping with exhaustion.

That man! Gideon had ruined his kingdom! Still, no one else would stand up to him if he could just get rid of Gideon! Then he could ride into town and watch as townspeople stepped aside for him. Nobody would stand in his way! His demented mind could not see the truth, believing too much in himself and not enough in reality. Clyde was unable to see his kingdom existed only in his mind.

Topping a small ridge, he paused to scan the area. A perfect place to set up an ambush!

Dismounting and grabbing the rifle from the boot, Clyde strutted back and forth on an outcropping looking over the meadow he just crossed. Stumbling, he lost his grip on the reigns of the almost demented horse, which suddenly jerked and, with freed reins, trotted away.

"Come back here!" Lurching toward the frothing horse, Clyde stumbled and fell as the animal ran into the distance, head held high to avoid stepping on the reins.

Clyde stood, yelling at the receding beast.

"Never mind! I'll have another horse in a little while. I'll come get you and teach you to run away when the king calls!"

Seeing where the trail entered on the far side, he raised his rifle, aimed and, satisfied, began to look for a place to hunker down. Gideon would come and he would shoot him as he entered the meadow!

A maniacal laugh erupted from Clyde Bowers as his mind once again crossed into another valley where things were different...so much different

Gideon knew he was falling behind Clyde. Winding further into the foothills, the trail became rocky and he was forced to slow and watch for likely places of concealment where Clyde might wait in ambush. Where and when were the only questions. It was Gideon's responsibility to anticipate and to turn the tables. Yet he could not do much more at the moment than watch the trail. Everything within him warned him Clyde's impulsiveness and sense of importance would cause him to make a play sooner than later. Reaching down, he pulled the rifle from the boot. A Winchester, it was well oiled and clean.

Suddenly, fickle ways of fate brought everything together in a sequence of moments in time.

In the first moment Gideon came to the top of a small saddle ridge overlooking the meadow. A couple of hundred yards wide, he scanned the far edge of the meadow, wary of ambush. Where he sat his horse was exposed and he cast his eyes quickly, wide-eyed and keyed up.

In the second moment a large and famished mountain rattlesnake, by some simple reptilian brain process, spotted the movement of a rabbit and chose to cross the trail in pursuit. Anticipation absorbed its focus.

In the very next moment the horse Gideon was riding, through some sort of innate sense of danger, looked down and saw the rattlesnake. Instincts widened its eyes and its nose flared. It jumped sideways and reared, prepared to bring its hooves down on the rattlesnake.

In a moment almost but not quite concurrent with the one before, two things happened which philosophers and clerics through the ages would debate for causation. First, Clyde pulled the trigger on his Winchester.

Second, because of the horse jumping from the rattlesnake, Gideon lurched sideways and grabbed for the saddle horn.

Lurching sideways, Gideon heard the sound of the rifle and felt the bullet as it passed his head and burned across his upper arm.

Hooves came down on the rattlesnake, ending its quest for food or anything else.

In the next moment, Gideon kicked from the saddle and landed in the rocks with his rifle in his hand and a wince from hitting the ground.

A double moment later Clyde cursed.

119

Clyde knew this day would bring death.

Gideon Henry knew the same. A grim determination filled his mind as he lay in the rocks. Hardness filled his heart and anger rose to just below the surface as he shifted against a large boulder and checked his loads. It was an anger that faded as Mary opened his heart and his life changed. Now the anger filled him again.

Anger was large in his life for many years, since that long ago day on the train when the face of his lifeless father stared back at him, a day of joy turned to destruction of a family. Yet, even amidst the recurrent anger, he rarely lost his ability to be calculating, to focus on the task at hand.

Clyde was nested somewhere above. As Gideon kicked from his horse, something in his mind registered a cluster of rocks across the valley. Leaning to peer around the boulder, in the instant before Clyde's second bullet blew rock splinters in his face, Gideon took in the meadow and the movement of Clyde's rifle barrel in the rocks. Clyde held a commanding position. But how long would Clyde remain?

Raking splinters from his face, Gideon glanced quickly around. It was clear there was no chance unless he could gain movement. His horse stood a hundred yards ahead, in the meadow. Attempting to reach it would leave him a sitting duck. Looking back, it was obvious that way was out, with thirty feet between him and the downward trail. Noting the still quivering rattlesnake, he instinctively pointed with his rifle until his mind registered the throes of an animal already dead.

Where there was one rattler there usually would be another nearby. More than once he heard of men stumbling unexpectedly across mountain rattlers in a bend of a trail and instinctively jumping or doing a sort of dance to get away and inadvertently bounding off the trail right into a nest of the reptiles. The result was not a pretty sight. Just the thought brought a shudder and a glance to the nearby brush.

To his right the woods loomed fifteen feet away, though it seemed like a mile. It was the only option. It was a slim option, but there was no other choice. Clyde had a good bead on him – if he was still in the rocks. Taking off his hat and slipping the brim around to the left, he jerked back as a bullet creased the brim.

He needed to gain a moment, to cause hesitation in Clyde. Moving his hat again to the left but higher and drawing a bullet again, he purposely dropped the hat to the ground at his left, as of a man suddenly down. An instant later Gideon sprung up and leapt to the right, making the trees with a desperate dive as Clyde's shots reached for him like burning fingers. Burning fingers laced with death.

Clyde cursed and the vile words echoed.

Crawling further into the woods, Gideon knew the game was now renewed, and planned his next move. It was possible Clyde remained in the rocks, awaiting some glimpse of his prey. At the same time, he did not want to underestimate Clyde's abilities. Anticipation of greater skill of his foes allowed him in the past to better complete his job. Most of the rogues he dealt with gained their reputations through an ability to manipulate and out think their foes. Just because a man – or a woman – went down some criminal path did not mean they were fools. On the contrary, Gideon found most incredibly intelligent.

It was now cat and mouse; hunter versus the hunted. That was the deadly game he was playing now. The only question was which of the two of them was the hunter. Gideon knew he must turn this situation so he was clearly in control – or at least to even the odds.

Working carefully to his right and remaining deep in the woods, he found a game trail, following for a quarter mile until he could see through the trees and brush bordering the woods. Standing motionless, he cast his eyes into the distance, through the gaps in the trees and the clearing ahead. Gideon settled in to watch, avoiding unnecessary movement.

After what seemed like hours but which was in reality more nearly fifteen minutes, his eyes registered a flicker. Just a passing shift in a gap where there had been but light. Still, it was out of place and his senses keyed.

Clyde! With attention ahead and far to the left of where Gideon actually stood, Clyde crept at the edge of the distant tree line. Though unable to get a solid glimpse of the man, Gideon knew this as the moment to turn the tables. Raising his Winchester slowly and taking a bead on the movement, Gideon blinked and squinted to separate the man from the mottled shadows and light.

Something within Clyde – perhaps a brief register in his peripheral vision, caused him to stop. At the same time a mere brush of a breeze caused a small branch to move into line, deflecting Gideon's bullet. It missed Clyde and blew bark from a tree instead. Clyde turned and ran frantically through the trees. Taking rough aim without expecting results, Gideon fired ahead of Clyde, missing but effectively turning the tide of the hunt. Clyde would know this was not one-sided. At the same time, Gideon knew the man was crazy and anything could happen.

And so it went through the afternoon. Gideon tracked Clyde's movements through his honed skills, while remaining wary of how easily an unstable mind or one bullet from a gun could turn the day. Effectively keeping Clyde moving back into the hills, still an occasional close shot reminded him Clyde was looking for opportunity. The man was not a coward, but worked constantly to find vantage over Gideon.

Nearing a point of boulders at the edge of the woods, Gideon sensed rather than heard movement and felt the bullet as it grazed his ribs. With a shout of jubilation, Clyde began to rush forward and jumped, wide-eyed, as Gideon's muzzle zeroed on him and fired. Shattering Clyde's rifle stock the bullet grazed upwards, cutting a furrow along his face. Blood spattered and Clyde lurched backwards, scampering on his knees into the rocks and wiping frantically with a sleeve to clear blood from his eyes.

Gideon paused and felt of his side and the blood there, wincing as his eyes focused ahead. Hearing Clyde's coarse movements, he crouched and warily followed the fading sounds.

Clyde was in a panicked state as he stumbled away. Sure he would get lead into Gideon back in those rocks, he only managed to wound him and not badly. Now he sought to get away, to put distance behind him, to regroup. His rifle ruined, a deranged Clyde pulled a pistol and checked the loads.

He was the king! This was his kingdom and all were to obey! He would take care of this Gideon, this one who dared defy his rights to the land and the respect and honor belonging to him! With Gideon dead, he would ride proudly to the ranch and take it back. Then he would dress in his finest, saddle his best horse and ride into Craswell. If anyone refused to show him respect…well, he would take care of that!

Yes! This must be settled today! He paused, panting, fingers still tingling from Gideon's bullet hitting the action of the rifle. Rubbing the fingers on his jeans, his other arm swiping the blood from his face, Clyde saw a cluster of boulders to his left and lurched over. His mind lingered between reality and falsehood, between danger at hand and his anticipated triumphant ride into town.

Reaching an opening in the boulders, Clyde realized it was a cave and, pulling his pistol, backed into the shadowed space, keeping his eye to the trail. Gideon needed to cross the space, or at least show himself on the trail.

Thirty yards away, Gideon peered around a boulder and jumped as Clyde's shot threw quartz shards through the air. Pulling his own pistol, he quickly chanced a shot back towards Clyde. Yet the man was indistinct in the cave opening and the shot was wide.

Clyde scampered backwards, deeper into the cave, waiting for Gideon to draw closer. Looking over his shoulder, he saw a shaft of light and spied a hole, deeper in and up, which would overlook the place where Gideon stood.

Quickly calculating, Clyde grinned in triumph. One good shot would end this! Clyde carefully moved back and stepped upwards to the light.

Sure enough! There was Gideon! The vantage of the hole put him to Gideon's right and so exposed Gideon to his shot. Smiling, he brought up his pistol and rested it on his other arm...waiting.

Gideon moved his head back and forth, catching a scent he had smelled before. Not fresh, but old and musky - and strong.

Clyde saw Gideon sniff the air and a gleeful smile broke though the blood covering his face and shirt. Resting his pistol on his arm and lining the sights on Gideon's shirtfront, Clyde began to squeeze the trigger.

It is a curious fact of the mind of man that Clyde's focus was so attuned to the death of Gideon that for more than a few moments he registered something else but failed to truly take notice.

Finally sensing movement, Clyde turned and paled, eyes wider than wide.

120

A primeval roar filled the air and echoed off rock walls.

Clyde's bullet ineffectively ricocheted through the cave as his guttural scream rent the air.

Enraged, the Grizzly roared again and swiped its massive claws forward. For only an instant, Clyde's mind registered missing claws.

Gideon hugged the rock as he heard the scream. Enraged roars filled the air.

Gideon found it difficult even to envision what was happening in the cave. Turning, he hurried down the hillside. In the distance, the roars continued.

An hour later, Gideon sat upon a log, weary beyond belief. Early evening was upon him and he knew he must rest and spend a cold night. Tomorrow he would begin the journey home. A unique thought but that is exactly what it was – home.

Gideon was a changed man. The weariness sagging his frame was more than physical. It was as if a journey was ending and a new journey beginning. The death of his father, the resulting death of his mother and the ensuing years of confusion, loss and bitterness seemed no longer important. Something new was springing forth within and perhaps it was partly Mary, partly the fight with Bowers and the truth of his life over the years. Finding the young girl in the alley was a defining moment. Perhaps it was a combination of many things causing the change.

It ended with the death of Clyde Bowers in the cave.

It didn't matter. He could not go back to the way of the past. There was now new life and new beginning. Could he embrace it? Gideon knew with all his heart he wanted to try.

Before long, deep dusk was upon him. An owl hooted. Rousing from his thoughts, he looked to the sky and rose, breaking dead twigs for a fire. Within a very few minutes the small fire brought both warmth and comfort. There was peace within, a sense of having dropped a heavy load from his shoulders, as if his heart now beat again after having stopped.

Mary.

This was his future.

The old was gone and the new lay before him.

In the morning he would hurry home. Mary would be worried. Somewhere he would find the horse. No matter, though.

He was at peace for the first time since his father's death.

Smiling, Gideon laid his head back against a tree.

It was the chuckle that awakened him. At first it seemed a part of a dream, then something broke through the deep weariness and he opened his eyes. The night was still young; the stars were coming out. He must have been asleep no more than an hour.

His bleary eyes opened wide to see a smirking Clyde sitting across the fire, pistol pointed at Gideon's middle.

121

lyde's eyes were like nothing Gideon had ever seen before. Whatever sanity once remained was no longer. Crazed eyes looked back at Gideon, reflecting the subtle glow of the low burning fire. Clyde spoke and even the voice was demented, coming as if from a distance. It was hoarse and weak.

"Surprised to see me, Gideon?" A chuckle came from somewhere deep. It was not an earthly chuckle, but something dark.

Gideon stared, slowly easing his hand downward.

Clyde moved the pistol and his thumb cocked the hammer.

"Don't even try it, Gideon. You'll never even clear leather and you know it."

"The bear...I heard you scream."

Clyde laughed, high-pitched and eerie. Then the raspy voice again.

"Yes, a moment of sheer terror. As you can see, the bear did manage to claw me." Shifting his left shoulder into the feeble firelight, Gideon saw the torn shoulder, skin hanging in ghastly shreds along with the shirt. For an instant, Gideon saw the white of bone. Blood dripped slowly but plentifully.

"You need a doctor, Clyde."

"No!" The pistol extended towards Gideon. Then a calmness came to Clyde's eyes and the pistol retracted. A small wince of pain crossed Clyde's face and was gone. "Put another branch on the fire, Gideon, but don't try anything."

Gideon reached slowly and placed a branch upon the fire. The flames licked at some dry pine needles and flared. Clyde never glanced down, keeping his eyes upon Gideon's face. Blood slowly spread over Clyde's shirtfront.

"The bear got me. It was the same bear. It was the bear what got pa. I recognized the missing claws. It knocked me down, but it knocked me into a crevice leading to a tunnel under the rock. I scrambled and it just about got me again." Clyde laughed again, but weaker. "That tunnel led out of the cave. That ol' bear kept trying to reach me from the inside, and there I was crawling to the outside. I got away – in case you didn't guess." Again the eerie laugh... though weaker.

"Let me bandage your arm, Clyde."

Crazed eyes spit angry, but weakening, fire. The gun sagged slightly, but still pointed towards Gideon.

"I'm dying, Gideon! You know it and I know it. But guess what? I'm not going alone! I couldn't be king for long, but you'll not be king for even a moment." His voice paused and he gasped in a spasm of pain. "You ruined my kingdom."

"You never had a kingdom"

A curious look crossed Clyde's face as his finger tightened on the trigger.

Gideon knew Clyde would fire in mere moments. His mind worked quickly. There was no chance of pulling a gun. All he had was a small rock palmed when feeding the fire.

"Do you know what happened with the bear, Clyde?"

"No."

Gideon suddenly looked puzzled and sniffed the air. Clyde's eyes widened.

"What are you doing, Gideon?" Clyde struggled to keep his eyes open.

"I smell something musty! The bear's coming back!"

Clyde laughed again. A branch broke in the woods. Clyde's eyes became platters and flickered to the woods. Gideon threw the rock and rolled to the side, coming to his hands and knees, ready to spring. In that moment of pause he looked at Clyde. The eyes were wide but the gun hand lay in his lap.

Clyde was dead.

Wanting to own the territory, now all he would own was a six-foot plot of mountain dirt.

In the darkness many miles away a bear, missing claws and bloodied, walked away, shaking its head to and fro, scenting the air and seeking an escape from the man-smell. There was too much noise here. Too many of those strange things that made noise and made him sting. Deeper into the mountains...

Early the next afternoon Gideon rode through the lowest hills. Though tired, he rode with a freedom, a difference in his manner perceptible to any who knew him. A subtle something was transformed.

Coming to a crossing of the trails – one to the ranch and the other to town – Gideon paused in thought.

Not long afterward he approached the batwings of the Gold Horse. Ol' Ridley sat outside in his usual spot, head tilted strangely.

Gideon nodded to the old man.

Before he could think, Ridley nodded back.

Both men grinned.

Squeaky batwings attracted eyes of regulars sitting around the room. Gideon took the room in with a sweep of his eyes, nodding. Nothing had changed, yet everything was changed. Motioning to the bartender, he slowly drank from the glass placed before him. Wiping his mouth and turning, heads followed as Gideon walked to the chessboard, paused, reached down and moved a piece.

Straightening his back and smiling, Gideon spoke softly.

"Checkmate."

The batwings squeaked once more.

ABOUT THE AUTHOR

Mark has always loved the old West. Spending his high school and college years in Idaho, he became enamored with the mountains and the characters of a more rugged life. With a B.A. in History from Boise State University and a Masters in Counseling Psychology from Ball State University, he has experience as counselor, seminar speaker, adjunct college faculty, pastor, hospice chaplain and now author. An avid reader all his life, Mark has spent countless hours with his favorite author, Louis L'Amour, and seeks to share the adventure and clear morals of the classic west. He currently resides in Indiana with his wife and two daughters.

Follow him on Facebook.

Made in the USA
Lexington, KY
17 June 2017